LILLIBURLERO

LILLIBURLERO

Sam Keery

Book Guild Publishing
Sussex, England

First published in Great Britain in 2012 by
The Book Guild Ltd
Pavilion View
19 New Road
Brighton, BN1 1UF

Typesetting in Baskerville by
Keyboard Services, Luton, Bedfordshire

Printed in Great Britain by
CPI Group (UK) Ltd, Croydon, CR0 4YY

A catalogue record for this book is available from
The British Library

ISBN 978 1 84624 731 6

1

It was his 50th birthday. He had spent the day on a pilgrimage of remembrance, re-visiting London streets in which he had lived or worked when he had first come to London full of dreams. Most of the buildings turned out to be smaller than he remembered them, or to have fewer steps up to them, or not to be balconied, or not to have a pillared portico, or not to have iron-railed windows, or to be on an avenue bare of trees, or to have windows from which there could not have been the view he would always associate with an episode of amorous significance, or to be at the top of a street and not the bottom, or to be in the middle and not on a corner, or not to be adjacent to or opposite or above or below a feature of London landscape with which he would always associate it, or even not to be anywhere near where he thought it was but somewhere else entirely. For some he searched in vain.

Being at heart a sentimental man there was more than one street on which he had stood before a building and wept a little, though choosing carefully a moment when no one was looking his way to see his tears or notice that the tilting of his head was not only to look up at windows which evoked the long ago but also to take a swift swig from a hip flask that appeared and disappeared in a dexterous accomplished movement, the result of much practice in public places.

And now, at nightfall, in an untidy room dominated by a desk and a typewriter, his hip flask stood empty beside a bottle of gin from which, come morning, it would be replenished to equip him for the needs of a more usual day – if it still had enough in it. Also beside the bottle was a small wine glass, the cubic capacity of which was exactly that of the measure used in bars for a single of spirits. He had of late taken to counting his daily drinks, which started, in so far as he could keep to it, not before one o'clock in the afternoon, a time of day that, on rising after troubled sleep, gave his mornings something to look forward to, when care would lift and the world would brighten.

He poured gin into the small glass, taking care not to overflow, at the same time filling it to the brim, as otherwise the tally of his daily intake to be noted in a diary he kept solely for that purpose would not be exact. Exactness was crucial. So long as he kept an exact count he would be in control. He was proud of having established control by counting, and his mind firmly resisted any classification of himself other than controlled drinker.

He flipped through the pages of the diary trying to remember the meaning of the days when the number was unusually high or low, whether they betokened happenings, celebrations, departures from the even tenor of his ways, meeting old drinking chums, wandering about London to see what else of his earlier years they had since pulled down, giving afternoon readings and advice to housewives' writing groups, or sex. They were, after all, only numbers, he mused, meaningless without other numbers, and yet, even with other numbers, reducing our totality to the correlation of numbers. The number of years lived; of words written; of words read; of miles walked between bars; of phone calls made; of bills received; of bowel movements; of hours of sleep; of funerals attended; of unsolicited manuscripts received; of magazine subscribers renewing; of condoms purchased; of haircuts; of acquaintances made; of tube and bus journeys; of centilitres of semen ejaculated; of death threats from Irish poets; of socks discarded; of near misses by vehicles; of clothes given to charities; of litres pissed; of bagel and salt beef takeaways; of dreams.

His dreams were now all variants of the same dream except that it was darkening. He had tried to put it on paper but quite failed to convey its darkness that still lingered even as he awakened from it. He even made it seem funny rather than disturbing, so deeply ingrained was his need as writer, editor, bar room raconteur to entertain when recounting anything, even a dream of being unable to get to where he wanted to go in a city both strange and vaguely familiar, where the buses had their destinations half rubbed out and the streets always curved away downhill from the direction he knew he should be going, and increasingly it was night with rain and sometimes fog.

He swallowed the gin at a gulp with only the merest of grimaces at its fieryness, noting the time so as to know when he could allow himself another, welcoming its renewal of the glow from his afternoon's drinking that had been diminishing. A thought struck him to help banish the sombreness of the nightly dream that awaited him and he smiled at the opportunity to present his problem in a way that would amuse. He pressed the record button on the cassette recorder and spoke into it in a still strong Belfast accent.

'When those whose researches require Irish drinkers to establish control put the question "are you a one bottle a day man or a two bottle?", they are using as a measure the standard 70 centilitre bottle of spirits so that if the Irish person to whom the question is addressed is in the habit of purchasing the larger litre bottle and takes a pint or two of beer as well, to say nothing of wine, then, even if he makes every effort to be truthful, which is not always the case, or if his memory is still A1 at Lloyds which also can not be taken for granted he would have to be tickety boo at arithmetic involving the decimal fractions if he is not to weaken the validity of the data...'

But then a doubt assailed him on this very point as he totted up the count for the day so far, adding to the quarter bottle contained in the hip flask what he had had in several public houses, in one or two of them for old times' sake, notwithstanding being dismayed at the philistine refurbishment. How many drinks had he had? He recalled bar scenes in order to remember. One there, yes, and one and a half there yes, and ... yes, and ... but which pub was that? Where the still attractive woman of mature years but not on her own had been flattered by his admiring scrutiny? Why couldn't he place it? Wasn't it after ... or ... when he came out of the tube and turned left ... no, that was the what's its name where the terrier dog begged on its hind legs for crisps and stout... So it must have been before he tried to find...

To help him locate the missing pub he unfolded a street map of London intending to trace the day's wanderings exactly, starting at one of the great railway termini that had been the point of arrival, not only for him, but for generations of London Irish. But the great city spread out before him distracted his gaze from where he had actually been that day to places he had not but which had as good a claim upon nostalgia. He fell into a reverie in which the recollection of these once familiar places was so strong that when he roused himself from it he found it hard to resist including them with those he had revisited, especially if he had been in their vicinities in the more recent past.

Well, it was the first time he had lost a pub! But wait, had he lost it, or merely mislaid it among the others? What if one of them had two bars, or a long bar that turned a corner into another different looking area? Perhaps the terrier dog pub and the woman who had given him the eye pub were one and the same. Was she drinking stout with crisps? Was it the terrier had given him the eye? Ha, ha! That's it, see the funny side. So what if the tally of drinks for this one day will be more inexact than was strictly required? It wasn't every day he had a 50th birthday. He would re-establish strict control on the second day of his second half century.

His attention returned to the map of London and the places in which he may or may not have drunk on this, his 50th birthday, and to one place in particular, in which was also situated, opposite a public house in which he had had his first drink of the day, a hospital, in which a consultant had held up X-rays to a bright screen and told him that they would like him to come inside so that they could do a probe.

It was a nineteenth century public house about which he and another waiting patient had joked, saying it had a very 'nipped in' look. Indeed they had nipped in themselves on the way. He told the other that the servants from all the big houses around that were now all bed-sits would have nipped in and come out wiping their mouths and saying they had been in to ask the time. Would have given the child of the house a sup too to make it sleep. No wonder, he commented, the upper classes of Kensington so prone to drink in later life from the servants ladling it into them. His fellow patient had said something about the staff of the hospital nipping in and what did he think of the way they came onto the wards from the operation theatres nowadays in green overalls and rubber boots and he made the other laugh though uneasily by saying it was like they had been hosed down after gutting pigs. But it was worse in the old days, he explained, remembering an article he had once printed by a feminist about this very hospital. Used to be a great lying in hospital. Very fashionable with the upper classes – or at least the husbands – even though it had one of the highest death rates for the mothers. Because it was a teaching hospital and the professors would go straight to delivering babies after cutting up corpses for the students without washing their hands. And wouldn't be told! Blamed the deaths on a 'mysterious debilitating miasma'. Wouldn't wash their hands no matter how many women died. But the women knew. By Jesus yes. Every evening the carriages and hansom cabs would drive round and round the hospital like a procession, the women trying to hold out till the professors went home and left the delivering to the junior doctors and midwives.

Thus did his propensity to turn everything into something of interest to readers or hearers manifest itself even on this occasion, the seriousness of which he pushed to the back of his mind as, after the consultation, he had wandered around London, drinking and reflecting upon his fifty years and his father's before that, reaching back into a past that had fashioned them all.

... fathers of ten children and more never saw their wives naked ... saying grace ... bible readings ... very stern with the wife and children ... after leading family prayers creeping up the attic to fornicate with the servant girl... London bed-sit rooms once witnessed the antics of your Victorian pater familias ... the hypocrisy, the brutality ... yet the other side of the coin too ... their songs ... my father still sang them ... those lovely sad sweet songs about parting and death...

He rummaged among a heap of cassettes and picked up one on which were such songs recorded by famous singers, most long dead. He often played it of late. He listened to it on his feet, sometimes walking up and down and joining in occasionally, imagining an old style London pub of the sort now nearly extinct, with a piano – a joanna – and a sentimental clientele. By the time it got near the end the hands of the clock told it him he was due another gin which added to the pleasure with which he heard the last item which was not a song but a well known hymn sung by a Welsh male voice choir, which he listened to with as much enjoyment, though purely for old times sake as he had long ceased to be a believer.

> When I survey the wondrous cross
> On which the prince of glory died

He hummed in chorus as he poured the gin to the very brim of the glass, wondering vaguely as always whether the surface of the gin curved upwards or downwards at its junction with the glass but this time, prompted by unbidden memories of science lessons at school, he kneeled down and put his eye to the rim. Yes! It definitely curved down, he decided. The level of the gin did seem to be slightly above the rim except at the rim itself. Yes, just a teeny bit. A mimmilitre, he murmured. A millimim, he tried again, something to do with calipery attraction, no, capliary... And yes, he remembered now, it was called a hibsicus, no hibsicus, no, starts with an emm ... the miscunem, the meniscus. Yes! Got it, sunshine.

Thrilling to a belated interest in scientific experiment he tried to place a ruler across the rim to see if the surface of the gin curved up or down, trying to remember which way was convex or concave. But he peered so closely that his nose touched the glass and knocked it over just as WHEN I SURVEY was ending. It flowed over an unsolicited m.s. from an aspiring poet, making the ink run. He cursed at the waste of good gin and, as he wiped up the mess and poured himself another, the tape ran on past the point where he would normally have switched it off. He was startled by a voice speaking. It was his own. He must have accidentally put the songs and hymns onto one of those

on which he recorded things he might one day knock into
shape for publication. Only one of those things on the
tape now remained. It was a kind of poem

One of the mistakes that the goyim make
Is assuming that skull caps will be provided free
At the funerals and weddings of Jews.
Paper ones, nothing fancy, you understand
Throw away kind like paper cups or hankies.
Then to your dismay there are none there
And your bare head affronts the synagogue
And is rebuked by the rabbi
Who considers it no excuse to be told lamely
That you thought there would be paper ones.
We can't keep up with paper ones, he says accusingly,
As if it is people like you
Who cause such a run on paper skull caps.

Startled by the abrupt change from Christianity to Judaism
he shook his head. No, no, he muttered. It was wrong. It
did not suit his mood of sentimental nostalgia for the
protestant culture in which he was rooted, his unbelief
notwithstanding. He did not want to think of ... another
culture ... memories ... a woman...

No, he said almost angrily, its all wrong ... could be
taken as anti Semitic ... I was never ... not after ... she...

He did things to the recorder and pressed a button,
erasing the poem for ever, banishing from his mind brief
dark images featuring the words 'they crucified our Lord'
and 'Auschwitz'.

He picked up another cassette from the heap that
contained things less disturbing. He stopped and started
it, shaking his head in wry amusement as he listened to
himself speak on matters dear to his heart. He started to
play a piece, thought better of it, hurried on, then changed

his mind and went back to it, listening glass in hand, and ear cocked in exaggerated attention.

'Ah, that's better! Say what you like about your fine malt whiskeys, your starred brandies, your best beers and stouts, your wines red and white with bubbles beading at the brim – and God forbid I should decry them that loved them not wisely but too well – but there's nothing like plain no nonsense gin to go straight to where it's needed urgently, desperately, life savingly.

'Come here till I tell you. Pull up that chair a bit closer. The secret of a happy life is not for the hoipolloi. Listen, here's Charles Lamb's cure for melancholy given to his friend Coleridge in Highgate. *Have a second glass to keep the first one company and a third to see that the first two got there all right and a fourth to announce that there is another on the way and a fifth to say it might not be the last.*

'Oh Dionysus, God of drink, lightener of darkness, warmer of the heart, dispeller of dread, hope bringer, dream nourisher, uplifter of my soul, gladly ride I in thy chariot, though it be pulled by tigers.

'Oh pied piper Dionysus, thy distant tune was early heard by a child at Belfast funerals loving the talk of drink-warmed mourners back from gravesides and by a child on a Belfast street pausing at the swing doors of bars to wonder at the joyful babble coming out on the bars' beery breaths.

'And oh there have been many bars. I did not know there would be so many. Bars for sighing lovers. Bars for no-hopers and for market porters. Bars for in-betweeners and not badders, for so-soers and could-be-worsers, Dockers' bars and bars for strippers. No singing bars and bars for pick-ups. Bars plush as well as plain. No dogs bars and bars with pianos.

'Oh Dionysus, inspirer of songs. And oh there were so many songs, so many glass-in-hand tunes and times that were not measured out in coffee spoons.

'For you befriended me when I was friendless and filled me with goodwill to all when there were none that loved me. I need thee, Oh I need thee, every hour I need thee. I need thee Oh my saviour, I come to thee.'

He switched it off, frowning. What happened to all the other bars, he muttered, there were far more of them than that. He replayed the bit about the bars thinking he might have missed them, but they were not there.

This is sure one helluva day for losing bars, he intoned in a mock American accent, imitating a one-time drinking crony, then resuming his own voice.

Yes, dammit I remember now ... there were ... bars for doers and for wistful wooers ... bars for chancers and for backward glancers ... bars for dreamers and for schemers ... bars for ruminators and procrastinators ... bars for now or neverers and for waverers...

'Et cetera,' he interrupted himself impatiently, adding 'and so on' in a more thoughtful voice which became a reflective murmur as he finished slowly and softly, 'and so forth,' staying quite still for a long time as he mused upon the course of his life and how distant the age of fifty had once seemed, how swiftly it had crept up on him.

He gazed at his bookshelves on which were several books bearing his name but they merged with the crowd of other books so that he had difficulty distinguishing them, especially his first, in order, for a moment or two, with the help of another gin, to try to recapture what it had felt like to be be young and newly published in London. A gin-warmed trace of excitement and innocence did indeed manifest itself fleetingly and he smiled and shook his head in a kind of compassion as he turned his gaze to survey a pile of would-be books on the floor, some beautifully presented in glossy covers, confident of impressing at once, others ragged and marked by many rebuffs but still grimly battling on towards what the unpublished regard as the glittering prize of print.

So many scribblers, he muttered, scribble, scribble, scribble. A.N. Other's critically acclaimed first novel. Remaindered. Out of print. Remaindered to critical acclaim. The yellowing clippings of acclaiming reviews. The forgotten yellowing acclaim for forgotten yellowing books...

He switched on the tape recorder again, starting and stopping it till he found what he was looking for. Against a background of chatter, laughter, and the clink of glasses a mock ecclesiastical voice began intoning and the babble quietened to an orderly occasional amused chorus of response.

Dearly beloved brethren, the scripture moveth us to acknowledge and confess our manifold sins against the word and the phrase and the sentence and the cadence of the line.
    From all offences against the comma and the semicolon:
    GOOD LORD DELIVER US.
    From all purple passages
    GOOD LORD DELIVER US.
    From all neglect, sloth, and hack reviews.
    GOOD LORD DELIVER US.
    For there is no health in us and style knows us not

He took another sip of gin and joined in the laughter on the tape. He wagged his finger at the pile of unsolicited manuscripts as if enjoining them to listen to what came next which might have been a Belfast clergyman reading a text of scripture.

For of them that do hunger and thirst to be published there are they that, being published, find it as of little account and do hunger and thirst after good reviews and when this availeth them naught neither with the multitude nor with the scholars turneth to the bringing out of magazines so that they may give or withhold from giving that which once was withheld from themselves.

11

SAM KEERY

For of the scribbling of manuscripts there is no end and we did make them that scribble sit humbly in our ante chambers or stand upon our stairs seeking audience with us that we might make them known onto men for great tellers of stories and great makers of verse or great judgers thereof. And we said onto them our pages presently are full and there is no more room therein, but if ye would be of service to us presently we would remember it in time to come when we took counsel among ourselves what to put in our pages for all men to see. And they said what would ye of us? And we said onto them take these our pages under thine arms and carry them to them that trade in news and reports and press them to put our pages on show that all men may see that the pages are good. And some scribblers did do it gladly yea through all the streets of Kensington and Fulham did they bear our pages, as far as the borders of Westminster did they bear them, even onto the heights of Hampstead did they make our pages known onto men. And there were others among them that tempered the wroth of the printers with coin for the printers were often exceeding wroth and would hold captive our pages till coin was given onto them. And there they of the scribblers that gave us our fill to eat and drink and would make merry with us, both they and their women, and their women we knew.

Here, I still have the auld Belfast bible twang do you notice? Sure it never leaves you.

The tape ran on, for a while half-heeded, as he gazed at the pile of unsolicited manuscripts, but only half seeingly, seeing instead the distant past. Only occasionally did he come out of reverie to listen more closely to something: a poem: a song: a reading from literature.

...happy are they that live in the dream of their own existence ... to whom the guiding star of their youth still shines from afar...

Ah, Hazlitt, he murmured, letting a tear fall.

Or a woman reading scripture in such a way as momentarily to banish melancholy. The voice was pleasant English middle

class and of mature years and might have been that of a
church deaconess, at first clear and steady.

I am the rose of Sharon and the lily of the valleys...

Ah, The Song of Solomon, he told himself nostalgically.

But she appeared to become more and more breathless,
reading in short spasms in which gasps began to appear
which, as the reading went on turned into whimpers and
eventually into little sobbing cries

... thy two breasts are like two young roes ... I opened
to my beloved...

And then her voice steadying and cool again but still
accompanied by gasps, not hers, male and rhythmic, ceasing
suddenly with a groan.

He poured another gin, swaying slightly, but not spilling
a drop, letting the tape run on through a medley of items,
some of them fragmentary. Then came what he had had
it in mind to look for in the first place before he got
diverted. His voice spoke softly, thoughtfully and sadly. He
listened carefully.

'Father, mother, street, city, religion. The basic identity
kit. Aunts, uncles, cousins. Kitted out with circle of
acquaintance ready made, proof of your existence. If people
enquired who you were they would be told your father's
trade, your mother's maiden name, an uncle's drinking
habits, another's late demise, and so on, clue upon clue,
until the enquirers created you from these basic elements
entirely to their satisfaction.

'Two parents, four grandparents, eight great grandparents,
sixteen great great grandparents, thirty two great great
great grandparents, sixty four great great great great
grandparents, one hundred and twenty eight great great
great great great grandparents ... and all their heirs, scions,
litters, spawns, lineages, families patriarchal, families
matrilinear, close families, falling out families, offshoots,
branches, throwbacks. All these are my begetting.

'Popery-hating shipwrights. Shipwright-denouncing true blue boilermakers. Skivvy-groping sons of the manse. High principled free thinking Jack London-reading iron turners. Off-the-bottle testimony-giving mill chimney riggers. Primitive methodist son-denied-daughter begetting copper-smiths. Paynight-boozing conjugal-rights-demanding dye-house charge hands. Mixed marriage flyfishing gasworks retort house deputies. Early rising pigdung-collecting public-house-waylaid market gardeners. Pay night house-to-house dashing stomach-pill-sucking insurance men. Daughter-spoiling piano-in-parlour brass foundry foremen. Titanic-recalling League and Covenant signers. Patent-shoed tango-gold-medallist pigeon fanciers. Stubbs's listed two shillings in the pound jobbing builders. Marriage-postponing still-on-their-mother's hands church choir baritones. Palm-reading journey-by-water-predicting secondsight-gifted widow women. Snuff-taking wet spinning room doffers. Pay night late-home-arriving fried-soda-bread-and-sexual-intercourse-requiring ropeworks foremen. Prize-terrier-fancying Church of Ireland aislemen. Wife-embittered temperance-promising bar-tempted damasc loom tenters. Wife's-money-started -up strict Brethren foundation garment manufacturers. Jesus-saved street-hymn-singing Pure Ice and Cold Storage brine tank men. Last Rose of Summer disappointed parlour tenors. Caught-at-it car-seat-copulating Gospel Hall preachers. One-armed parley-voo Somme survivors. Dried-out prayed-for public-house-passing daughter-escorted cabinet makers. Discreet french-letter dispensing pew-renting pharmacists. Shop-girl pestering Baptist green grocers. Funeral-brandy-declining off-the-drink doctor-warned RUC sergeants. Golden-voiced Danny Boy-singing never sober mother's-heart breaking favourite sons. Carrying-on monumental stone masons. First-World-War-gassed pigeon club clock stewards. Irish Guards regimental boxing champions. Illegitimate grandmother-reared presbyterian

14

coalmen. Courteous hat-tipping public-house-side-entrance-users. Bible-thumping wife beaters. Last chance till-tempted barmen. Saturday night knee-trembling-brylcremed maiden-head-taking shipwright platers. Blind done-by-feel dogshow-judging second wife seekers. Born again motor car dealers. Plaza Ballroom copulation-minded foxtrotting rivetters. Closing-time Gunga Din reciters. Hushed-up maintenance-paying solicitors' sons. Four-under-par clubhouse-bar-lingering Great Northern Railway signal men. Summer evening long-grass fornicating skivvy-fancying pig men. Choirgirl-eyeing sermon-bored youths. One-lung tubercular melodeon players. Typist-tickling Church of Ireland assistant mill managers. Derby-winner-tipping sugar-borrowing Rookery dwelling women. Henry Ford-quoting hedge-clipping freemasons. Mother guarded church-confirmation-party french-kissing daughters. Drink ruined cattle dealers. Servantgirl-molesting Church of Ireland organists. Dickens-loving gas meter readers. Gin-sipping man-foolish once beautiful yarn winders. Near-the-mark women-customer-bantering market stall men. Melancholy chess-playing bachelor ship chandler's clerks. Four-dog-pack greyhound walkers. Seaside-landlady-marrying grown-up-children-disinheriting Presbyterian widowers. Tropical-fish fancying Orange Lodge masters. Come-up-from-nothing daughter shaming speculative builders. Church-music-loving God-doubting bespoke shoemakers. Old school brotherhood-of-man-believing Keir Hardie revering toolmaker trade unionists. Yellow-whiskered last-of-their kind wheel wrights. Pensioned hard-times-remembering bleach green spreaders. Spion Kop recounting bandy-legged ex-Boer War horse troopers. Last of the-the bearded venerable ponycart lamp oil men.'

He switched it off to pace unsteadily up and down, musing upon the richness of his heritage. The stories that are there, he reflected only scratched the surface in my books ... inexhaustible mine ... all human life ... not finished yet, sunny Jim ... no, by Jesus, we're not beaten yet, my old china ... could still kick the arses of the fucking Eng. Lit. little shits...'

One of the pubs he had called at after the hospital had a sign depicting, not the more common rural allusions to harvests, farm animals, wild animals of the chase, but a magnificent Victorian railway locomotive, and around the walls of the bar were old photos of the great age of steam, with railwaymen on them facing the camera squarely, arms folded in the confident old fashioned way, just like that of his engine driver grandfather in the Great Northern yards in Belfast, standing beside an engine that might well have been working forty years later when he himself had first come to London and worked among such engines in the Great Western yards near Paddington. Such a mighty span of time had the age of steam encompassed, lingering into the age of computers. He had even debated in his mind whether to go to the Science Museum and look at the mill engines and spinning frames of the industrial revolution that had gone into the making of him. Warmed by the gin he had looked around at the pictures of Victorian engines and out of the window at the Victorian houses of London and felt sentimentally close to his roots. He now tried to remember a poem of his about the age of steam that had been published years before called MADE IN BELFAST but could only recall two verses and was not sure in which order they came.

Mill chimneys framed in our school room windows
The Titanic on our parlour walls
Bushmills Whiskey up on the hoardings
Though Your Sins Be Scarlet in the Gospel Halls.

16

Genesis, Exodus, Alpha and Omega
And *The Lord Is My Shepherd* over our bed
The map of the world behind our teacher
And all that was *Ours* on it coloured red.

There's more of it, he murmured to himself, if only I could remember it. Quite proud of it once. What did I do with it? Have to have a good clear out to find it again. Worth reprinting together with a good boot up the crotch of the Eng. Lit. mafia. Have to make sure the brainless goons know that the 'made in Belfast' refers not just to ships and linen but people. I got the bible into MADE IN BELFAST and the parlours with pianos and the old songs I used to still hear sung and loved them though they were old fashioned even then.

He would have liked to have sung one of the sad sweet songs from the age of steam but what came into his head was one of its famous hymns ABIDE WITH ME ... swift to its close ebbs out life's little day...

When he visited the toilets for a swig of gin from his hip flask in the interests of economy he was directed to them by a pointing hand that must have been there since the pub was built. They made him think of his formative years and the old pointing hand signs all over Belfast that directed with stern but reassuring authority, especially WAY OUT.

Was there, he wondered, a way out now? Way out, exit, exodus. Genesis, Exodus, Leviticus, Numbers, he muttered. Deuteronomy comes next but couldn't say Deuteronomy in childhood because of stammer later cured by sex and gin, not necessarily in that order. Not being able to say Deuteronomy cast long shadow. Hide it. Pretend to forget what comes next? But what when prompted? Danger. The cruel herd. But divert mockers onto another. Find a proxy. Join jeerers and persecutors. Become adroit diverter.

17

SAM KEERY

Wariness the key. Wary warder off. Ever wary ever since. Sorry now.

> Who's sorry now, who's sorry now
> Who's something something your vow...

Was that a quick step? Can't do it unless. Never got past slow waltz and quickstep on the ballroom floors of Belfast and London. I failed the hurdle of ... Deuteronomy ... puberty ... the fox trot ... living...

When was MADE IN BELFAST? Was it before that other time? No, it must have been after that because the time before that was when I was still – I nearly said at home in Belfast. Was I ever at home in Belfast? Was I ever at home anywhere? Was I ever anywhere? Was I ever? Was I I?

Had to get out? Yes. No other way except WAY OUT. Follow the pointing hand. Exit. Exodus. No re-admission.

> Good byee, good byee, wipe the tear, baby dear
> From your eyee

Genesis, Exodus. But took my Genesis with me. Stuck with it for keeps. By the waters of Babylon remembering Zion.

He switched on the recorder again but fell asleep before it reached the last thing on it.

'I. I land. Island. Ireland. Godland. Prodland. Prayland. Sayland. Nayland. Norland. Nor Ireland not Ireland. Scot Ireland. Prot Ireland. My not Ireland yet Ireland not yet Ireland bit Ireland Brit Ireland.

'I unbelieving bit Brit Ireland leaving elsewhere dwelling far wandering Ireland rememberer.'

18

2

One night before a poetry reading he had a new variant of his dream of being lost in surroundings that were strange versions of familiar ones. Names would be called out which he tried to answer to as they seemed to resemble the pseudonym under which he wrote, being similarly constructed out of place names of his native place. He could not make out if these were alternative pseudonyms which he might have been wiser to use instead of the one that he had stuck to through thick and thin, for richer or poorer, in sickness or in health, or whether it was being put to him that it was not too late to make a fresh start, even now, when the pages of his calendar with a page for every day were fluttering off two and three at a time with proverbs on them such as 'neither a borrower nor a lender be' which enraged him with their bourgeois smugness. His names were being called out at gatherings, prize-givings, award ceremonies, honorary degrees in Eng. Lit.

> Chichester D Banbridge!
> Connor Deny Braidwater!
> C Dundonald Bushmills!
> Crumlin D Blackmountain!
> C Dungannon Boyne!

He struggled to let them know the correct version so that he could claim what should have been rightfully his, but more and more names were shouted out by masters of ceremonies, except that some of the names were of a kind that he would never have made up, not even as a callow youth when he had received rejection slips under the impressive nom de plume of Harrison J Westbury before he had settled for place names. Suspicion gave way to anger when a bit of hush was called for

Clandeboye D Bleachgreen!

The fuckers were taking the piss. He struggled out of sleep seeming to be shouting, though in reality only muttering his real pseudonym Colin Divis Blackstaff, though sufficiently uncertain of it to be reassured by finding it on the book he took from his shelf from which to select a poem for the reading that afternoon.

The poetry reading was taking place in a Scout hall in Fulham around the walls of which were posters about woodcraft and knots. Many in the gathering were poets come from near and far to read their work. Just behind where they stood to read was a huge poster with the words of the Scout Law which gave an unusual flavour to the words of some of the poems being read, including those from The Collected Poems of one of the readers – a college lecturer who had put out a pile of copies for sale on a chair at the door – as they seemed full of drinking, fornication and four letter words, leading those who had not seen him in the flesh to expect a Dylan Thomas/Brendan Behan type of roaring boy which was not the case as he was an inconspicuous quiet man of about 50, though a young woman student he had in tow could *perhaps* have testified to the Jack-the-lad virility celebrated in his poems, a remark made a shade too loudly in a Belfast accent by another man of about 50 to a woman of mature years still slim and good looking. The Belfast man, editor of the *Clerkenwell*

Review, might be able to get her into print, and perhaps, with a bit of luck, into bed. Her laughter at CD's quip was encouraging with respect to the latter as was her looking not displeased when he told her during a changeover at the rostrum that one of the compensations of getting older for *emotionally mature* men was becoming aware how attractive older women can be, a line he used with varying success these days. During the interval he pointed out to her the publisher of The Collected Poems, a small provincial house. Not Faber & Faber, he said in his rather carrying Belfast voice, though good enough to dazzle his female Eng. Lit. students. One of the perks of academic life – the young women students, he added with perhaps just a shade of bitterness that ran the risk of slightly undoing the softening up done by his praise of older women but he made her laugh again when he said that maybe there was a talent scout from Faber & Faber here tonight as poetry was now one of the performing arts and Faber & Faber auditioned poets these days like song and dance turns – don't call us we'll call you. He excused himself to go to the toilet to prepare himself for his own performance at the rostrum by taking a long swig from a hip flask of gin in one of the cubicles. On the way out he took a small green Cub cap hanging on a peg and stuffed it in his pocket with a smile.

While he was away the young woman student sitting with Collected Poems asked indignantly who that awful Irishman was making those remarks. It is CD Blackstaff, said Collected Poems with distaste, seemingly sober at this stage presumably to impress the wellheeled lady he is currently battening upon. Aren't you Seedy, he said softly as CD reappeared and headed straight for the rostrum without waiting for the polite applause for the previous reader to stop. If it's Seedy's Walt Whitman turn that he's been putting readings to sleep with for years you'll wish you hadn't come my dear, it's like the bloody book of Genesis.

When CD took the rostrum he whipped out the tiny Cub's cap and perched it on the top of his head half turning toward the Scout Law with upraised hand. 'I promise,' he read, 'to smile and whistle under all circumstances and not to use bad language,' at which the audience laughed in appreciation of his dig at Collected Poems.

The audience now being warmed up by his little joke, and himself warmed up by the gin – and also by the hope of a bit of youknowwhat later if he played his cards right – CD placed before him a single grubby sheet that had obviously been around a bit and Collected Poems whispered acidly that mercifully, it was a shorter one than he had feared – probably one of Seedy's back street Louis MacNeice pastiches which I have had the satisfaction of dismissing with contempt in...

AHEM, admonished CD loudly, snatching off the Cub cap as if to take a swipe at Collected Poems, and then, after replacing it and putting on a pair of spectacles mended with adhesive tape he began reading from the page before him.

AVE ATQUE VALE

(Until recent times there lived at the end of Barnet High Street two sisters who were the last of the Royal House of Tudor)

My father's old aunt was the last of *her* line.
I was allowed to play her gramophone to forget the
    odour of her room
But not to sit on a chair like a throne they called a
    commode
Nor take down the picture of the Union of Iron
    Turners
To draw its tallchimneyed mills and ocean liners
And sturdy workmen clasping hands across a sea.
I played *I Dreamt That I Dwelt In Marble Halls*

While my mother listened eagerly to the right way of it
On who was who; on second wives and property not
    left out right
On seed and breed and generation and where people
    were buried.

She once came to our house despite her bulk and
    infirmity.
I watched in awe the furniture pushed about to steer
    her in.
People shouting directions, the cat booted astonished
    from the hearth.
It was like some great ship being brought to dock
The fuss half real, half laid on for ceremony.
That was his father's aunt, my mother said of me with
    satisfaction
And faces turned surprised to study me and murmured
Well now! Goodness knows! Dearie me!
Seeming to saddle me with complicity in her monstrous
    creation.

Others too reported similar momentous visits
That must have been some kind of leavetaking grand
    tour.
The last was to the cemetery and her husband's grave.
But not to take her leave. No.
I heard about it at her funeral ham tea. How
A gravedigger she had a word with had
Told her not to worry missus, she'd be all right. How
To reassure her so that she took to her bed content,
    had
Put the rod in to show her there was room.
The audience was unsure that this was the end until CD
produced the Cub cap and made a show of holding it out
for coins at which a few tittered uneasily and gave a few

claps of applause. Two male poets rushed towards the rostrum but stopped halfway as CD invited what he described as a bright new talent to read a poem he was proud to be going to publish in the next issue of the *Clerkenwell Review*. Judith Walsh-Massingham, he announced, in the manner of a master of ceremonies and he beckoned to her impatiently as she at first tried to protest but then saw that it would be less embarrassing to obey the summons. She read in a pleasant educated voice a very nice little poem about the Suffolk landscape and sky which left a pleasing delicate impression as of a good water colour copy of a minor Constable. Its brevity also pleased so that Judith, to her delight, was applauded with a genuine warmth. It gave her a tiny little taste of acclaim that was quite exciting and made her drop instantly her intention of remonstrating with CD for not warning her he was going to do that. And she was going to get into print! How nice. What a pity Colin drank so much. His breath always smelt of spirits. He would be quite nice if he did not. He must have been a good looking man once before he got his... She did not like the name beer belly. What was it the French called the paunch Frenchman got from wine? Oh yes. Cussion d'amour. A love cushion. Well! Oh dear, he's off again somewhere. To have another little tot of spirits? Isn't his nose red enough! I'll get away as quickly as I can, she thought, otherwise he'll start misbehaving himself.

In the toilets CD was replacing the Cub cap on the peg and his hip flask in his pocket. Collected Poems was at the urinal.

Ah, said CD, a chance to consult the fountainhead. I'm trying to track down a love poem I saw in an anthology once and I forget whose. It's about a rural swain called Alfred and his girl Sue making love in the churchyard on a grassy mound that is Alfred's grandfather's grave. There's a stanza that goes something like this:

With his grandfather cold beneath him
And Alfred hot on top
Something something something
She rose to meet the life to come.

Try Hardy, said Collected poems coldly.

Doesn't sound like Hardy to me, said CD doubtfully and then went on, here's something else in your Eng. Lit. department line, I want an article on Jack Judge, the composer of the song *Tipperary*, the greatest marching song the world has ever known. What about one of your students doing a bit of research – would get them into print. Could slip in a mention of yourself you know 'without whose unfailing help etc.'

Oh, I hardly think it's quite our line, said Collected Poems distastefully, buttoning up his flies.

But you see, said CD excitedly, there's a mystery there. It was never published, never sung by big name music hall singers, so how did it catch on for God's sake. Poor old Jack Judge who composed it and sung it never got a penny. Good bit of research there. Osmosis in Art, he suggested as a title.

As Collected Poems shook his head and tried to leave CD blocked his path and leaned his face confidentially to his ear.

How's your menopause these days. Still getting your ... ah ... your tutorials I see, he whispered with exaggerated leering innuendo, motioning with his head in the direction of the girl student in the hall.

Leave me in peace, said Collected Poems wearily but grandly, make good love to your woman and leave me in peace.

Before making his exit he still had to endure CD miming the writing down of his words repeating them at writing speed, make ... good love...

Oh, very good, CD called after him admiringly, the mantle of Earnest Hemingway, play it close to the horns boyo.

Already he was mentally fashioning the little encounter into a good anecdote for literary drinking acquaintances, modifying some features to make it tell better such as that he had been standing alongside the Sex Poet and had told him ('says I') he should give a plaster cast of his credentials to the Natural History museum until the originals become available.

When he returned to Judith he would have liked to tell her that Collected Poems had just referred to her as 'your woman' but he thought better of it when he saw that she was still in the spiritual afterglow of a good reading in which she had succeeded, for a moment or two, in conveying something of her love for the flat wide-skied Suffolk countryside. On seeing her to the tube he had to be content with a little kiss on the cheek and an ambiguous though sweet smile when he looked at her wistfully and quoted The Book of Judith at her, '... for Judith, daughter of Merari, made him weak with the beauty of her countenance.'

But perhaps it was just as well. He was in a drinking mood and would consume a lot more drink before the evening was out and knew only too well the truth of Shakespeare's adage about drink provoking the desire but taking away the performance. Besides that he was also in the mood for easy careless company rather than intimate companionship – for which he had little gift – and what better place to find it than a bar full of Londoners, cheerful, gregarious, and anonymous. He walked through Fulham towards the river, passing several public houses, put off by the throbbing disco music blaring raucously to lure in the mindless young and intending to enter the first that gave out only the babble of voices talking. He crossed Battersea Bridge and glanced down at the swirls and eddies of the grey waters of the

Thames on an ebb flood tide bearing restless debris to the sea and he wondered about endings and beginnings and death and drowning and suicide. He turned down an unfamiliar side street near the famous home for stray dogs and smiled at the subdued chorus of yelps, whines, and barks of its residents. He saw nearby an interesting looking public house with the sign 'The Angel'. Its ornate Victorian Gothic style of architecture with turrets, pillars, and tiles around the entrance suggested immediately the word 'palace', a one time gin palace that had been the focal point of the surrounding streets of drab artisan's houses some of which were now being tarted up to sell to a very different class to whom they were becoming fashionable. When he went inside CD's expert eye spotted signs of refurbishing to cater for the modern tastes, including loudspeakers on the walls for barbaric disco though the wires protruding from them had, mercifully, not yet been connected. In a corner was a battered upright piano with the bottom panel missing so that the strings showed. A small elderly man began tinkling at it experimentally and a group of older people playing dominoes at a table shouted up the names of songs encouragingly. After a while a tough looking old man with a surprisingly sweet voice began to sing as he played his cards and moved his dominoes and some of the others joined in. CD listened with pleasure. His musical tastes had been early and permanently affected by gramophone records of songs from the English and American music halls as well as by the tuneful hymns he had heard so often in church or in meeting houses and Gospel Halls. As the drink spread its glow through his veins and he listened benignly to the sometimes half-hearted sometimes lusty community singing he seemed to hear not only the songs being sung such as 'We'll Meet Again' or 'Underneath The Arches' but, faintly as a background others from his childhood: 'I Dream of Jeannie'; 'The Old Rugged Cross' . . .

27

Then the pianist played the first bars of 'Tipperary'. The old sweet voiced dominoes player sang some of the words and stopped to take a pull from his beer. CD spoke to him about the odd and pathetic mystery of the greatest marching song the world has ever known which was not composed as a song for war or soldiers. The old man agreed it was a bleeding shame and thanked CD for telling him about Jack Judge the composer. But he could offer no opinion on how it had come to be taken up so swiftly by men on the march, by regiments, armies, peoples.

Sponteous, said CD earnestly and then tried again, spontaneous osmosis. His speech was beginning to be affected by drink. He began to speak in the slow deliberate manner required to avoid slurring.

Research is needed, he said slowly and solemnly, it is crying out for research, as I represented very forcibly to someone in a position to have it carried out this very day not a mile away from where you are sitting in that chair.

Many voices around him took up the famous song.

> Farewell Piccadilly, goodbye Leicester Square
> It's a long long way to Tipperary
> But my heart lies there.

Judge and Williams, went on CD though no one was listening, Williams was a cripple and Judge a small time music hall singer. It was 1912, the year of the Titanic. Judge must have sung it at the bottom of the bill round the halls in Manchester but how many people would have heard it? It was never published, never recorded. Yet a nation went to war singing it. Judge and Williams never got a penny.

> What's the use of worrying
> It never was worth while

28

Williams, continued CD to nobody in particular, died just after the war, but Judge lived for many years in a back street two up two down in Salford with a card in the window that said 'Jack Judge, Composer of Tipperary'. CD's voice took on a note of awe as he came to the thing that most deeply impressed him. They say, said CD sorrowfully, that that card looked no different to other cards in other windows in that street: 'Boots Mended'; 'Room to let'.

> Pack up your troubles in your old kitbag
> And smile, smile, smile.

I am determined, said CD, to put that injustice right in the pages of the *Clerkenwell Review*. Here, he said to the old man back at his dominoes, do you think the British Legion would put up funds for the research? Dammit, the greatest marching song in the world.

Nah, said the old man contemptuously, they did sweet eff all for me about my back that I got done in with the Signals.

The time for research is short, said CD very slowly, as people old enough to recall the years 1912 to 1914 are being gathered in by the rate greaper.

The rate what? said the old man.

The great reaper, said CD, thinking he was merely repeating what he had just said. Time's winged chariot. Sergeant Death feeling your collar. Abide with me. Show me the way to go home.

They were singing that right now and CD joined in.

> I had a little drink about an hour ago
> And it went right to my head.

He rose to go to the loo. There he discovered that the

hip flask of gin in his pocket still had an inch or two in it and he finished it off at a swallow. He walked a little unsteadily into the evening streets vaguely wanting something but not sure what. Jellied eels? Sex? Mozart's violin concerto in G? Chopped chicken livers and rye bread at Bloom's? Another drink, another pub? Yes. He re-crossed the river by Chelsea bridge with a step that felt as light as air, and he smiled as his mind rummaged with pleasure among a rag bag of drink-associated words.

Bottoms up. Cheers. Here's mud in your eye. Next year in Jerusalem. Slanchen. Mother's ruin. The Demon Rum. John Barleycorn. Guinness is good for you. Great stuff this Bass. In vino veritas.

> Hark the temperance bells are ringing
> Joyous music fills the air

One for the road. Name your poison. The auld uncle on the methylated. Bubbles beading at the brim. You'll have one yourself. Paralytic. In good form. The anti-treating league. Father dear father won't you come home. Bushmills Whiskey the spirit of the age. Hitting the bottle. For medicinal purposes only.

> Sweet hope in the home of the drunkard has risen
> Where the darkness of sorrow too long held his reign

Pissed as a newt. Signing the pledge. Linked to the door by the taxi man. Not a drop is sold till it's seven years old. Tied houses. Empties in every corner of the house.

> Toil on the morning cometh
> The port you yet shall win
> And all the bells of God shall ring
> The ship of temperance in.

CD smiled fondly as time-mellowed fragments of his Belfast protestant culture competed for his benevolence. Those Gospel hymns belted out in tin-roofed tabernacles. He should have invoked them at the poetry reading. He should have engaged in a bit of a cod for an epilogue. It had occurred to him, but Judith might not have liked it. Next time he would. He would invite the catholic Irish poets – there are always catholic Irish poets at readings – to share certain feelings aroused by the sound of a Belfast gospel hall joyously not letting the devil have all the best tunes, well knowing that catholic Ireland is embarrassed by any publicity given to the fact that there is more than one culture in Ireland. Ha ha! He laughed pleasedly at the prospect of putting however small a toe up the priest-ridden crotch of the cultural arrogance of catholic Ireland. Ah, he would say, inviting them to confess to it. It takes you back like Proust's madeleine, doesn't it indeed, the sound of the old favourite protestant hymns heard in exile, eh? How oft have you stopped to linger pensively at the meeting place of a London Christian sect, the light of other days around you from the sound of the singing. Especially the women's voices. The sound of women's sweet voices belting out the old Sankey favourites is especially rousing, is it not, eh? More than once have you gone on your way hoping your excitement will not be visible to the pagan multitudes of the great metrollops as, with hand in pocket, you manoevre your downward-trapped erection to let it lie less noticeably up the belly, but even so, bearing it uncomfortably on bus or tube with a spot of involuntarily emitted semen showing faintly through the material of your trousers. Eh? Eh?

From Transcript of Court Proceedings.

C.D. Blackstaff appeared before magistrates at Kensington

District Court charged with a breach of the peace at Fulham
Road Pentecostal Tabernacle. Mr Blackstaff, whose
occupation was given as Man of Letters, was said to have
interrupted a service on 21st October and to have committed
an assault with a hymn book, causing actual bodily harm.
Elder of the Church Samuel Bumpers said that the Defendant
entered the Tabernacle smelling of drink during the breaking
of bread, but was allowed to take a seat at the back and
was furnished with a book of sacred songs and solos. The
Defendant stood up several times during the service to
make requests for hymn numbers other than those
announced and attempted to sing them himself, urging
the Brethren to join in. Police were called after the Defendant
threw a hymn book at the lead singer of The Verily, a
gospel group, causing bruising around the eye. PC Moresby
of South Kensington Police Station, said that the Defendant
was making a disturbance in an Irish accent with drink
taken, and had said that he would refuse to leave the
premises until they sang the hymn He's The Lily of the
Valley in the old way, and minimum force had to be used
to take the Defendant to South Kensington Police Station
where he was charged.

Mr McCardle, defending, said his client would not contest
the prosecution's evidence, and was deeply sorry for what
he had done, but had pleaded NOT GUILTY in order to
put before the Court extenuating circumstances. His client
was a widely known writer in his field, which was the
protestant culture of his native Belfast, where he had been
brought up in a God-fearing home. He had entered Fulham
Road Pentecostal Tabernacle with the deepest respect in
order to listen to the hymn singing, which would remind
him of his formative years. It was unfortunate that the
hymn singing on this occasion was being led by what is
called a Group, a collection of energetic young persons
who shout, yell and prance about to the beating of drums

electrically amplified in a manner identical to that which, as the Court knows, has alienated those of our generation from the popular music of today. His client was very upset to hear a favourite hymn from childhood being rendered in this manner, which his client considered blasphemous. He would add that his client was under great stress following the closure of a magazine dedicated to the raising of artistic standards in the young. Testimonials of good character from Lady Judith Walsh-Manningham, widow of Lt. General Walsh-Manningham KCVD, and from Nigel Lambton, an Actuary in the service of a leading insurance company, would be placed before the Court.

Mr Lovibond from the Bench said he had to take a very serious view of the police being called to a place of worship. However sad it might be that what he himself had often referred to as 'noise pollution' in the name of music should have now, it seemed, spread to religious gatherings. However, he could not have traditionalists causing breaches of the peace. He would advise Mr Blackstaff to confine his religious observances to churches where they still worshipped in a civilised manner. If he would remain behind after the Court rose, he would let him have the name of someone who could help him find a meeting house where they still accompanied their singing on the harmonium. Regretfully, he had no option but to impose a fine of ten pounds, and bind the defendant over in two sureties of twenty pounds.

3

There was another means, besides keeping a count of his drinks, by which he sought to impose order and control upon the disorder of his ways and that was by giving an account of himself into his tape recorder with a vague view to composing his memoirs. The cassettes accumulated unlabelled since he had originally intended to have them typed as he filled them but his intention had not yet been put into effect even though he could easily have found a willing typist among the authors of the unsolicited writings which littered his room, eager for his approval. This was partly because he found that he rather enjoyed playing back a cassette taken at random from the growing pile like a lucky dip and listening to something he had half forgotten, so that in the brief interval of not remembering having spoken a phrase that was rather good he could enjoy moments of the pleasure one gets on listening to someone speak well on a subject of interest. As well as that he had the bar room raconteur's gift of mimicry which would of course be lost on the silent page.

One evening with a quota of gin inside him to top up the intake in several bars, both totted up in his diary with what he believed was meticulous accuracy, it amused him to speak into his recorder in a persona not his own. He mimicked the presenter of a popular television programme called THIS IS YOUR LIFE in which a famous person, supposedly unsuspecting, is ambushed, lured to a studio, and made to listen to their life history read to them from a large black book in a stern voice, almost accusatory, like

an indictment, even when the facts, supported incontro-
vertibly by witnesses, were not discreditable. So he too
stood before his recorder as if confronting a defendant
and in an accent not his own and with only the merest
hint of being inebriated, he accused himself of the following
facts.

Your first earnings from writing were at the age of sixteen
for unpublished work commissioned privately by a patron,
a well read protestant male getting on in years who made
your acquaintance at the threepenny and sixpenny end of
the bookstall outside the second hand bookshop in
Smithfield market run by the woman with the bus conductor's
money satchel which she would rattle from time to time
to remind the browsers that the books were for sale for
modest sums. You had just purchased for sixpence the
Essays of William Hazlitt that appeared to have been a
school prize in the year 1905 to a boy in the sixth form
of the Royal Belfast Academical Institution whose name
you later adopted as one of your literary pseudonyms. He
initiated a conversation with you in which he spoke
authoritatively about Hazlitt's work as well as that of Rabelais
and the Marquis de Sade. He invited you to partake of
refreshments at the fish and chips shop adjoining Robinson's
bar, where, behind the cover of his hand he poured
something from a small bottle into his lemonade saying it
was for his old complaint. He recommended you to read
Hazlitt's Liber Amoris about Hazlitt's frustrated and half
consummated affair with his landlady's daughter Sarah
Walker which shocked the readers of that time expurgated
though it was. He said that an unexpurgated version would
be just the kind of thing 'naughty boys like you would
love'. There was something in the tone in which he said
'naughty boys' that alarmed you. Had he been sitting beside
you in the back seat of a cinema you would have got up
abruptly and left as you had done the previous year in the

Hippodrome opposite Robinson's bar when a man getting
on in years had bought you an ice cream and then attempted
to masturbate you during the burning of Atlanta in Gone
With The Wind. But in fact it was a very different proposition
he put to you after eliciting from you a confession of
literary ambition, virginity and lustful imaginings. He
enquired if you never tried writing down these imaginings.
As a literary exercise of course. Practising the craft of
words. He said that the intensity of the urges involved gave
a unique vividness to that branch of juvenilia, which, he
assured you had been practised by many famous writers
and poets including Leo Tolstoy, Thomas Hardy and Alfred,
Lord Tennyson, though, inevitably, little of it had survived
due to the vandalism of prudish executors. He said that
if you met him the following week at the same second
hand bookstall with a couple of pages he would pay you
well in addition to giving you valuable literary criticism
and fish and chips. So every Saturday you handed over to
him two foolscap pages of your sexual fantasies. He was
always what, in your innocence, you thought of as being
late, but was more likely a precaution to make sure that
you came alone and not accompanied by burly male relatives
intent upon chastisement and perhaps prosecution. You
never learnt his name nor where he lived and your one
attempt to follow him in dark glasses with your collar
turned up ended abruptly when a shopkeeper into whose
window you were feigning to stare intently while your
literary patron did up a shoelace emerged from the shop
and subjected you to verbal abuse which included the claim
that you needed your arse kicked. From the manner adopted
by your patron, his knowledge of literature – and the
technical advice with which he guided you away from your
first clumsy erotic fantastications for which he paid you
only sixpence to more satisfyingly plausible fictions about
real women and girls known to you for which he gave you

a shilling you surmised that he had been a teacher, possibly
– though this was based only on a remark made as he
doctored his fish and chip shop lemonade for his old
complaint – in the Royal Belfast Academical Institution.
You found that there was no need to write furtively in
great privacy; your school English homework gave a perfect
opportunity to scribble away without arousing curiosity
though taking care to keep separate the two somewhat
different literary forms.

The earliest pieces for which your patron rewarded you
with more than sixpence were influenced by the advice of
Anton Chekov *write about what you know* quoted by the
correspondence course you were paying for in monthly
instalments entitled 'You too can write for big money'. So
you wrote about the solitary act except that you made it
no longer solitary. Remembering the times just after puberty
when boys had exposed and fumbled with your private
parts you set down these experiences but you changed the
sex of those who had explored your body and you made
the fumblings more purposeful and carried to a concluding
climax. At first this was only half successful since your
female partners in these acts were creatures of fantasy such
as the beautiful and mysterious woman in a veil who bought
you ice cream in the back seats of the Hippodrome and
masturbated you with a silk gloved hand during the burning
of Atlanta in Gone With The Wind. You were later to do
a more effective version in which the woman was a real
person: the unmarried daughter of a Church of Ireland
monumental stone mason for whom your father made
boots and whom people criticised behind his back for not
letting her marry despite her good looks. But in the
meantime you pleased your patron with pieces set at puberty
involving females of your acquaintance: cousins; neighbours;
girls at school. The first piece to get your fee raised to
the ten shillings level described you being forced by a

cousin and her friend in the girl guides to serve as a model
for them to exhibit your private parts to other girls for a
charge of sixpence increased to one shilling if they wished
to stay for what was called 'The Demonstration'. This was
when they masturbated you to show what the stuff that
makes babies is like, accompanying the demonstration with
confidently stated though dubious facts such as that once
your thing got rubbed it had to go on till the stuff came
out or else it would go into your system and poison you
or give you shingles; that it took so much out of you that
you could hardly walk for an hour afterwards and sometimes
needed beef tea or egg beat up in warm milk; that the
stuff was so strong it would kill warts; that the reason the
girls weren't allowed to bring their dogs with them was
that they would be put on heat if they smelt it and that a
woman who made up cures from handed-down recipes put
it into the cure for baldness that some of their fathers
used.

This milestone piece was followed by more on the same
theme. There was the strapping sixth form daughter of
the police sergeant across the road whose father encouraged
her scientific inclinations by buying her a microscope. With
this she studied spermatozoa forcibly extracted from you
twice on a Sunday afternoon despite your protests that
such a short interval would impair your health. There was
the still good looking mother of a classmate who accidentally
dropped a pot of stew on your lap and had to make sure
you had suffered no serious injury, giving you her breast
to suck as she established this conclusively.

After a time your patron suggested you be bolder and
extend your range closer to the act itself. Surely, he said,
a good looking boy like you must have tried things with
girls. It was a day he did not have his remedial bottle with
him and you had to wait outside Robinson's while he got
something for his old complaint. He said it was sometimes

the boy who was too timid to effect penetration of the girl. He said he had once known such a boy and he produced some pages of typing, frayed and yellowing, which he said might be of guidance but would not allow you to take away though you would have liked to as it was indeed interesting. It was about two thirteen-year-old cousins, a boy and a girl, in a rambling house after a family funeral. The two are sent out of the way to the lumber attic to look for treasure among ancient bric a brac while the adults argue about property and who was to get what. The treasure the boy finds is the girl's body which she allows him to explore in delighted wonder, knowing he will be too timid to do more than insert his finger in awe into her beautiful sexual organ. But in fact he goes a little further. With one hand between her legs and the other between his own through his pocket he suddenly puts his mouth to hers to do more than kiss as, with a convulsive sob, he floods his saliva into her mouth and this she accepts and swallows without demur as the voices below are suddenly raised in anger over what should have been in the will.

Even on a hurried reading of this ragged well thumbed piece you felt a stirring of the loins that was a tribute to the quality of its eroticism and you had your first taste of a writer's bitter jealousy for the superior work of another in the same field, a feeling the manifestations of which not only in yourself but in others you were to become sadly familiar with in later years. You demanded almost angrily to know who had written it but your patron pocketed it very hastily and would only hint that it had been written by a now distinguished man of letters who might still be identified by the detail in the descriptions of the things the children discover in the lumber room – before they discover each other. You did not have the temerity to say that you hoped he was taking similar care of your own work in which you had left people and places with their real names. But perhaps the main effect of reading this and perhaps the one intended was to spur you to compete, and indeed on your next rendezvous you turned up with your most effective piece. At first sight it was an imitation of what had inspired it even down to two thirteen-year-old cousins. But in fact it was taken mostly from memory and was nearly true. Your cousin and yourself. She had been evacuated to a farm in County Antrim after Belfast was bombed in the war and you also stayed there in the school holidays. One summer the two of you made a bathing pool out of an old flax retting dam. In your written version the two of you did not keep a promise to each other not to look when one day you bathed nude together. And so the girl saw what she should not have seen which was what the boy should not have had – an erection. Spontaneously they start to wrestle while wet and the girl feels something hard pushing and rubbing against her. She knows she should push the boy away but goes on wrestling with him till suddenly he gives a little cry and goes limp in her arms and when they rise to dry themselves, now hiding their nakedness in guilt and shame the girl sees, half in disgust half in fascination, grey droplets of a glutinous fluid upon her belly and thighs which she wipes away with such force that the marks are still there when she is getting ready for church the following Sunday. Your patron was delighted and wanted more like it but you had tired of the theme of puberty and turned to one more in tune with your immediate longings. You wrote boldly of full sexual initiation. You wrote it as usual as you did your homework on the living room table but in the very presence of the woman who featured in it, a contralto in your church choir who had called to give your father his part in an anthem to be sung at some special service or other. Although of your parents' generation and inclined to stoutness she was quite fancyable and had often unknowingly alleviated the tedium of church for you when you got into a pew facing the women in the choir. In this piece you hit upon a technique used by some of the greatest writers to cover up some weakness, an inability to do something other lesser writers do easily and by disguising it or avoiding it turn it into a strength. In your case it was inexperience of what you were attempting to describe. So in your narrative of being seduced by a church chorister when she was looking after you during a crisis in your family she came to your bed at night with no more light than that from a window blind made luminous by a street lamp, showing you nothing of herself, playing the dominant role, taking your virginity unmistakably indeed but allowing you to confess no more accurate knowledge of female anatomy than before, especially as you plausibly claimed also to have been too timid to touch her with your hands in the place of which you were most ignorant even after it had irradiated your being with swoon inducing sweetness.

But alas. This piece had unfortunate consequences. When your patron took the foolscap pages from you and unfolded them he was so put out by what he saw that he dropped the bottle of remedy for his old complaint with a crash instead of shielding it from view. What you had handed him was a translation from Caesar's Gallic Wars which should have gone to your latin teacher Miss Batefield, a severe lady nearing retirement age, to whom, through carelessness you must have submitted your very plausible account of being initiated by one whom Miss Batefield may well have heard singing the contralto solos in Handel's Messiah not to mention Land Of Hope And Glory from the bandstand in the park on V E Day.

We now have a difficulty, squire. There is a hiatus, sunshine. Evidence is ambiguous, confusing and conflicting on what happened next. Waters have been muddied, veils drawn, witnesses got at. We were forced to fall back upon a method of research frowned upon by the Biographers Friendly Society who have struck members off the register for practising it on the Q T.

At this point CD, staggering slightly, picked up an unsolicited manuscript and tried to drape it round his head like a shawl. He cupped his hands round his eyes to concentrate his gaze into the bottle of gin as if it were a fortune teller's globe. He put on a falsetto voice. I am getting agitated figures some gesticulating. Voices are coming through, some angry and shouting. I am getting a figure in an academic gown; a fish frying basket, a bus with Finaghy on it being hurriedly boarded. There is a voice coming through 'you will take geography for the remainder of the term instead of latin'. Is that your headmaster? What is he doing with the fish frier? Is there some coded message there? I'm getting Bing Crosby singing White Christmas and a gold plated fountain pen. What can that mean? Ah yes, a Christmas present. There is a woman's voice coming through very angry 'was this what you were bought that pen for ... should take a stick to you ... not to be trusted with pen and paper'. Is that your mother? I'm getting the academic gown again with a schoolgirl in the back seats of the Hippodrome. Does that mean you had your headmaster at it too? But surely that was a later phase of your work not your juvenalia, this is most confusing. I'm getting a white aproned figure and an angry voice 'no drink allowed ... corrupting a minor with drink ... get the police to ye ... need your arses kicked the pair of you'. I'm getting another figure in white, a bride, a virgin? No, its a church of Ireland minister in the back seat of the Hippodrome with the choir contralto but surely that was your more mature work, these waters are very muddied. There is the same woman's voice coming through quoting scripture 'he that looketh at a woman with lust in his eyes also committeth adultery'. I'm getting a cobble stoned arcade, secondhand bookshops with school books, schoolboys and schoolgirls with lists of set books including Caesar's Gallic Wars and retired schoolteachers with Royal Belfast Academical Institution on their blazer badges passing among them with fish and chip frying baskets, propositions, and free gold plated fountain pens. There is deep symbolism in that which I will get to the bottom of don't you worry, my old china. But where is this leading, how was this affair brought to a conclusion. The picture is darkening. I'm getting only spilt bottles; academic gowns; fish frying; hands moving up and down in back seats of cinemas. The voices coming through are getting faint. I'm getting very faintly a man and a woman arguing, 'will go no further if... ah, you know, young fellows growing up ... no excuse for lust ... blackguarding a respectable woman ... could have got jail ... her father in the masonic...' I'm getting ... nothing ... damn all ... its all gone.

What was your first published work? Did it concern epic themes: Courage; Betrayal; Passion; Art; Religion, Politics, Women, The Human Condition? No. *A Visit to Guinness Brewery, Dublin* in the school magazine. A subsequent piece entitled *A Visit to Bushmills Distillery* was turned down without explanation, your first rejection of many. The facts and figures about the production and consumption of stout and whiskey failed to capture the readers' imagination. The equation Carbohydrate + Yeast = Alcohol + Carbon Dioxide did not, for others, have a mathematical elegance. Few took delight in the pleasing words, some strange, others used strangely. Mash, gravity, proof spirit, ethyl, butyl, propyl. It is true that there were one or two sentences here and there that had a bit of life in them such as the one about the huge fermentation vats at the Guinness

Brewery in Dublin: 'The lake of foam never still but heaving, sighing, breathing, making long po-ooh and pah-ah ploppings like the exhalations from a million flabby lips' but the rest was too dry.

Need it have been so? What about that publican your father got the Guinness visitor's passes from? Raided by the police for after hours drinking. A gambling den as well. The RUC constable badly bruised by the jostling he got from the gamblers grabbing at the piles of money on the table, the women worse than the men. Yes, Women. Was it only the card school the women were there for? Eh? Eh? Oh there was talk. Now that would have put a bit of colour in the school magazine, And the publican an atheist, proclaimingly openly he believed in nothing. Not long after that dying a notorious sinner's death, gambling and drinking to the last, propped up in bed playing poker, barely able to hold the cards from the cancer, denying God to the end. A bit of human interest there you could have worked in. That correspondence course you signed up for a year or two later on How To Write For Big Money and never finished, the one that sent you the solicitor's letter for its instalment money, told you about *the human interest* and quoted Chekhov on that very point. Less of discoursing on jacket condenser and coil condenser stills, fractional distilling out of the methyls, butyls and propyls and a more *human interest* What about your father showing you up in the hospitality room of Guinness Brewery at the end of the guided tour eh? Refusing a second glass on account of 'the auld stomach'. And *farting*. Fears that he might let one off had never been far from the mind of our budding Hazlitt of Form IV, and, as the touring party had looked into the fermenting vat from the viewing platform listening with awe to the poohing pahing plops 'from the million flabby lips' you had thought 'do it here, if you are going to do it, do it here'. But no, he had to wait for the quiet of the hospitality room. And with such *satisfaction*. The agonies that fathers cause their teenage sons! Mind you, you're going a bit that way yourself now. Oh it's been noticed, Sunny Jim, don't you kid yourself: the shifting onto one buttock on the bar stool to try to ease the sphincter open a crack for silent exhalation – not always successful – though five out of ten for trying to keep it out of earshot.

But was there not another literary effort round about that time also rejected? Moreover not a dry technical treatise but movingly eloquent, passionate, from the heart. On the subject of circumcision no less. Write about what you know, Chekhov had said in that correspondence course and you certainly knew about that, oh too damned well you knew. Tell us about it while I get you another sup of gin – ethyl alchohol incidentally, your butlys and propyls would have killed you a damned sight quicker than this is doing. Tell us why you wrote to the press about it with such feeling.

Because it was a disgrace in a so called civilised age! Dear Sir, I wrote, I am aware that this is not a Moslem country with strict segregation of the sexes but... Oh I told them straight. I called for the matron to be struck off the register for allowing it to happen. Surely, I wrote, in a country calling itself civilised other arrangements could be made for this operation with some regard for its delicate nature. I am, I said, considering making a complaint to the British Medical Association about the callous indifference to the sensitivity of youth shown by our family doctor notwithstanding his well known service in the first world war. Oh I let them have it, squire! What? Did they take too much off? Oh ha ha. Listen buster, I was seventeen. At that age one is shy, vulnerable, One's private parts are never more private than at seventeen. One's natural modesty is then compounded by feelings of shame, guilt and sin. One glances surreptitiously at one's peers in changing rooms and public conveniences and seeks reassurance from the measuring tape or the ruler alas not always forthcoming. One fears divine retribution for certain solitary acts in the form of stunted growth, pimples, mental impairment, blindness. One is alarmed by symptoms and manifestations on one's private parts which one hopes will disappear if one is good. One consults the *Daily Mail* Home Doctor in vain. One widens one's research in the public library. A great amount of information is acquired. One learns of strange devices patented by English school masters claimed to cure the habit. Illustrations are studied of the symptoms of venereal disease including the terminal stages of syphilis. One feels oneself to be leprous, outcast. Then just when one is about to end it all one's research is rewarded. Later one is hard put to it to recall under which entry, foreskin or prepuce, both cross referenced to circumcision, one at last tracked it down. One's relief is blissful. One can now go to one's family doctor in a glow of virtue vindicated. Confidently one enters the surgery not so much to consult as to confirm, expecting to be congratulated upon the accuracy of one's diagnosis, perhaps even to air one's recently acquired scholarship, letting fall a remark or two upon the religious aspect as for instance that Jewish Rabbis are equipped with a special instrument though some could perform the circumcision as swiftly upon babies with a sharpened thumbnail. But one reckoned without the crassness of a family doctor of the old school, though perhaps it should have prepared one for what was to follow in the public ward of the hospital. What? No he didn't use his thumbnail! Listen squire, in I march to his surgery expecting to see *him*. On his own, buster, on his own. Well you don't expect spectators, do you? *Young women* spectators. Well one young woman. Yours truly here has picked an evening when the old bugger has a learner in to watch! Come on, come on, he says, waving a paw at my flies, lets have a bloody look at it. Bluff military type, never done cursing. I'm damned, says he, but you couldn't have left that much bloody longer – and waves me into the light so that the girl could see! How's that, old sport, for sparing the feelings of blushing youth, for awareness of the poetry of awakening manhood? The old ward sister in the Infirmary knew better than that. I'll do that patient's dressings nurse, she would call out sharply when one of the young nurses headed my way, and if they asked why she told them off, 'I said *I'll* do it, nurse,' says she very sharp. Oh a bit of discipline is good to see isn't it, squire? Make the young bitches do what they're told. Far too bloody lenient with them, no wonder the world is in the state it's in. So what was I writing to the papers about? Ah well, you see the old ward sister wasn't on duty the next evening. Where, I enquire with an outward nonchalance I am far from feeling, is sister so-and-so? Off-duty, I'm informed by this much younger sister. Has she left instructions, says I with mounting apprehension? What instructions, says she impatiently. And what could I say? The instruction that I was to have my dressings changed only by an older woman I wanted to tell that bitch. Then, guess what, my old china? You'll never believe this could happen a mere bus ride away from the centre of Belfast, a city believing itself civilised. What? One's eye was suddenly arrested by touches of bright colour among the austere white uniforms of the nursing staff. One is informed the reason for it. It is the Red Cross and St John's Ambulance Brigade evening. When they come in to help and to watch! And who is among them, pal? None other than two young ladies whom yours truly here has been worshipping from afar, making sheep's eyes at, too shy to declare his true feelings when they met at socials and parties. What? Just in it for the pretty uniform? Oh right on, sunshine, right on. And very fetching they looked too. Am aware, I said in my letters to the press and other bodies, am aware that voluntary medical organisations perform a useful function at Sports fixtures and public gatherings and that probably not all of them join just to get the attractive costume. But, I said, the male surgical wards of our hospitals are no place for the amateur, however enthusiastic. Oh, I told them, squire, I let them have it straight, old pal. No advocate, I said, of strict segregation of the sexes, nevertheless, I asked, are the most intimate parts of the male body to be exposed to the *untrained* eye and even the *unskilled* attentions of young persons of the opposite sex? Will it, I enquired, with telling sarcasm, be girl guides next? Where, I demanded to know, do the churches stand? Oh, I laid into them, sport, I bloody well hammered them! What? Protest? Sign oneself out in high dudgeon? Call for screens? One thinks of these things afterwards, squire, esprit d'escalier, the French call it. But at the time one lay transfixed, one gritted one's teeth, one mentally composed letters of complaint to the Belfast Telegraph, the Northern Whig, the British Medical Association, The Royal College of Nursing, the Queen Mother, the Royal Black Institution, while all that was beautiful in Belfast's maidenhood ranged themselves round one's bed and demurely lowered their eyes.

In his troubled sleep he dreamt of women in uniform, not nurses, but Salvation Army women. A bar he had been in the previous evening had been visited by two of them selling the War Cry. In his dream they approached CD's bed where he lay circumcised singing temperance hymns. One of the women was slim and good looking, a fact about which CD spoke into what appeared to be a recorder. '... no great risk to public order being inspected by the big sergeant major one past the menopause but that other cutie ... General Booth never intended charmers like this one to enter the danger zone ... might get a one gun salute ... John Henry standing to attention ... that marine in the next bed circumcised in Gibraltar ... told me he burst his stitches twice ... nurses had to slap at it with a cold dishcloth first...'

The Salvation Army girls had only a faint notion what he was talking about until he addressed the slender pretty one in a stronger voice.

'I'll show you if you show me, darling,' he said loudly, 'You can't say fairer than that, can you. Ah go on, just pull your skirt up and give us a wee flash, dear, it won't take a minute.'

The shocked women fled back to the group and began singing loudly a temperance hymn in praise of water. They sang it with a mixture of indignation at the Demon drink and joyful assurance that its devotees would get as much of a kick from water.

> It nerves the hand to deeds of might
> It wakes the heart to gladness
> It breathes a psalm of pure delight
> And charms us all from sadness

Young women seemed to be advancing towards him bearing gifts of mountain streams, babbling brooks, white enamel buckets of clear spring water from County Antrim. Among the Salvation Army uniforms were those of nurses, some with red crosses, and then they all seemed to fade away again into the shadows of sleep.

4

The biographical details on the jackets of his out of print books did not always agree with each other regarding what should have been simple facts such as his age, when he had left school, when he had come to London, what jobs he had done. He had, of course, as is the custom in the book trade, written them himself. Only his first book jacket mentioned insurance. Thereafter he had preferred to draw attention to his having been such things as a railway shunter, a hospital porter, a barman, since book readers are more likely than not to be women in the suburbs with dull husbands in jobs like insurance. Nevertheless the great gothic building of the Bulwark Assurance Company had been one of those he had visited on his pilgrimage of remembrance the day of his 50th birthday and he had slipped into it unnoticed to wander its corridors in search of mementoes of what he sometimes referred to as his 'previous existence', though finding few that had survived the years. But one department still in the same place was that which looked after the London properties of which the company was landlord, these being marked in red on a huge street map of the capital that dominated an entire wall. He had used to walk through this department for the purpose of discreetly marvelling at how many famous streets had blocks of red.

'And all that was *ours* on it coloured red,' he mused nostalgically, recalling the Belfast schoolrooms of his boyhood and the British Empire in red on the oilskin maps of the world, London at its heart, and then the money at the heart of London. Commerce, trade, rates of exchange.

Pitman's Commercial English. He had kept his copy for old time's sake. Written for clerks at the height of Empire. Still studied in the twilight of Empire. Clerks everywhere including in the mill offices of Belfast learnt punctuation, the use of the semi colon, the letter of enquiry, the reply to complaint, the placing of orders, the salutation, the complimentary close. London to Bombay. Lisbon to London. Belfast to London... In good English too. Like the navigation guides for ships' officers whose good simple prose was admired by Joseph Conrad. Out of fashion today. Good prose a thing of the past. Hardly read a thing these days where the writer should not have been made to take a course in Pitman's Commercial English. A good article there if I could find the time. That fellow who sent me his rubbishy novel who wants to work part time on the magazine unpaid. Terrible prose. An actuary on the Bulwark too. Might have passed him in the corridors without knowing.

He reflected on the unlikely coincidences that had people's lives touching and crossing. The Victorian writers thought nothing of it. Coincidence an essential element of their melodramas.

He took a swift swig of gin from his hip flask in a hushed corridor flanked by panels of fine wood in which were solid doors with brass nameplates all the more quietly impressive for being small. The Legal Department. Another piece of good prose came back to him from his previous existence. 'A contract is an agreement freely entered into by two or more parties to do or to withold from doing...' He inspected the nameplates. No. Such a long time ago. Long over and done with. Not a trace left of them.

In which, however, he was not entirely correct...

Mr Major from Belfast was a company solicitor specialising in insurance contracts. He had been widowed for about twenty years and for most of them lived alone in a flat off Fleet street visited only occasionally by his unmarried mathematician daughter Lucy who managed to combine being an actuary in The Bulwark Assurance Company with being unconventional in dress and behaviour which her father did not approve of. 'You don't dress like that at the office?' he once asked her and when she said she did he had said, shocked, 'Good God!' When he died after his seventieth birthday she was amazed to discover that he had been a collector of erotica. On clearing out his study she was confronted by an aspect of her conservative church going father she would never have suspected. There was a clockwork toy which set in motion a male and female figure first to dance to tinkling music and then to copulate – after ingeniously revealing the progressive arousal of the male. However although this object and several others were the most immediately noticeable it was magazines which formed the bulk of the collection, especially one magazine called EROS which was bound into sets for many years. The most recent issue had been in 1962. Probably the Lady Chatterley judgement which had made such publications no longer unlawful had also made them old fashioned and obsolete. It had been a very expensive magazine and each copy appeared to be individually numbered which seemed to indicate that it had circulated privately to a select readership. Some of the issues contained colour plates of paintings some of which were said to have been commissioned centuries ago from reputable artists for very private viewing by princes, Cardinals and Popes. From the signs of certain pages being more well turned than others it was clear that Mr Major, who came from a strict protestant home, had especially appreciated the paintings with classical biblical subjects involving sex such as Samson and Delilah, Judith and Holofernes, Susanna and the elders, and so on, in which the ladies had had restored to them the pubic hair normally denied them by conventional art (Delilah's bush was as thick as Samson's) and male figures displayed their arousal with a truth to life never seen in an art gallery. Two plates in particular had the pages around them very worn. One was at first sight based upon Rembrandt's picture of Bathseba at her toilet on her rooftop being lusted after by King David on a distant roof except that on this one David is much nearer and is plainly masturbating. The other was of the Garden of Eden done in the Holbein manner except that Adam is about to penetrate Eve. The picture was called 'Genesis'. Mr Major was obviously just as fond of anything with a religious connection in the other contents. Lucy found a sheaf of photocopied pages which, from their well thumbed condition, she guessed he had taken with him on journeys or trips without having to take the magazines. Lucy skimmed through some of the shorter pieces thinking with shocked wonder of her father's solitary widowhood and speculating what else he might have got up to. The flat bore no trace of a woman's presence or influence, being clean where cleanliness mattered, as in toilets and sinks, dusty and dowdy where it did not. And ominously, there were several empty gin bottles around as well as one half full in his study with a solitary glass. She picked up one piece by a 'C.D.B' entitled 'Second Coming':

'... still virgin at the age of 39 ... initiated by a man who came about insurance while her father was at church vestry meeting.. never seen an erection before ... smaller than masturbatory fantasies ... hurt less than expected ... but little pleasure till near end when he climaxed ... took time to overcome shock of what she had done ... began to dwell on certain images ... not only shame but excitement ... man rising from her, penis subsiding but still tumescent ... glistening with wet ... bead of semen ... very naughty fantasy to suck it hard again ... one of those women who

could pleasure herself by crossing legs and squeezing thighs
together ... began to do it in church ... pick out man in
choir or congregation ... suck a peppermint ... only a
slight flush ... the Rector as very special treat ... tall
imposing man of 60 ... forbidding manner ... note of
harsh chastisement in sermons ... Deborah sitting upright
in pew gazing at Rector ... only slightly growing flush ...
saliva flowing well round peppermint ... in theatre of her
mind ... Rector's white surplice hitched up round waist
... just risen from her ... dangly but still enlarged ...
glistening wetly ... drop of semen ... kneeling before him
... swell in her mouth for his second coming...'

Well! She would have to try it sometime! Next meeting
of the Computer Priority committee. That stern looking
white haired man, what's his name from what's that
department always goes to the bottom of the queue
Unclaimed Policies. Rather dishy. Yum. Yum. No but really
she just might show the piece to Fred, her clergyman friend
who wore leather jackets, rode a motor bike and pretended
to be unshockable. She would say it had turned up at a
meeting of the Women's Institute where they had discussed
the motion 'are men necessary'. Fred, in spite of his Hell's
Angel appearance was very high church, well into candles,
incense, leaning towards Rome.

She picked out another piece, also by this C.D.B. person,
entitled 'Madonna' and read more attentively:

'David sometimes glanced at goodlooking boys of about
17 with a slight stirring of the loins not because he was gay
but from nostalgia. At his boys' school his friend Harry had
once played the part of Mary in a nativity play. Delicate
featured Harry had looked so pretty in make up and wig
that David had taken him to an empty classroom and kissed
him full on the mouth to which Harry had responded so
eagerly that they had a session of mutual masturbation.
After that whenever they got the chance of having one of

their homes to themselves they would pleasure each other though with the variation that for David Harry would put cream on his thighs and press them together to give the sensation of a vagina and David would gaze down on the beautiful girl boy's face and fantasise the joy of first consummation still to come. On one memorable occasion at Harry's place Harry combined his madonna make up with some of his mother's underwear and also one of her little hats with a veil which so added to his allure that David had to be shushed in case the neighbours would hear him cry out as the vagina thighs took his seed into the beautiful mother of God and into all the girls he dreamed of.

'But as time went by these sessions became fewer. On the one hand David was trying for the "real thing" and on the other Harry was probably finding youths for whom he did not have to pretend to be a girl. However when, at last, David had his first experience with a girl he was disappointed that it was nowhere near as good as his half real fantasies with Harry. As time went by and he became more experienced with a succession of girl friends and two marriages his pleasure improved but never quite came up to the standard set by those romps with the madonna. Many years later in middle age he would sharpen his love-making with his wife by getting her to close her thighs when she lay under him, partly to tighten her vagina widened by child-bearing, but also for another reason. Looking down on his wife's face through half closed eyes in soft light he could mentally transform it into that of a boy madonna between whose lubricated thighs he could let old virgin fantasies run riot again about the joy from women that was still to come and yet at the same time allow words learnt at childhood Sunday school to murmur at the back of his mind: "Tell it not in Gath, publish it not in the streets of Askelon ... thy love to me was wonderful, passing the love of women".'

Oh dear. Had her father a homosexual side to him?

Boys? Hanging round Gents' toilets? Bisexual? Lucy had two gay men friends from whom she had learnt that there was a lot of it about. Those biblical scenes in EROS. The male wares displayed in full working order. Her two friends would have appreciated some of those pictures at least as much as normal men. She could hear them jokingly envy and offer to change places with the famous old testament women about to be 'known'. 'Oh aren't you lucky, ducky,' they would chortle at The Rape of Tamar. Not that she was going to let them see the pictures as they were far too indiscreet.

She wondered who this C.D.B. party was whose writings her father was so partial to since much of the photocopied material had those initials as author. Then as she leafed through more of it she caught the name Belfast several times as well as other words associated with her father's homeplace: preacher, Gospel Hall, pews, hymns. There were passages of explicit sex even steamier than in 'Second Coming' which, though it had not mentioned Belfast, clearly had a Belfast ring to it. Lucy had been taken to Belfast on visits as a child and had not enjoyed them. She had resented being taken to church there by her parents when she did not have to go in London and of being instructed to hide that fact from her grandparents, especially her grandmother, a puritanical old biddy who would not let them start a meal without a lengthy grace. Her grandmother had been a semi-invalid since Lucy's father was a child. She rose everyday at noon to bring down with her an enamel spitoon into which she had hawked phlegm during the night and which she once left standing in the kitchen for Lucy to come across before she knew what was in it and thought it was jelly. Ugh! Every time she came across those particualar biblical texts framed on her grandmother's walls – sometimes on the board of a synagogue near her flat – she thought of that awful spitoon. Yes, thought Lucy, there must have been awful lot of repressed feelings in the Belfast bible belt of her father's time though if C.D.B. was to be believed not all of it was repressed. She skimmed through another C.D.B. tale of sin and lust among the church goers and keepers of the protestant sabbath. It was called 'Handmaidens of the Lord':

Dinah and Ruth ... unmarried ... ageing parents ... keen fans of charismatic Gospel preachers ... stayed behind to collect hymn books and to give Mr Clark sex ... God's will... Mr Clark's wife an invalid ... prayed with them beforehand ... knew which one from texts in prayers about a patriarch's wives and it said which one he lay with ... made sure they had nice knickers on ... his handmaidens ... in room at back ... only prettier Dinah's breasts were exposed ... let us now be one flesh in the Lord Jesus ... disapproved of them showing signs of arousal ... filled with the holy spirit when Mr Clark ejaculated ... both in turn on nights of fervent preaching and calling out of 'hallelujah' by enthusiastic congregation ... never took off his trousers ... wrapped handkerchief round it on withdrawal ... Ruth's mouth if she had period but not Dinah's...'

Charming! The feminist in Lucy longed to put her smart pointed shoes swiftly into Mr Clark's groin. And C.D.B.'s. And Men's generally. What had her father got from this stuff?

She would destroy the lot. It took several trips to the flat to dispose of the many copies of EROS. She dumped some into the communal refuse bins at her father's building and some into bins at her own and some at her office where there was always a huge skip filling with waste computer printout. There was something appropriate about EROS's old fashioned club gentlemen's and clergymen's porn being carried off to the knackers on the tide of computer print out.

The clockwork couple turned out to be quite a valuable antique. One of her gay men friends knew a man who knew a man at London's leading antique auction rooms. It was by a well known German 18th century clock and music-box maker and must have been specially commissioned. It was worth nine hundred pounds.

Then, emptying the rest of the book shelves into tea chests, she came across several booklets on alcoholism. She wondered again about those gin bottles and the single drinking glass in the study while all the other glasses were collecting dust at the back of a cupboard. He had never shown any sign of being inebriated the few times a year she met him; but then, as one of the booklets said, some alcoholics never do even while getting through over a bottle a day – spreading it over the day and always just sober enough to pass for sober. Was this another life of his she had never known?

Something fell out of the alcoholism booklets. It was several pages of typing, folded and stapled. Across the top was scribbled in unfamiliar handwriting 'I don't think we should print this'. Who was we? And why should her father have it? Was he involved in putting out that corny old magazine for sex-starved vicars? Had he put money into it? He certainly hadn't left her much. But surely there would have been some evidence of that among his papers? Oh to hell with it! She was getting fed up with the whole business. She was about to tear it up and consign it to the plastic bin liner along with the old business correspondence and paid bills when it occurred to her to wonder why it was so unsuitable to print? Not enough religious obscenity for the dog collar readership? Not enough of a turn on for the old bachelors married and single too scared to get themselves a real live woman? Who was it by? But of course! Who else! Our firm favourite of the dirty minded old church goers. C.D.B. himself. But as she read it she realised it was indeed different to the other stuff. When she had finished it she was frowning in distaste but of a different kind to what she had felt for the other stories. She clicked her tongue in disgust. Of course you couldn't print that, she said, you old fool, so why keep it? She tore it angrily into shreds. A little while later she had cleared away all traces of her father's other lives.

WHO WHOM? By C. D. Blackstaff:
But let us look more closely, probe deeper into this matter of your beginnings, your provenance, what made you what you are, which is, to put it to you with the candour of a friendly enough well wisher, a failure at every damned thing there is, including fornication, marriage, adultery and literature, a near impotent old lecher with – let us not mince our words – a strong weakness for drink. What was that biblical text you have long raised a laugh with, glass in hand, in many a London bar? 'He that is wounded in the stones or hath his privy member cut off shall not enter into the congregation of the Lord.' And raised more than a laugh. Sometimes a pint and a chaser or two when incredulity was unwise enough to put its money where its mouth was. Deuteronomy twenty-three verse one. Though it has to be said that, sadly, not all bars and public houses in London are equipped with bibles for the settling of bets on holy scripture. Oh they should have known better than to challenge a Belfast protestant on the texts of the King James version, though on the other hand they might be forgiven for not detecting the one time bible scholar in the dirty minded old bar fly pestering decent middle-aged women trying to have a quiet gin and tonic, 'I don't believe I know your ladies' Christian names' in your rasping Belfast accent, hat off to them, smarmy leer to the fore, you hopeless old lost cause of a no-damned-good-at-it womaniser, having to make do with a flash of knickers when the ladies

uncross their legs or get up to go. Let us look into this more closely. Were you, metaphorically speaking of course, early wounded in the stones?

Who *was* your father? Your numerous drinking acquaintances at different times, places and milieus both literary and non-literary have formed different impressions of his identity from what you have let be known. A Baths and Lodging Houses Superintendent? A Pig Marketing Board Chairman? A Coroner? A Clerk of Sessions? An Alderman? A City Treasurer? A Chief Constable? An Assistance Board Principal? All, it would seem, men of power and influence, able to overawe, intimidate, command favours? Let us look more closely into this, dig deeper. What else do these figures of authority have in common? Were they or their like not also mighty preachers of the Word throughout Belfast's many Gospel Halls, Tabernacles, Citadels, Bethels and Missions? Ah ha! Our quest begins. Your parents were born again Christians, grace at meals saying, bedtime bible reading, old testament version of creation believing, refusing to let you play cowboys and Indians or read Billy Bunter or go to the cinema or listen to the radio except to hear the news and the weather forecast though you sometimes flouted these prohibitions, earning rebukes couched in quotations from the scriptures uttered at table in the lengthy saying of grace especially at that time of your life called puberty. Remember you being adjured to take to the Lord temptations of the flesh, your horror at the injunction to take heed of the anger of the Lord at Onan who cast his seed upon the ground? But were your guilty secrets only of yourself? Ah ha! We are getting warmer. Did you not kneel in prayer asking the Lord to stop it? What was it that you took to the Lord Jesus in prayer? The bed? In your parents' room above? When you slept in the parlour, your room commandeered for visitors? And sometimes heard bed noises? Creaking?

Regular? Rhythmic? Heard only faintly until puberty?
Seeming louder then? Oh how our senses sharpen at
puberty! Louder still on certain nights following evenings
of particularly fervent preaching and hymn singing? Your
feeble protests about 'the bed' when sent to sleep in the
parlour not understood? But we are still some way from
the heart of the matter. Let us get closer. Was there not
an occasion, a great mission campaign perhaps, when, as
usual, the faithful competed jealously for the privilege of
putting up the great preacher and it was won by your
home? How your mother cooked and baked and was in a
glow of happiness when he fell upon the food with relish!
And go on, admit it, you were in awe of him yourself with
his loud musical voice, his harsh handsome face that sweated
when he ate or prayed. Remember those women carried
out of the Gospel Hall in a faint, so overpowering was his
vision of redemption? *Handmaidens of the Lord* he called
them. You liked the word handmaiden didn't you? Eh?
You often in moments of solitary lust had a maiden in
your hand didn't you, eh? Or a wife. The wives and
handmaidens of the old testament so oft referred to in
the nightly bible readings. The doings of the patriarchs
your favourite passages, their comings and goings especially
their comings, eh? Sarah the wife of Abraham giving him
Hagar her handmaid to lie with ... *then again Abraham took
a wife and her name was Ketura* ... Esau taking Malahath
the daughter of Ishmael to wife as well as Judith and
Basheba ... Jacob's wife Rachel giving him her handmaid
Bilhah to wife and his other wife Leah giving him also her
handmaid Zilpah ... *and Jacob went in onto her.* Orpah.
Ruth. Hannah. Peninah. Abigail. Abishag the Shunamite.
Vashti. Esther. The patriarchs got plenty of exercise eh?
Not much seed spilt on the ground in that lot? Fancied
being a patriarch didn't you? A patriarch aged fifteen years,
stern, feared, revered, obeyed, submissive women provided

to pleasure you? When you heard the names of the biblical wives and handmaidens spoken in deeply reverent but passionate male voices was your mind not filled with images of flowing garments, swaying maidens with pitchers on their heads, camels, city walls, the Lord speaking onto his servant, tents, bedchambers in which patriarchs rose from couches with their robes hitched up to their waists, their sperm-dripping penises dangly but still tumescent and glistening with the wet of vaginas? Eh? But we digress. Let us return to the matter we began with. This famous preacher man. Your parents fawning on him. No small bedroom for *him* with the window looking onto the yard of the Horse Shoe Bar! *He* had to have your parents' bedroom, new sheets from Anderson Macauleys, your father driving him about like royalty in the back seat of the Morris Eight, you having to bus, bike, or walk it to the Gospel Halls and mission tents he packed full to overflowing every night of the week he was there. But you remember something else do you not? Ah ha! We are nearly there! You on the settee downstairs nearly asleep, post *hand* maiden drowsy, when suddenly you heard it. IT. The bed above. Creaking. Not irregularly as might betoken a heavy man shifting and turning. Oh no. Oh God no. Oh Christ have mercy on us no. *Rhythmic.* Creak, creak, creak, creak. One, two, three, four, ... sixteen ... Were your prayers answered at or about thirty two? Was that less or more than the count you were accustomed to? Did it stop as abruptly? Except that just when you were desperately attempting to form some alternative explanation it started up again. One, two, three, four, ... and half an hour later yet again. And half a century later you are still wondering, are you not, you tippling old porn scribbler? Yes, lets open another bottle. No, it's gin, not whisky. Stop trying to keep up the pose of the discerning drinker who knows his malts. You'd sup the wringings of a barman's dishcloth!

5

He gave a talk to a writing group in Earls Court. THE AUTOBIOGRAPHICAL FIRST NOVEL. There was a woman of mature years in the group who would have qualified for the description 'matronly' but for her dark sexy eyes. He adopted the style of an authoritative academic able to impress students, especially female ones. He was gratified to see her eagerly scribbling down his words. As his gaze roved over the group it lingered discreetly on her as he spoke and he saw that she was flattered.

'The autobiographical content of many writers' first books is due not only to the urge to put on record their early life experiences but also because the material seems more readily workable for beginners' skills. Perhaps deceptively so, though in having to solve the problems that arise in using the memories of childhood for fiction, the writer upgrades his . . .'

He deftly inserted an 'or her' not in his text and caught her eye as he did so, repeating his tactic at other places.

'. . . or her skill from beginner to improver. He or she discovers that many experiences sacred to memory cannot be made interesting to others. Children are small creatures to whom everything is larger than life, whether the cold of winter, or the heat of summer, or the appearances and mannerisms of adults. We know that tables were not bigger then than now from the unavoidable evidence that it is we who grew in size. But what of the eccentricities of the adults who towered over us, impressing their blemishes, deformities and absurdities indelibly upon the memory.

Some dwindle into ordinariness when we try to capture them upon the cold unindulgent page; others swell and bloat into unbelievable caricatures. The autobiographical novelist is at first almost overwhelmed by an abundance of material. But when he or she tries to use it most of it crumbles away in his or her hands...'

The 'he or she' and the 'his or her' that he substituted for the he and his in his text made heavy going of what should have been a simple sentence of plain English. Quite fucked it up, in fact, he thought, as he perpetrated the atrocity for the sake of a bit of what he hadn't had much of lately...

'... but writing about childhood is usually more successful than that about youth. St Augustine has put his finger on the reason for this. "The child I was is long since dead, and yet, O Lord, I live". Childhood ends, is over and done with, and, because it has been completed, it can be remembered objectively, and therefore interestingly. But youth is a different matter. Its unfinished business trails after us like a ball and chain for the rest of our lives, making it difficult to write about unemotionally. A child knows who it is. Its parents are so and so; it lives on a certain street, goes to a certain school, has an uncle fond of a drink, a granny who plays bingo. That is its identity which it happily accepts. Who was the child James Joyce? He was the one whose grandparents were rich, whose relatives quarrelled over Parnell and the church in front of the servants, but something happened to the family money and he had to be taken away from the famous school... We identify him easily. But who was the youth James Joyce? Well, he was the one whose mission in life was changed from a call to the priesthood by a transfiguring spiritual experience – seeing a girl on a beach in her knickers – after which he *would not serve*, but would *forge the conscience of his race*, and so on. WHO?...'

He caught her eye on the phrase 'in her knickers', and she gave a little smile. After the talk he offered to read her novel about girlhood in Rhodesia, and went with her to her flat in Fulham to collect it. Later that evening, he looked at it and consoled himself for what had happened at the flat with the thought that having her manuscript meant he would get another chance when he would make sure he went easy on the gin. How foolish of him, that the first thing he did in her flat was to go to the loo for a long snifter on top of what he had already to warm him up for the talk. And then she gave him another big drink on top of that again. Was it any damned wonder he had not been able to rise to the occasion? And why not just leave it at that and retire with dignity intact to live to fight another day? Oh no. Big mouth not only has to let her try to turn him on in ways that she knew, but has to come out with suggestions of his own, such as her reading the SONG OF SOLOMON while he explored and caressed her. Afterwards in the gents of a bar he had startled a neighbour at the urinal by glaring down at his manhood and muttering loudly 'neither fucking use nor ornament any more.'

And yet the discussion they had had in the bar about childhood being concerned with the outer world, youth the inner, had been interesting and had deserved to be regarded by him as more than a kind of sexual foreplay. They had found things in common between girlhood in Bulawayo and boyhood in Belfast. Churchgoing, Anglican Hymns. And the Afrikaans song SARIE MARAIS which he had asked her if she knew the words of. He had once known an Afrikaans girl when he had first come to London who used to sing it when she had had a few drinks, and he still whistled it because it reminded him of his first bedsittingroom in Kensington. She did indeed know the words and had written them down for him. He sang them,

65

SAM KEERY

confidence restored by the evening's gin, as he paced up
and down his room.

> Bring my terug
> Na die ou transvaal
> Dar waar my Sarie woon
> Daronder in die mielies
> By die ou doringboom
> Dar woon my Sarie Marais

For some reason too complex to pursue, a song from a
culture not his own in a language he did not understand
suited his drinking mood. He sang it from time to time
in between confiding to his recorder more notes for an
autobiography.

... that doll I was carrying whose was it? We must have
been coming from granny's. I wouldn't let go of it. They
must have got it off me when I fell asleep. They must have
got it off me to give back to whosoever it was, maybe that
wee girl my mother gave me a skelping for taking off her
knickers. I didn't know I was doing anything wrong. I
didn't know either how long it would be. Oh God, how
long before I would get doing that again. Where was it I
was carrying that doll? There was a street lamp and a big
building and it was my father carrying me. Where were
the rest of them? Not like him to be carrying me through
the streets on his own. It was at that corner where the
Labour Exchange was and there was nothing before or
after, just me and my father and the light of the lamp the
old gas lamps with the bar at the top you could tie a rope
to and swing round. We would argue over whose rope it
was and whose lamp it was and whose street it was. It
wasn't fair, we said. Fair was the word most often on our

66

lips. Not getting that doll, that was my first memory. It was wanting what they were not going to let me have and it's been that way ever since. Who was that fellow who said something wise about that, was it Barnum or Henry Ford? My father could come out with a famous saying on anything he liked. The one about the singer that Barnum found greater than Jenny Lind, but would never get anywhere because of stage fright. Oh you get nowhere without cheek and boldness my father said. I wish now I had let him tell me about the woman long before my mother that time I was moping over that girl down the street that wouldn't have me and I was thinking of ending it all. Oh better men than you have been wrecked by a woman before now he says I was wrecked up myself once for years. But I didn't want to hear. I wonder who she was might have been my mother. No I would have been somebody else not me at all. I wonder what that would have been like. I suppose it wouldn't have started like it did with that doll I tried to grab and hang on to through the night streets with my father by the light of that lamp. I wonder was she one of the girls on that photo of the football team my father played for among the photos in the biscuit tin. I should have asked my aunt Lily. She would come out with anything. Like that time my mother and her and my aunt Martha didn't know I was in the kitchen. I couldn't believe my ears what they said about the church organist just married to the big woman that sang I Know That My Redeemer Liveth in the Messiah. Very stuck up they said. Would sail past you in the street. Oh she'll have another organ to contend with now says my aunt Lily with a laugh. I nearly fainted with the horror of it my mother and my aunts talking like that. Oh she will indeed my mother and my aunt Martha agreed with such grim satisfaction the hair rose on the back of my neck. I could hardly take it in. I never told a soul about it not even that psychiatrist in

Holywell. Is there anything in your early life you are not able to confront and I told him no. Perhaps more recently he says think deeply and I told him about Sandra. I was in love at seventeen and couldn't believe my ears the time she got up from a chair and let out such a fart worse than my father. A lovely girl farting like that I couldn't take it in. She never batted an eyelid. Just like MacFarquahar-Forbes the time the sole of his shoe came away in Claridges he was that hard up but the cheek of a regiment. The trick cyclist said the idealisation of women indicates a fear of castration and an oedipus complex. My aunt Lily would have said a good dose of salts. My mother said you never knew where to put your face with Lily. She would open her blouse on the tram and give them the breast till they were nearly four. My uncle gave her one nearly every year and him only half her size but had them all scared of him. She was a big easygoing woman always at the door gossiping. It was a half door. Aunt Lily's half door was the last one on her street before they pulled all those houses down. Very sociable devices half doors. Aunt Lily would lean her elbows on it all day but that old way of life was nearly past even then. An age of transition I suppose you would call it now. Radios and gas mantles and half doors and new bungalows with electric cookers and thatched cottages with cranes over the hearth at the end of our road and mother and me at the Ideal Home Exhibition in the Kings Hall looking at vacuum cleaners and that yard we played in of the two old wheelwrights. We loved it when they lit the fire all round the iron rim to get it on and the steam when the water went over it. Their white whiskers were yellow round the mouth was that from age or chewing tobacco. And the motor garage on the corner where we begged old tubes to swim with on the river and the song The Lambeth Walk the time of Munich and Hitler. No songs like that now. There used to be pianos in half the houses you went into. A song that caught on could sell a million sheets. My aunt Lily could play my granny's piano by ear. Lily of Laguna. It was only supposed to be for hymns after granny took up with the Elimites. Good songs mean nothing to the young nowadays its all drums shouting and screaming these days. I'd love to stamp it out with tear gas and alsation dogs. Oh but they are the future people say I hope I don't live to see it far worse than the old fogeyism my father preached against. Out of the frying pan into the fire no wonder you're not safe on the streets after dark all that jumping and gyrating to tomtoms. Used to be what the savages did round the camp fires before the United States cavalry came riding in and we cheered in the matinees so hard they had to stop the picture and bring Sticky Sloan the doorman to quieten us in bicycle clips and mac over the uniform with the epaullettes. Little did we know the next generation would be prancing in a frenzy getting their ears damaged. My god they call it music getting them worked up to vandalise telephones and public lavatories. That telephone kiosk on our street never once vandalised all through the war and the blackout. All those American soldiers and yet women not a bit scared to go out at nights not like now. We used to pick up used french letters on sticks but I can't call to mind a case of rape and you could go out with your back door on the latch and leave the coalman his money on the kitchen table. That article I got into Orion on The New Alternative: Barbarism. Who would have thought it possible to take other roads than socialism or capitalism. Letters to the editor denouncing me. Calls himself a socialist with the disgusting nostalgia for the thirties what about Ellen Wilkinson the dole the hunger marches rickets the means test not the first renegade in the class struggle. I never got paid for the article. So sorry my coeditor away two signatures required on cheques be back shortly. Oh I know that trick I could teach them a dozen variations on it now myself. The printers the hardest to put off. The advertisers could be a bit tricky too they would send you solicitor's letter dear sir have reason to believe circulation figures incorrect infringing such and such of trade description act if refund not forthcoming. Aunt Lily was always in debt having things re-possessed for not keeping up the payments but happy go lucky her house always packed with neighbour women in curlers and slippers. You wouldn't know what half of them were there for. There was more tea drunk at Lily's than a cafe she was always sending round to my mother for milk or tea or sugar. A big buxom woman she must have been a good looker once no wonder he gave her one every year for years. They say it was a love match my grandfather tried to stop didn't think him good enough for Lily until one day he raised his hand to her for still seeing him and she said you can't stop me for I'm his wife and she drew something up from her bosom on the end of a string. It was a wedding ring. The pair of them had got married in secret. I heard that when Lily was dying she kept moving her hands and people thought it was the way dying people sometimes do to push something away but my father said no it was Lily being young again and drawing up her wedding ring on the end of a string to defy her father. I should have found out more about that before they all died off. He was such a skinny little man to be big Lily's love with a soupstrainer moustache. He had been an apprentice on the Titanic. A blacksmith. You wouldn't think they would have blacksmiths in the shipyard but they did nor that they could be skinny little men like him. I think they came under the boilermaker's union. I wish I had found out more before I left, a pity the young are not more interested in the older generation till they are getting on in years themselves and it is too late. He used to get drunk every Saturday night I wonder is that how he gave her so many children. There was a picture of the Titanic in their parlour had pride of place among the family photos. They used to put the orange arch across the street at Lily's house maybe she handed out tea to them like she did the army convoys in the war. They say a couple of orangemen would sit all night in Lily's house with guns to guard it. I used to hear my father talk about Carson's time and the Volunteers against Home Rule and Winston Churchill chased out of Belfast for sending a battleship into Belfast Lough against the Volunteers. I wish I had found out more about that time from my father. He paraded along with the rest and signed the solemn league and covenant at the city hall. He said he was young at the time though he had set up a shoemaking shop with an apprentice. He must have been a good catch as a husband in those hard times yet he married late. It must have been that first unhappy love put him off. I wonder who she was. He never marched with the orangemen, he had a row with my mother about the state of our old torn union jack he poked out over the shop for form's sake on the 12th July. He would go on about the hooligans and the mobs and she said it was time we had a new flag as the people were saying it was his catholic customers and he had been bought. She was more conservative than him she was shocked when Winston Churchill lost the 1945 election. I should have written a portrait of him like Hazlitt did of his father. I used to play in his workshop listening to him thinking and talking to himself. He loved thinking so much he would stop hammering a shoe to think instead with the hammer halted in the air like a statue and I would make a banging noise to bring him out of it and he would start hammering again and sing one of the old time songs. He had a good voice and good diction from singing Handel's Messiah in the church choir. The neighbours once thought he was the wireless and tried to get the station the songs were

71

coming from. They call it catharsis writing about it to get it out of your system. A load of ballocks it just brings it back. I should have cultivated the imagination more and not heeded the damned reviewers whose praise is worse than blame who said that? And siren voices luring us to doom. Why not use your gift for the erotic to pay the rent says MacFarquahar-Forbes while writing work of literary merit. There was more groping than copula vera, the hors d'oeuvres tastier than the main dish. I should have stuck to Hazlitt. I could have done it too and wrote about steam coaches on the roads killed off by the stage coach interests, or the composer of Tipperary not getting a penny. The young pen veers wildly in the presence of genius who said that? But it veers more wildly in some presences than in others. Mine veered to Hazlitt when I read Liber Amoris. That prickteasing landlady's daughter Sarah Walker. He put down as much of it as he could without him and the printers going to jail but THE FIGHT the best piece of journalism ever written. I never tire of it. The English master did not think much of it. He was called Rogers. I was happier in the first school before the scholarship where we read Lamb's tales from Shakespeare and parsed sentences into subject, predicate and object and the red biddy woman came round once a year to warn us of the perils of the demon drink. I was good at composition. Miss Pym showed my composition to the inspectors. I should have written a composition about her in the style of Hazlitt. I never did get feeling that girl in the row behind who her cousin Len said moved forward in her seat for him to feel and if I changed places would let me too but Miss Pym said why have you two changed places. Miss Pym's brother was a unionist MP. The cane was never out of her hands. Was it Len's cousin was the ringleader of the girls got that old tinsmith into trouble where my mother got her saucepans repaired? They were getting their Picture House matinee

money off him for letting him have a look. They didn't
prosecute for they couldn't get any of the wee madams to
say he had done more than look, poor old bastard. We
used to play in his workshop but weren't allowed to after
that. I wrote too much about the secret underlife of
protestant Belfast. I should have done more on the
spirituality of boyhood and its solitary exaltations. Those
summer Fridays the sky so blue no more school till Monday
and being moved to tears by Robert Louis Stevenson's
*home is the sailor home from the sea and the hunter home from
the hill* in our school reader, and standing still in the
evening mist at the river to listen to a man walking a dog
whistling as beautiful as a nightingale *I dream of Jeannie
with the light brown hair* the whistling fading away into the
summer twilight. He must have had a great ear to whistle
like that. I have always envied people with the gift for
song. The old songs able to sit down at a pub Joanna and
get a sing song going. I never could do more than join in
and stand the player a beer. I got nowhere with that banjo
I bought in Smithfield the chords painful on your fingers.
I got it on H.P. I put the signature of that tailor down the
street on the H.P. form. Such a row, my mother saying
not a wink of sleep did she have that night wondering had
she brought a forger into the world. The shop I got the
banjo in was opposite that bookshop where I found Hazlitt
on the stall outside later on. The high water mark of the
English language Keats said of Hazlitt. I felt sorry for the
old man who worked in that shop that day the pair of
schoolmasters denied him his little show of erudition when
he said shyly elementary and beginners not necessarily
synonymous terms if you know what I mean and they
snarled back yes it means the same thing the poor old
bastard's face dropped. Such brutality, I would have loved
to kick their arses. Hazlitt knew how to slap down the high
and mighty. His meat-grinding style Keats called it. He had

a go at Byron for his aristocratic spirit. *Even when he espouses the cause of liberty as now in Greece,* that made you feel sorry for him, and Shelley on the loony left who would support no cause unless it be guaranteed to bring the millennium. There were three basic banjo chords in C major, C F and G. *Way down upon the Swanee River.* I always marvel how the banjo men in the jazz bands can do it all by ear. I sold that banjo for half nothing before the H.P. payments were finished, there were more rows and that tailor wanting to know if I was trying to get him put in jail. I wonder was it true that story I put him into for MacFarquahar-Forbes from the talk at the time how soon he married his woman assistant after his wife died. His wife had been an invalid for years upstairs, the tailor and the woman assistant together in the shop every day. I made up things the neighbour women would say about his unseemly haste to install her, the flowers hardly withered in his first wife's grave, based on that time I heard aunt Lily and my mother and the others talking about the organist and the soprano who worked in the butchers. Oh, she had been pressing more than his trousers! Oh she had been warming more than his irons! Oh he had threaded more than her needles for her! Oh she had been more than good with his buttons. I got – how much was it for that one? – would be about three hundred pounds in today's money ditto for another one from the same stable I worked a rich seam of rich Belfast underlife. I tried it once or twice with the London Irish of Kilburn but all catholic Irish there, it only worked when I used a protestant though no religion in it. It's funny only a catholic could get catholics right their culture so based on their religion. Except for that story I did about the vice ring in the railway shunting yards at Paddington. How long was I there it's so long ago? The shunters and greasers all catholic Irish some of them not long off the boat their only assets wives and daughters. That little

Cornish foreman like an eastern potentate in the carriage
and wagon office you have to cross the lines to reach. It
was before everybody had a car and went on Spanish
package holidays. Travel still an adventure and places you
had never seen romantic. I used to like the names on the
carriages The Cornish Riviera Express, Bristol, Newberry,
Reading, Holyhead, Truro. Was it Newberry Hazlitt saw
the prize fight that went forty rounds on the heath with
the quality in their coaches betting a hundred thousand
pounds. The Irish all arrived by Holyhead. It was still the
age of steam. The lovely big Western locomotives you
nearly wanted to pat on their flanks standing hissing on
the roads, the drivers too proud to pass the time of day
and treated the Irish like dirt. It was like the caste system
the untouchables. Except Irish women they would touch
all right. I should have written about it like Hazlitt instead
of steamy fiction. I had to invent a station. MacFarquahar-
Forbes even made me take out Brunel's name as it would
have identified Paddington. How much did I get for that
one? I thought it was munificence I bought myself a silk
shirt I was a snappy dresser then. It got ruined in the
launderette. Refused compensation. Silk should be cold
washed they said not boiled. Where was I working then?
So many jobs then night shifts day shifts, life's rich tapestry.
I think it was the insurance again. Had tried it in Belfast
with the Bulwark just before I got out. I never told Lambton
I was once in the Bulwark too. It doesn't do to let them
know too much about the previous existence before the
booktrade and the magazines. I wonder how these Eng Lit
fellows going straight from college into teaching back to
school again can have anythings to write about. They have
experience of damn all but the ivory towers and hanky
panky in the common room. They can't keep their hands
off the women students, the chancellors getting their leg
over too, one of the perks of academe I suppose. Power

of any sort a great aphrodisiac to the women. It was a revelation what poets will do to get their stuff into print. As bad as the Irish shunters and greasers except maybe draw the line at daughters and then again maybe not. I used to read the book reviews going through the empty trains for the papers left behind in the first class you could always tell a train that had called at stations near the posh schools along the Thames. *Jolly fine boating weather, hay on the harvest breeze, blade on the feather, your shoulders between our knees* and me not noticing I would always agree with the reviewer about stuff I had never read. Till years later in the game myself. You had to be careful getting down from the carriages in the yards. No platform and the shunters moving stock anywhere. That fellow that was killed getting down; they took up a collection. Some of the Irish greasers had accents I took for Welsh so thick and lilting they must have been from the bogs. What a change for them the middle of London. Always borrowing money to tide them over. They say the little Cornish man in charge of carriages and wagons kept an account book. I wondered about that time I went in. His door was locked and I heard a woman say something in an Irish accent. MacFarquahar-Forbes said the publishers got protests from the Railwaymens Union and Irish priests. Good God I says alarmed. No, no not at all MacFarquahar-Forbes says, excellent publicity if only we could stir up a bit more. My father would have come out with a saying about that. *If you don't advertise your goods the bailiffs will advertise them for you.* He was right. You get nowhere not upsetting people. I was too concerned trying to entertain and amuse playing the Irish jester the English love. Did you hear about the Irishman who thought that oral sex was talking about it? I used to make up jokes like that by the yard. That time I sold some to Softheart and Flint. I wonder what happened to them. All that auditioning. Bright young hopefuls like myself sure they were ready for lift off into the big time. Setbacks mean nothing when you're young full of years. Everything an adventure. Even nearly dying an adventure with the tube up my nose in St Mary Abbott's hospital. I was operated on by that 'bone man' he called himself. Orthopaedics. In the middle of the night. The gut men not in until the morning and that might be too late. He was an American. Talked like Hemingway. I guess we ought to get in there and do something, he says, whaddya say? Can I have something for the pain, I said. Sure, he said. I suppose he saved my life. A bone man not a gut man and Prunty at the bedside with the coat off the shoulder like a cloak one eyebrow raised quizzically. Are they treating you all right in here, one eye on the nurses giving them his best profile. I wonder where she is now that night nurse I used to look forward to her eyes very close when she changed the tube frowning in concentration and her lovely dark eyes and brows with the little wrinkle from concentrating so hard. There was once she had trouble with the tube and there was the shine of perspiration on her white forehead and her breath on my cheek. She came out with me once afterwards. She had never heard of chopped liver and Schnitzel and didn't know it was Jewish food. What show did I take her to? Had that song in it my father used to sing *Delia Oh Delia*. I couldn't get in to South Pacific. She told me she was engaged. Prunty asked in amazement you didn't let it go at that oh dear oh dear I can teach you nothing oh ye of little faith for Christ's sake if she went out with you and her engaged it meant more than if she wasn't I can take you nowhere this reflects upon the Prunty school of charm branches everywhere one opening shortly in your neighbourhood. He changed his name to Bronte when I told him the Brontes were Pruntys from Ballynahinch. Women fell for him whatever his name: young ones; older ones; bog Irish ones; posh English ones. Sometimes he

77

found it more of a nuisance than not and would rather have read poetry or acted. *Now is the winter of our discontent.* We always want what we can't have. If only nature would match our talents with our personalities or writers' talents with their experiences, maybe the same thing. What was it Flaubert said about experiences being a writer's only material and works of genius only happen when talent and material are exactly suited. You can count me out there buster though I did have a go and I'm not finished yet by Christ; there's a bit of mileage in me yet if I could cut back on the hard stuff. Where did I get that from? Not from my father. He was not a drinking man but a thinking man. He loved thinking and philosophising, talking to himself about the state the world was in. He got angry with God sometimes. The Jews say that is the most religious thought of all. I never realised till he was long dead how much of me is in him. He loved the old hymns and the old songs. The old music hall songs. The sad sweet Victorian ballads about parting and death. He was always singing them. I loved them too. Put me out of step with my own time . Have stayed that way ever since. I wonder now about that first memory of mine, him carrying me out of the dark into the light. Have I been carrying him ever since towards the dark again...'

At this point he let the tape run on silently as he fell into a reverie from which he roused himself with another measure of gin.

Beginnings, beginnings, he sighed, where did it all begin? In the beginning was the word. Nothing exists until it is described. And the void was filled with words ... Word hunters and gatherers ... word shifters ... wordsmiths ... word wheeler dealers ... wordsmith hirers. And the word was ... made flesh ... MacFarquahar-Forbes ... a peddler of word pleasure for flesh pleasure ... flesh words for selfpleasurers... should put up a sign, I told him ... and lo, in the fullness of time ... Mac Farquahar-Forbes Associates, fiction, belles lettres, biography... 10% Home, 15% Foreign, no callers without appointment, no unsolicited manuscripts. All those manuscripts. One in every bedsit. More carried in every day. Not one writers' agent in the whole of Kensington, he said. I am fulfilling a need, said MacFarquahar-Forbes. Modest reading fees, advice given. Please clarify the he's in para three page eighteen: is the third he the same as the first he or the second he? House rule for the possessive case of names ending in ess. House rule for this that and the other especially the other. Thou shalt. Thou shalt not.

Blessed are they that have cheek for they shall inherit the earth and a public school accent helps. A white shirt and tie and a public school accent and nobody notices the arse out of your trousers. Let us go in here to talk about your work, says MacFarquahar-Forbes. The Savoy Hotel. Cool as a cucumber. Not five shillings between the pair of us. But it was porter, would you have a copy of the New York Tribune by any chance. Was it Eton MacFarquahar-Forbes went to? No, was at. You say at a public school. Me quaking in trepidation that they'd charge us with false pretences when the porter in the gents' brushed my collar after a piss and I didn't tip him. He had the cheek of a bloody regiment as my father would have said. Over a couple of half pints of beer he would discuss manuscripts for hours in the public rooms of London's top hotels. Sitting near that big open fire in Claridges. Lovely warm blaze. I say, porter, this is last Tuesday's edition of the Washington Post, surely Claridges take the airmail edition? All that was before the Lady Chatterley judgement when you had to dot dot dot nudge wink in the sex scenes but if you knew your business it was all the better for exciting the readers' imagination. Have you any more like this, says MacFarquahar-Forbes, I've got a chum who might take it if there's more. More? No problem. Sandra Laffin. The lovely Sandra. Poor bloody bitch. She must be as old as me now. That time she was downstairs in her nightie and I might have but didn't. Made up for it since – on paper. As well she doesn't know the times I've had her poked by church elders, gospel preachers, curates, choirmasters and vestrymen. I went round after school to do her father's wage book and she was still in her flannel nightie on the settee reading a paper back romance before Mills and Boon. *Will shy staff nurse Mary win the love of handsome brain surgeon Rupert with a past despite the scheming of beautiful but unscrupulous ward sister Kay?* She was all flushed and excited – had most probably been masturbating and me too green when she snatched something off me and held it behind her back for me to wrestle with her to get it back, her eyes shining. We were about seventeen. She was a beauty and naked under that flannel nightie. She probably wanted me to finish off with my hand what she had been doing knowing she could stop me doing more and still be virga intacta when her mother came back or her father Alfie rushed in for a cup of tea full of money worries. *Dear Mr Laffin, your account now stands at so much we regret no more goods on account pro tem.* I remember more business latin now than school latin. Alfie that morning committed the terrible offence of letting out a four letter word and taking a swipe at Sandra's backside for being a lazy bitch while his men were stopped from getting stuff at builders' merchants until he paid something on account *inter alia.* He knew he had done wrong and would pay for it! Sandra shouting. Her mother arrived and started shouting. A neighbour in to join in the shouting. I felt sorry for him. I used that scene several times in different ways. Sandra would be comforted under the flannel nightie. There, there, this will soothe you. Naughty daddy using bad language and spanking lovely Sandra. They'll put off him getting saved at the Gospel Hall. More prayer meetings for bad daddy. No supper for bad daddy this evening. He'll have to get himself a fish and chip from Fusco's. There, there, this will comfort lovely Sandra, safe in the arms of Jesus, safe on his gentle breast, and still *virga intacta, inter alia, pro tem.*

You have a gift for the puritan erotic, said MacFarquahar-Forbes. Powerfully erotic, said the Edinburgh Review. My first review. The expurgated version, before the Lady Chatterley judgement.

Dearly beloved brethren the scripture moveth us to confess our manifold sins and wickedness. The wickedness of marketing poor Sandra for the D.I.Y. trade.

So shall the King greatly desire thy beauty for he is the Lord. She shall be brought forth onto the King in raiment of needlework and clothing of wrought gold.

Those sexy bits in the Old Testament I used to read to while away the sermon. All different today. Explicit sex scenes and four letter words obligatory. As Virgina Woolf said: every sentence has to have its little heap of manure. Not in the swim unless you describe the sex act in minute detail never mind never having witnessed it. That time I opened Prunty's door and there it was! The pair of them at it naked and it looked so funny I couldn't help laughing. I once tried to make use of that and wrote it up as comic. Oh no, said MacFarquahar-Forbes, there is no market for that sort of treatment. Back to sin and lust in the Belfast Bible belt and Sandra pleasuring the men of God. I said to Prunty do you know that one of the cheeks of your bum is bigger than the other you must be favouring it when you are on the job. I didn't think he would take me seriously till I saw him at the mirror naked holding up another mirror. I should have stuck to Hazlitt and been a brilliant essayist. Who was it said Hazlitt was the high water mark of the English language? Keats, I think, when he also said we are all mighty fine fellows but none of us can write like Mister Hazlitt. That time I took Prunty to Soho to look for Hazlitt's grave and he quizzed the tarts very man of the world about their prices. You are sitting on a fortune my dear could you direct us to St Annes church. Gave us an old fashioned look and pointed to a distant spire. The dreaming spires of Soho said Prunty, putting on the literary. But the spire was all that was left from the bombing in the war. Prunty picked up something from the ground. Alas poor Hazlitt we knew him well. He took elocution lessons to get rid of his Belfast accent. I wonder if his looks wore well. I used to joke about his best profile. Never sleep on the right side of the woman and avoid artificial light from the north east quarter. But MacFarquahar-Forbes didn't like it when I used that time Prunty arrived back with the big barmaid who nearly did him an injury. Ah, don't do that doll, don't do that, he starts shouting, you'll break it! I wonder is that possible? Isn't it just blood, a tumescence? But no market for jokey treatment, has to be dead serious to be titillating, said MacFarquahar-Forbes. Like my story Coronation Day. Had celebration drink in Claridges with one of his chums. We're into the U.S. market, he says. Twenty per cent to MacFarquahar-Forbes. Not Sandra that time but Mrs Lamont. That time in Mrs Lamont's boarding house in Maida Vale. The first place I stayed in London. Big peroxide blonde Dublin woman with great legs. So am I a protestant woman she said when I told her what I was. It was odd to hear her say the protestant prayer book responses in the broad Dublin accent when she took me to the Anglican church in Maida Vale. All the men in the house catholics from the south. Some of them fancied her. Had enough paddies in Dublin, she said. I thought she just wanted to mother me till the evening she took me to the Metropolitan Empire on the Edgware road. Last music hall in London. Pale shadow of former glory. Lavatory jokes and jugglers. Was knocked down a year or two later. I wonder if Jack Judge ever sung Tipperary there? I tried to write a piece on the sad state of the place in manner of Hazlitt but MacFarquahar-Forbes only wanted stuff like Coronation Day. Mrs Lamont knocked at the door of my room the evening when we got back from watching the coronation. Here, she said, do you see what I found in that tart's room after I got rid of her? And showed me a packet of french letters. Don't be such a shy boy, she says, and puts one on me. Next Sunday in church when the minister recited *From fornication and all other deadly sin*, Mrs Lamont joined in the response confidently in the Dublin accent, *Good Lord Deliver us*. Had a daughter of sixteen. I helped her with her homework. Simultaneous equations. Mother kept a strict eye on her. Don't you take advantage, she says. If she makes you feel that way you come to me or I'll skin you. I never told Prunty about her. Let him think I was greener than I was. You are carrying a load of dirty water, he says, that time we tried to visit Hazlitt's grave among the tarts of Soho. Never heard of that expression before for going without it. I daren't tell him about Mrs Lamont buying me things, taking me out, charging me less rent, putting make up on me when we came back from the coronation. I didn't like to say no. Very strong willed woman. Big Kerry men from the building sites as meek with her as poodles. Just a bit of eye shadow, she says, where's the harm. At first made out it was no different to her eejit of a son's duck's arse haircut. Then just a touch of lipstick. Children must have been out. Everybody out watching the coronation. If only I had a wig, she said. It was before the wigs came in along with the mini skirts. But even without the wig she had me done up like a girl. I wrote Coronation Day after Prunty left. He never knew me as a writer. Couldn't have shown him that one anyway. Would have known it was me in it. Would

have been shocked at me lying all dolled up under Mrs
Lamont like that. Couldn't be as explicit in Coronation
Day as you could after the Lady Chatterley judgement but
easy enough to let the reader picture what was going on.
That Irish magazine editor who wrote to the magazine it
was in saying he had passed the obscene material to the
London police and hoped the prosecution would demand
and get a custodial sentence. A magazine for catholic family
reading, editor Father Mick McQuaid, S.J. MacFarquahar-
Forbes edited out some of it and got me to put the sex
bits in poetic prose. Beautiful words make the erotic very
effective, he said. Antithesis. Mustn't be crude if we are
to court the literary market. Prunty would not have approved.
Anything other than the missionary position a perversion.
Brought up like that in Belfast. Maybe it wore off like the
Belfast accent. Wonder if he ever made it onto the stage.
Never heard of him as an actor. Doesn't mean he wasn't.
It's like writers. Fame for the few and for the very few.
Those theatrical photos of himself he had done. His best
profile. Admiring himself in the shop windows when you
were with him on the street. Can see him hanging round
the agencies. That flamboyant way actors have even when
hard up. The sole of a shoe coming away from the upper
but an eye catching silk cravat. Press a card on you. The
parts they have been in. Back from fabulously successful
season in Tasmania. Available for bookings. Agent so and
so. MacFarquahar-Forbes Associates. No, that's not right,
he would handle the playwrights not the players.

Was I MacFarquahar-Forbes' first writer to make it into
the book pages of the big papers? I was before Maguire
but there was that Aussie chum of Maguire's, always getting
into fights, they made his taking the-lid-off-life-in-Gundagai
novel into a movie. When did Maguire appear? You've
been reviewed in the Observer, says MacFarquahar-Forbes
one day. What Observer, I ask. Good God man, there's

only one Observer, he says. I thought you might have meant the Ballymena Observer, I says, dinna fash yersel, mon. That's how the old people of Ballymena talked when I was a boy. A wheen o' folk in the kirk the nicht. The Scots dialect of Antrim had long died out in Belfast. I had to explain it to Prunty when I tried for a cod to get him to read Robbie Burns for his elocution exercises. I've got you into paperback, says MacFarquahar-Forbes, lets wet the contract. So many wets. Was that how it started? He was always reaching for the glasses and the bottle. Graduated from a shelf to a drinks cabinet. That tiny office he took above the fish and chip shop in Hogarth Place with the drinks cabinet jammed behind the desk and the bed sit scribblers on the stairs clutching manuscripts. The way he could swing round in the chair from the drinks cabinet with two glasses in his fingers and a bottle in the other hand in one swift action...'

He switched the recorder off to swallow another gin and to reflect. The Afrikaans song Sarie Marais was still running in his head. He thought of the brief encounter that had stayed in his mind over the years and began describing it in a reflective murmur.

'I discussed the racial question while dining out with a beautiful South African girl after dancing to the music of the Joe Loss orchestra, afterwards making love...'

He laughed derisively.

'Come off it, sunny Jim. In vino veritas, sport. Let's have a bit of veritas, sunshine. She chatted you up in a ladies' excuse in Hammersmith Palais. She embarrassed you over fish and chips in Joe Lyons because the black girl wiping the tables was not showing her proper respect. You failed to penetrate her in an Earls Court third floor back single because of tightening of the vagina about which she said her boy friend back in Jo'Burg hadn't been able to get his thing in either. She drank a lot of your British Sherry and sang Sarie Marais very loudly until thumping on the wall made you stop her...'

Still, he thought, why had he never used it for a short story? Humorous possibilities ... bent it badly trying to get it in ... No, MacFarquahar-Forbes was right ... no market for that treatment ... they can't wank if they are amused ... but other possibilities ... not Afrikaaner but true blue protestant loyalist ... but then couldn't sing Sarie Marais ... what about singing Lilliburlero after tanking her up on gin ... a Kilburn bedsit ... catholic Irish thumping on the wall ... no ... has to be Sarie Marais ... but why not both...'

The idea of *both* excited him enough to resist the onset of sleep for long enough to jot down some notes on the back of the piece of paper on which the Rhodesian woman had scribbled the words of Sarie Marais, but he nodded off over them into a dream.

The notes said: length two to two and a half thou; Orangemen's day, the twelfth of July Hyde Park Orange Lodge from South Africa...

He dreamt of a vast gathering, bowler-hatted and orange-sashed; contingents arriving from all corners of the Empire with banners and bands. The Jo'burg L.O.L No. 1 is played in through Marble Arch to the tune of Sarie Marais from a girls' melodeon band wearing flannel nighties under a banner that proclaims VIRGA INTACTA PRO TEM. Their huge Lambeg drum is supported, not on the belly of a drummer, but on the back of a black girl who is sometimes flailed along with the drum. The Jo'burg brethren appear to walk bowlegged and when they line up along a hedge to piss they tell each other ruefully in Afrikaans that they hadn't been able to get it in either. The drummer appears to be Sandra Laflfin who insists on marching the band up

the Edgware Road to let the Kilburn Irish collectors for
Sinn Fein know that if that didn't do we'd cut them in
two and give them a taste of the Orange and Blue but she
is persuaded to go instead to Mrs Lamont's boarding house
where the Hyde Park platform speakers – Irish protestant
Bishops and ministers of the Dutch Reformed Church
attempt to penetrate her but give up groaning in pain and
bang angrily on the walls of the room to Mrs Lamont, who
tanks her up with gin to dress her up as a young man
whom he recognises as himself taking notes for a nice little
earner, length two to two and a half thou for MacFarquahar-
Forbes Associates, home ten per cent, foreign fifteen per
cent, no unsolicited manuscripts.

He awoke hearing himself say yes, that's it sunshine,
there's a bit of mileage in us yet, by Jesus.

6

An invitation arrived to read one of his short stories at a writers' workshop for aspiring authors run by a successful novelist who had once been a drinking chum. It contained a hint, humorous but firm, to turn up sober. Perhaps it was this that made him decide not to pick a story from his published work but to write a new one, to prove that there was still a bit mileage in him yet by Jesus. In fact the story was one that had been kicking around in his head for many years in several different forms, settings, viewpoints. The morning of the day before the workshop he put it onto paper quickly and with hardly a correction.

It led the reader into what seemed to be an account of children enjoying a public holiday accompanied by their teachers. But gradually the reader would be made uneasy as to the nature of the holiday and what was being celebrated and would begin to guess that something dark and terrible is to take place, perhaps something to do with the crucifixion, perhaps an allegory of it. And partly it is. It is a village in Poland during the war. Nuns are marshalling the excited schoolchildren to wave their crosses at a procession that is about to pass along the village street. It is the day the SS have come to escort the Jews to the railway station and the cattle trucks. THEY CRUCIFIED OUR LORD.

He would have liked that as a title but that would have given away the story too soon. So he called it simply THE PROCESSION. He had once thought of setting it in an imaginary wartime Ireland under German occupation but there are no Irish towns or villages with Jewish ghettoes or even enough Jews to make up a procession. Conversely he might have kept it closer to the true account by a survivor of Auschwitz he had once known who had been in such a procession through a Polish village along with his family and relatives all of whom been murdered. But that viewpoint had proved unimaginable. The day before the reading he suddenly saw what to do, which was to draw upon his own childhood memories of public celebrations and to put his well remembered feelings of excitement into a catholic Polish boy. It is through the boy and his chums showing off their knowingness in sniggering asides made behind a nun's back that the reader is first made to suspect what is about to take place. The nun, based upon one of his teachers, sternly rebukes the boys' rowdiness, especially when one of them remarks something about 'up the chimney', for to her it is a very solemn and sacred occasion, and her own obvious excitement is entirely religious. THEY CRUCIFIED OUR LORD.

The night after he wrote it his dream of lost wanderings was visited by boys of his schooldays, glimpsed standing on the pavements of half familar streets that yet led him to where he did not want to go, streets he was wandering down the centre of, trying to take comfort from being alone, and therefore, he hoped, less likely to be confused with a group that was ahead of him, or perhaps behind, but still finding it necessary to protest that, although circumcised, he was not one of *them*, and holding up to try to prove it Hymns Ancient and Modern, but on awakening in a sweat of fear still unsure whether he had convinced them.

The disturbing dream made him undecided whether to read it to the workshop, and he took with him another that he might read instead, one that had been published several times over the years and had once been included in a text book collection for a literature course at an

American university, '...a wonderful eye for the comedy of failure...' it said in the course notes.

The workshop was in a city college in which the novelist running the writing course was a lecturer. CD's mood when he arrived had been somewhat lightened by a few beers in a nearby bar, far less than usual on these occasions even when souped up with a swig from his hip flask in the college toilets just before he went into the lecture room in which the workshop had already started. The novelist-academic chairman looked relieved to see CD as he had him down to read before the coffee break when CD might well have something other than coffee. He was addressing a large group of would-be writers of all ages, but more women than men.

'...the short story ... quite different form ... not abbreviated novel... Chekhov ... Hemingway...'

CD had heard it all before and only half-listened, still undecided which story to read. Then the speaker referred to the Irish contribution to the art of the short story.

'...James Joyce's Dubliners ... arguably the best short stories ever written in English...'

He had heard that before too and would normally have let it pass.

'Tell them he was banned in Ireland by the censorship up till five years ago, ha, ha,' he interrupted.

The speaker ignored the interruption, supported by the obvious disapproval of it by the audience and the other writers waiting to read their stuff. He made no mention of Joyce's treatment by catholic Ireland, but as soon as his talk ended he quickly called upon CD to read his contribution. It would divert him from further disruption and he would probably slope off soon afterwards in need of more drink as he was easily bored by literary discussion. This decided CD. He would read *The Procession*.

The novelist/academic who introduced CD to the

audience did not, of course, let them know that he had engaged CD for quite a small fee. He presented the high points of CD's career in the form of impressive quotes from reviews without mentioning that they mostly referred to work long out of print. This had the desired effect. The audience got ready to admire and watch out for things they should try to do themselves.

The brief portraits of the boys and the nun went down very well, done as they were with a kind of malicious affection from memories of his schooldays. Hopper Dawson the gullible fool; Bliff English of the knowing aside; thin pious Miss Harvey. And of course, himself. The audience liked them. There was a woman who seemed particularly appreciative. Not young but still quite fancyable. She might be good for a drink and even a bit of how's your father... He aimed the story especially at her, forgetting what it was about, concentrating only on its effectiveness.

But as its dark meaning began to be suggested and the audience's warmth cooled she was the first to show signs of uneasiness. At the point where a Polish Bliff English sniggered an aside about '...up the chimney...' and the nature of the approaching procession is unmistakable even before the sight of German SS helmets, she seemed to raise her hand in dismay and opened her mouth, shocked.

When the story ended she looked aound at the others as if expecting someone to say something but there was only an uncomfortable silence. The organiser, embarrassed by something so different to what he had expected, struggled to say something to cope with it.

'The ... the ... holocaust,' he stammered, '...is a ... a ... very difficult subject to ... to ... some would say impossible...'

He was interrupted. The woman was on her feet.

'I didn't come here today,' she cried in an Irish accent, 'to have my religion insulted.'

CD and the woman began arguing, the organiser trying in vain to re-establish his authority. As she grew angrier she grew reckless in her choice of words. Lies, she shouted, she would not listen to lies about her church. CD at first answered her as angrily but when she shouted something about 'they' and 'them' he knew that she had lost control and all he had to do was to prompt her to question his Irishness.

'I'm as Irish as you,' he said, 'can you not tell I'm from Belfast?'

'Oh, they have them there too,' she cried harshly, but realising in the same instant, even before the gasp that went round the room, that she should not have said it. She gathered up her notebooks and rushed out.

The organiser hastily introduced the next contributor without any discussion of CD's story. Nobody wanted it. It was too embarrassing and uncomfortable. They all wanted to forget it. CD slipped away quietly. Even with a big swig of gin inside him he was unable to sort out his mixed feelings. And he had thought she might be Jewish! He had thought that might be why she looked unhappy during the reading. And he had thought she might be good for a bit of... He suddenly thought of another woman, and of the piece by her he was publishing.

'Anglo-Saxon and old English in Place names' by Judith Walsh Massingham:

...Ham as in Clapham, Manningham etc. The oldest meaning seems to be homeplace and is the ancestor of the word home but in many instances it is impossible to distinguish it from hamm meaning 'meadowland by a river'...

He would have liked a crowded bar full of loud talk, laughter, the horses on the telly, an old fashioned juke box with old fashioned pop tunes: Crosby, Sinatra, even Elvis. But it was between opening times. He had a couple of hours to kill.

He had half-promised to meet at opening time a young man from a city bookmakers in the vicinity who, like many others that inundate magazines with their writings, have a second very private identity, a secret life kept from friends and colleagues with its own dreams and aspirations – especially that of getting into print. He might be good for a few drinks and perhaps a donation to the Friends Of The *Clerkenwell Review* club if – as the young sometimes are – he would be overawed by the large folded card which CD presented to such people displaying the high points of CD's literary career in the form of impressive quotes from reviews though omitting the dates which would have revealed that they referred to books long out of print. Indeed he had that morning spoken on his own behalf to someone who Read for a publishing house but had been given no more than a vague promise to look at some of his stories and poems photocopied from the yellowing pages of books and journals in which they had been published many years before.

He whiled away the time browsing at London's oldest open air secondhand bookstall laid out on ancient four-wheeled market stalls permanently parked along the kerb opposite the Daily Worker and the gin distillery. He took his place among the silent serious men turning over huge leather bound copies of *The Times* from the 19th century or carefully examining editions of children's comics dating from their own childhood. In his own case memories of boyhood were more readily evoked by the pile of wartime *Picture Post*s and *War Illustrated*s which his mother used to bring home with the shopping all those years ago. He passed on to a section setting out old directories and one large thick red one instantly caught his eye. Belfast & Ulster Directory 1942. He leafed through it with interest as he spotted old familiar names of towns, villages, schools, mills, churches, streets, marshalled alphabetically in military order.

It amused him to order a place in the A's to identify itself.

Wartime Ahoghill two paces forward! AttenSHUN!

Ahoghill. County Antrim. Population 751. Shops' half holiday Wednesday. One RUC Barracks with one sergeant and four men. Five places of worship: one Church of Ireland; two presbyterian; one Roman catholic; one Gospel Hall. One Petty sessions clerk. One Medical Officer and registrar. One sub post office, first delivery eight a.m. One creamery. One motor and cycle agent. Two provision merchants. One butcher. One blacksmith. One newsagent. One member of parliament: Captain the Hon. Terence Marne O'Neill, Glebe House. One licensed premises. One draper. And, thought CD, one farm suitable for summer holidaying of town boy, offering wireless to hear war news on, panoramic view across Braid Valley to Slemish Mountain, spectacles of rural life: turf being cut at moss; bull servicing cows; the spraying of potato fields; pigs being killed with sledgehammer and knife, pretty girl of boy's age to be naughty with.

CD raised his eyes from the directory and gazed absently at the dome of nearby St Paul's Cathedral as he recollected.

There was Vera Lynn singing *There'll be Blue Birds Over The White Cliffs of Dover Tomorrow When the World is Free* on the wireless with the glass batteries that my uncle got charged in the motor garage off The Diamond and my aunt brushing the griddle with a goose wing before baking soda bread and fadge and my uncle's head against the cow's flank in the byre pulling the teats and the hiss hiss of the milk into the white bucket and the slobbering suck of the calves' gums on your fingers and reading *War Illustrated* and *Picture Post* on the sofa hoping not to be asked to carry water to the cows' trough in the field and being homesick for Belfast and missing smoking in the air raid shelters with the used french letters in them and going to the shop in Ahoghill for the papers owned by the fat man with the split in his trousers at the backside when he stooped and trying to make a model of a Stuka dive bomber in the shed with the bench beside the meal barrels and thinking the Ahoghill people very ignorant because they could not identify German aircraft from the silhouettes for observers in *War Illustrated* and taking down my cousin's knickers to see her pussy in various sheds, barns, outhouses and the bedroom at night with the summer twilight outside and the people laughing and talking in the room below us and riding on the neighbour's carts bringing in the hay and sitting on the gate pillar in the warm sun looking across the fields to the spires of Ballymena and Slemish Mountain like a box and my Aunt pissing into a grate in the meal shed not knowing I could see her through a hole in the wall and my cousin coming to my bed at night when the people got noisy downstairs and my uncle cutting my aunt's hair making her neck scrawny and the hens rushing towards her when she opened the back door and standing among men after church on Sunday looking over a field of lint to price it and thinking how plain and ill-favoured their wives were not like my pretty cousin and my aunt getting ready for church with her black coat and hat and her peppermints and her prayer book and the blue white glowing ash of the turf fire in the thatched cottage up the lane with the hearth crane and the white enamel bucket of cold spring water and secretly admiring the girl of the house wishing I could take off her knickers like my cousin's and put in my finger and my uncle's sheep dog being shown the whip for a misdemeanour and crawling out heartbroken to whine at the door till my aunt ordered my uncle to tell it it was all right when it was all joy abounding and holding the goat's horns to stop it butting and learning the scotch words like ca' canny and wheen and thole and dinna fash yoursel and being afraid to put my thing into my cousin's pussy in bed one night when a throng of people were singing and laughing and shouting old scandal downstairs...

But the trout, dammit, the famous troutstream of Ahoghill, he prompted himself impatiently. All that tickling promised in the prospectus. A figment of my imagination?

No. A figment of memory. They doubted it when I brought it up years later. But I swear there is a stream near Ahoghill in the County of Antrim, where, when I was very little, I saw a stooping man standing in the water watching it motionless until he lifted out a silver-shining fish in his bare hands.

It was still half an hour till the bars opened. He debated whether to slip into a nearby public convenience and have a swig from the flask of gin. It was a rather smart little flask of leather covered silver curved to fit snugly against a buttock while resting on a shooting stick at a steeplechase or point to point. He had found it in a lavatory of a large country house at a literary weekend for poets and writers though whether it had been one of them who mislaid it he never troubled to enquire. It had been on the window ledge looking at him as he took a snifter from a quarter bottle to get into form for his own performance.

He glanced over the books on the cheap barrow and idly picked up 'Hitler and the German High Command 1939–1945'. It was nearly new. Probably heavily remaindered after poor sales. CD knew all too well about publishers clearing their shelves of a nonrunner and he felt an impulse of fellow feeling for a writer given the rasberry by the great reading public. He flipped over the pages keeping an eye on his watch, suddenly he started back in consternation.

'Fucking Christ almighty,' he exclaimed incredulously as he read: Lisburn. Long river meadows. Meeting of Hitler and German High Command, Obersaltzburg, New Years Day 1941. Colonel Kurt Student of 11th Airborne Corps

outlines plan for diversionary paratroop attack on Northern
Ireland in support of Wehrmacht bridgeheads at Brighton
and Eastbourne. Northern Ireland vital to British convoys
in Atlantic. RAF would have to be diverted. Long river
meadows at Lisburn suitable for landing aircraft. Hitler
very interested. Becomes excited. High Command cautious,
already committed to operation Barbarossa, invasion of
Soviet Union. Can they do both? Hitler yes. High Command
no. Except Colonel Student (later to capture Crete in just
such an attack). Hitler lectures them on boldness, Napoleon,
luck, faith in his destiny. Hitler displeased. Orders the
maps of Ireland out. Sees Student alone. Defers final
decision.

Well hell roast you Colonel Kurt Student you kraut
arsehole! Those river fields had evolved over the ages for
the summer pasturing of cattle, for courting couples, for
Sunday poker schools, for walking greyhound dogs, above
all for the pursuits of boyhood, *my* boyhood, you German
vermin. Fucking Jesus, I got a ME 109 for Christmas that
time you aryan master race bag of crap. Being smaller they
were cheaper in the model shop in Wellington Place than
the Heinkel bomber I really wanted. They could also land
on grass. They would have landed not far from my grannies
you Deutchscheisseuntermensch. How many Jews did you
put in the oven you goosestepping German excrement?
Oh but I'm sure you know them that did and don't think
any the less of them for it you lump of German shit. Oh
here, I can just see it, the quiet plain clothes men arriving
in Belfast (Ah, sure you couldn't wish for nicer neighbours)
to look at the birth registers: *More than one grandparent a
Jew.*

Item in London evening newspaper under sub heading
'Irish Author in row at St Paul's'. Irish writer Mr Donard

Blackwell of Penywern Road Earls Court appeared before
Clerkenwell Magistrates charged with disturbing the peace.
PC Copley of Holborn Police station said that he was called
to St Paul's Cathedral following a complaint of the theft
of church property and of threatening behaviour. He found
defendant in possession of a prayer book marked St Paul's
on the steps smelling of drink. Hans Schmidt of Stuttgart,
West Germany, made a statement to him which PC Copley
had taken down and got signed by Thomas Winstanley,
verger of St Paul's, who was also appearing as a witness.
Mr Schmidt said that defendant kept pushing into his coach
party being photographed in front of Cathedral shouting
unpleasant things about Auschwitz and giving Hitler salute.
When asked not to do this by Mr Schmidt defendant had
struck him on the ear with a large book causing much
pain. Defendant had been taken to Holborn Police station
where he had been unable to walk a straight line to the
satisfaction of the duty sergeant and two officers and was
charged. Mr Winstanley said in evidence that in his capacity
as verger he had been called to a disturbance in a pew in
the west transept where defendant was waving a Cathedral
prayer book and shouting that they had ruined the 23rd
Psalm that he had learnt at Sunday school. When asked
to leave he became abusive and only did so when another
verger came to assist at great inconvenience having to close
the turnstile to the whispering gallery and to lock up the
money in order to do so. Witness formed the impression
that defendant had drink taken. Defendant refused to give
up prayer book saying he wanted to see what else they
had ruined before complaining to the Archbishop of
Canterbury and was followed outside where the altercation
with German visitors occurred. Mr Batfield, solicitor for
defendant, said his client denied being abusive to Mr
Winstanley and would contend he had merely invited Mr
Winstanley to agree that the translations of Tyndale and

Coverdale used in the King James version of 1601 were superior to the new version in the Cathedral pews. He also denied theft as the book was of no value to him and he was only taking it to the door to look at it in better light intending to return it after perusal of parts of it he knew by heart from the King James version having been raised in a Godfearing protestant home in a loyalist district in the Belfast area worshipping in the church of Ireland, which, as the court knew, uses the Anglican service. A group was blocking the cathedral exit and he had to push his way through them in the course of which he was jostled in such a way that the prayer book came into contact with someone's head. The court might like to read a character testimonial from Lady Walsh-Manningham of Manningham Hall, Suffolk, widow of Lt. General Walsh-Manningham MC, KCVO and also one from Nigel Lambton, an actuary with a leading Insurance company.

From the Bench Mr Ridley said that, as a church member himself, he could understand the strength of feeling regarding the attempts to do away with the incomparable beauty of the prayer book of Cranmer in the name of so-called progress but he nevertheless thought it deplorable that the police had been involved and he had no option but to take a stern view of the defendant allowing his feelings on the matter to get out of control and he would therefore bind him over to be of good behaviour in two sureties of ten pounds.

Extract from Literary magazine *Clerkenwell Review*, Editor Colin Divis Blackstaff, entitled 'Brushed by the Wing of History':

Long river meadow ... cattle standing at water's edge ruminating in the cool of the evening ... mist on water ... quiet broken by faint ripple of moorhen or water vole

... solitary boy surveying with pride and love the idyllic scene ... Belfast hills nearby ... far Mourne mountains ... aware of being figure in landscape setting of 23rd Psalm: The Lord is my shepherd I shall not want, He maketh me to lie down in green pastures, He leadeth me beside the still waters ... never again be so happy as on those Lagan river fields, as oblivious of the precariousness of our world as the cattle that came down to drink in the cool of the evening like in a painting by Constable. In those wartime boyhood skies of cloudless blue we saw no shadow, heard no faint beating of that dark wing that surely hovered over us before, seeking larger prey, it wheeled toward Barbarossa and passed us by.

7

When a man with a Belfast accent was spotted by a sharp-eyed member of the staff taking a swift swig from a hip flask while browsing the bibles in the showroom of the British and Foreign Bible Society and showing signs of being amused, it was understandable that he was thought to be acting suspiciously, and was about to be asked to leave when, surprisingly, he purchased a bible in a foreign tongue, and left without any trouble to the staff who, relieved, exchanged raised eyebrows and looks of the we-get-some-right-ones-in-this-game kind. What had amused CD were passages in the bible translated into Pidgin English such as 'Him big boss fella he go walkabout'. But the bible he went out with was not in pidgin, tempted though he had been to buy it as a source of material with which to amuse drinking cronies, but in Spanish. That evening, after he had entered what he hoped would be an accurate count of his drinks which included an estimate of what he might expect to have before bed, a period when counting became unreliable, he enjoyed a session with his tape recorder and the Spanish bible, in which he invoked the presence of a one time drinking crony whose copy had exasperated many editors, being typed on an ancient machine that jumped a space on the letter O so that for instance soon became so on – and so on.

CD began by singing a verse of Oft In A Stilly Night with great feeling:

> Fond memory brings the light
> Of other days around me.

La Santa Biblia, he continued. Revised, it says on the
the front, by Cipriano de Valera in 1601 – of which more
anon, as they say. About the same time as our King James
version, which, by a remarkable circumstance I also have
before me to assist fond memory.
And the whole earth was of one language and of one speech ...
una sola lenguay unas mismas palabras. Genesis 11.1.
Languages are a punishment for original sin in the garden
of Eden. Therefore is the name of it called Babel. Nuestro
padre que es en los cielos. That's the Lord's Prayer in
Spanish. Belfast College of Technology 1947. The Matric
exam. That is where it was held. I did well in the Spanish
paper. En el Colegio de la Technologia, Belfast, Irlanda del
Norte. No that's not the Lord's Prayer, you're having me
on! Proust's Madeleine, man, Proust's Madeleine, something
that takes you back, recreates the past, makes you feel young
again! You must oft in a stilly night have seen the light of
other days yourself. Say to me uno, dos, tres, cuatro or soy,
eres, es and so on, and, – I confess it freely – I am a callow
youth again, the sap rising, much troubled by ... fear of ...
loss of vital forces ... going blind. Las muchachas, senor,
comprendes? Las mujeres, hombre, no es verdad? Da-Da-
Dum-Dum-Dum. The Tango, amigo. The Plaza. No, the
Belfast dance hall of that name. Si, si. Saturday night. Noche
de la samedi. Picture the scene. Group of callow youths
lounging at edge of dance floor surveying the talent. Muy
interesado en las chicas. No, wrong word interesado. You
wouldn't have a Spanish dictionary about your person for
le mot juste? Oh, I didn't get to where I am today without
an uncanny feel for le mot juste! Da-da-Dum-Dum-Dum.
Callow youths telling each other it was hardly worth a fellow's
while coming. Disparaging the talent. Comparing the Plaza
unfavourably with other Belfast dance halls, where, it was
argued unanimously, a fellow would have to be deformed
not to get off his mark, get his onions, sometimes referred

102

to as his greens, on a Saturday night. Da-da-Dum-Dum-Dum. Ah, youth, youth. That which, while it is still expected, is already gone, in a sigh, in a flash. Do you not know your Conrad? Eng. Lit. paper 1947. Are we in the Plaza or el Colegio de la Technologia? The Plaza, no readmission, no jitterbugging, callow youth mentally rehearsing basic steps of your slow waltz and your quick-step while out on the floor, Brylcremed Lisburn dog fancier Freezy Fitzsimmons, pencil-moustached, patentshoed, many partnered bachelor, suavely executed a Buenos Aires brothel dance based upon the Bull Fight, to the disapproval of unpartnered callow youth. Da-da-Dum-Dum-Dum. You didn't know that? That Freezy walked greyhounds, had cups for the tango and paso doble and skilfully avoided marriage? Oh, the BA brothel origins? Have I been there? You mean, of course, the familiarity implied in the abbreviation BA? Could I not have acquired the knowledge from Belfast's principal centre of learning? No, not El Colegio de la Technologia, emphatically not, never mind it being known *you know where* as Nuestra Senora de las Technologias. What do you mean, its only in Madrid they make *Our Lady of jokes?* Belfast centre of learning? Queen's University? You must be joking! That cramming shop! That bourgeois grind! Am I left wing? You mean my use of the word bourgeois perjoratively? Oh, let's keep politics out of it, old hand, never you bloody mind the May Day I had one pole of a banner in the march past Downing Street singing the INTERNATIONALE. The cultural heart of Belfast, the Athens of the north, the place where callow youth could discover the pleasures of the mind and disillusioned age find consolation – yes all right, all right – was none other than, where else but, the one and only SMITHFIELD. What? You thought it was what? A flea market? A secondhand junk souk. Oh, how travelled we are, a real breath of the East in the way you said that, eh? Yes, I know PJI buy-any-thing-Kavanagh was its best known establishment to the hoi polloi. Granted people would say try Smithfield when spare parts were needed for veteran mangles, family heirloom hot-waterbottles, gramophones. Yes, yes, but those who pressed further into the cobblestoned arcades would be rewarded with treasures of the mind. Books, my learned friend, books. In many languages, ancient and modern. What? Dogeared Latin primers? School children with their lists of set books? Do you think I spent the happiest hours of my life poking about for second-hand algebras and grammars? What about what? Ballroom Dancing by Victor Sylvester? Shyness cured or your money back? Self-confidence in three months? I too was a sevenstone weakling by Charles Atlas? *How to Win Friends and Influence People* by Dale Carnegie? The books my mother found behind the wardrobe on gynaecology and the menopause, and wanted to know who was trying to corrupt me? Well yes, callow youth feels its way, has not yet learnt to discriminate. La Santa Biblia. What? No, it's not a book on the menopause! It's the Holy Bible. In Spanish. Discovered in Smithfield the year I sat the Matric at the aforementioned examination centre. Da-da-Dum-Dum-Dum, Ole! El Colegio de la Technologia. There was this plumber. No, not sitting the Matric! Gospel Hall man, born again, awaiting the call to the mission field in South America. In Genesi's Fish and Chip Saloon. No, he wasn't awaiting the call there! That's where I bumped into him. After a happy browse in Smithfield, dreaming my dreams, turning the pages of old books, as, indeed so had he. *Here he passed his days, repining and resigned.* What? Hazlitt, man, do you not know your Hazlitt? On his father, '... the sacred name JEHOVAH in capitals, pressed down by the weight of style, worn to the last thinness of the understanding, glimpses ... glimmering notions ... palm trees hovering in the horizon and processions of camels at the distance of three thousand years ... questions as to the date of the Creation, predictions of the end of all things ... a dream of infinity and eternity, of death, the resurrection, a judgement to come.' Oh, here, it wasn't only the Kama Sutra and French printed brown paper covered versions of Lady Chatterley that callow youth found in Smithfield! The born again plumber? I've got something here would interest you, says he, tapping a pile of books he sets on the table, but waiting till he lays into a plate of fish and chips and a bottle of lemonade, which he describes as a wee snack till he gets home for his tea, saying, as he belched loudly that he was more dry than hungry. Bap and Cy. What? Born Again Plumber and Callow Youth. The party of the first part hereinafter referred to as Bap and the party of the second part referred to as Cy. I swear this is a true statement. Have you done much swearing in your time? Terrible lot of swearing goes on at the courts, and don't I bloody know it! Writs, affidavits, submissions all have to be sworn. You have to get your statement sworn and stamped. A clerk in an office holds up a card in front of you that says I swear this is a true statement unless you say you are not religious, whereupon the clerk rummages about for one that says, 'I affirm'. What? Oh, more than you've had hot dinners! The things you hear at the swearing office! Like one time queuing up behind this solicitor and his client. 'I suppose,' says the client, 'I'll have to pay for that woman's tights?' 'What woman?' says the solicitor. 'The one that served that paper on me,' says boyo. 'She was a solicitor?' says his lawyer, greatly agitated, 'what – what did you do to her tights?' 'She caught them on the bicycle in the hall,' says the litigant gloomily. 'Oh, ha ha,' the other laughs weakly in understandable relief. Oh, here, I could tell you some good stories about the courts … what? Oh, Bap and Cy? Where did we leave them? Oh, yes. Fresh from their separate forays into Belfast's principal centre of learning they had each made their separate ways to Genesi's Fish and Chip Saloon quite near to where Freezy Fitzsimmons' mother still had him on her hands at an age reputed to be the wrong side of forty. What? Not relevant? I am merely adding local colour to aid veracity; Freezy's pigeon loft being very familiar locally, as were his greyhounds, his patent shoes, Ronald Colman moustache and ballroom prizes. Da-da-Dum-Dum-Dum. Santa Biblia? Bap kept that to the last. Let Cy leaf through his other finds while he washed down his fish and chips with a quart of lemonade and commented that that class of drink was inclined to be a wee bit high. Relevant? Of course. A man of large appetites. What? The flesh, man, the flesh! It was why he was still awaiting the call, though long married, why the other books that Cy idly perused were to do with countries like Venezuela, their peoples, climates, diseases, their brave protestant mission stations. He had shelffuls of them at home already, but kept collecting more, including Spanish grammars, and got Cy to give him lessons. *If the soldiers should enter the city the mayor may flee.* Future conditional tense followed by subjunctive. Cy's grasp not one hundred per cent either. Stronger on the imperative. *Sacristan! Bring out the relics!* The wife knew. What? That it was the daughter Cy was interested in. Lovely girl. Oh, many's the Gospel meeting Cy sat through for her sake, the sap rising! Washed in the blood of the lamb. Michael, row the boat ashore, hallelujah. But risen only, never ... spilled ... at least not... Not like Bap the younger. What? Sorry, I was lost in a reverie about Bap's undoing at the hands of the serpent in the garden. Lord, the woman tempted me. Used to hear my mother and the aunts whispering about it. Bap the fiery young preacher making a name round the Gospel Halls; ready to be sent to Wales to train as a missionary. Then you'll see now why the quart of lemonade and the wee snack of a plate full of fish and chips between meals was relevant. *The flesh laid him low.* This summer seaside mission tent in Ballycastle. Conversions galore. Troops of hymn singing women on the sands. What? You can't hear

me? I'm imitating the way my mother and the aunts used
to lower their voices to a whisper and mouth at each other
like I'm doing now. Can you make it out? *Had to* get married
soon after. And here, come here till I tell you, *they said* it
was *two girls*. Are you with me now about the relevance of
the way he swigged that flagon of lemonade and burped in
Fusco's? Oh, I had a keen eye for human frailty even then!
Yes, two of them. How did the Brethren sort than one out?
Oh, quien sabe, amigo, quien sabe? Sobre sus rodillos,
rezando! What? On their knees in prayer, man, what else
would it mean? I still have the twang, do you notice after
all these years? That is what Bap would say to Cy, 'you have
the twang,' he would say. 'Here,' he said to Cy that day in
Fusco's, 'I have something here would interest you,' tapping
meaningfully the book he had been keeping back till he
settled his stomach with a good belch. La Santa Biblia. The
Holy Bible. Translated into Spanish from the Hebrew and
the Greek in 1602 by a fellow called De Valera. Notice how
casually I mentioned the name? As if it were a mere incidental
detail. To see how you would react. Surely you must be
familiar with our protestant demonology? In which the name
of De Valera was second only to the anti-Christ in Rome.
De Valera, Prime Minister of the Irish Free State, dedicated
to making Ireland and its institutions the most catholic in
the world, prime bogeyman of our protestant Ulster, No
Surrender, No Pope Here, British and proud of it, Oh God
Our Help In Ages Past, Remember Derry's Walls, Lero,
Lero, Lilliburlero, Lilliburlero Bullen a La. *Devileerie* was
how protestant children learnt to pronounce it on their
mothers' laps. So you can appreciate the promptness with
which Cy exploited the possibilities for callow mirth and
wit at the expense of the traditions in which he had been
reared to the chagrin of Bap. What? Oh, it's pronounced
ang not *in*, is it? Oh, so Bap was chagranged, not chagrinned,
was he? Oh, je beg votre pardon pour mon pig ignorance!

Maybe somebody should have told Bap that to encourage
the efforts of the working classes at self-improvement? 'You
thought,' our self-improvement for the working classes wallah
would have said to Bap, 'you thought you were chagrinned
when Cy thought it very funny to speak of conducting
Shankill Road church services with a De Valera bible, of
Sandy Row Orange Lodge masters having the new banner
blessed with a De Valera bible and so on and so forth, but
you weren't, you were chagranged.' How did Bap express
this chagrang? With dignity. Reminding Cy that it was still
God's word. What effect? Oh, instant! Cy was easily deflated,
especially by a father of one of several girls with whom Cy
was in love. What, sucking up? The term is a bit strong
considering that the sap was rising fast, but his apparently
voluntary presence in Gospel Halls and meetings had been
noted and contrasted with his previous marked preference
for more secular interests, such as the dance hall and the
back seat of the cinema. What conclusion was reached about
this? That there was in fact no contradiction. How was this
conclusion greeted? With amusement in general. And by
his mother in particular? By giving him what would nowadays
be described as 'sexual counselling'. What form did this
take? By the following words: 'If you get some poor girl
into trouble your father will take a stick to you, and if he
doesn't, I will – do you understand?' Did he take heed? He
did. By resolving upon chastity? No, by endeavouring to
purchase a contraceptive in four chemists shops. With what
success? None. He emerged from each with, respectively, a
toothbrush, a bar of scented soap, a blackhead squeezer
and a packet of breath sweeteners. Oh, he got one in the
end. From a catholic. What? You thought *they* didn't use
the rubber goods? So did Cy. How? It was an unsolicited
gift. The circumstances are not relevant and would be a
tiresome digression. Was the gift put to immediate use?
Only to alter his state to one of readiness. Did its presence

reassure him? No. What effect did it have? A gradually forming ring-shaped indentation on the surface of his wallet, impressing itself upon his gaze every time he took it from his pocket. Did this occur at Fusco's Fish and Chip Saloon? It did. When? In proffering payment to Giovanni Fusco. With what effect? The usual one. Reminding him of his virginity. Was this reminder purely abstract in nature? No, it consisted of mental images of an erotic nature including a very recent memory of Bap's daughter's thigh. Was she not a devout brethren? Indeed so, and had made it unmistakably clear to Cy that only the path of Christ crucified would lead him to *you know what*. What, flashing her thighs at him in the name of the Lord? No! He had felt them. No, no! Pressed unavoidably against his own in a car conveying a party of them from a meeting at which a famous evangelist who had been through Peru by mule and canoe had failed to impress Bap, who had found fault with his interpretation of his texts and set out the correct meanings all the way home in the car. What? By mule and canoe through Peru would make quite a good clerihew? Oh, it is a firm favourite in my Collected Poems. Santa Biblia in Fusco's? Oh yes. Bap was eager to hear some of his favourite passages of scripture in Spanish. 'Ah, go on,' he said to Cy, 'you have the twang.' Notwithstanding it being a De Valera Bible and the extreme probability that even if no actual relative of Devileerie, the 1602 fellow was nevertheless of the Roman faith, a devotee of the Scarlet Woman, The Mother of Harlots, The Great Whore of Babylon? Indeed so. Cy had already hinted at its unsuitability for protestant worship in loyalist localities, but Bap's life-long dream had been stirred afresh, and he brushed such considerations aside. What? I said Bap was jugando cerca los cuernos! Playing it close to the horns. Da-da-Dum-Dum-Dum. Ole! Bap tiene los cojones! Do you not think so? That he had them, what? Balls, man, balls! Getting Cy to read aloud from a De Valera bible not a stone's throw from an Orange Hall, a Masonic Hall, a Presbyterian church, an Elimite Tabernacle! 'Go on,' he urged Cy, 'you have the twang!' And Cy? I can do no more than quote something I jotted down later. Another prose poem? No, but asked for at readings, am thinking of issuing it on my latest album.

The youth read self-consciously at first, wishing he had the strength of character to refuse, painfully aware of four other customers as well as one of the Fuscos watching them curiously, especially when the Salvationist plumber began emitting heartfelt groans of religious fervour as though he were in a Gospel Hall. But strangely, the passages which the latter requested were mostly those which the youth himself would have looked up in curiosity to see how the Spanish compared with what he had learnt by heart in Sunday School or had impressed itself upon his memory in church lessons because of the beauty of the words. For the first time in their acquaintance, he felt a sense of something shared. No longer embarrassed by his companion's loud sighs and murmurs of almost sensual enjoyment, his own interest quickened and he spoke louder, in the best Spanish accent he could muster, trying to infuse into the Spanish something of the sonorous grandeur of the King James version, hardly knowing which was which as the old familiar biblical English reverberated in his mind alongside the Spanish.

Jehovah es mi pastor; nada me faltara... The Lord is my shepherd, I shall not want... Si yo hablase lenguas humanas y angelicas y no tengo amor ... Though I speak with the tongues of men and of angels ... En la casa de mi padre muchas moradas hay... In my father's house are many mansions.

The big, middle-aged, heavy eating plumber still bore

traces of the young crowddrawing hotgospeller he had once been, and they now became more than traces as he listened avidly with half-closed eyes, envisioning distant peoples with Indian features hearkening to the WORD, half believing that he was receiving a *sign* from the Lord that a call to the mission field might still come.

Benjamino Fusco, or it might have been Pietro or Giovanni whom the locals could not tell apart because of the confusing Italian characteristic of changing straight from beautiful angelic boys into plump balding young men with no intervening phase, also drew nearer, perhaps attracted by the sounds of a language that resembled that of his own, and he too listened, though wistfully, longing for his homeland.

The four other customers were not together, and had no common bond that might have allowed them to form a response other than puzzlement and a slight awe, though even so the powerful figure of the plumber might in any case have deterred amusement. They ate their food quietly, taking care not to clink their cutlery or the vinegar bottle – especially, though they would not have recognised the texts – during the final readings from the Revelation According to St John.

And I saw a new heaven and a new earth... Vi un cielo nuevo y una tierra nueva... And God shall wipe away all tears... Enjugara Dios toda lagrima de los ojos de ellos ... I am Alpha and Omega, saith the Lord, the beginning and the end... Yo soy el Alpha y la Omega, el principio y el fin.

And the youth? Strangely excited, only dimly sensing why, hardly caring, knowing only that it was pleasurable. Something to do with power. The power of words. The power it gave to orators, preachers, actors. The admiration of audiences. Being listened to raptly. The youth formed audiences in his mind listening to him in rapt admiration, and among the upturned admiring faces were those of pretty girls, not necessarily at – though including the possibility of – a religious gathering.

Through the window at which they sat could be seen a bend of the Lagan canal as it passed between a mill and a coal quay, the outlines of which softened in the gathering dusk until the mill might have been a feature of the natural landscape, and the coal quay a simple and primitive landing stage on a great waterway, so that the youth was also stirred by longing for travel and adventure. A coil of the Lagan canal slid through tropical rain forest in which gaudily coloured birds screamed from branch to branch. Turgid with the soil of the Andes, the LaganOrinoco swept round the bend at Fusco's and rolled on to the Spanish Main.

CD played it back, listening so intently that he forgot where he was and knocked back a measure of gin with the covert hand-shielded swiftness he would use in a public place, musing upon – how would he put it? – the confessions of a bible-loving unbeliever, yet not certain in unbelief. When the believer has doubts there are those to counsel him but when the unbeliever has doubts who is there to reassure him in his unbelief? Omar Khayyam, beloved of immortal youth? How does he go?

> For up and down, above, below
> Tis nothing but a magic shadow show
> Played in a box whose candle is the sun
> Round which we phantom figures come and go.

At which CD permitted himself a little jest to break into his reverie. Not, he exhorted, to be confused with the cockney poet Omar God, he, he!

LILLIBURLERO

There should be pills for it, he laughed, fending off the desolation under everything. The immensity of the universe in empty space ... what is emptiness? Is it nothing ... how can nothing contain everything ... the magic shadow show ... but wouldn't have missed it for anything all the same ... too soon over ... programme changed often ... worst thing will be not knowing what happens next...

Sleep overtook him and he first dreamt of pills. Magic pills to ward off sleep. Offered in verse.

Take the dream pills says the bringer of night
But sleep not yet says a figure in white,
Wait yet for the magic shadow show
And see your phantoms come and go.

He is a boy back in Belfast, in bed on the edge of sleep, trying to imagine what his father's workshop looks like unseen. Time and again he mentally travels to the door of the workshop to throw it open suddenly and so capture the instant of seeing. But he is never quick enough. The things in the workshop assume their forms at the moment of being observed and there forever eludes him that other mysterious form, the one they had the instant before and he wonders if things not being looked at exist. But then the red, white, and blue dream pill called Lilliburlero, to be taken with 50 centilitres of gin, explodes to reveal the workshop in a radiance of eternity. The bench, the great sewing machine, the heaps of lasts and sheets of leather, are not to be viewed from one side or the other but from every side at once, from every point of view simultaneously and with a fourth dimension of time expanding them to indefinite size. It is what God sees. The wooden lasts for mill managers' shoes; RUC Sergeants' boots; publicans' brogues; special fittings for solicitors with bunions, undertakers with fallen arches; church choir sopranos with ingrowing toe nails; lasts for black patents for tango gold medallists and for soft brown kids for Bulwark Assurance Company district managers. Some of them belong to those he had heard his father talk to himself about and have names on them such as Napoleon; Julius Caesar; Barnum; Henry Ford; Lloyd George and Isambard Kingdom Brunel. These the boy had made into ships by hammering lace holes into them for portholes and calling them *The Victory*; *The Great Eastern* and *The Titanic*.

All these are rushing off at the speed of light towards where the voices of women sing of shoes.

> What kind of shoes are those you wear
> Oh my Lord,
> That you can ride upon the air
> Oh my Lord,
> These shoes I wear are Gospel shoes
> Oh my Lord,
> And you can wear them if you choose
> Oh my Lord,
> He's the lily of the valley
> Oh my Lord,
> King Jesus in the chariot rides
> Oh my Lord,

No! don't get in that chariot! Don't want ... that awful for ever and ever without end ... shut the workshop door quick before it ... get back to bed and hug the doll they wouldn't let you keep ... Alpha and Omega above the bed the beginning and the end ... not that terrible music of beginningless unending void ... all the timepasts somewhere still a here and now in lightyeared space ... all the spacetimes racing through the galaxies in the chariotlight ... how many spacetimed me's being beamed across the ether ... pasts of cities, Belfasts, Londons by the thousand million ...

multi timespaced Belfasts all singing all whirling to the edge of time space... Belfast One, Andromeda ... Belf Two, Orion ... Bel Three, Centaur ... B Four, Taurus ... AlphaBelfast a black hole from which light cannot escape ... all singwhirling timebackwards ... don't want that terrible whiteness ... or is it blackness ... or black whiteness ... or white blackness ... take your pick ... take your time... want my last time ... last with black holes time ... a black laceholed last time ... before the blank whole...

8

As on several other occasions when he fell down the details of his fall were unclear in CD's mind. Had he been going into or coming out of the tube station? Was it Brixton tube station? What had he been doing at Brixton? And the woman who had helped him up? Was she a passing stranger or had he been with her? Was the fall before or after the tube station? Was it her bed he had fallen out of when he got up from on top of her? But in Brixton? Not Bethnal Green or Whitechapel? Had she not given him bagels and salt beef? No, that had been the other time he fell, details of which were also unclear. Now he came to think about it had there not been a little gold cross? On a chain round her neck. There looking up at him all the time he was on top of her? C of E. That would be more Brixton than east end. Unless catholic. Irish? In which case Kilburn tube more likely. But do catholic Irish women keep on their crucifixes when they take their clothes off for sex? English catholic then? Or in between. High church. That high Anglican woman church bellringer who wrote about her team and the bellringing league the year before? No, she was Muswell Hill not Brixton. Or could it have been a Star of David not a cross? Could a Star of David look like a cross between her breasts with two of its points in shadow? Was that other time he fell not in fact this time and vice versa?

Well anyway, crucifix or Star of David, Brixton or Whitechapel, the consequence was the same. He could not use his typewriter with a sprained wrist. Always his right hand. Could he not fall on his left for a change? Nothing for it but dictate a cassette for the typing agency again from the notes that only he could decipher.

Being in a gin-mellowed humorous mood he began the cassette by addressing the recorder as if it were a shorthand secretary sent by the agency, intending to wipe off this preface before giving it in.

'You must be my new amanuensis, dear. Have you worked for indisposed literary gentlemen before, taking down their masterpieces? You'll be asked to take down nothing else you don't want to here, honey, don't you worry your pretty head. I'm not Frank Harris dictating "My Life and Loves". Oh No. No question of you rushing out of the room shocked at being asked to write down willy measurements before and after coitus. Oh none of that here! Never mind that George Bernard Shaw had a soft spot for the old lecher, a magazine editor in his time like myself. By the way you're the spitting image of Sandra Laffin, you're not her daughter or her grand daughter are you? Oh just as well you're not, sweetheart, as you'll be taking down a dramatic piece in which Sandra's father is depicted with what the *Times Literary Supplement* has often referred to as my "ruthless unsentimentality". Are you sitting comfortably, pet? Those trousers you have on look very tight surely they must be cutting into you? Yes. Very wise to unzip them. Mind you don't catch your lovely hair in the zip! No no, it won't distract me at all. My literary skill will, if anything be sharpened. The muse and the libido are on good terms in Art as I demonstrated in my famous essay "The Pen and the Penis". Look at Goethe and WB Yeats to say nothing of John Donne. Toyed with their members as they wrote. But you'll know all about "burgeoning masterpieces and bulging codpieces" from your A levels in Eng. Lit. Oh here, ask not for whom the codpiece bulges, it bulges for thee, eh, what, ha ha.

Write this: Taken down by an amanuensis bearing an uncanny resemblance to Sandra Laffin for whom the author risked going blind at the age of seventeen.

SCENE One. The assembly hall of a Belfast girls' school. It is speech day. A high camera on wide angle does a take of the array of heads below. Zooming closer it pans from back of hall to platform along rows of girls' faces whose smooth stillness as they gaze impassively ahead gives them a look of purity and innocence that is, however, occasionally belied when the camera lingers to peer lower and reveal things being passed covertly from one gym tunic lap to another: notes; photos of male pop singers; rude drawings.

There is the sound of a speech being made, at first faintly, but then loudly enough for fragments to be heard referring to the building work that has been going on at the school.

'... well done school ... the daily noise of saw and hammer ... examination results unaffected...'

Cut to medley of scenes: Bricklayer expertly tossing brick to turn it over for chopping in two with a single strike of trowel. Girls at desks diligently conjugating French irregular verbs unheeding of the sounds of labour and men's voices at the window. Carpenter with pencil behind his ear appraising a joint of perfect fit. Everywhere that plumb line, spirit level and rule are applied are seen to pass the test of sound and satisfying workmanship. Girls at their desks are studiously solving simultaneous equations unheeding of hodman mounting ladder at window.

Cut back to assembly hall. Camera completes panning of girls and arrives at platform on which are seated a row of adults at a long table. A large clergyman is speaking.

Cut to further medley of shots of builders working while clergyman speaks in Ballymena accent. Each shot includes a phrase or two from his speech

'... building of the temple ... erecting stout walls of faith

... cedars of Lebanon ... twenty cubits ... twelve foundations of grace ... lintels marked with the blood of the lamb ... cornerstone of a proud protestant people...'

Dissolve to shot of same speaker on an open air platform in a field, the only words audible being '... our covenanter forefathers ... the walls of Deny ... the antiChrist in Rome...' A short-skirted girls' flute band is marching into the field playing *Lilliburlero* led by a very pretty drum major who is throwing her ornate staff into the air and catching it again.

Cut to brief shot of bowler hatted orangemen pissing against a hedge and singing in tune with the flutes the words '... Lero, lero, lulliburlero, lulliburlero, ballin a la ... and if that doesn't do, we'll cut them in two, we'll give them a taste of the orange and blue...'

Cut back to assembly hall where headmistress is delivering end of closing speech.

'... and three special cheers for our League winning netball team who carried on in the very thick of it, refusing to be distracted by the workmen all around them ... School hip, hip...'

Cut to scene in half demolished gymnasium. Very short-skirted senior girls contending for the ball are leaping and stooping so close to men in a foundation trench that the men could nearly have reached up and touched ... Camera at trench level to give workmen's view of a medley of girls' thighs and knickers. Other shot to show men making groaning noises to let each other know the discomfort of virility as lovely girls leap towards them, flushed and panting, arms outstretched.

Cut to arrival of van marked A. Laffin, Building contractor. Alfie Laffin jumps out almost before the van has stopped. He is a dark complexioned man with a shifty look and five o'clock shadow. He runs towards the half built wall of the gymnasium whipping out his rule and spirit level. Everywhere he looks he finds evidence of bad workmanship: bricks split wrongly and discarded; a doorframe out of plumb; good timber sawed wrongly and thrown aside to boil tea mugs on a fire. He stalks about glowering and whingeing and as he leaves he shouts back that the first man's breath he smells drink on will get his fucking cards, God forgive them for making him swear like that. Cut to show bricklayer who looks like WC Fields with drinker's nose.

Cut to scene of two girls practising at the net, their leapings and stoopings covertly watched by the workmen. One is the same as the drum major. She is Sandra Laffin, daughter of the contractor, voluptuous in form, provocative in movement. The other is, although handsome, more demure.

The effect of the girls' sinuous gryrations round the netball goal is most felt by a young carpenter with the vigour of hot youth surging through his veins and bulging at the seams with manhood and muscularity. When the two old bricklayers with assorted ailments complain about there being no block and tackle to manoeuvre into its place a huge oaken beam shaped like a cross our bold young carpenter, one eye on the prancing maidens, boasts that he could do it himself. Other men express doubt and concern, some urging him not to try, others challenging him to prove his words. Money appears, bets are laid, work stops. The two girls stop their leaping and stooping to watch and sit down gracefully at the foot of the goal post. The young man half kneels with arms outstretched and three others lay the cross-like frame on his back. He slowly rises, steadies himself for a few seconds and then takes first one step and then another.

Cut to close up of his face. It is anguished yet transfigured. Down his forehead hang sweat-matted curls that might be a crown of thorns.

Cut to girls kneeling, meekly watching. The shot to be

composed with the two Marys at the foot of the cross in mind. The girls faces are to express sorrow and adoration.

Cut to the two old bricklayers with assorted ailments standing apart like disapproving pharisees. The one with the red drinker's nose like WC Fields is saying something scornful into the other's ear.

'... seen pups like him get a cooling before now.'

Dissolve as third cheer sounds for the netball team.

'School, hip, hip.'

'Hooray.'

MAKE UP AND SPECIAL CINEMATIC EFFECTS.

Great attention must be paid to Alfie Laffin's unshaven visage. This has the effect of making him look more shifty and villainous than he actually is. Brief flash backs must be used to demonstrate that it is his misfortune to be cursed with a stubble which defies any razor but a cut throat and would require him to rise earlier than is his wont in order to shave without bloodshed. There is also to be another brief scene of Alfie in a barber's chair, blissfully relaxed, his jaws emerging smooth and gleaming as if being sculpted by the cut throat razor from lead or gun metal. This second flash back to be ambiguous as regards reality by including the following details:

The glass shelves which the barber's chair faces display the usual bottles and packets of french letters. The bottles however, are not those of hair lotions and pomades but of gin, whiskey, rum and brandy.

The person shaving him is female. She is about the same age as Alfie but still retaining some of her former bold good looks now aided by heavy make up, dyed hair, huge ear rings, bangles, necklaces, bracelets, all these ornaments being shockingly made up of crucifixes, prayer beads, miniature pictures of bleeding hearts and madonnas which go jingle jangle as she lathers and scrapes and then palps and thrums her fingers on his cheeks to his sighs of pleasure. She represents TEMPTATION both in herself as the Anti Christ of Rome, the Scarlet Woman, the Whore of Babylon, and also in her wares. A close up to show Alfie darting shifty sidelong looks. Firstly at the bottles since he has recently again signed the pledge for another attempt at salvation in his wife's Gospel Hall. Secondly at the little packets of you know what. Thirdly at the mirror in which the painted papish Jezebel getting on in years but still with a bit of mileage in her smiles enigmatically as he relishes his secondmost sensual moments – being shaved. A third flash back to suggest that the woman is real and is the wife of a catholic publican whose premises Alfie once frequented for the double purpose of getting drunk and covertly admiring her.

The five second shot of the two girls kneeling at the netball post is to have a two second shot suggesting how they might appear to the young carpenter staggering under the beam and perhaps also to the bricklayer with the drinker's nose. In this shot Sandra Laffin is more definitely given the part of Mary Magdalene. This is done by showing her heavily made up and wearing much jewellery: bangles, ear rings, and even bracelets on her ankles, all of which serve to highlight the simplicity of her single shift-like garment which she begins to remove as the shot ends.

The Ballymena accent specified for the presbyterian minister is very important. It must not be thought that this would have significance only for the people of Ulster. Far from it. Every country has its Ballymena, every region even. There is one in France, in the Punjab, in the Ukraine, in Tennessee, its accent immediately recognisable as that of the townified farmer, the peasant who has been to school, the butt of the sophisticated, easy to underestimate, ultimately formidable. Abraham Lincoln was from an American Ballymena, Nikita Kruschev from a Russian one. Casting must test actors' ability to do this accent convincingly.

This virtually rules out southern Irish actors, who, for some reason that has never been satisfactorily explained are quite unable to imitate a northern accent of any kind let alone a Ballymena one. Indeed the English are better at it and casting might like to consider that English comedian, whats his name, who tours the halls in a dog collar shouting at his audiences through a loud hailer in a Ballymena accent that I would mark him as high as nine out often for.'

CD played it back with great satisfaction. He thought of one or two one-time drinking cronies who had had something to do with TV and to whom he would send the typescript. He thought it called for another gin and as he sipped it it amused him to do a final teasing of the notional secretary, intending to remove it along with the preface.

'Just one last thing before you go, dear. You look so like Sandra Laffin why don't you audition for the part? Tell them I sent you. Oh here, I still have a bit of pull round the independent studios whatever BBC might say about me. And listen, before that I'll get you on to the MacFarquahar-Forbes office netball team for a bit of realistic practice in Lincoln's Inn at bending down for the ball and jumping up at the goal in short skirts. You'll find there's always a group of middle aged men in raincoats there will let you know by their expressions when you are doing it right. Then about that two second shot of you in bangles and a nightie as Mary Magdalene. Just a word of historical background. In Roman times prostitutes sometimes shaved off the pubic hair and replaced it by a painted red triangle like a pointing arrow. There'll be just a quick flash as you remove your shift. Just enough to get heads turning towards the TV in the public houses with arguments breaking out. Never! It bloody was! Couldn't have been! Ask him then! Oh here, I know how to get the audiences, it was me that was the first ... Hey, where are you going dear, I haven't finished yet! Here, come back. Hi!'

Ha, ha, laughed CD, and then, more seriously, fell into musing over his piece for TV, thinking of some of the real people and incidents on which it was partly based. So absorbed did he become in his reverie about the past that he forgot to erase the bits of codding not intended to go to the agency.

The Typing and Secretarial agency used by CD purely because it was nearby happened to be one of London's oldest and most respectable. As well as literary works it specialised in theses and dissertations and its clientele included economists and theologians. At one time its ladies were renowned for being able to decipher the worst of handwriting, but this skill was no longer in as much demand now that most of the clients supplied them with work dictated onto cassettes. These require a stricter system of control than manuscripts to prevent them being mislaid or returned attached to the wrong typescript. It had now been some years since this had happened and the system had then been tightened to make it what was thought to be virtually impossible. What made it worse when it did happen again was that it should have involved CD's cassette and that of Dr Peabody, an academic theologian of considerable standing who was said to have the ear of Lambeth Palace. The mistake appears to have been the result of several coincidental factors starting off with the fact that Trish, the typist doing Dr Peabody's thesis on the identity of the author of the Revelation of St John the Divine, had previously done work for CD, so that when Vi called over to her that she had got a right naughty one from 'that Irishman of yours' Trish had to have a listen for a bit of a giggle. Exactly how this led to CD's cassette being labelled PEABODY/D13F was never clarified. However, it was Dr Peabody himself who unwittingly blew the incident up out of all proportion. Being a stickler for accuracy but at the same time very busy on another thesis he gave the task of checking the typescript against his own words and typing instructions regarding punctuation to one of his divinity students, saying with his austere wintry smile 'you might even learn something'. By the time the agency had been made aware of their blunder by an absolutely livid Dr Peabody threatening legal action he had good reason to believe that others besides the student had listened to the cassette, a copy of which he suspected was still circulating around the faculty and not only at student level. Despite a statement by him prominently displayed on noticeboards to discourage those who thought it a light matter he occasionally overheard a colleague say something like '... would never have believed that Peabody could do an Irish accent so well...'

CD did not complain about getting Dr Peabody's cassette instead of his own. Indeed he kept it a few days before returning it and listened to it with great interest in the evenings with a bible open beside the bottle of gin.

9

Of the two sides to him: the solitary drinker and the gregarious bar room raconteur, the solitary began to gain the upper hand. He drank in bars where he would meet no one he knew and he spoke more and more to his recorder, glass in hand. But at the same time the drinking habits of many years were so ingrained that he often needed to conjure up a drinking companion from the past to stimulate his flow, so that there were cassettes on which, although his was the only voice, there appeared to be others present and making remarks but audible only to the speaker.

Oh for the land of lost content that will not come again. What? Boyhood, my old china, boyhood. Do you not know your Housman? Puberty the high water mark of our lives did we but know it at the time. You don't believe that? Ever looked into the LIFE TABLES of the insurance companies? In which all the ages of man are set out? No? Then guess the age they pronounce the best, that at which the human male reaches his peak, at which he is least likely to die. No, not that. No, wrong again, sunshine. It is TWELVE. After puberty it is down hill all the way.

Would you like to hear my poem about it? Not even if there's another drink to wash it down? Ahem!

What untold tales there are in family photos,
Young women peering out from under cloche hats
Along a seaside promenade.

In the company of young men in baggy flannels
One very sporty with a little tash.
Who turn out to be your mother and your auntie Lil
And your uncle Bert but not your father.
The blurred young girl who would have been another
   aunt
If her chest had not been weak
The school football team and that's your father with
   the ball
Next the boy whose son got jail for fraud.
The lovely baby on the sofa who sold insurance
And beat his wife
And you? That smiling open boy so confident in his
   charm?
That scowling youth skulking at the back?
And so short a time between.

What? Should beef it up a bit from the Life Tables. No. But maybe I should have brought Stanley into it. Stanley should have been a warning that AFTER TWELVE would undo so many. Pale earnest Stanley. I see him now. Palely loitering. Against the playground wall. Who was who? The belle dame sans Merci? Oh she was a sexy wee bitch called Edna. Pretty sweet voiced Edna of the dark and melting eyes. You like that? Oh here, I can turn a phrase with the best of them. I fancied Edna myself. Had my first ... come here till I tell you ... my first *nocturnal emissions* over Edna. Stanley? Oh, he never took me into his confidence on such matters, though, as I have already stressed, he was unduly pale. I see him now. I see the blackstone wall with the cemetery though for catholics on the other side, then the mill, and the blue hills beyond. On the wall the girls had started to chalk those love circles in which it was stated as a bald fact that so and so loved so and so. I see now Stanley's lip trembling with earnestness as he whispered things to me about the charmer Edna. Of the dark and flashing eyes? Of course. And the occasional flash of knickers? Well, now you come to mention it, yes, but it was not the belle dame's charms that Stanley drew my attention to, following me around, buttonholing me everywhere, taking me aside, whispering in my ear. Quite the contrary. Did I not know this about her, had I not heard that? That she was a sly bitch, a teacher's telltale pet? Why did he blackguard her to me? Good question, squire. Jealousy is the answer. A love circle that said she loved him she had contemptuously rubbed out but when they put my name in she let it stand. Oh I was not then as you see me now. I was a bonny lad of twelve, accepting my popularity with the girls as no more than my due. Oh here, sunshine, if you had seen me then you would have shaken your head with a wry smile and said to yourself 'that likely lad is going to get a cooling before long by Jesus, as well for him he hasn't looked into the Life Tables of the insurance companies or it would wipe that pleased with himself smile from his face.' What, Stanley? Oh yes where was I? Stanley saw me as a rival he could not outshine so he tried to put me off her instead. Such a straw to clutch at! I got sick of him sidling up to me with some new discreditable fact. First it was things everybody but me was supposed to know and how could I be so blind? Then it would be something nobody knew but him and I had to be sworn to secrecy it was so awful. I tried to keep out of his way he was so obsessed. Did he never try to woo her by more conventional methods? His only idea of that was to push a bag of sweets roughly into her hand from time to time and you would see her and the other wee bitches chewing and laughing. One day they pushed her against me in the corridor for me to kiss and I am sorry to say I enjoyed his hurt white face as much as they did. It maddened him. He followed me about after that with the perseverance of the besotted. At last he was going to reveal something about her he could only hint at. Oh, if I knew what it was he knew it would cure me of loving her. I can still see his meaningful looks and telling nods to make me curious about this ace up his sleeve. I was supposed to press him to tell. In the end he wore me down. Ah what the bloody hell is it now, I said, what are you fucking-well persecuting me about. I displayed an early gift for language? Oh, here sunshine, I have been reviewed in the Times Literary Supplement. I see him now, deadly earnest, lip shaking. What? Done the palely loitering bit against the playground wall? This was not the playground wall, which, as I emphasised earlier to exploit the symbolism, was black. What we have now is *white* and the symbolism is again masterly. Oh here, skipper, the Times Literary Supplement ... What? Oh yes, white. Well, where Stanley had cornered me was where the young ones were having their white mugs of hot milk. Now hot milk forms a skin that is dry and wrinkled on top. The young ones were plucking off their milk skins with exaggerated disgust. Oogh! Aagh! To the despair of our dinner lady. Where are you throwing them skins, she shouted unavailingly as the brats hurled them into the cloakroom wash hand basins just as we had done in our time. Above this bedlam Stanley hissed in my ear *'Edna washes herself in her own piss to make herself good looking.'* I looked at him appalled, His tormented jealousy repelled me. I knew nothing then of the canker of unrequited passion. *Her and only her, that one and none other* was beyond my comprehension. Perhaps it still is – to my sorrow, but that is a different kind of sorrow. I wanted only to be way from him, away from where the milk skins on their wet sides glistened like living membranes torn from the flesh of pallid creatures denied the light. I wanted to be out in the playground again, out in the sun, among the games and the teasing girls for a little while more.

What? Who? Ah, you mean St Augustine, squire. *The child*

129

I was is long since dead, and yet, Oh Lord, I live. What does it mean? Puberty, sunshine, puberty. The frontier second only to death in its finality, the bringing down of a curtain that makes childhood a previous existence. In the boy of twelve we catch fleetingly a glimpse of the man he might become but will not, of the uttermost to which he will struggle but fall short, often by far. Who said that? I just did buster. A nice bit of fancy prose there for the Society of Actuaries or the Sporting Life don't you think, skipper?

Ah yes, I was wondering when you'd get around to asking that. My first time, eh? Get us another glass and I'll tell you. Are you sitting comfortably, chief?

I was twelve. No, don't look amazed. All will become clear as my narrative develops, my old china.

That night at my aunt's there were so many staying that I slept on a makeshift bed in the same room as my cousins, three sisters, who were all in the big double bed against the wall. The eldest, Vera, was the same age as myself. She was very good looking with big dark eyes and a temper. It must have been thought she and I would not get up to anything with the younger ones there to tell on us if we did. For a while we lay awake in the darkness listening to the voices below which were too muffled by the floor to be distinct except for the occasional merrily shouted piece of wit at absent friends' expense. We knew that my uncle would have got the bottle out from the belly of the grandfather clock and that those who would at first utter shocked protests at the amounts in their glasses would put up less resistance when they were replenished. The darkness too turned us into disembodied voices and encouraged us to be daring in what we said as we chatted softly before sleep. Vera commented on something we heard them shouting and laughing about below which was that blind Patterson the piano tuner was thinking of advertising for a wife. How would he know what the women would look

like, Vera wondered slyly, and I said in the same sly way
– by feeling them. At which she and the next oldest giggled
while the young one said disgustedly, that's dirty, and then
fell asleep. After a while I suggested to Vera that I could
be blind Patterson if she would come in with me, and she
and her sister began a whispered argument that was more
like some kind of bargain being struck the terms of which
I could not hear until the whispering stopped abruptly and
she felt her way in beside me. We just lay together for a
while, unsure what to do except cuddle, until she put her
mouth to mine and kept it there. I simply lay there in her
arms, mouth to mouth but with an erection that throbbed
pleasantly as it had often done since infancy on many
occasions and had done no more than that, except that
this time it was against the belly of a lovely girl and my
hand was touching her between her legs but too timid to
explore more than a very little way and in awe at what I
was doing. We lay like that face to face for quite a while.
Then downstairs my father began to sing. It was the old
sad love song 'Bonny Mary of Argyle'. For some reason it
made me roll on top of her our mouths still together. It
was when my father got to the last verse which always
made him sing it quavering with emotion that something
began happening to me that had never happened before.
Instead of my erection just aching away pleasantly as it
rubbed against Vera, first it and then the whole of me
seemed to melt away in waves of sweetness. I can still
remember it vividly. Wave upon wave, getting bigger,
reverberating like sound, dizzying me, as my father finished
on a high note. I must have made sounds and convulsive
movements that frightened Vera for she threw me off her
and left me. In a dreamy state I heard her and her sister
whisper together about the meaning of it, Vera denying
angrily that she had hurt me and claiming I had had some
kind of fit. It was the arrival of puberty, my old china, my

SAM KEERY

first orgasm, and here, I tell you what, sunshine, it was the best I will ever have.'

At this point CD recalled an article he had once published by a dropped-out trainee priest on the grounds for annulment of marriage laid down by the religious courts of the past and it amused him to repeat bits of dog latin and business latin to represent catholic ecclesiastic experts on coitus going into solemn conclave on virginity and whether his arrival at puberty was to be deemed a true score or a bounce off the goalposts.

'... virginibus puerisque ... orgasmus primus pubertii ... nisi bonum... virga intacta pro tem...

He intoned gravely and imitated the swinging of incense.

'... broken hymen not conclusive ... childhood accidents ... things pushed up...'

Then he remembered the old wives. The wives of mature years employed by the religious authorities in cases of alleged non consummation whether wilful or arising from impotence. He put on a high chant.

'... the three wives will testify to the court that the husband was or was not able in their presence to have full coitus with the wife without unnatural acts or potions ... premature exterior ejaculation ... semen not to a depth of one finger joint ... second attempt allowed within five hours ... bread and wine only, no garlic ... such children to be declared bastards without inheritance ... cases requiring fine judgement to be referred to Rome...' He muses thoughtfully.

... shelffuls of books in the Vatican from the fourteenth century on the sex act ... every angle you could think of and some you wouldn't ... and, here, my old china, all written by celibate churchmen under vows of chastity, ha, ha ... What? You think it must be a collection of old wives' tales, eh? Not to get your leg over when church bells doth toll the dead ... concoctions to get your pecker up to be taken when the moon is full ... dandy lion root, sweet basil and thyme? WRONG, squire, WRONG. Accurate, detailed and compendious. Sex manual people could still learn from them today if they knew latin and knew somebody in the curia to let them see the library.

What? The last impotence trial before they were abolished for 'inciting the lewdness of the multitude'? Oh that was the best bit. Paris. Sixteen something. This Count. Accused by the Countess of impotence even though they had children and he was a notorious womaniser. Church reluctant to take it up because of implications on inheritance if children not his. But he insisted because of the slur on his reputation. HIM! The greatest rake in Paris. A five times a night man! He demanded to have the test, made a festival of it, wine barrels in the street under the windows to be broached when the three wives announced ... But ... time passed ... the mob got impatient and broached the wine anyway ... went into extra time ... mob shouting up advice at the windows. Got nought out of ten from the three wives. Oh hubris, hubris, Not even referred to Rome for fine-point adjudication. I wanted that fellow to do a follow up article on how come celibate churchmen could write treatises on all the ins and outs of doing it: poor penetration; premature ejaculation; frigidity; vaginismus, but we fell out over a postdated cheque.

What? Vera? Ah, poor Vera ... heard life wasn't kind to her ... naughty beautiful Vera full of life ... loved dressing up and doing song and dance turns ... big dark eyes like a lovely Jewess ... looking forward so much to life ... life let her down ... her beauty and bright eagerness long gone ...

And Stanley? ... God knows ... poor Stanley ... virginibus puerisque ... oh for the land of lost content that will not come again ... for a little while more ...

133

10

The lot of a magazine editor who is counting his drinks is not an easy one, especially for the last issue. The last of the year. The Christmas number. On top of the usual chore of making the small amount of contributions, wheedled, for old times' sake, from writers known to the public, seem more than is the case, there is the need to put in something Christmassy other than Santa Claus and holly on the cover. CD fancied something in the yuletide line that had a bit of an edge to it, that would make a nice astringent accompaniment to the drinks and funny hats. He was considering an article by a one time divinity student now into poetry, bit part acting and fetishism involving canes. CD had once caught sight of him on a TV screen in a bar playing a Russian general in an advertisement for fish fingers. The article by the ex-theologian-actor-poet was about the nativity.

'And it came to pass that there went out a decree from Caesar Augustus that all the world should be taxed … every one into his own city … Joseph … up from Galilee … onto Bethlehem … Mary being great with child … brought forth in a manger … no room at the inn.'

But Augustus never issued such a decree. Even if he had, Roman tax collectors, just like ours, did not care where you were born, only where you lived at the time of the tax. Joseph would not have had to go to Bethlehem. And Roman taxes were not poll taxes but property taxes. Joseph would not have had to take Mary with him…

That the nativity story which is found in only one of the

Gospels, Luke, is a myth has been known since history began to be studied properly, but by then the people had become so attached to it that theologians had not liked to take it away from them, or to draw attention to the curious fact that the story of Christ's birth on which Christianity's most celebrated festival is based is not essential to doctrine unlike the story of his death.

Yes. A nice little Christmas cracker which CD had improved by judicious editing. He left out the irrelevance to doctrine. Let the herberts work that out for themselves, he decided. This, together with some adjustments to the style, had given the piece a somewhat mocking tone not intended by the writer, still a high church Anglican. CD might soup it up a bit more with an enthusiastic endorsement from a militant atheist whom he had met at the secular funeral of a controversial Scottish poet where they played 'I Did It My Way' instead of a hymn.

By the time he had got enough material for the last issue of the year the Christmas season was well under way and it was hardly possible to pass a shop from which there did not come wafting out the strains of Adeste Fideles to lure in trade.

The Christmas season can be the undoing of a controlled drinker, so many are the occasions for festive conviviality. In the case of controlled drinker Blackstaff, the strict counting of his drinks for his diary so necessary for control was further undermined by an additional reason for celebration. An anthology had just come out to catch the Christmas book trade and an extract from one of CD's out of print books was in it. The extract, though only ten pages long, nevertheless put him into print again and therefore entitled him to an invitation to the Christmas party of the publisher, one of London's most prestigious. The party was attended not only by the literati but by leading politicians and their wives. Even so, the mobile steps in the library had been prudently removed to put out of reach the higher shelves holding the publishing house's first editions of famous books now in the canon of literature, and directors of the company circulated to engage flatteringly in conversation those like CD whom they did not know in order to discreetly ensure that they were not interlopers.

Hired waiters in black jackets assisted by waitresses in white blouses also circulated with trays, the waiters dispensing drinks and canapes, the waitresses collecting empty glasses, a system which CD ignored by repeatedly exchanging an empty glass for a full one without stopping the waiters in a swift practised movement that impressed though did not please the waiters. He moved glass in hand around the crowded rooms looking for those with whom he could exchange more than a nod of vague recognition and who would give him the opportunity to confirm the English notion of the Irish as good drinking companions. A young poet, described in reviews as 'a craftsman of the perceptually charged metaphor,' who owed to CD his first appearance in print, rushed towards him with hand outstretched – a rush that carried him straight past CD to give an effusive greeting to a figure of importance, an Irish poet and professor of Eng. Lit 'a staggeringly original poetic effloresence' of international fame renowned for his 'presence', whom the publishers had recently transported by helicopter to several packed readings far apart on the same day.

The drinks, of which he had now lost count, insulated CD against any feeling other than sardonic amusement and he looked keenly around for someone to share it with. It was in the library he found Maguire studying the first editions. Frank Maguire: ex-merchant seaman; literary rough diamond; novelist of the telling-it-like-it-is school; poet; womaniser; one time drinking chum of the famous; and, above all, one time bar room raconteur before good bar talk was ruined by disco noise for the mindless young.

Maguire was also from Belfast but his accent was overlaid with American from a long spell in New York where his nose had been broken in a bar brawl, over, it was said, the awfulness of modern poetry.

After the long-time-no-see enthusiastic greetings they shared a laugh about the best selling poet, referring to the striking full length portrait poster of the staggeringly original poetic effloresence in all the bookshop windows.

'... marketed by his publicity machine dressed up as a pigprodding bullock whacking livestock dealer about to spit on his hands for the handshake deal at a fair ... to promote his latest best selling collection in the catholic bog-Irish school...'

It prompted them to revive an old game based on the jargon of Eng. Lit. reviews that they had used to play in bars and at parties frequented by the literary set. Maguire spotted a poet he knew sucking up to the presenter of a TV arts progamme.

– A fastidiously brooding sensibility – he pronounced, and they both roared with laughter.

CD in turn identified another.

– A celebrator of the filtered personal spasm.

Before they tired of it the crowded library had heard loud allusions to: a post structuralist of relentless fecundity; a compelling permutational experimenter in open exploratory form; an unabashed truth teller; an arhitectomic purist; a multi-layered Empsonian and a memorably terse picker of verbal scabs.

There had been a time when they could have set a literary bar in a roar with this act but the people around them were less amused so CD tried an Irish Christmas joke to better effect.

IRISH BOY CHILD. Mother, did the boy Jesus get toys at Christmas?

IRISH MOTHER. No, he was born in a manger and

they were too poor to put anything in his stocking at Christmas. He was not spoiled like you.

The laughter this earned drew some attention from the groups gathered round big name writers. Some good jokes and stories later CD and Maguire had a small group of their own listening appreciatively when Maguire related a wartime experience at sea.

'We were in a Mediterranean convoy just off the North African coast when our ship was torpedoed. Captain McWhirter from Belfast orders us into the boats but waits for the second officer and two seamen who had gone below. Some don't want to wait.

Permission to lower, sir, the ship is listing twenty degrees. This ship, says Captain McWhirter, is not listin' twenty degrees. This ship will be listin' twenty degrees when I say it's listin' twenty degrees. Hold the boats.

All masters of merchant ships in the war were issued with revolvers and Captain McWhirter has his prominently on show. Minutes pass and we all get worried more than somewhat. Permission to lower, sir, the ship is sinking fast. This ship, says Captain McWhirter, is not sinkin' fast. This ship will be sinkin' fast when I say it's sinkin' fast. Hold the boats.

The Captain has his revolver drawn by now. Even so, things are about to take a nasty turn when the missing people appear. They are struggling with a wardrobe. Mr Wilson, the second officer, is a very fancy dresser, and has bought a lot of dude clothes in Buenos Aires that it would break his heart to lose and hence money has changed hands to get the wardrobe into a boat.

Captain McWhirter is annoyed more than somewhat.

(At this point Maguire puts on an exaggerated Belfast accent)

Mr Wilson, he says, I have known ship's officers that put the ship first, and I have known ship's officers that put the crew first, but damn me if I have ever known ship's officers that put fancy suits of clothes first. If you come near this boat with that wardrobe I'll shoot ye so I will, I'll shoot ye. Lower away.

But more money must have changed hands because when we pull away from the ship there is the wardrobe sticking up in one of the boats and second officer Wilson with his arms round it.

Well then a Free French destroyer stops to pick us up for Chrisssake! We are flabbergasted. When a ship in convoy is torpedoed escorts never stop for Jesus sake! They put on speed. They whizz round dropping goddamned bangers on the sub not to make targets of themselves. Goddamned warships cost a helluva lot more than merchantmen for Chrissake!

But it is not so much the breach of naval regulations that has us pissed off more than somewhat. It is also that we have been torpedoed on a calm sea within sight of Tangier towards the lights of which we were rowing eagerly before the goddamned Free French boat interfered. The red light district of Tangier is well known to all sailors and some of us haven't had a woman for two months. The Free French destroyer is not hailed warmly. Words are exchanged. Fuck off gestures are made. Captain McWhirter has again to draw his revolver. And in all the kerfuffle second Officer Wilson's wardrobe slips over the side and is received into the bosom of the deep for Chrissake! Later, on the destroyer I hear him speak of the matter. I go down on my bended knees, he says, and thank my maker I did not have the Captain's gun or I might have shed human blood.'

CD led the laughs and announced that cassettes of that and other great sea stories could be had from the Joseph Conrad Society for two tots of rum and a twist of baccy.

The group around CD and Maguire was now augmented by people who had edged closer from other groups to listen.

Passing waiters had entire trays of drinks disposed of at a stroke. CD and Maguire led an animated discussion the theme of which was that while the prose department of literature was still connected by however long a chain with what the man in the street read for Chrissake, modern poetry had broken that connection and was now only for a goddammed gang of Eng. Lit. academic wankers who couldn't rhyme a goddammed Christmas card for a cod. TS Eliot's esteem for Kipling was quoted as well as his poetry itself. A young woman junior editor just down from varsity with an English degree who had never before heard literature debated with oaths and even four letter words was obviously rather taken with the novelty and it was obvious to CD that Maguire might well score before the night was out, while he himself had his eye on a woman writer of children's stories who had laughed harder than anybody at his quip about Conrad. There were pained looks from other groups when Maguire loudly recited verses of Dangerous Dan McGrew from Robert Service's Songs of A Sourdough to prove some literary point about the ballad.

> Now a bunch of the boys were whooping it up
> In the Mamalute saloon
> And the kid that handles the music box
> Was hitting a ragtime tune...

CD listened with a touch of wistful sadness. How they had once whooped it up when he first came to London! Was it really so long ago? The noise around him seemed to retreat as, for a moment or two, he detached himself and listened instead to echoes of his past and felt some breath of cold as he thought of how time seemed to be rushing away from him since his fiftieth birthday. Needing warmth again he rejoined Maguire for a bit of whooping it up one time more. Maguire was saying something about

good plain English being the hardest of all to do for
Chrissake and that every writer should have a shrine to
Hazlitt. It gave CD his cue.

'My First Acquaintance With Poets,' he said, enunciating
Hazlitt's famous essay about Coleridge in a reminiscent
tone and emphasising the *my* in a way that suggested it
was his own first acquaintance he meant. He told them
about it.

'It was during a Belfast Arts Festival when I was a callow
youth collecting rejection slips. My then patron, a retired
schoolmaster called Blair who was a bit of a ganser macher
in the literary life of the Athens of the North sent word
that Louis McNeice would be at his house at a certain time
on a certain evening and would I bring some of my stuff
to read to him. "Cocoa only", it said. It always said that
on invitations to his "little evenings". He would not
encourage the national weakness, he said. So along I go,
convinced I was about to be launched on my literary career.
I find the living room packed with poets thinking they are
going to be launched by the famous poet. But no McNeice
or Blair at the appointed time and the poets all sitting on
whatever they could find to sit on as close as possible to
a large armchair and a smaller one that the wife and
daughter said to keep free. Nobody near those chairs dares
move for fear of losing their place not even to go for a
piss. One, two hours tick by. The big chair is like a throne
to us waiting for Royalty and hating each other. Such
hatred. You could have cut the atmosphere with a knife,
though maybe it was just because it was new to me then,
and I'm so used to it now I don't notice it anymore.
However, at long last a taxi draws up. Through the window
we watch four figures approach the door including the
taxi driver who is helping to link one of the others who
can't walk. No that wasn't McNeice. Oh he could still walk.
So could another fellow we heard was the Festival poetry

organiser. It was "cocoa only" Blair who was paralytic. We heard him throwing up somewhere at the back of the house. Anyway, McNeice sinks into the big soft armchair with a brief case on his lap that he keeps trying to open. The poetry organiser, just about able to stand straight, starts to make a rambling speech of welcome. The poets all have their stuff out at the ready. MacNeice looks straight at me. "Here boy," he says in his posh public school accent, "here boy, I do not fancy your college tucker, so I have taken the liberty of bringing my own." He makes about six attempts to sit upright before he succeeds. Then he dives into the briefcase and takes out something in a newspaper. It is a pair of fresh herrings. "They are already gutted," he says. "I insisted on them being gutted."'

Maguire loved it and let out a huge guffaw as did about half of those who heard it, the other half however, looking stony-faced with disapproval.

Although CD had lost count of how many drinks he had had, those in the increasing group gathered around him and Maguire were privately impressed by how well the two, could, as the phrase goes, hold their liquor, especially as they ate only a little smoked salmon from the excellent sideboard, explaining loudly in mock complaint that it was the only goddammed kosher nosh on the table – CD wondering aloud if he had had anything since breakfast and then if he had had breakfast. Maguire claimed that you got a better goddammed high on an empty stomach anyway for Chrissake.

The group did not know if CD was serious when he announced he was going to change the format of his magazine. Break new ground. First literary tabloid in London. A gossip page. An agony auntie. Tips for the unpublished. An etymology quizz with popular appeal. Question: what is the origin of the word club as in tennis club? Answer: same as in club a weapon. People out late

142

in violent 18th century London *clubbed home together*. Good stuff eh? And how about a crossword? Clues like:

A great Russian writer whose youthful pastime was raping serf girls on his father's estate.

An English novelist who was a nasty little squirt who regularly beat up his fat German wife.

A Welsh poet described as an incontinent clothes pilferer.

A woman writer who died senile in the geriatric ward of a London hospital unknown to the staff as the inventor of the stream of consciousness.

This last clue had most of the group guessing. The young lady with the degree in English who had found all the other clues dead easy was stumped by this one which made CD look slyly pleased. Maguire was enthusiastic. He added eagerly his own suggestions. What about headlines for the tell-it-and-be-damned exposures. Ho, ho, said CD and together they concocted, with a little help from the younger members of their circle things like:

THE NOBEL PRIZE AND THE MAFIA. A Swede comes forward.

NO DRINK LICENCE FOR POETRY SOCIETY. Police objections.

SEX WITH VIRGINIA WOOLF. Bloomsbury milkman's exclusive story.

POET LAUREATE SENSATION. Four letter words in Queen Mother's birthday poem. Palace statement expected.

HARVARD WIVES GROPED BY DYLAN THOMAS. Now it can be told.

FR LEAVIS WROTE FOR MILLS AND BOON. Sensational disclosures by lady friend.

WB YEATS TV BIOGRAPHY ROW. Cuts in gym slip sex scenes demanded by Taoiseach. Union Jack burnt on stage of Abbey Theatre.

JOYCE DROPPED FROM OXFORD SYLLABUS. Tear gas used to disperse PhDs. Provost injured. Drink blamed.

TS ELIOT'S WANDERING HANDS. Ex-Faber tea lady speaks out.

And, shouted Maguire, as people in the crowded library started exchanging looks of distaste, how about a top twenty page?

Compiled, cut in CD, from the number of PhDs done on them together with other factors by our literary actuary from a leading Insurance Company Yeats down two, Joyce unchanged, Larkin up five.

Hell no, Maguire objected, more like the sports pages. He put on the voice of an on course bookmaker and intoned rapidly:

Blake, Browning and Byron of Ballymacarret six to four bar one. Coleridge, Chatterton and Chaucer of Cregagh failed the dope test. Dickinson, Dryden and Donne of Dundonald up three at Ladbroke's. Hopkins, Hardy and Herrick of Hilden under starters' orders. Lamb, Landor and Longfellow of Ligoniel disqualified by the jockey club. Milton, Marlow and Moore of Malone in the two thirty at Newmarket. Sassoon, Swinburne and Shelley of the Shankill fancied over five furlongs.

CD led the applause and announced to the staring party goers that by Jesus protestant Belfast could still show the world a thing or two, that they weren't finished yet sunshine, not by a long chalk.

But there comes a point when even seasoned boozers like CD and Maguire should take more water with it on empty stomachs if shennanigans are to be avoided in which Important People are involved and it gets into the press. It really started to get out of hand when the two Belfastmen thought the company would be vastly entertained by them pretending to be the public address system at a big literary event.

'Testing, testing, testing. One. Two. Three. Four. Five. NO POPE HERE. Sixseveneightnineten. REMEMBER THE ALAMO. Roger and out.

Here is an important announcement for those with unpublished novels. Would those at the front go to the back and those at the back go to the front and those in the middle stand well clear of the front ones going back and the back ones going front. Thank you for your co-operation.

Would the Irish poets holding orange and blue tickets with numbers whose last digit is not greater than nine and is divisible by itself *not* go to the gymnasium with their urine specimens for charisma and fitness testing unless asked to do so by Faber and Faber marshalls in green coats with numbers greater than zero.

Would those with tickets for the sold out lecture on the Book Of Kells please amend an error in the programme. 'The Art of the Mediaeval Fornicator' should read 'Rubricator'.

Would entrants for the Ezra Pound prize for the best tobacco-chawing-well-I'll-be-goldarned-ole-rocking-chair-hill-billy poem about usury please note that they must not have more than one grandparent a Jew.'

An Eng. Lit. academic who wrote books on Pound made a loud exclamation of protest and was asked by CD how he could think Pound's Jew baiting filth poetry. The Auschwitz Cantos, jeered CD and when the academic remonstrated further Maguire asked him if he would like to step outside. People thought that was the point where the publishers should have intervened and asked the pair to leave.

There was no truth in the reports next day in the tabloids that two Irish Americans, singing Irish nationalist songs had assaulted an ex-cabinet minister. It was in fact a well known protestant hymn that they sang: 'When I Survey The Wondrous Cross'. CD and Maguire were recalling nostalgically the names of hymns from their Belfast protestant upbringing and that hymn, unlike other old

145

favourites has two tunes the rival merits of which they put to the test by singing the first verse to each tune. Moreover this occurred before the arrival of a party consisting of an ex-cabinet minister, his wife and his literary agent MacFarquahar-Forbes who was promoting the memoirs of the politician, a controversial figure who in office had married a pop singer 40 years his junior. The ex-cabinet minister did not suffer any injury. It was in fact MacFarquahar-Forbes who suffered some abrasions to his face though of a minor nature requiring only sticking plaster. Nor was this due to his being assaulted. This story was put about by people who left the library before it happened – people who had been deterred from remonstrating with the two Belfastmen partly by fear of ridicule and partly by the pugilistic impression made by Maguire's battered looks.

What actually happened was that MacFarquahar-Forbes returned CD's warm first name greeting with only a cursory nod and then turned his back. This proved to be a mistake as he might otherwise have been able to avoid being accidentally struck by a large heavy first edition from the higher out-of-bounds shelves which CD had managed to reach by standing on Maguire's back in order to settle the question as to whether it was The Seven Pillars Of Wisdom by Lawrence of Arabia. The shelf was so tightly packed that, in pulling at the volume hard it came out all of a sudden so that he fell off Maguire while the Seven Pillars Of Wisdom went flying in the direction of MacFarquahar-Forbes who would have been felled to the floor had not the impact driven him, clutching a full glass of wine, against the ex-cabinet minister and his young wife who, as luck would have it were nibbling at smoked salmon and potato salad at that moment. It was their first literary party. It is perhaps not surprising, considering how fate seems to watch over the inebriated, that CD and Maguire emerged virtually unscathed from the cascade of first editions that rained down upon them – except for a dig in the ribs from George Bernard Shaw and a poke on the buttocks from JB Priestley.

The two Belfastmen were of course asked to leave, mention being made of the police. They complied good humouredly but not before they made a pantomime with a scriptural allusion: Samson bringing down the pillars of the temple upon the goddammed Philistines. It was later said to be all the fault of the chief editor (Eton and Baliol) because, being a one time chum of Maguire's when they were both hospital kitchen porters, he had not liked to get rid of him when he should.

By Jesus, they sure had whooped it up, they agreed on the pavement outside, only slightly unsteady on their feet, wondering where they could whoop it up some more. But someone else had followed them out of the publishers. It was the young Eng. Lit. woman who had not known that the inventor of the stream of consciousness was Dorothy Richardson. She said she would get a taxi, but looking only at Maguire.

As they got into the taxi there was just a suggestion in Maguire's manner that he might have preferred to whoop it a bit more with CD who saw him and the young woman off with bantering pleasantries about middle aged libido. Can get a Japanese one to strap on these days, boyo. Keep taking the tablets. Must keep in touch.

But he knew that they would not.

As CD wandered alone through the night streets towards more gin and dream troubled sleep he mused.

Funny word, touch. Touched your heart. Touched for a fiver. A touch of class. Lost your touch. Out of touch...

Should have told that one about ... so much untold ... might yet still ... if ... so iffy ... the iffiness of the great untold if...

11

Nigel Lambton, unpaid assistant editor of the *Clerkenwell Review*, normally found it easy to use the photocopiers of his employer, The Bulwark Assurance Company, in the service of Art and he did not expect it to be any less so on Christmas Eve when the office parties got noisily under way with drinks, crackers and pastries cooked by the ladies. However for that very reason it attracted unwelcome attention from revellers who thought he was working. Leave it, old chap, they called to him. Here, have some of Linda's goodies – I meant your mince pies dear! He was forced by this attention away from several copiers otherwise well situated for his purpose. Those managers and heads of departments normally most strict about company rules and behaviour were now so imbued with the seasonal shedding of inhibitions that, glass in hand, they shouted at him convivially to stop that *work*, and waved him away from copiers. Is that man working, ho, ho. Chuck it, old sport, Armistice declared at eleven a.m. ha, ha. Don't break the ceasefire, lad, he, he. Take that man's rank and number, yuh, yuh. It was only when the drink had begun to do its work to encourage the staff, especially the male staff, to concentrate on the opportunities to be different to their normal office selves and do things like getting the girls a bit squiffy and shouting double entendres at them, or even, with a bit of luck, touch them up in corners, that Nigel started to get his copying done. He was copying two things. One was his novel 'Rules of Engagement', the story of a love affair between the son in a family business and the daughter of a strike leading shop steward. The other was of the *Clerkenwell Review* of which they had insufficient printed copies to send to all subscribers. He fended off facetious party banter by shouting back that it was for the KGB, the Flat Earth Society, The Come Again Massage Parlour. As usual he did it in small batches at different machines, ranging widely over the great brick Gothic edifice that was one of London's landmarks. He found that the Christmas jollifications had reversed the workday situation with regard to certain quiet nooks and corners where his favourite copiers were sighted. When he turned into a pillared and shaded alcove off the carpeted vestibule of the Legal Department he came suddenly upon a bald headed man in a pin stripe suit and a plump woman of mature years kissing passionately with the woman's tongue obviously thrust into her partner's mouth as far as it would go. So sorry, murmured Nigel, and then, less audibly as he retreated, it must taste different to the trumpet recalling when he had seen them a few days before in the church of St Sepulchre Without Newgate, the man performing 'The Trumpet Shall Sound' from Handel's Messiah and the woman singing the lead soprano part. Opposite another copier in the corridor of Unsettled Deaths (Ireland) was a lift which opened suddenly and a group of middle aged men emerged from it supporting a colleague who, it appeared from their indignant remarks, would have been perfectly OK if it had not been for old Ackroyd's home made elderberry wine – awful, definitely cloudy, God was yours like that too, and pulls rank on you if you try to refuse, had that young actuary sick in the toilets, young what's his name, father in Estates with the hare lip, daren't say no, how on earth were they going to get a taxi for old Charlie on Christmas eve. Oh God we'll have to get him to the rest room on Mezzanine, what about a company car ... They stared at Nigel with such hostility that he gathered up his stuff and left. As he did so old Charlie slid from them to sit on the floor with outstretched legs, shaking his head and repeating in an awful whisper 'unfermented yeast, unfermented yeast'.

The reason that about fifty copies of Vol 2 No 12 of the *Clerkenwell Review* were having to be produced by the copiers of the Bulwark Assurance Company rather than being printed was due to the illness of the editor CD Blackstaff and there was a small notice to this effect. The notice did not, of course, explain that this was because only Blackstaff, with the experience of several magazines behind him, knew how to farm out an issue around several printers just starting up in business who could be persuaded not to press for a substantial deposit before printing. Vol 2 No 12 contained a larger number of misprints than usual because CD had omitted a proofreading stage in order to get fifteen hundred copies rushed out while the boss of a small printing firm in Clerkenwell was sick and the young foreman perceived CD as a promising new customer. Over the previous week Nigel had copied most of the outstanding issue and it was only now when the last fifteen bulged safely in his ancient briefcase with handle mended by rope that he relaxed. He returned to his department where they had run out of soft drinks and were knocking back neat gin. They exhorted him to do the same as they uproariously pulled the girls' crackers for them, read their cracker jokes for them ('What did the Irishman say to...') and helped them put on their funny hats. Nigel's proud feeling of mission accomplished might have encouraged him to join more wholeheartedly in these celebrations had he not just noticed that his own name as assistant editor was misspelt 'Tampton'. Oh well, might have been worse – Tampon'. He recalled with foreboding previous issues when disgruntled contributors had had cause to complain. *Nots* coming out as *nows* and viceversa thereby reversing the meaning were bad enough but were nothing to real horrors such as when the word cult was spelt with an *n*. A cunt figure. His imagist admirers made a cunt of him. Nigel turned the pages hastily to the poetry section where that sort of thing can cause real anguish, especially if the contributor has also been persuaded to put money into the magazine – an aspect of editing for which CD had an impressive talent and which Nigel suspected him of practising on a larger scale than he would admit to. But there appeared to be no obvious howlers. There was a suspiciously conventional arrangement of lines in a Douglas Grantly poem about – so far as you could tell – whimpering snow flakes in Brompton cemetery. Wasn't it Grantly who wrote long instructions about where each line was to be positioned and – oh God – shouldn't whimpering be *whispering?* Nigel sipped again at his half tumberful of gin just as the benevolent warmth the first sip had generated began to compensate for the stinging bite of the raw spirit and gave consideration to the question whether snow flakes could whimper. In the opinion of a reasonable person that is. The man on the Clapham bus. What was it Wordsworth said about what Hazlitt said about what Samuel Johnston said about meaning in poetry? Oh well, too late now. Que sera sera. Water under the bridge. Nigel went to the toilet and filled up his glass with water at a wash hand basin. Whispering grass the trees don't need to know, he sang softly, doing an old fashioned ballroom spin turn with an arm round an imaginary partner. His girl friend was a keen ballroom dancer. He became aware he was not alone.

A figure stood brooding at the closed door of one of the cubicles even though all the other doors were ajar. It was St John Tutley, pronounced Sinjin. He was well known throughout the office from having his picture often in the company magazine, being, along with Lucy Major, one of the leading lights in the Dramatic Society. He was a stocky bald man who could play the male heavy in a wig and was also a contributor to the magazine on Wine. He had been pictured in it recently at a tasting of the homemade wines entered for the annual Arts and Crafts exhibition looking so thoughtful with a glass at his cheek that it was as if he was listening to what it had to say to him. He let Nigel's singing and dancing pass without comment and explained gloomily in his somewhat mannered actor's diction that he was the victim of unusual circumstances. Having answered a call of nature he had left his briefcase behind in the cubicle and had hastened back whereupon to his consternation the cubicle was now engaged by someone who refused either to communicate or to come out. Unfermented yeast perhaps, suggested Nigel, is his name Charlie?

It's all right Charlie, he shouted, you can come out now, old Ackroyd's been drowned in a butt of parsnip wine and it's Appellation Controllé from now on don't you worry.

Oh for God's sake, said St John, be serious, the man could have had a seizure. And I need my revue pretty damned quick.

Revue? said Nigel.

My Noel Coward numbers arranged for the New Year pantomime. I was about to get it copied for distribution to the cast to study over Christmas. SHOULD WE GET SECURITY TO BREAK THE DOOR DOWN? St John enunciated very slowly and loudly in his famous reach-the-back-seats word chewing style for the benefit of the silent and immobile occupant.

Here, said Nigel, emboldened by the gin, why don't you people put on some decent stuff like Ibsen or Chekhov for a change?

Nigel then went straight on to quote from a piece that he had written in Vol 2 No 3 of the *Clerkenwell Review*, '... it is a common mistake of amateur dramatic societies to suppose that thrillers and farces are easier than serious drama when in fact they often demand timing and stage business which only the pros can manage successfully whereas the simplicity of some of the great...'

Nigel's peroration was interrupted not so much by St John starting indignantly to put him in his place as by the noisy entry of a group wearing funny hats and blowing into those humorous devices which unroll with a farting noise. They stood at the urinal whooping and chortling about someone called Barbara who 'carried all before her' and discussing which public house to repair to to continue their revelries. One of them wore a false nose secured by an elastic band round his head. Nigel hailed him cordially.

Hey, said Nigel, that thing you wrote for the Bulwark magazine that won third prize in that competition. Very good. Been meaning to ask how ... er...

Cor, said red nose, half proudly half contemptuously, I was just taking the piss. Silly bloody competition. HOW I GOT TO THE OFFICE IN THE RAILWAY STRIKE. Blimey. All the crawlers and bum lickers got their pens out 'Look what a good boy am I, sir'. Could have knocked me down with a feather. Streuth. Third blooming prize!

Yes, but your play on words, said Nigel, I've been meaning to ask where ... er...

Nigel cast about unsuccessfully for a diplomatic way of asking how a clerk whose speech often betrayed his humble cockney origins with such phrases as 'we wasn't' or ''e did an' all' and who appeared to have read nothing but the vulgar tabloids could have managed such clever play upon words as '... crossed the Red Sea in The Dhow Jones Index ... Port Said Aswam the Nile but Mrs Sippy's Vulgar boatman ...'.

Joyce, said Nigel, trying again, you read James Joyce, do you?

Get off, said red nose with a laugh.

But er that Dhow Jones Index, said Nigel admiringly – recalling heated arguments he had had with literary snobs in an Earls Court writing group who had refused to concede Nigel's claim that the spirit of art could choose such an unlikely vehicle to manifest itself – and that Mediterranean bit with the storm 'may deter any 'un' and what was that Irish dromedary in Arabia?

The Irish drummer Derry Walls, said red nose, good one that, eh?

But red nose's companions were impatient for the joyful hubbub of the Christmas decorated bars and pulled him away before Nigel could explore further his talent for Joycean word play. He might follow it up after Christmas, perhaps even publish 'How I got to the office in the strike' in the next issue of the *Clerkenwell Review* – if there was a next issue ... if CD was still ill ... if the printers could be appeased with a part payment of the debt ... if ... He fell to thinking so deeply about the problems and opportunities (Editor N. Lambton) of Vol 4 No 1 that he absently said yes to St John's precisely enunciated request to remain where he was till St John fetched SECURITY but went out immediately after he had swallowed the rest of the gin at a gulp and felt it warm him, firing his resolve to take over the magazine for at least one issue with his name as EDITOR. He strode through the corridors savouring phrases on the blurb of his novel '...and edited, for a time, the *Clerkenwell Review*'. Thus heartened, another bold idea took hold. Why not take the copy of his novel to the Agents right now? Yes! Who dares wins. He was passing the glass panels of an office with typewriters in it which the occupants had abandoned for Christmas revels elsewhere. He typed 'J MacFarquahar-Forbes Associates, Author's Agents' and then 'Dear Mr MacFarquahar-Forbes, I ... enclose m.s. ... my friend and colleague Mr Blackstaff...'

Would it be wise to refer to CD's claim to have known him when he started up with, so CD said, 'one pair of trousers, one manuscript – mine – a basement bedsit, a coin box phone in the hall, a public school tie and the cheek of a regiment'?

... asks to be remembered to you and to wish you the

joys of the season ... prevented by illness ... suggested I let your Agency see it first ... extracts published in *Clerkenwell Review* ... warmly received.

He decided not to refer to having actually met MacFarquahar-Forbes in The Fox in Knightsbridge where CD had briefly introduced him to a fleshy pink faced man in an expensive pinstriped suit carrying shopping bags marked Harrods for a youngish woman with beautiful hair and heavy make up who, to Nigel's embarrassment, had coldly vetoed CD's invitation to have one on him by saying to her companion 'you've had quite enough already, darling', and then pointedly not being amused at CD's awful jokes about chewing garlic to put off the breathalysers.

'For the personal attention of Mr MacFarquahar-Forbes' he typed on the envelope which he taped to the folder containing his novel and hurried out into the busy streets. Near the Office he paused at a building on which there was a plaque stating that Thomas Chatterton the poet had died there by his own hand on 24th August 1770 aged only eighteen. Nigel had passed it many times before with only a glance until CD had shown him a book of literary correspondence in which were a few letters the boy poet Chatterton had written from that address to his family in the country, letters full of his triumphs and conquests of literary London, his commissions from the booksellers, praise from famous men, promising his sister silks and cloths for gowns and asking her to tell him what colours ... when in fact he had sold nothing and was starving ... Let that be a warning to you, CD had said. CD had had a skinful, had called them all names: publishers, agents, the fucking so-called reading public that won't spend the price of a Chinese takeaway on a paperback unless it's a best seller. They were all whores or whorehouses. London the great whorehouse. When Nigel parted from him outside Hennekey's in High Holborn CD was singing.

155

But for all that I found there I might as well be
Where the mountains of Mourne sweep down to the
   sea.

The Agency was in a quiet tree lined square in Bloomsbury. A brass plate beside a Georgian door with a fanlight said J. MACFARQUAHAR-FORBES ASSOCIATES, Authors Agents. The foyer had a floor of fine black and white stone tiles on which the feet made a pleasing rich sound. The reception desk was deserted and from a corridor came the sound of people laughing and talking to the clink of glasses. Here too Christmas was being celebrated by flaunting the abandonment of work. Nigel pressed the bell but no one answered immediately. As he waited he studied a large book case containing what he guessed to be the books of writers looked after by the Agency. Among them there were famous serious writers and popular best sellers as well as others less well known but all brought out by leading London publishers. As Nigel's eye traversed the shelves with all the bitter sweet envy of the unpublished but hope-buoyed aspirer to literary fame he spotted a familiar title. 'Lilliburlero' by CD Blackstaff. He had seen it before but somehow it looked more impressive here so that he had a twinge of guilt for pretending to CD that he had admired it when in fact he had not even finished it, finding the scenes of low class Belfast protestant life conflicting with his conception of Irishness and Irish writing nurtured by the monopoly-claiming Art of catholic Ireland. He took it down and opened it, looking at the technical data page with new interest. Reprinted twice. Well! So it had been a good little seller for a while. You never knew with CD and some of the claims he made – which were bogus, which true.

   At that moment a group of men in expensive overcoats swept in from the street in a reek of cigar smoke – one of them looking very like the man whom CD had introduced Nigel to as 'Jack' who was complaining humorously about the Cafe Royal's wine list going down the hill since Oscar Wilde. That Puligny-Montrachet ... fruity finish but lacking in authority. Lets have a glass of real brandy in my office to cleanse the old palate he shouted to the loud approval of the others. They left lying open the office door and from the foyer Nigel could just glimpse a stretch of wood panelling with a large oil painting which might have been of the Impressionist school. Their voices carried, haw hawing over jokes and anecdotes from the trade in books.

'... cried all the way to the bank about what the film people did to his novel ... the one about the Irishman who thought that oral sex was talking about it ... got him incarcerated in a villa in Fiesole with a minder under orders not to let him out for a drink till he finishes ... was only getting twelve and a half per cent after fifteen thousand hardback when she came to us would you believe ... critics here gave him a right going over but it's gone into three editions already in the States ... German rights not worth a fart it's only the French who read...'

A girl appeared at the reception desk. She looked doubtfully at Nigel's parcel. Was Mr MacFarquahar-Forbes expecting it, she wanted to know.

I've met him, said Nigel in the same kind of loud confident voice that was emanating from the richly furbished office and was gratified to see it work. Respectfully she picked up his typescript to take it inside. If he's not too tied up I wouldn't mind a word with him, Nigel called after her but not to worry if he can't.

She stopped to attend to a man who had just come in and Nigel sat down again. The man muttered something indistinct and then took the seat beside Nigel. He was a nondescript looking man dressed in jeans and windcheater and carrying a plastic shopping bag, probably a messenger. Nigel paid him little attention as he pondered whether to wait. Better not push it too far, he thought. He had got his book past the door after all. Half the battle, CD was always saying, getting somebody to look at it.

The girl went to the panelled room and did not come out, presumably because there was another door into the general office. An outburst of guffawing at what seemed another Irish joke died away and was replaced by the sound of more serious but quieter talk that did not carry. Mr Macfarquahar-Forbes then came out of the office and, beaming broadly, came hurrying towards where Nigel sat, a gold ringed hand extended in greeting. Nigel gaped, electrified, his mind a whirl of images in which his m.s. had metamorphosed into one of the books on the showcase the blurb garnished with choice phrases culled from critical acclaim '...holds a clear mirror up to our age – *Times Literary Supplement* ... powerful evocation of pride and prejudice – *Observer* ... a brilliant new talent who may well change the way we see ourselves today – *New Statesman...*'

Nigel half rose from his seat at the same moment as the shabby man beside him stood up.

'Dicky,' shouted Mr MacFarquahar-Forbes in greeting, affably pumping the shabby man's hand vigorously before ushering him almost paternally into the office.

'... got Knopf fighting it out with Scribner's at the moment ... about three hundred thousand yesterday evening ... dollars I'm afraid but it's only ten a.m. New York time...'

Then the door was very firmly closed.

It would be Christmas Day in a few hours and he had left undone those things which he ought to have done. He still had to visit CD in St Mary Abbotts hospital; ring Angela about going down to Purley to have Christmas dinner with her and her parents; open the Review mail he had collected from the P.O. Box No. Was it four gin and tonics he had had or five? Damned poets kept plying him with drink to print their stuff now he was acting editor. He should have kept out of the Kings Head. Seething with poets. A density of five poets to every square yard, a bard on every bar stool exuding manuscripts from every orifice. The George almost as bad though more prose merchants there. Is there a bed sit in Kensington that you couldn't flush a manuscript out of? Still, it was not unflattering to have them grovelling round one. The way they slavered when I said I might want a couple of reviews. Like dangling meat over hungry dogs. Wuff wuff. Aren't there still two or three review copies that CD wheedled out of the publishers? How they rushed to get me another gin! And that fellow in the Kings Head with the PhD on Blake and works at scaffold erecting, Simon whats his name that CD printed in July, what was it that girl called over to him: 'Any good erections lately?' God! Said he could get me fixed up there. Should I have? Haven't had ... since Angela two weeks ago. But that girl looked as if she would expect a fellow to be ... a great stud. That other time when ... I couldn't. Awful. Felt terrible about poor Angela too. Wish Angela liked it more. Mother's letter wanting to know when I'm going to settle down. You'll soon be thirty, she said. Angela musn't leave it too late to start her family. Thirty. Only a few things in print. First novel still unpublished. It was *five* gins I had. This is my 6th. Those bloody scribblers pouring alcohol into you and offering you women to get you to take their stuff. Occupational hazards of being an Editor. No wonder CD has a drink problem and has to be dried out every now and then. Not as many women scribblers in bedsit land or maybe keep their heads down. Plenty out in the suburbs though. That letter CD showed me. Unfulfilled housewife in a Writing Group in Lewisham wanting to meet him to show him her stuff. 'Photo enclosed.' Probably showed him more than her manuscripts. He was probably too pissed. Would have had to put a splint on it. Frightfully shaming when that happens. Angela didn't like CD. Said he kept looking up her clothes every chance he got. Wish Angela would shave her pubic hair again. Said the stubble chafed her. Not much chance tomorrow. Her father running around the house looking for things like he does. But when they're full of turkey and pud? A quick knee trembler after the Queen's speech? Those hair clippers I got in the CND jumble sale. Wouldn't chafe that much dammit. I wonder if there's a letter in this lot among the printer's bills offering the Editor sex in return for taking a poem? Hey, there's one with nice writing. Wonder if it's from a dissatisfied suburban housewife in a writing group. 'Dear Editor ... photo enclosed ... could meet on my aerobics day ... would be so grateful...' Well let's see.

Dear Mr Blackstaff,
I hope you can print my poems soon. It is now six months since I sent them along with the cheque for twenty pounds as requested. The one about the magpie killing the squirrel in our garden I sent to 'Wildlife' last October. I believe in that. I believe a poem about horse racing should be printed on the sport pages for the punters to read. I call that Involvement Oriented or IO for short. I went to a hare coursing meet with a friend who has a lurcher dog. That is how 'Kill' came to be written. I have got many more IO poems if you are interested though I don't think I could afford to send any more money. The four IO poems I sent you are the best so far. I nearly sent 'Stock Car Racing' to a poetry competition in our local paper but it might not have been legal after letting you have it. My girl friend's father said it would have won. He is security guard at a supermarket. He let me watch him catch a shoplifter. That's where I got 'Shoplifter'. He is looking forward to reading it in the *Clerkenwell*

Review. He knows Earls Court well as he once ran a gymnasium there.
   Yours sincerely
   R. Croker

Christ! No keep cool, don't panic. This is where the P.O. Box No comes in handy. Damn CD and his tricks. What a way to get finance. Could get you a good thumping. I need at least one more issue. '... and was editor of The Earls Court Review...' Wonder if MacFarquahar-Forbes will take on 'Rules Of Engagement'. Hey, why don't I get a job in publishing. Yes. Write to all the publishing houses. 'Dear Sir ... familar with all aspects of editing ... exercising judgement on merit of submitted m.s....' Why not. Get into the book world, get to know people. Definitely. Meanwhile get another issue together. Get the finance somehow. Angela's father? And material. That 'How I got to the Office in the strike'. Discover new talent perhaps. Port Said Aswam the Nile but Mrs Sippy's Vulgar boatman... Quite easy really when you get the hang of it. Why does Joyce intimidate everybody with his cleverness? A good article there. Shakespeare doesn't do that to people. Milton didn't say I'm not as good as Shakeaspeare so no point in writing Paradise Lost. Yes. I've so many good ideas. Might consider that Ezra Pound article from that Blake PhD chap 'any good erections lately' Simon whatshis name that CD has been sitting on. A bit strong on Pound's rabid anti-semitism and Nazi collaborating. 'A Pound of Auschwitz'. CD said it would have all the PhDs on Pound come round to kick the shit out of him. Anyway CD's judgement on the blink now. Past it. Had his chances. A has been. That stuff of his own he let me have for next issue. Not too sure. Let's have another look if I can dig it out of this damned case. Another gin first. Angustura this time. Like the pretty pink colour. No, just water please. Oh make it

SAM KEERY

a double. Well now, let's see Seedy's bit for our lit crit…
Hey, CD stands for Christmas Day. Why didn't he call
himself that too? Christmas Day Blackstaff. Ah. Here we
are. By C Day Blackstaff. Two pieces. We'll bring our
editorial judgement to bear upon the short story first.

MORNING SERVICE by CD Blackstaff

'The Blairs were the last to arrive for morning service and
as they walked up the aisle to their pew the second Mrs
Blair was agreeably aware of women's jealous glances directed
at the new hat which set off nicely her wavy hair that she
now got styled every week since the much older builder's
merchant and church vestryman widower had married her
six months previously despite the bitter opposition of his
married sons and daughters. She took in with satisfaction
the long glance from the big buxom soprano in the choir
opposite the Blairs' pew who had had her eye on him herself
and might indeed have got him if something about her
didn't tell you that she thought at his age it would be just
good cooking and companionship. Well! As she rose to sing
the first hymn the second Mrs Blair looked impassively at
the plump choir singer waiting for the organ and thought
half wryly half amusedly, 'Oh you would have had another
organ to wait for, dear,' as she recalled the reason for them
nearly being late. She was putting on her new hat ready for
church unlike Mr Blair still in his shirt which he suddenly
raised and said 'Ah would you look at the state I'm in,
woman,' showing her his thing sticking out wagging and
nodding at her, it must have been the hat, so that there was
nothing for it but to lift up her dress to her waist and crouch
across the bed with her backside up for him to come into
her from behind standing so as not to disturb the hat she
had just arranged so nicely and warning him to use the
cloth when he pulled out of her at the finish so as not to
stain her lovely new bed cover and squeezing her thighs

162

together to grip him tight and make him finish quicker, the randy old bull. As she joined in the hymn lustily she thought she would have to begin training him to let her relieve him with her hand when the urge came on him at awkward times like that or even that other way too shocking for some to even think about. As the second Mrs Blair thought about it the soprano woman opposite was in full throat on the line Oh Come Emanuel which kept her mouth open and rounded. 'Plain cooking and companionship how are you! Oh you'd have had more than plain cooking in your mouth, my dear with this old ram. You'd have had more than church peppermints to suck with this old boar to keep sweet.' And as they got to the line with Oh Israel in it she thought about that package holiday to the Holy Land with coach tours to Bethlehem and on the way home three days seeing the pyramids...'

Nigel pursed his lips in distaste though at exactly what he was a little uneasy since RULES OF ENGAGEMENT contained the obligatory explicit sex scenes now required by the market. Let us, he announced to the imaginary editorial committee at which he was in the chair, let us instead take another look at Seedy's so called poem:

BED SIT LAND

Cohabiting Yorkshire housekeepers partial to gin. Promiscuous South African girls from Jo'Burg in front doubles affronted by coloured man in back single. Metropolitan Empire doormen boasting of sex with actresses in landing singles next the loo. Wandering-eye wife-watched Polish landlords. Unpublished New Apocalypse poets giving readings in basement singles with hands blackened from the tyre factory. Broken nosed old Glasgow communists recalling Maxton and strikes in book filled front singles. Top floor elderly tennis coaches in trouble over boys. Milk-stealing Old Etonian morgue attendants in second floor backs. Lyons dish washers practising Mozart violin concertos in basement singles. Girls from Leeds with men in attic singles. Audition-attending telephone-jumpy comedians rehearsing jokes and behind with the rent in first floor backs. Socialist landladies giving rooms and sex to visiting Nigerian trade unionists in ground floor doubles. Unexhibited jew-and-niggerhating water colourists in top floor backs. Respectable prostitutes taking in short times in third floor fronts with wash hand basin. Communist Irish girls explaining Marx's theory of surplus value in ground floor front doubles. Gas meter-fiddling prolific writers of unperformed plays in garden singles. Scots called Macbeth hoarding cigarette ash in saucers in top floor backs. Manuscript-bearing new arrivals from Somerset in landing singles with no table. Auditioned shirt-borrowing pop singers vanishing with gas meter money from basement backs. Mazobiscuits-offering communist Jewish barbers waiting for the revolution in pamphlet-strewn second floor backs. Ex-Wigmore Hall concert pianists with canary in third floor singles. Marijuana-offering cabinet ministers' sons with barmaids in fourth floor singles. Secular Society members proffering anti-God leaflets in landing fronts. Self-published Imagist poets on remand for shoplifting in basement backs. Stamp collecting failed priests in...

And burnt-out boozed-up Belfast prod ex novelists in...! No. I don't think so. My judgement says not. No use being an Editor if you allow sentiment to influence judgement. Won't tell him just now. Must go over and see him now. Should I bring him a bottle? God no. Not the way he is. Not even a Puligny-Montrachet with a fruity finish but lacking in Authority. Tell him I saw MacFarquahar-Forbes. Sent his best wishes. Well. Tells some whoppers himself does old CD. Hey, that Sally Ann girl selling the War Cry in the George a real cutie – and she knows it. Christ I'd shake her tambourine anytime. Would Angela put on a

Sally Ann bonnet? Theatrical Costumiers have them off Shaftesbury Avenue. Take those clippers down anyway. Old CD loved those hymns they sing up the alley at the tube. Prods as bad as the micks about religion. Just comes out differently. CD explained it in Henekey's. Prods read the bible for themselves. Micks don't. Only their priests. Prods a bit like the Hindus. Anybody can start up a sect. Micks more like the Muslims. Regimented. All do the same thing, think the same thing. An article there maybe. No, better keep out of it. Don't want an IRA letter bomb before I get my first book out. Must get started soon. Angela wants a family. Do I? A row of books by Nigel Lambton. Sir, these are my children. That book of CD's in MacFarquahar-Forbes glass case. 'Lilliburlero'. Two reprints. Must feel wonderful. Over the moon. Out of this world. Euphoria.

A jangling bell broke jaggedly into his reverie. It was closing time.

TIME PLEASE, the barman shouted, YOUR EMPTY GLASSES PLEASE.

The bar staff, anxious to get to their beds, encouraged the lingering drinkers to drink up by switching off the Christmas tree and the carols, emptying ash trays into a bucket in a cloud of cigarette ash, using dish clcoths to wipe tables on which there were still glasses with drink in them, and in Nigel's case standing accusingly at his side till he gulped down a nearly full glass of gin and tonic.

He walked out unsteadily into the night, his head a mish mash of Joycean word play, Angela's shorn pubis, the boy poet Chatterton, the words of an old English carol he had sung as a boy chorister before his voice broke *Oh I wonder as I wander all under the sky*, and how absolutely marvellous it would be when his novel would be critically acclaimed and...

What shelebrations, he muttered, what pish ups. What glissorious shiss ups. What pissorious euphorics. What gluppish glory. And a bottle of sin for old CD.

12

It was Christmas evening in Earls Court. Literary activity was at a low ebb. Unfinished poems, plays, novels and short stories lay unworked on in many a bedsitter while their tenants visited their families for festive season quarrelling and recriminating and to borrow money. But a hard core stayed put to keep the lamp burning. A meeting of The New Writing group, though much depleted, was taking place in a second floor front double in Philbeach Gardens. Had it been two houses further down the street the room would have been that in which CD Blackstaff had once been visited by the muse though none was aware of this remarkable coincidence.

Only four young men were present: two poets, a playwright and an autobiographical novelist who was re-writing for the third time to try to get his father right. Disappointingly there were no women, either literary or just women even though Ted, the one reworking his father, could usually supply a chambermaid or two from the Knightsbridge Hotel in which he was at present a porter for the Christmas season. He had however brought a whole salami, a carrier bag full of Russian salad, and a bottle of gin with the hotel stamp on it.

'Oh thou who didst with pitfall and with gin,' intoned Simon as he went out to forage for ice. 'Beset the road I was to wander in.'

'My God,' said Vivian in an appalled tone, 'is that the sort of crap he's writing?' Vivian was a very modernist poet and never used capital letters even for names so that he was always in conflict with typists and editors who put the capitals back.

'No, that's from the Rubaiyat of Omar Khayyam,' Ted said. He finished the verse. 'Wilt thou with predestination round enmesh me and impute my fall to sin.'

'Oh that crap,' said Vivian.

'I like it,' Ted said defiantly.

This was passed over in silence by the two poets until Roger, a stage hand at the Duke of York who had a PhD in mathematics and wrote metaphysical poetry about n-dimensional space remarked condescendingly that Omar Khayyam had been quite a useful mathematician. The Binomial theorem is his, Roger added. You know, he went on, as of something everyone knew, the expansion of a plus b to the power n. Sometimes called Omar Khayyam's theorem.

From downstairs came the sound of dogs yapping, a woman's voice chastising them, and Simon's voice, though indistinct, then silence for such a time that the three speculated about what was keeping him. Was Mrs Dodson the housekeeper having her wicked way with him? Not in front of the dogs surely? Oh dogs wouldn't stop them these days, said Vivian, who claimed to be for ever being accosted by women. He said that the woman in the room next to his tried to rape him every Saturday morning after launderette and the more he tried to put her off the more maddened by lust for him she became which one found awfully tiresome.

'Two tea chests full,' announced Simon in tones of dismay and wonder as he entered the room with a bowl of ice.

'Manuscripts,' he explained, 'two bloody tea chests stuffed to bursting with bloody manuscripts. Her husband's. Died a year ago. His war experiences. At it every evening for years. Wants me to look it over before she throws it out. Phew!'

It might be easier to move out, they advised him. As they started drinking they competed in making up images of Simon up to his ankles in a pool of pages the level of which rose faster than he could read.

Simon was a temporary sub editor on the local weekly newspaper. He had left university without a degree in geology because he didn't like the subject. His play about a homosexual affair between a student and his tutor was no further forward due to Christmas.

Christmas, they agreed, was a bad time for getting your stuff written. Too many Christmas parties and pissups. Too much shagging. Vivian said he had nearly worn his out. Ted said he would have got his father right by now if it hadn't been for bloody Christmas. He read a chapter to them in which a boy who is scared of the dark is made to sit for hours in a large cupboard at the end of an upstairs corridor. His father sounds a right sod, they said. Yes, but what kind of sod, he asked them, to test whether he had got him right. When they used adjectives like cruel, sadistic, Ted flung down his manuscript angrily and said no, no, he wasn't *that* kind of sod, that he still hadn't got him right. Keep that chapter though they said, some of it isn't bad. Oh I keep it all, he said. It occurred to more than one of the others – though no one would have been so tactless as to say so – that his first tea chest must be filling up quite nicely.

'I'm reviewing the latest Graham Greene for the Clerkenwell,' said Simon, 'Lambton asked me in the King's Head last Tuesday.'

'Oh snap,' Vivian said, 'he took two of my poems in the Lord Nelson on Monday.'

'He's going to put back the capitals you take off,' Roger said grimly, 'he told that Blake fellow he's going to make his presence felt on the poetry section.'

Vivian said that there'd be one hell of a row if he did.

168

He wants to watch it mucking about with people's stuff or he just might get a beer glass in his face.

'He's such a repressed suburban bourgeois,' Roger said contemptuously.

Ted said but surely it doesn't matter. You can't hear the capitals when you read which made Vivian so angry he nearly said something cutting about getting Ted's father right but instead said coldy that novelists had no ear and couldn't be expected to understand.

'Lambton is drunk with power,' said Vivian, 'Old CD should hear about him and what he's doing to the Clerkenwell.'

'A woman in the King's head,' said Roger, 'says that Lambton is impotent. Which would account for his power complex.'

'What exactly is wrong with CD?' Ted asked.

Nobody knew exactly. Simon had heard an ulcer, Roger a dicky heart, Vivian that prostate business old men get. Finishes them with sex, he added. But they agreed that too much living it up at publishers' parties and book launches must take its toll. Ted said that he had seen CD at the MacFarquahar-Forbes Christmas party that the hotel had done the catering for. Tucking in and bending the elbow. He did not add that CD had called him George and asked him how his father was coming on these days. He said that CD had been one of the last to leave. Him and some American. They had had to be asked twice to stop singing 'We are poor little lambs that have gone astray'. They were on to hymns when they staggered out.

'It could be syphilis,' Roger said slowly, 'congenital syphilis is endemic in the Belfast area where he comes from.'

'This salami,' said Simon appreciatively, 'is very good. Damn turkey and sprouts, say I.'

'Yes. Very bourgeois fare,' agreed Roger.

'It looks like a dildo,' said Vivian, laughing so much he choked.

'Perhaps not only looks...' Roger said, frowning. They stared at him.

'Oh, you know, Byron's story,' he said. No, they did not know, and urged him to go on, though a little apprehensively.

'This young man in Venice,' said Roger, 'saw his sister using a salami for a certain purpose in the kitchen. When the salami later appeared on the dinner table the young man rose and bowed to it saying "Vi riverisco mio cognato. I salute thee, brother in law".'

'Charming,' said Vivian, pushing his plate away in disgust and Ted said angrily that it was the last time he'd bring any grub and was mollified only by Roger and Simon eating Vivian's portion as well as their own.

Roger read a short metaphysical poem about planes of being trailing luminosity through nothingness which he said had been listed tenth in the Muswell Hill Arts Centre competition and published by them later.

'I don't understand nothing,' Ted said.

'Wot, you don't know nuffink?' Simon queried in a cockney accent.

'No, no,' said Ted impatiently, 'the concept of nothing. What *is* nothing?'

'You can't say nothing *is*,' said Vivian, under the impression that he had just made a profound philosophical discovery, 'you can only say nothing is *not*.'

'The boy in my book,' said Ted, 'keeps asking his father what nothing is and if empty space is nothing and when his father says yes the boy asks how that can be since space goes on for ever and ever.'

Ted made an encircling gesture with his arms to enclose millions of light years of space and then asked the kind of question the boy asked in his novel.

'How can nothing be so big? Nothing must be *something*.'

'It does not go on for ever,' Roger said, 'it is curved and bounded.'

Then what, they asked him, is on the other side of the boundary? Roger spotted the trap but not how to extricate himself from it easily. He avoided saying 'nothing' but only by taking refuge in a claim that it could only be expressed mathematically and he reminded them of Malvolio's theorem about space-time. But they were not going to let him off so lightly, especially Ted, still smarting over the salami story.

'If there is nothing after the end of space, and space is nothing,' he said, 'then space comes after the end of space and so goes on forever.'

Simon and Vivian applauded loudly. The drinks were beginning to make them boisterous. Roger had to shout to make his protests about logical fallacies heard. Vivian came to his rescue somewhat as he still had it in for Ted for his crass insensitivity about Vivian's abolition of capital letters. He asked slyly if the boy in Ted's book talked like that a lot, and Ted said yes.

'Christ,' said Vivian, 'no wonder they put him in a cupboard.'

'We all have our dark cupboards,' said Simon sadly, shaking his head sentimentally. He filled up their glasses under the idea that they had not yet had much whereas its effect was merely being delayed by the food.

There was the sound of a telephone ringing downstairs in the hallway and a little after it stopped the buzzer above Simon's door rattled brokenly. He rushed out to take the call.

'Guess who?' he said on returning, 'Lambton. Wants a favour. Guess what? Wants me to go and see CD. Was supposed to go himself. But is at his fiancee's in Purley. To tell him the issue is all out.'

'Bloody nerve,' said Vivian 'CD's errand boy is trying on the crown for size. Listen, I'll come with you. I want to tell him about what Lambton's up to behind his back on the poetry pages.'

'No, no,' said Simom deprecatingly, 'not at this time. Season of goodwill.'

'A *"fiancee"*!' Roger repeated incredulously, '*in Purley*. How utterly bourgeois. How absolutely stomach turning petty bourgeois.'

'Yes, well,' said Simon, 'er ... there you are.'

The hospital was on the Fulham Road. They would have a last one for the road before Simon set out. The last one for the road went down so well that they had several more. Why didn't he take old CD a drop, they suggested. It was Christmas, dammit. A couple of snifters, hang it all. Yes. Take him that half of gin. Could cheer up the patients with his prod Irish drollery. A little of what you fancy does you good. Simon said a glimpse of heaven in the tavern caught better than in the temple lost outright and Ted said old Omar Khayyam hit the nail on the head there all right. He said this so fiercely and stood up to raise his glass in salute that Roger and Vivian thought it prudent to make a slight glass raising gesture to avoid trouble.

There was a rapping at the door. It was a good looking young woman who said, 'Mum said you can have them now. You know. The tea chests of Dad's stuff you want to look at.' Simon tried to say 'Oh, er, when I get time, er. not just now...' but Vivian and Roger were eyeing the girl admiringly, in Roger's case lasciviously. They jumped up and offered to help and the girl said it was ever so kind of them. Simon and Ted remained, drinking silently.

A little later loud voices on the stairs were heard shouting directions of the kind associated with furniture removing and Roger backed cautiously into Simon's room supporting a tea chest with Vivian at the other end and the pretty young woman watching them encouragingly as they lowered it slowly to the floor.

'Just one more to go,' Roger shouted cheerfully as they went out.

Simon stared disconsolately at the tea chest while Ted rummaged among the contents: notebooks of every size; sheets ruled and unruled held together by rubber bands, some of them marked HM Prison, Wandsworth which Ted held up with raised eyebrows and then browsing somewhere else said, 'Did you know that when they take out your appendix in the army they give you a local anaesthetic and a pair of dark glasses.'

The tea chests party reappeared. The second tea chest was heavier than the first having more hard backed notebooks and they gouged a deep score on the wallpaper when Vivian, who was showing signs of inebriation, confused his left with Roger's left when Roger at the rear this time shouted directions to steer him in. Roger was by this time calling the girl Melanie in tones of warm intimacy and he insisted upon seeing her safely downstairs to her mother's. As they were leaving she said the only time her mum had tried to read some of it she was in it. He put everything in it, Roger, she said wonderingly. Reading about herself affected her more than the photo album. Funny, isn't it, Roger. They heard Roger on the landing explaining this. 'Words are more powerful than visual images, Melanie, the pen is more evocative than pictures. That is why poetry...' The sound trailed away.

'Jesus,' said Vivian.

'Christ,' said Ted.

'God,' said Simon, shaking his head deploringly.

In the time they waited before deciding that Roger was not cominng back Ted read out bits from the tea chest. The style was that of someone giving formal evidence or making a report however personal the subject matter. Vivian laughed immoderately every time he predicted accurately a well worn cliche. When they grew tired of this Simon said slowly with great sadness, 'Poor bastard. Poor bloody bastard.' But he meant something more than that, something also to do with themselves, with their own literary hopes and dreams.

'I have to get this gin over to CD,' he said. Yes, and the message, they said, the message. What was it again, he asked them. 'The issue is all out,' they told him. He repeated it to make sure he had it.

Vivian left. Ted lingered to avoid leaving with Vivian. He accompanied Simon to the corner of Philbeach Gardens. He was more at ease in the absence of Roger and Vivian. Damned poets, he said, ruining poetry. *You can't hear capital letters*, he repeated scornfully, my arse.

'Yes, well,' Simon said, 'there you are. In my father's house are many mansions.'

'Your father?' said Ted, but Simon shook his head and muttered something about a quotation from the New Testament.

'I'm aiming for spring,' said Ted, 'to be ready to submit. If I can get my father right.'

'Ah. Our spring list, our summer catalogue, our winter new writers,' said Simon, 'publishers' calendars do not have months but seasons.'

'Oh Christ,' said Simon in dismay, 'Lambton didn't say which ward. That effing hospital is so big you can get lost. Christ.'

But Ted had started to sing. It was not only the drink that loosened his inhibitions but the absence of highbrow poets. He had a pleasant voice.

> We are poor little lambs that have lost our way,
> Ba, ba, ba.
> We are little black sheep that have gone astray
> Ba, ba, ba.

Simon embarrassedly took his leave and walked off thinking of the Rubaiyat of Omar Khayyam. All about wine. So why did he switch to gin in that one verse? *Oh thou who didst with pitfall and with gin.* Oh, of course. Rhymes with sin, wine doesn't. This drop of sin for old CD. Went in for sin, I'm told. Never read his stuff. Old hat now, I expect. Had many a sinful skinful. What was I to tell him? Lambton's issue is now out. No. the issue is now all Lambton. Something like that.

13

In the hospital opposite the nipped in pub a senior registrar accompanied by a junior house doctor came and looked at the chart hanging on CD's bed. The registrar asked loudly of the sick man how are we now Mr Blackstaff in the bedside manner of one with his name down for a consultancy but elicited little coherent response. The registrar referred to the case file opened for him by his junior colleague which said under DIAGNOSIS: Cirrhosis of the Liver. He queried something that was unclear. Was the patient reckoned to be a one-bottle-a-day or a two-bottle-a-day man? Claimed to be a half-bottle-a-day man, perhaps an Irish half, said the young doctor with a laugh. The senior registrar was not amused. His name was Read O'Shaughnessy. Perhaps he was displeased by the slur upon a race which had a half share in him; perhaps he was not going to allow levity on the wards from a pup of house doctor just out of medical school; perhaps he liked a drink himself. But as they moved away he abashed the junior with a brief lecture on the disease as if rebuking ignorance.

... no direct link between cirrhosis of the liver and alcohol ... enlargement of the liver to deal with alcholic toxicity not morbid in itself though may predispose to attack ... possible more direct cause the poor diet usually accompanying alcoholism, in particular protein and vitamin deficiency...

A tube into CD's arm connected him to a bottle at the

176

top of the bed. It simplified everything, giving him release. No need now to try to remember when he had last eaten and how many drinks he had had and if he had them with strangers or acquaintances or a woman and if he had had them in bars or public conveniences or libraries or in the pews of empty city churches or alone in his room listening to his memoirs trying to tell him what his life had been about. The bottle took care of all that and more.

From it there seemed to flow into his veins a steady drip, drip of voices, figures, places, dreams. There was a chair at his bedside in which it seemed to him that someone sat. No matter that when he looked to see who it was the chair would be empty since he knew that it would be there again when he looked away. Other figures that stood or moved around him were sometimes familiar, sometimes not, though in those who were not he sometimes detected what might have been a lingering time worn likeness to people who had perhaps deserved better of him, or who had given him the opportunity or been given it by him of making life quite other to what it had become. As well as the flickering figures around him he himself flitted in and out of places in which he watched previous versions of himself mostly with serene detatchment but sometimes with regret for what would never be.

Some of the figures addressed him. The first to do so appeared to be carrying a battered briefcase with an improvised handle made of rope. He came down the ward peering closely at each patient's chart in turn in the manner of one well used to tracking down birth, marriage and death certificates, book lists of extinct publishers, book reviews in old numbers of the *Times Literary Supplement*. He inspected CD's chart and pulled a face of wry congratulation.

Always the last damned one you look at, he said, rolling his eyes resignedly. His accent was that of Belfast, in which,

SAM KEERY

as he took the place of the dark figure on the bedside chair, he said that his feet were killing him. He propped his card up on the bedside locker. This said that he was a bibliobiographical data researcher, obituarist and autobiography ghoster and listed among those who used his services were: Who's Who; *The Times* obituary column; the Vatican Index; The Bulwark Assurance Company. The card also claimed to have written the non-authorised biographies of several Irish poets and a self made born again second hand car dealer.

He opened his case and took out a hip flask and a bottle of gin, which, with a long knowing wink at CD he connected to the intravenous tube and then ducked down out of sight to take a swift swig from the hip flask before again rummaging in the old case for a fistful of papers which he brandished at CD.

The goddammed crap they tell you in this game, sunshine, he complained contemptuously. He struck a page as an example but paused before quoting it to dart a quick look round to ensure confidentiality.

'... two paper rounds at the age of ten, now on the board of six publishers, who dares wins, ... has gone ten rounds with James Joyce and had Chekhov on the ropes...' he read, rolling his eyes again before suddenly swinging up the hip flask to his lips and away again so swiftly that although all heads turned to look at him suspiciously he was too quick for them to be certain and he stared them all out boldly before striking the pages again and reading another titbit from them with angry scorn.

'... they laughed when I told them I was going to win the Noble Prize someday...'

He took another now-you-see-it-now-you-don't gulp before getting down to business which was to check the ticked boxes and statements attested as true on a Bulwark Assurance Company form for Irish policies. In a rapid monotone he

178

ran through the ones deemed more or less correct by the actuaries.

'... religious observance; betting shop attendance; antimodernist; homosexual/lesbian/straight; King James Version; pill/condom/ interuterine device/coitus inter-ruptus/total chastity; bailiff repossessions; unsolicited manu-scripts; wife swapping; out of print books ... the YES/NO DO YOU BLAME THE BRITISH cross check on religious observance ticked as stipulated against: leaking roof; acne; unrequited love; greenfly; impotence; manuscripts rejected; haemorrhoids; the law's delay; premature ejaculation; ingratitude; old age.

We can't have you fucking up their life tables, my old china, he said, taking another swift swig before holding up a section of the form that was blank. It was headed LOVES/FRIENDSHIPS in BELFAST. He raised his eyebrows.

Ah well, said CD, you put these things off, don't you, until ... First it's until you grow up and then it's until you find out who you are, get the hang of things, get into the swim, chart your course, study the possibilities, weigh up the options, consider the alternatives, read all about it first.

Did you do much reading about life, asked the bibliobiographical data researcher.

Sure I liked nothing better. I would have done more but for the distractions.

Such as?

Ah, you know how it is. The eventualities that did not arise, the contingencies that never occurred; the crises that did not take place – just one damned thing after another...

The bibliobiographical obituarist grew impatient as he held up another section not filled in.

You're holding out on us, skipper, he accused. Damn all can I find in the way of decrees nisi and absolute, summonses for maintenance, joint title deeds, land registry entries, sweet FA for the wedding photos section, the smiling couple, the boot tied to the getaway car, the words of love then spoken, the eyes that shone now dimmed and gone, the cheerful hearts now broken. Dammit, not even a will leaving her the second best bed.

'It don't signify, my dear,' CD murmured softly.

The biblibiographical obituarist repeated these words slowly and suspiciously as if he had come across them before somewhere. He tossed back another swig from the hip flask and frowned in concentration. Then he pointed accusingly at CD. 'Got it,' he said confidently, 'under DEATH BED UTTERANCES Charles James Fox the parliamentarian. Sweet liberty was all his cry. His last words to his weeping mistress. *It don't signify, my dear.*'

He undid the makeshift rope handle of his battered briefcase and took out Bulwark Assurance Company biography forms. There were two kinds, plain and fancy. After some hesitation he decided on fancy, but reluctantly. 'I tell you what, squire,' he said, wanting to be reasonable, 'I'll put down that you stained the white radiance of eternity. How about it, sport?'

But CD heard him only faintly as other figures, other scenes, shimmered around him.

'It don't signify,' he repeated in a drowsy murmur, 'it don't signify.'

The presence in the chair never seen directly was always dark but not unbenign, the keeper of the bottle, the dispenser of dreams, the giver of release.

14

It seems to the stricken Belfast man of letters that he is attended by shadowy figures. They are Oxbridge classicists seeking to enlist him in their bitter struggle with the Oxbridge modernists for control of the syllabus and the laying down of the colleges' port. They push forward a beautiful naked woman to whisper to him enticingly of a revamped EROS magazine, classy, classical, full of erotica from the classics. She has striking Semitic features and short hair giving her profile the beauty of a queen of ancient Egypt painted on the walls of a royal tomb in a pyramid in the Valley of the Kings. She will be on the front cover kneeling before a sacred cat, with earrings of Isis and Osiris. Is she Nefertiti, sister-wife of the Pharaoh Akanaten? She will not say. Her mission is to murmur sweet voiced promises of advertising revenue; printers' bills taken care of and of error free typescripts each accompanied by a case of Gordon's Gin and a dozen of Taylor '29 Port. Softly whispering enticements, she breathes fragrant fragments from the classics not found in the schools editions that would surely make EROS a nice little earner in the catholic seminaries among the onanist takers of vows of chastity and on the stalls at the Bishop's conference called to acrimonious debate on the ordination of women.

'... and when Alexander The Great married a Persian Princess, 10,000 of his soldiers were ordered to couple with Persian women on his wedding night simultaneously with him at the stroke of midnight...

'... and Pasiphae, wife of Minos, King of Crete, put a

curse upon him for his adulteries, so that he ejaculated scorpions, serpents and noxious millipedes which devoured women's vitals until he put a goat's bladder into them to protect them...

'... and did you know how the goddess of love, Venus to the Romans, Aphrodite to the Greeks, came about? It was because Uranus raped his mother the earth goddess in her sleep causing her to give birth to the Titans, and she was so angry she gave the youngest Titan, Cronus, a sickle, with which to castrate Uranus when he was asleep. Cronus sliced off Uranus's testicles and threw them in the sea and it was from the semen in them that Aphrodite (foam born), goddess of desire, was made.'

Eagerly he bends his ear to her tit bits from the classics which she cunningly extends to include juicy anecdotes concerning the God of his fatherland not widely promulgated on either side of its religious divide or taught in the Sunday schools of his childhood.

'... and there were sects such as the Manichaens and the Cathars who sprinkled their communion bread with semen obtained, some said, by female hands...'

He is so excited by this he struggles up in bed. Three columns on that, he coughs enthusiastically, Lever-Martin ecclesiastical typeface and the caps illuminated by Nefertiti in different coital positions would shift another five thousand copies at least to the box number rectories, presbyteries, manses, chapels, Lord's Day Observance Society and Brethren tract distributors.

He calls for his deputy editor.

Hey, Lambton, is that you? Why the black suit and hard hat? We're not finsihed yet, sunny Jim! You can stuff the Bulwark photocopiers, we've got the Dreaming Spires Press now, my old china! Here, take a look at our cover girl for the next issue. How would you like to give *her* pubic hair a short back and sides, eh? Ah sure everybody knows about you barbering Angela from you telling it to the third prize in the strictest confidence over a beer at the Hackney Poetry Festival, where's the harm in a wee fetish or two and it keeps the hairs out of your mouth as well. But here, who does this beautiful Semite put you in mind of, eh? I thought at first she had the Akenaten nose and eyes from her mother's side but ... Who? Mary Magdalene? Oh here, a bit of a problem there, squire. You'll split the classicists and let in the modernists. You'll have Oxford and Cambridge at each other's throats. Oxford keeps the 'e' in Magdalene, Cambridge drops it and says Maudlin. Christ, they've heard you, you have them at it already! Listen to them. They're all pissed from mixing the gin with the Taylor '29, they call it a Corpus Christi cocktail with a dash of Manichaen communion semen.

'... the only classics you know anything about are the Derby and the St Leger, you wanker, heh, heh ... and up yours too, you arsehole...'

Classy classicists classifying the classics for the classes. First class. Second class. Third class. Steerage class. Saloon class. Working class. Longtailed class. Bantamweight class. Class of '42. Miss Pym's class.

Miss Pym, sprung from a noble sire, seed of Zeus, earth shaker. Sammy Jackson of the loud war cry. Edna of the braided tresses. Stanley, pale of face, stricken by Eros. Fitzsimmons minor, fleet of foot. Betty of the white arms. Sid Gorman, favourite of Poseidon, destroyer of ships. Cissie Coulter, steadfast in virginity. Nina, fair-tressed nymph. Jack, subtle in wit. Lorna, comliest of maidens. Bertie Marlow, of the evil counsel, practised in deceits ... heh, heh,...

Oh here, sunshine, I had a thorough grounding in the classics. Come here till I tell you about Bertie Marlow.

*　　*　　*

I was a very impressionable boy and full of imagination. The story in our class reader of the Gorgon Medusa with snakes for hair whom it was death to look upon except in the reflection of a burnished shield appealed to me very strongly. Eagerly I pointed out Medusa-like girls with curls or ringlets and would shield my eyes in horror or go rigid as if struck down dead. I tried to start a street game which involved advancing backwards upon girls like big Cissie who had a mop of ginger curls, while gazing into a bin lid. I tried to get big Cissie nicknamed Gorgon, but to my annoyance they started calling *me* Gorgon instead, despite my angry protests. I was particularly angry with Bertie Marlow over the Gorgon affair. Sly Bertie had led me on, had pointed out big Cissie to me, had even suggested the bin lid, and then turned round and led the campaign to get people to nickname me Gorgon. Hello Gorgon. Here comes the bold Gorgon. Lend us your comics, Gorgon. So assiduously did sneaky Bertie Marlow *Gorgon* me that it caught on for a while and lasted long enough for it to take wing like some windbourne seed over the school walls into the streets beyond, where however, it suffered a mutation to Gordon. Years afterwards, my mother would sometimes be puzzled by people who knew us only slightly referring to me as Gordon and when she mentioned this I would remember the school reader in Miss Pym's class with its stories of the gods and half gods, not only of the Greeks, but of the Norsemen, of Valhalla and Wodin and Thor, of the half-god Loki the troublemaker, patron of slyness and treachery. I tried to get sly Bertie Marlow nicknamed Loki, though in vain. Not because of the Medusa affair. It was because of the affair of the frog.

There was another story in that reader about a big mechanical frog made by a poor clockmaker. It could jump over a city wall at dead of night with soldiers inside it to rescue a beautiful princess from her wicked uncle.

'We have one of them at home, Gorgon,' Bertie whispered at me from the desk behind. What was more, if I went home with them after school, I could have it.

'Get stuffed,' I whispered back derisively. The Marlows lived in the railway cottages near the goods sidings where there were definitely not any beautiful princesses, muskets, drums. I did a two fingered gesture at him behind my back, which is not as easy as it sounds.

'Honest,' whispered Bertie, and followed this at intervals with 'Cross my heart,' 'May God strike me blind,' and other attestations to truthfulness, some of them so fearful in the penalties invoked that it was impossible not to be somewhat impressed.

'Ask Ned,' said Bertie. Ned was his elder brother.

At break in the playground Bertie led me over to Ned for confirmation.

'Certainly we have,' said Ned scornfully, as if angry with Bertie for caring who believed it or not.

'It come off a fairground,' he added in an indifferent take-it-or-leave-it tone that insidiously undermined disbelief.

Fairground. So I was not being asked to swallow drums, fifes and princesses? My interest quickened in spite of the too obvious pleasure on Bertie's face at having aroused it. Then when Ned, with brutal candour, said dismissively that it was only a two-seater, the reduction in scale, far from being a disappointment, on the contrary helped along the process of being persuaded that there might be something in it after all.

Bertie placed his hand about three feet from the ground and said, 'It could jump that height with Gorgon in it, couldn't it Ned.'

'Away to hell,' said Ned angrily, though not to contradict, far from it. He gestured impatiently at the playground wall.

'It could clear that bloody wall, so it could.'

'And Gorgon can have it,' Bertie prompted, 'can't he, Ned?'

'Him or anybody else,' said Ned, impatiently turning away, 'first come, first served.'

Bertie watched triumphantly as my scepticism melted away and was replaced by eagerness to acquire so delectable a possession.

When we reached the railway cottages after school, Mr Marlow was digging his garden in his railway clothes, still wearing his bicycle clips. His bicycle was against the window. Mr Marlow was famous for being inseparable from his bicycle. He went everywhere on it, even to the public house. When he rode his bicycle home from the public house he pedalled so slowly that the bicycle nearly came to a stop and he would be about to fall over when he would turn the wheel sharply and start pedalling again just in time. People said it was like an act in a circus.

Circus. Fairground. Two-seater. The association was irresistible and exciting. I greeted Mr Marlow with unusual warmth.

'Hello Gordon,' said Mr Marlow as Bertie and Ned went in to carry out the frog.

The curtains moved at the window along the sash of which was a row of little ornaments. I saw a hand do something to them. Then Bertie and Ned appeared. Bertie watched me, smiling, as Ned, with an ironical bow, handed me a small object. It was a little delft frog on which it said 'Present from Portrush'.

Quite gravely I accepted it, turned, and walked away. Only when I was out of their sight did I give vent to disappointment and rage. Rage at myself for being made gullible by acquisitiveness. Rage at Bertie Marlow. I turned down an alleyway alongside the playground wall of our school. There was no one about.

'Fuck you,' I shouted, 'fuck you, Bertie bloody Marlow. Fuck you, Loki Marlow. Fuck the lot of you.'

I hurled the little seaside gewgaw high into the air. It

sailed over the wall at almost the very spot where Ned had said it could clear the wall with me in it.

I was allowed a single moment of mollifying satisfaction before the sound – musical almost – of breaking glass filled me with horror, I nearly started to run wildly in panic, till I remembered just in time that no one had actually *seen* me do it. I emerged from the alleyway with that sweet angelic look which had served me so well in the past, and might, with a bit of luck, see me through this latest affair in perfect innocence.

He would have liked to fend off sleep long enough to hear the outcome of a debate that might be taking place on whether to allow this as a grounding in the classics. Voices mingled with the clink of glass, the sound of flowing and pouring, and a swishing sound that might have been a cane. Perhaps it was the swigging of college port at high table or the urinal flushing in his old school toilets or the modernists stoning the stained glass windows of wherever it was that the classicists were gathered for a boozeup or tides breaking over empty bottles on a deserted beach or something else entirely too far off to understand.

15

The ward was full of evening visitors. Because of the festive season the restriction on the number of visitors around a bed had been relaxed and at one of the beds a small crowd had gathered. It was that of a dark skinned gentleman who was apparently far from satisfied at the treatment he was receiving and was inclined to blame his assembled relatives for having persuaded him to have his operation carried out under the National Health rather than in a private clinic. This could be inferred even though he and those around him conversed volubly in one of the languages of the Indian sub continent from the many English words tossed casually but distinctly into the swift flow of Hindi or Gujerati.

'...sleeping pill ... jolly damned bad ... brown bread too by jove ... wait for bed pan ... go private by God...'

At one point he produced a half full bottle of urine and invited them to pass it around to inspect the colour so that they could see for themselves what it meant not to go private, and, suitably chastened, they began arguing among themselves volubly during which other English words and phrases popped up, startlingly familiar in their exotic settings.

To the sick Belfastman drifting in and out of sleep their voices evoked confused associations from years past going back to the schoolroom and the oilskin maps of the world showing the once mighty British Empire in red. It seemed to him that a heated debate was taking place on how empires end and why and if the decline is gradual and what marks their final demise.

'... damned salt tax by jove ... that Kipling fellow ...
non violent protest ... dominion over palm and pine ...
Mahatma Ghandi gave up sexual intercourse by god ...
second world war ... Britain's difficulty India's opportunity
by jove ... Nehru not sound on cow question ... when
dawn comes up like thunder on the road to Mandalay...'

The sick Belfastman struggles into a half sitting position.

No, he tries to tell them loudly but manages only a
whisper. No, not India. Not 1945. Later. I'll tell you when
the British Empire ended. I was there when it happened.
I took a picture. Where is it. Can't be in my mother's
biscuit tin with the rest. No. Later. Ah there it is!

He points triumphantly at the white wall of the ward
above the bed of the Indian gentleman on which there
appears to be a flickering image in monochrome as if from
a projector. It seems to be the enlargement of an old
snapshot though the flickering sometimes faintly animates
it with a suggestion of movement. The snapshot seems to
have been taken over the heads of a crowd some of whom
are holding banners towards a raised plinth around a
monument with a huge carved lion to the side of a speaker
with a microphone to whom the flickering imparts the
illusion of gesticulation. Several heads are turning to smile
up at the camera, one that of a beautiful young woman
with Semitic features.

He tries to raise himself to point. Trafalgar Square, 1956,
he explains in a half shouting whisper. The Suez affair.
We took to the streets. Bliss was it in that dawn and to
be young was very heaven. Well, it was for some. Should
have been for me...

In the picture on the wall the flickers enliven the lovely
features of the Jewish girl smiling up at the taker of the
snapshot of a moment of history and of happiness. The
sick Belfastman calls to her but a dark figure at the bedside
says softly, not yet. Other voices are heard, louder and

disputatious. They are drunken historians and history tutors arguing over whether he should be invited to give an eye witness account to The Decline and Fall Society in Oxford before it is too late. Some say there's nothing like a good *telling it like it was paper* to keep you awake after a liquid tutorial but others say contemptuously that that fellow will give nothing away. He's not an editor for nothing. He'll edit whatever version of himself he wants to leave to posterity. He'll edit himself out of any scenes of squalor, acts of meanness or spite, times of near despair. But the ayes have it and there is a call for a bit of hush for the sick Belfastman to tell it like it was when the British Empire passed away.

'When Nasser nationalised the Suez Canal in the long hot summer of 1956, girls at parties in the bed-sitting rooms of Earls Court said excitedly that there was going to be another war. The Yanks would come over, they said, and lots of lovely officers would be about. However other bed-sit girls took a different view and handed out leaflets at street meetings and protest rallies denouncing imperialism and the Eden government. Two girls from the house where I had a first floor single sold the Daily Worker at the tube station, calling out things like "Stop Eden's war ... the only paper of the workers," to the dismay of gentlemen from the City in bowler hats, one of whom I saw reproach her sorrowfully in the manner of Gladstone trying to rescue a woman from prostitution. An elderly gentleman with a room on the second floor was quite shocked. He half whispered to Danny Prunty and me that Mrs Pusey the old housekeeper had told him that one of the girl's fathers was a general and her brother was at Eton. He was something in the administration of the Church of England and had all the old middle-class courtesies, such as addressing you by your surname in order to avoid the rudeness of presumptuous familiarity.

'Who would have believed it, Prunty,' he said mournfully to Danny, who was a backstreet Belfast Catholic, 'a girl from a good family, eh, Prunty?'

When the Church of England man came upon a group of us loudly debating the Suez crisis on the landing, and ventured the remark that perhaps Mr Eden was waving the big stick too soon, he was brutally rebuffed.

'He's an imperialist,' they said scornfully. Ancient and mildewed heads and other big game trophies looked down at us from the walls of the landing and there was everywhere a musty smell of age and decay. It was probably one of the last bed-sit houses in Kensington still lived in by a member of the family for whom it had once been home, though I did not discover that for some time. One night I heard voices outside my door and when I opened it I was startled by the sight of a tall old lady in a moulting but bright brown fur coat who called past me into my room, 'Alice, Alice, do come down, there is news from India,' while old Mrs Pusey behind her shook her head at me to pay no attention before gently leading her away. Just after the start of the Suez affair I saw two men in black conferring softly in the hall and when I went to pay the rent Mrs Pusey said that Miss Lovibond was dead. I gathered she had been the old lady in the fur coat. She was to be interred in the family vault in Brompton cemetery.

'So convenient, you know,' said Mrs Pusey with firm cheerfulness.

You could see the railings and some of the taller monuments of Brompton Cemetery from the corner of the street. I once wandered in and strolled along the avenues of the tombs of London's illustrious dead: Admirals, Judges, Inventors, Colonial Administrators. On several there were additional tributes in strange swirling scripts from the grateful subject peoples. There was one in Chinese which made me suddenly remember where I had once before encountered the name Lovibond. It was in St Mary Abbot's hospital and there had been a little old man in the bed opposite mine called Mr Lovibond, very well spoken but hard up. He had been *most awfully obliged* to me for giving him some cigarettes and, when he saw I was reading Stevenson's TRAVELS WITH A DONKEY, told me he had done that sort of thing himself, don't you know. In China. He said he had walked across China with a donkey. Had to shoot the beggar in Chang Ming, he said with the same firm cheerfulness with which Mrs Pusey had described Brompton Cemetery as convenient. Was he, I wondered, what they used to call, in the days of Empire, an *old China Hand*? I tried to remember where else I had seen the name Lovibond, perhaps on jars or bottles in the kitchens of my childhood: coffee perhaps, or ginger or rice or tea? Strolling through the cemetery, I came across a vault, though not the Lovibonds', with a clipper ship carved in stone above the portals. It was like a little house, having a strangely snug-looking front door with a glass panel Inside there seemed at first to be a cosy little room, in the middle of which there was a table and a chair, except that on the shelves lining the walls were coffins. On the table was a jam pot containing freshly withered flowers.

When Mrs Pusey referred to wills going to probate and family having to be traced I was tempted to ask about the old China Hand in St Mary Abbot's Hospital but it was none of my business. The house was to be sold. We would all have to go.

'Won't we,' she shouted down cheerfully to her two little pug dogs, goggle-eyed and snuffling cantankerously in case they were left out of the conversation, 'we'll all have to go, won't we.'

Men with briefcases were shown round our rooms from

time to time, making furtive notes. One of them worried over the identification of item: *head with curved horns.* The fact that we all lived in the imminence to quit gave an extra flavour of change to that Suez summer when Nasser's dark face smiled down upon us from the hoardings, gone jowly with middle age but still floridly handsome with the little lady killer moustache.

The communist girls on the third floor gave us leaflets explaining that Suez was part of the class struggle everywhere. Everything, it appeared, was part of the class struggle, even Northern Ireland. They gave Danny leaflets on the Irish problem and he learnt to his surprise that Finton Lalor had been a kind of early communist before Marx. Danny had thought that Finton Lalor was the name of a band. The Finton Lalor Hibernian Pipe Band. Danny had only just arrived in London to work in the hotel trade and was still apt to be overawed by girls of the middle and upper classes having not yet had it proved to him that their anatomy was identical to that of the cockney girls he picked up easy as wink in Hammersmith Palais and whose voices spoke his name plaintively on the telephone in the hall. Tell him Barbara. Tell him Doreen. He combined Irish good looks with a puritan resentment against women for being desirable which women found irresistible.

I showed Danny around the famous sights of London and we were lucky enough to view Downing Street on a day when there was a flurry of comings and goings over Suez. The police kept us well back but we witnessed the swerving arrival of black limousines and the slamming of their doors. Someone was hurried into number ten amid a posse of tough-looking men who glanced all around them as they moved. The man in the centre was grey-faced, vaguely familiar from his picture in the news.

'Hey, that's Foster Dulles, the American State Secretary,' I said to Danny and added half ironically that we were being brushed by the wing of history. He liked the phrase and got me to repeat it. He was rapidly shedding his broad Belfast accent, though not by Englifying it into that awful Ulster cockney which grates on the ear in both London and Ulster. More subtly, he exploited the resemblances in the Ulster accent to North American and old Mrs Pusey had delighted him by enquiring if he was a Canadian. He addressed the girls on the hallway phone as *doll*. 'OK, see you around, doll,' he would say, as he brought the latest affair to an end. 'Brushed by the wing of history, doll,' I heard him tell another in just the right tone of raillery to convey an impression of knowledgeability and sophistication. Perhaps she was the pretty little blonde I found in the third floor kitchen one morning doing his washing and worrying aloud what she'd tell her mother for being out all night. She wanted me to persuade Danny to go home with her. If only he'd go home with her, she said wistfully, convinced that if her mum met him she would understand.

Soon he no longer needed my tutelage and he knew more about London's west end or 'the town' or 'up west' as he called it than I did. Instead of Hammersmith Palais girls or scrubbers, as he called them it was chambermaids and waitresses from the big hotels. At bed-sit parties he was in great demand for being able to supply delicacies such as smoked salmon and women. He reported seeing many of the famous in the hotels he worked in: The Savoy, Claridges, Browns. Sightings of the statesmen who were in the news about the Suez crisis no longer gave him the slightest thrill of being *brushed by the wing of history*. It seemed that government ministers and politicians like Nehru, Selwyn Lloyd, Foster Dulles, were two a penny in the hotel trade.

The girls on the hallway phone who asked you to tell him Doreen, tell him Barbara now called him not Danny but *Mark*. He thought Mark had more *class*. He sometimes pulled faces at me behind people's backs to get me not to call him Danny. He took a great fancy to reading poetry from some of my books, especially from the plain rhyming verse department of English literature of which his Irish catholic education must have starved him. He learnt Coleridge's 'Rime of the Ancient Mariner' off by heart, and Fitzgerald's 'Omar Khayyam'. He was particularly fond of reciting such verses imbued with the sad sweet hedonism of youth, celebrating the joy of life shadowed by its brevity.

> Dreaming when Dawn's left hand was in the sky
> I heard a voice within the tavern cry
> 'Awake, my little ones and fill the cup,
> Before life's liquor in its cup be dry.'

He was apt to call on me with smoked salmon and gin after he had been to confession though he would pretend he had been to the public library. The combination of confession and gin made him very candid and poetical. He recited poetry and spoke openly about changing his name. It seemed that he would have preferred to be Ralph or Christopher; there was some objection to Ralph I can not remember perhaps it was that catholics have to have a saint's name and he was not sure about a St Ralph whose bona fides might not, being English, be in favour with the Irish hierarchy. Christopher, on the other hand, would be made common by people shortening it to Chris. I agreed it was a crying shame what shortening could do to some very classy names. Stephen – Steve; Joseph – Joe; and of course Daniel – Danny. He was quite indignant on the subject and attributed it to the darker side of human nature, with its urge to drag down, deface, defile. I recalled a boy named Alfred who was actually called Alfred not Alfie but it must have needed great strength of character. Whereas there was nothing the bums could do about Mark. He had clearly given the matter some thought and I said that after all if his famous namesakes could do it why not him? 'What famous namesakes?' he asked and I said, 'Why, the Brontës, of course.' Emily. Charlotte. *Wuthering Heights* and all that. He had liked the Laurence Olivier film version so much that he got the book out of the library and went about being very Heathcliff till it wore off.

'Brontë,' I told him, 'is fancy for Prunty.'

'Ah, you're codding me,' he said.

I maintained it was true and what was more that they came from Ballynahinch in County Down but he said I was taking the piss out of him. Lapsing into broad Belfast, the old Danny once more, he said that I was right oul' cod so I was, though he was intrigued when I said I would look it up in the reference library next time I was there to prove it to him

When I got home next evening he was waiting to take me to the reference library. To speed things up he cooked me an omelette. I had never seen one flipped before and it was most impressive. I told him I could visualise him one day performing at table, vanishing in a sheet of flame after they toss in the brandy the way they do, to the ohs and ahs of the ladies, reappearing immaculate and urbane, not a hair singed. Perhaps his own restaurant. Prunty's. Around St James's.

He had never used reference books before, yet he found it while I was still searching. He was very bright. I was looking in the wrong places, in the literary reference books, all about the *works* of. He wandered off around the shelves and came back with a biographical dictionary. He pointed at the entries. BRONTË, Charlotte.. BRONTË, Emily ... BRONTË, Patrick, father of..Yes! There it was. Clergyman, ne Prunty ... humble Irish origins ... Ballynahinch...

'The oul' father,' I said in broad Belfast, 'the oul' father made it up for a bit of a cod.'

But Danny, or Mark, as I now had to call him knew better. Not for a bit of a cod but for a bit of *class*. And how! One of the most romantic names in English literature. Done with just a touch to the spelling. That 'e' with the two dots, hinting at origins exotic and mysterious. Made authentic by the true mystery of great art.

'You've been a Brontë all along,' I said, 'without knowing.'

A few days later I noticed a letter addressed to M. Brontë on the hall table. The handwriting seemed suspiciously like his own Similar letters continued to arrive several times as he savoured the *class* of having been 'a Brontë' all along.

He became very familiar with the third floor communist girls, especially the general's daughter with the brother at Eton, Jennifer. The girls gave a party to celebrate some high day in the communist calendar – The Paris Commune or the Tolpuddle Martyrs or something – at which Jennifer showed him off so much some of the visiting comrades were confused into thinking he was a new convert. When I spoke to Jennifer about the oncomimg big Trafalgar Square demonstration against the invasion of Egypt her attention kept wandering to where he was and once when he sat down beside her with his collar ruffled she smoothed it back for him with movements in which the pleasure of touching him were so manifest as to be shameless and would, I suspect, have been so whether he was a Prunty or a Brontë. I was less successful with the other communist girl Miriam, who was Jewish and beautiful.

'Hasn't Mark got the same lilt as Harry at Cambridge?' a woman called to her husband, who asked her if she was sure dear, and wasn't Harry from Canada, but the woman insisted and appealed to the others to hear Mark's lilt just like Harry's. They spoke to him with grave concern about what it was like to come from a fascist state like Northern Ireland, and when he looked puzzled sympathised with him over the special powers of the police there. The secret arrest, they condoled. The midnight knock, they sighed understandingly. They wondered solemnly how long it would be before Northern Ireland fascism spread to Britain. They quoted to each other the Marxist texts such as a nation that oppresses others cannot itself be free. When Mark allowed them to infer quite wrongly that he might be an atheist though from the catholic side they thought this very Irish, very *sweet* to be a catholic atheist not a protestant one, and wasn't he just like Harry at Cambridge, and wasn't it *sweet* the way he said *fillum* for film? When the other women made a fuss of him Jennifer looked unhappy and when I tried to make a joke about the tell-him-Doreen-tell-him-Barbara messages on the hallway phone she made sure it died out feebly by staring at me coldly.

I wondered what he made of the comrades, bearing in mind that the Irish hierarchy held communism in such horror and I chaffed him about it later. But he misunderstood and thought I disapproved. He chided me for not 'getting around' and 'taking in' things. A young guy should 'take in' these things, he said, meaning in the educational sense, as helping to make a young guy well-informed, interesting, one who had been 'around'.

'Never refuse an experience,' he advised me with a smile not yet as ironic and urbane as it later became when it was accompanied by the raising of one eyebrow which I knew for a fact he practised at the mirror for I had caught him at it. He said I shouldn't have created a disturbance at that leftie party, singing like that, a right carry on, he could take me nowhere with a drop of drink in me, what did I want to go singing hymns for?

But he had misunderstood. My hymn singing had been a witty and perceptive comment. Surely he saw that? It occurred after there had been a great deal of talk, for our benefit, about how naive they had all been before they became 'class conscious'; shaking their heads in wry amusement over how gullible they had been before they learnt about the 'class struggle', how they had swallowed their schoolbook history without a thought, how they had believed what they read in the 'bourgeois press', how *petit bourgeois*' they had been before. The word before kept recurring. They used to think this before. They used to believe that. It reminded me of something, this fond harping on some great watershed experience dividing a life into *before* and *after*. Suddenly I had got it. Sinners. Jesus saves. Though your sins be scarlet. The born again sects where the followers are 'saved'. The testimony giving of those who have dwelt in darkness but have seen a great light. Those to whom truth has been revealed and are set apart because of it, the *elect*. Boldened by gin, I remember starting to sing at what I thought was a very apt moment when Miriam described how a pamphlet on Marxism and Women's Fashions had changed her life.

> What a friend we have in Jesus
> All our sins and griefs to bear

'You were pissed,' Mark told me, 'they thought you were a bible nutter. It was a right oul' cod so it was.'

I was a little put out by this but we made it up with the help of gin and smoked salmon. I must say I was becoming very discerning about smoked salmon, its correct oiliness, texture and colour and could now tell the classy posh hotel variety at a glance – to think I had once regarded the blotting paper stuff in the corner delicatessen as good! But when I playfully slapped him on the back he let out a cry of pain. He showed me why. There were these marks on his back. Where fingers had gripped him arched like claws.

'Bloody women,' he said ruefully and almost angrily, as if the puritan in him was disgusted at them *all* being like that, at there being none with virtue among them. What, even Jennifer?, I wondered. Did public school girls from the shires with a brother at Eton also scratch him in their passion? When she and Miriam sold the Daily Worker at the tube staion or gave out leaflets on the Suez crisis at street meetings they looked as prim and high-minded as Salvation Army girls selling their 'War Cry' or shaking their tambourines. I made a little witticism which I thought quite good, putting on the Church of England man's manner of addressing him as Prunty.

'It helps in these cases, Prunty,' I said, 'to think of others worse off than ourselves.'

We laughed so much we nearly spilt the gin and he had to keep his back turned from me in case I thoughtlessly rubbed it in what a cross he had to bear. He said I was a right oul' cod and should go on the stage.

I asked him if he was not worried about her father the general horsewhipping him. 'Like he did that bounder at his club for insulting the regiment,' I said. I made up another brother who was a Cambridge rowing blue. Was he not alarmed in case a crew of rowing hearties wrecked his room? A fellow's sister, dash it, and a bounder! He did laugh a little at this but he also checked with Jennifer that there was no truth in it. Her father the general had cancer and while she had another brother besides the one at Eton he was still wetting the bed at a school which Danny – sorry, Mark – mistook the type for the name. I explained what a prep school was but he preferred Jennifer's description. 'Where they boasted how much their people had stolen from the workers.'

'Did she say that?' I said doubtfully, till light dawned. 'She just meant rich,' I said, 'Karl Marx. All wealth is created by work. That sort of thing. Stolen from the workers.'

'That's what that doll said,' he confirmed, with an ironical smile to show he kept an open mind.

He reported another Marxist pronouncement by *that doll* after the gas meter affair. The gas meter in the third floor kitchen was rifled. Mrs Pusey had wanted to call the police. I had heard the clatter of feet on the stairs and caught a glimpse from behind of a youth whom we all suspected of being one of the Church of England man's boys. He often had visits from boys. One evening his door had been ajar as I passed, and I saw two leering young louts tormenting him by throwing something he valued from one to another as he vainly tried to rescue it, but he shut the door firmly to stop me witnessing any more of his humiliation. Over the gas meter business he made me concede that I had merely presumed it was one of his young friends. Jennifer and Miriam, whose room was nearest the meter would not deign to interest themselves in something so squalidly petit bourgeois. Jennifer told Mark that they refused on principle to assist the class of landlord exploiters.

At first I wondered when she said these things to him, what with his odd hotel hours and her busy *Daily Worker* selling, her leafleting about Suez and fund raising for the party by means of jumble sales, at which, so far as I could see, the comrades sold each other their old clothes or bought them back again. Perhaps it was pillow talk in his room at night. I thought guiltily of the toilet next to his back single which was the cheapest in the house, and of how carelessly we flushed it in the wee small hours.

Then came the uprising against the communists in Hungary and the news was filled with Budapest as well as Suez. The lights went up in Kensington Odeon to reveal boy scouts with collecting boxes for the Hungarian freedom fighters; they were stationed in all the aisles, making escape impossible. Earnest debates went on in Jennifer and Miriam's room over the party line. You could hear them at it as you passed by. Sometimes when they had visitors it continued on the landing. One evening Mark and I went into the kitchen to find Jennifer there with a bundle of Daily Workers and a young man carrying one of those portable speaking platforms they used for street meetings. They were indignant about the hostility they were encountering because of Hungary and put it down to the whipping up of anti-soviet hysteria by the jackals of Fleet Street, the hyenas of the bourgeois press.

'Counter revolution you say, eh doll?' said Mark, cocking an ironic eyebrow. It seemed to have a more silencing effect than heckling.

The tenants gradually began to move out, the older people first, anxious not to leave it too late: it is only the young who find homelessness an adventure. We helped the Church of England man carry down his bits and pieces to a taxi and he shook hands with us in the hallway.

'How nice to have known you, Prunty,' he said courteously.

'Ships that pass in the night,' said Mark, 'and hail each other in passing.'

There was something in the way he said it that was new; a clarity of diction, every word distinct, quite different from the old warm Belfast slurry. I suspected he was practising elocution. I got it out of him on his next confession evening over the gin and smoked salmon. Yes, he was taking in a session or two at these studios in Hanover Street that you hired by the hour. There were musicians, singers. Oh yes, and comedians. *I say, I say, I say who was that lady I saw you with last night? That was no lady, that was my wife.* He said I should take in a looksee and hear them all at it. *La Donna e Mobile.* It's a right old cod, he said and I noticed he said old not oul'. Unaccustomed as I am to public speaking. He said that a guy had to have a bit of class to get anywhere in this *man's* town.

This confession evening was to be our last. He too was moving out to what he called a new 'pad'. Where, I surmised, he would be Mark Brontë right from what he called square one. It was just after the big rally in Trafalgar Square to protest against the British and French invasion of Egypt. He went with me to 'take it in'. He had recently taken in a symphony concert, a Soho club where transvestites gathered and a Chelsea party where they all smoked reefers and knew everybody in television. We heard the great orator Aneuran Bevan denounce Anthony Eden in his Welsh lilt, mocking the Suez affair as the last twitching of the lion's tail, an old motheaten joke lion. 'Was Eden,' he scoffed, 'the front end or the arse end?' All around us were banners and placards. I drew Mark's attention to one held high by a contingent of Kilburn Irish: *British Out of Ireland* but he was more interested in the efforts of a small counter-demonstration swathed in union jacks and singing 'Land of Hope and Glory' protected by a cordon of police; from time to time we heard faintly their speaker with a loud hailer saying in an indignant cockney accent something about putting the Great back into Britain again. It was all very exhilarating.

The house by then was half empty and I explored the vacant rooms. In the basement I found a small room that had never been let. It was nearest the private park at the back to which there was an iron gate, rusted and locked. The room was full of ancient deck-chairs, crumbling parasols, a set of croquet hoops and mallets and a huge archery target with the stuffing coming out, which, on a whim, I looked behind and found an old album of family photographs. I tried to guess which of the little girls or young women in the group pictures might be the old woman in the moth eaten fur coat who had called into my room. 'Alice, Alice, do come down, there is news from India.' In several of the yellowing photos people rode in a kind of cab on top of an elephant. One snapshot took my fancy: a man in a tropical helmet and shorts bestriding a donkey in a humorous pose, sticking his legs out exaggeratedly in a way that let you know he was used to very different mounts. The hunt. Cavalry. Perhaps polo. I wondered about the old China hand in St Mary Abbot's hospital.

'Hey,' I said to Danny, Mark, Prunty, Bronte the night of our last confession evening, after we had drunk various toasts to this and that: Auld Lang Syne; Mud in your eye; Next year in Jerusalem; and of course to Patrick Prunty, the founding Bronte father, the oul' fella himself, 'hey, let's have a verse or two of that Boat Song, is it Eton or Harrow? For a bit of a cod.'

I did not expect it to catch on with us as well as it did. But there are certain songs, and indeed hymns, which are very rousing after a glass or two – as anyone will agree who has heard drunken soldiers sing 'The Old Rugged Cross' with heartfelt emotion. We started the song somewhat falteringly and I expected it to peter out after the first verse but instead we were belting it out full throat, squatting on the floor in line and making rowing movements. There were thumps on the ceiling and a rapping at the door. 'One more time,' shouted Danny, 'one more time.'

> Jolly boating weather
> And a hay-harvest breeze
> Blade on the feather
> Shade off the trees
> Swing, swing together
> With your bodies between our knees.

Jennifer was at the door when I managed to get it open. She gave me a ferocious what-have-you-been-doing-to-him glare of the kind that only doting mothers or lovers are capable of to which I responded with a little witticism that I thought rather good. I put on a sergeant major's parade ground bullying manner.

'Git yore nails cut,' I barked at her and then he and I fell down laughing.

'Ah, he's a right old cod, so he is,' I heard him say as she helped him to his room.

I was the last tenant to leave. I studied the Rooms Vacant cards in the newsagents' windows. No Irish. No Coloured. No linen. Suit business gent out all day. Share K & B. One room I went to look at was already taken and the landlord was sympathetic to the point of indignation that he had to turn me away. It was all because of *them*, he said, that nice young men like me had a job to get rooms. It was the chinks and the yellowbellies, he said, so enraged on my behalf, as to be guilty of a tautology. He stood watching me walk away. I knew he longed to put the Great back into Britain again.

But I got fixed up. The evening before I left I wandered about the empty house wondering about things. The big game heads had all gone leaving bright patches on the faded and peeling walls. They had been thrown into a scrap lorry along with the old iron. But the garden room had not been cleared and I was in it looking again at the bric a brac and old family photos from the days of empire when the door bell rang. It was Jennifer. Could she have a talk with me. She looked very different in the light of my room. I had never seen her smartly dressed before. Stylish suit. High heeled shoes with matching handbag. Nice little hat. Gloves. She couldn't have been on her *Daily Worker* pitch dressed like that. I made some feeble joke to that effect. No, she said, she had been to church. I thought she meant some wedding or other among her rich connections, the kind where the women are rigged out by Bond Street and the men are in tails and toppers.

'It was for Mark,' she said.

SAM KEERY

I tried to imagine possible errands to a church undertaken on his behalf by such an emissary but they were all absurd. And where did I come into it?

I was to let him know ... that she had meant it ... she really had. She opened her Bond Street handbag and took out a small black book. The last time she had shown me a book it had been Engels' 'Condition of the Working Class in England'. This was quite different. It was for the instruction of those wishing to be received into the Roman Catholic Church. I was to tell him when I saw him. I had no other purpose. She talked of him for a long time. It seemed to be some kind of relief to her to talk of him to someone who knew him. She was hardly aware of my presence. I had difficulty getting her to go. I thought sadly of tell-him-Doreen-tell-him-Barbara and perhaps inaccurately of Lenin's famous pamplet 'Who Whom?'

I would miss our little gin and smoked salmon confession evenings, singsongs, recitations. He had gone off with my 'Omar Khayyam'. Perhaps he recited it in the Hanover Street studios to help along being 'a Brontë' of *Wuthering Heights*.

> Gin that can with logic absolute
> The two and seventy jarring sects confute,
> The subtle alchemist that in a trice
> Life's leaden metal into gold transmute.

The murmuring Belfastman has been listened to in silence by old Etonian communists, the Indian extended family around the bed opposite, the bibliobiographical obituarists and even the drunken historians and history tutors of Oxford who however are the first to challenge the veracity of this account of the death of empire. This they do with a certain amount of malicious high table teasing.

'Been telling little fibs, haven't you sunshine ... The pasteurised version, eh, squire ... edited out the Jewish bint, didn't you, sport ... took away your party card too, didn't they, skipper ... did you ever get your leg over her, my old china...'

One of them – almost certainly the senior history tutor who had sussed out that the high table port for which the college was renowned was in fact elderberry – put it to him straight, pulling down his lower eyelid to show him a bloodshot eyeball. 'Aint no green in my eye, guv,' he said.

But a dark looming figure near the bed is oddly familiar. Jowly with middle age but still handsome with the little lady killer moustache ... Surely it can't be ... Gamul Abdul Nasser ... No. He couldn't raise one eyebrow like that ironically unless he practised in front of a mirror. No. It's ... but ... it must be ... Prunty ... playing Nasser in Christmas pantomime ... so he got his Equity card ... never made it to the top ... hasn't worn well ... hope he's not going to give me that showbiz gush, a wonderful wonderful tour of Tasmania, darling...

The sick man of letters from Belfast struggles up in the bed to speak to the ageing actor of the time when for a little while they had been young together.

Hey, Danny, listen sunshine, I know it wasn't exactly like that but poet's licence my old china, you know how it is in this game.

Gamal Abdul Nasser's raised eyebrow rises further and he softly and ironically recites in an actor's mannered diction in which there is a lingering trace of a Belfast accent.

Ah love could thou and I with some fate conspire To grasp this sorry scheme of things entire Would we not shatter it to bits And then remould it nearer to the heart's desire?

'Ah Christ, Danny, you're a right auld cod ... come here

till I tell you ... did you ever hear about me and Miriam ... after you left ... Hey, I went back to look at that house in Philbeach Gardens the other day ... you and Jennifer and me and Miriam were happy ... well nearly for a little while ... until the world ... remember how sunny and bright the street was then ... darker now ... all shaded ... couldn't understand it at first ... thought memory faulty ... you know how it is ... everything bright shining when we were young ... no it's the trees ... when we were younger so were they ... can't see that front double from the street anymore ... used to get the sun in the morning ... the Sultan's turret I called it from your recitations ... how did it go ... morning ... puts the stars to flight ... caught the Sultan's turret in a noose of light ... and now ... the darkness deepens Lord with me abide ... and Miriam and me ... hey Danny why didn't I learn to raise an eyebrow and try to make her laugh ... why did I not ... when we argued ... Marx's Theory of Surplus value ... kiss her quiet ... kiss away the party line on Ireland ... hey, sunshine did you know I joined the Communist Party just to get Miriam ...'

At the mention of *the Party* a mixed rabble of literary and history academic hacks, Party branch subscription secretaries and others whose business is unclear erupts onto the ward and mill around the bed effing and blinding. The sick Belfastman breaks off from addressing the player of Abdul Gamal Nasser and in a clearer more steady voice calls for hush so that he can make an important statement at which the bibliobiographical obituarist pushes his way through the rabble with a tape recorder hidden in a urine bottle and a microphone cunningly disguised as an oxygen mask.

The sick man of letters from Belfast speaks.

'First I want to put the record straight about them taking away my party card in 1956. There have been inaccurate

and misleading accounts of this. It has been said I caused
disturbances at branch meetings and carried on with the
women comrades. I have had to send solicitors' letters to
two well known book reviewers as well as the literary editors
of the papers concerned and litigation against an
unauthorised biography is still going on.

The fact is I was forced out of the party because I was
a protestant. Oh that's not what you'd find in the records
in King Street. Oh Jesus no! It will be '. . . uncomradely
behaviour to a fraternal party delegate . . . views incompatible
with socialist anti-colonialism . . .' What that means is views
incompatible with the catholic Irish view of the Ulster
problem which is the only view the English left wing ever
hears.

Listen, all I did was to try to put a question to a speaker
from the Irish Connolly Association who had come to the
Earls Court branch to get a resolution passed: 'British Out
of North Ireland'. What about the million protestants of
Scottish and English stock who want to stay British, I asked.
Well! I had broken a taboo. I had sullied the sacred ark
of the covenant. I had farted in church.

But let me give you the background. It was my first and
only year in politics. Time of Suez and Hungary. Big protest
rallies in Trafalgar Square. Singing the Internationale going
up Whitehall. The Kilburn Irish holding up their placards
on Northern Ireland along with the rest of them and I
wishing them no ill-will, being all of us young and changing
the world at the heart of Empire. Bliss was it in that dawn
to be alive and to be young was very heaven. There were
nationalists from every quarter and socialists of every hue.
Everything, it seemed, was up for question. Well, not quite
everything. The catholic Irish version of the Northern
Ireland question was not to be questioned.

The resolution 'British Out of North Ireland' was supposed
to be passed unanimously. The central executive in King

Street decides and then the branches vote unanimously. I had already been a bit uncomfortable when we voted unanimously to approve the Soviet invasion of Hungary and the execution of Imry Nagy as a counter revolutionary. I'm glad now the poor bugger was already shot. Oh bliss was it in that dawn ... blithely dishing out death sentences. And I might have put up with being a bit more uncomfortable over the 'British Out' resolution and voted for it too. I might have enjoyed a bit of a gesture of rebellion against my upbringing especially as it did not seem likely to come about and even if it did what better way to loosen the grip of the church on the life of catholic Ireland than by having to fit a million truculent protestants into its laws and institutions? So I waited for the Connolly comrade to say something to that effect and he could have had my vote and a drink afterwards to wash it down. But no. He spoke only of the British and with bitterness and hatred. The British occupation of North Ireland was, he told the comrades, no different to the German occupation of Europe in the war. Oh I couldn't swallow that. I objected. What about the million protestants, I asked, are they and not the British the biggest obstacle to a United Ireland. Well! The Connolly fellow was so taken aback it was obvious he had never had to answer this before. Oh, says he, trying to laugh, I see we're taking Orangemen into the CP now. I'm not an Orangeman, says I, I'm as good a socialist as you and I object to you telling the comrades here that the only thing keeping Northern Ireland British is the British army. Why don't you answer my question, I said. Oh, says he, the protestants are culturally confused, they lack a cultural identity. The British Irish, ha, ha, he says, looking round for the comrades to join in the laugh, as if it was enough just to say the words to demonstrate their absurdity. What you mean, says I, is that they lack a *catholic* cultural identity. Oh, they do indeed, says I, but they don't feel the least bit culturally confused from not playling hurley on Sundays after mass. Oh, out of order, comrade chairman, he shouts, this is no place for orange bigotry. Comrade chairman, I object to being told I lack a cultural identity because I'm not a catholic nationalist. Our secretary here, says I, is Scottish. Comrade secretary, I asked him, do you feel culturally confused for being Scottish and British? And the secretary looked a bit uncomfortable for he and I had got pissed on Burns night when I had impressed him with my knowledge of broad Scots picked up from my presbyterian relatives in Ballymena where the old people still said things like 'ca canny' or 'dinna fash yersel' mon', or 'a wheen o' folk in the kirk the nicht'. Comrade Chairman, I cannot vote for this resolution as it is based upon the arrogant assumption that the only Irish culture is catholic. That must have been the first time the comrades had ever heard a protestant point of view and they did not like it any more than the fellow from the Connolly, though for different reasons – or maybe one reason was the same. Nobody likes you for telling them that something they thought was simple is not simple. The old army K.I.S.S. Keep it stupid and simple. Operating manual, troops, for the use of. And what could be simpler than 'British Out'. It was a time when other simplicities nearer to the comrades' hearts were being questioned. Kruschev had just denounced Stalin. At our piss up on Burns night our secretary had nearly cried. All the years, says he, that I've been defending the Soviet Union against the lies in the bourgeois press and now Kruschev comes along and says, comrades, all those lies were true. Oh the British comrades had enough boats being rocked, they weren't going to upset the Irish too. The vote has to be unanimous, they said, it's the party line. No, I said. This will have to go to King Street, they said. Like a case of heresy referred to Rome.

So, hey, all you biographers, politico-literary histioriographers, foreword and preface writers, lengthy footnote addicts, hack reviewers, post graduate thesis merchants, American fast buck reference book con men – for fuck's sake get it right.'

For a moment or two there is a babble of angry voices in which the Oxbridge history tutors and those whose business was unclear but who turn out to be the executive of the Communist party can be heard wrangling and brawling with much effing and blinding on the part of the fellow with the chair in Scepticism at Corpus Christi who manages to identify the one point on which the disputing parties are all agreed: that something is still being edited out.

'What about fucking whassername, sunshine,' he demands just before falling down, stoned out of his mind on high table elderberry port. The others begin to repeat the name but less and less loudly until they are softly whispering over and over: Miriam... Miriam... Miriam, their shadowy forms fading away until only Abdul Gamal Nasser is left, one eyebrow raised ironically and holding a guitar on which he picks out softly a tune that has poignant significance for his one time room mate.

'Yes,' whispered the latter sadly, 'but I can't remember the words. They'll come to me in a minute. And it had two tunes. We used to argue which one was the right one. You bought a steel stringed guitar. I learnt the chords of C, F and G on it. Hey, Danny, there's nothing left of that time now. The duffel coats, the girls in pony tails, everybody arguing about Suez and learning the guitar to sing ballads in coffee bars. "Barbara Allen": "The Foggy Foggy Dew". That ballad you're still playing the wrong tune to was all the rage. Everytime I see something about Karl Marx or Suez or Hungary it comes into my head along with bits of both the tunes and some of the words. There was a line: *The water is wide, I can not cross oe'r.* The rest of it will come to me in a minute. Do you remember when Miriam brought us some chopped liver from home and we spread it on the potato bread you got a parcel of from Belfast and we joked about being "culturally confused"?'

Did Jennifer tell you Miriam and I had long arguments over the party line 'British Out of North Ireland'? We used to argue in that coffee bar with the ballad singer and the candle light. Why, I asked her, if she was British Jewish couldn't I be British Irish? Because the Irish people don't want to be British, she said. Which Irish people, I said, Are the Northern Protestants not a people too? And we argued for hours about what is a people, what is a nation, what is a culture.

Hey, why did I not just make love to her like you did with Jennifer and to hell with problems of nationhood and national identity? Did it get back to you some of what was said in the bitter arguments Miriam and I had on the party line on Ireland? Her parents were Polish Jews. All her relations in Poland were murdered by the Germans. With, I told her, the assistance of the virulently anti-semitic Catholic church. Did you hear about me telling her that? If her people were village Jews, I told her, then the catholic villagers probably turned out to see them being taken away. The village probably made a holiday of it with the priests and the nuns getting the children to show the Jews their crosses and accuse them of crucifying our Lord as they were marched to the cattle trucks at the station. She cried when I told her that. There's how to woo a lovely Jewish girl! Another right passion killer was when I told her about the neutral Irish government in the war mourning the death of Adolph Hitler with the flags at half mast and De Valera conveying his condolences to the German ambassador at the very time we were seeing newsreels in Belfast showing the stacks of Jewish corpses in the camps; the bones; the ashes; the ovens; the still living skeletons. There's nice pillow talk for you! And yet I just wanted to take her beautiful face in my hands and...

Why did I join the bloody Party to get her and then I didn't get her anyway and the party line on Ireland broke up you and me as well. You and I never discussed the national question. We thought we cared nothing for it and were, in any case scrupulous in observing the conventions of behaviour for 'mixed company' that govern relations between catholics and protestants in our native city. But it must have got back to you...

Hey, Danny, do you know what Miriam reminded me of? Just a bit. Those Belfast girls in the born again sects that you would pursue into prayer meetings and even offer to get yourself saved. No, you wouldn't know them. There's no exact equivalent in your religion. They would quote scripture at you while you were petting – take their tongue out of your mouth when you tried to do more than that and say 'Yoke ye not unevenly with unbelievers' meaning if you want a bit of you know what you'll have to be born again in the Lord! When Miriam took me to my first party meeting I had the same feeling I had as when a Belfast girl I once fancied took me to a Gospel Hall. I nearly said to Miriam afterwards that I half expected the comrades to kneel in prayer for my early conversion. I wish I had said things like that to her, tried to make her laugh, took life easier, fooled around, made Irishisms of the sacred Marxist texts like you did.

But there was once when Miriam and I ... It was after that day on the river. Do you not remember it? When the four of us just fooled around? Took a basket of food and beer to Richmond. It comes back to me often. Didn't seem special at the time. But it was, oh it was. That school rowing crew with the master on the bicycle on the path shouting at them through a loud hailer. I say, put more back into it Charlton-Deedly minor.' We all took it up and

214

shouted at Charlton-Deedly minor to put more back into it and the master nearly fell off the bicycle and they got their oars tangled and had to stop. We hired a boat and you said you could row but you couldn't and we got honked by the pleasure steamers with the girls shrieking and laughing. That lovely lunch on that island they call an eyot. The jokes about kosher Irish bacon and soda bread and lying in the sun watching all the different kinds of boats go by: the big packed packed tripper steamers from London honking the little boats for room to pass; the giggling girls in boats they couldn't row; the serious rowing crews that would suddenly flash into the midst of the summer afternoon frivolity with such comical purposefulness we fell about laughing: IN OUT, IN OUT, IN OUT. Running through Hampton Court looking for a toilet from all that beer we had, you far worse than the girls. You're nearly there, we said when we saw CLOSET, just keep your legs closed, but it was Cardinal Wolsey's closet and we nearly pissed ourselves laughing. I did all the rowing back to Richmond on the ebb tide and you sang, your voice not as good without the guitar but nice all the same. That one of Elvis Presley's. *Are You Lonesome Tonight?* I knew I was not going to be lonesome that night. The evening sun on the river and the splash of oars and songs and lovely Miriam and I ... that night.

It wasn't long after Hampton Court we broke up. Ships that pass in the night. Jewish, Falls Road Catholic, King Billy Protestant, English public school.

It's all long gone. Suez, Hungary, Bliss was it in that dawn. That street is all in shadow now. The darkness deepens, Lord with me abide. But that day shines like a jewel. When we took life easy like the grass grows on the weirs. That boat. Rowing. Its coming back to me now. That song about crossing water. You preferred the other tune to the one the fellow sung it to in the coffee bar where they were all arguing about Nasser and Suez and imperialism and calling TS Eliot a fascist and Miriam and I argued about what is a people and what is a nation instead of taking her in my arms to learn more Yiddish love words to whisper to her, my bubbeleh, my little bubbee.

> The water is wide I can not cross oe'r
> And neither have I wings to fly
> Give me some boat that will carry two
> That boat shall row my love and I.

A new surge of voices, intermingled. Gujerati and Belfast dialect and Academic effing and blinding and Pitman's Commercial English and The Eton Boat Song and Medical whitecoated chit chat: auxiliary muscles respiration; sphygmomanometer; pulse; heart beat. The voices are a wave of sound. But on an ebbing tide. The voices blending as they recede, the different modes of speech seeming to merge into one that is at first all of them and then none of them but another that unites their differences: Hebrew, but by then so distant that only the rhythm of the wailing from the devastated schtetls of Poland and the last chanting of murdered cantors in the pogrommed shuls of the Ukraine enables him to catch faintly the name of Miriam and the words for love almost lost amongst the murmurings that go dub-dub-a-dub, dub-dub-a-dub like a faltering heart beat.

16

The proprietor-editor of the *Clerkenwell Review* dreams of being at the centre of much activity in which screens are drawn and apparatus installed so that the hand of him who has brought the magazine thus far may still be upon the helm to steer it clear of reefs and rocks into safe harbour. From the street below the window comes the sound of women's voices singing.

> We have an anchor that keeps the soul
> Steadfast and sure while the billows roll

Nurses with case notes question the people waiting to see the proprietor-editor on important business and there is an altercation in Gujerati about being made to wait for a bed pan not like going private by jove. Some of the nurses are in Red Cross uniforms and directed by the irascible Dr Harrison who, fresh from a field casualty station on the Somme with the Ulster Division, recognises the dark figure at the bedside and sends him packing with the words 'away to hell out of it you whore's get' uttered in a middle class Belfast accent. Mr Blackstaff's waiting clients include the Chief Actuary of the Bulwark Assurance Company who is also a member of the Lincoln's Inn Shabby Raincoat Girls' Netball League Fan Club who has come to discuss an investment by the Bulwark risk capital fund in the *Clerkenwell Review* on behalf of the tanner-a-week-on-the-auld-aunt wee burial policies of the Shankill Road district; a party of middle aged school girls led by Miss

Pym the headmistress of CD's first school come to give their case histories for the special features pages and poets who have turned up without appointments but with attractive leather covered hip flasks of gin with the Walsh-Massingham crest on them. These and many others are being marshalled by Sticky Sloan, the doorman of Lisburn Picture House in puce uniform with epaulettes and bicycle clips, who keeps them from leaning against the window of Fusco's Fish & Chip Saloon with appropriate gestures of his white gloved hands.

Despite voluble protests in Gujerati or Hindi Miss Pym ushers one of the middle aged school girls behind the screens and manoevres her into a chair with her cane, which, as usual, is frayed at the end from much use.

'Her composition is called "VE Night On Our Street",' says Miss Pym grimly, gnashing her teeth and showering saliva over the paper which the schoolgirl of mature years has shamefacedly produced. Miss Pym leaves shaking her head and clicking her tongue in disgust.

The wise proprietor-editor of the *Clerkenwell Review* adopts a kindly tone to put the menopausal schoolgirl at her ease by mentioning streets, dance halls, back row seats of cinemas and Gospel Halls, shop doorways and back alleys, the names of which oft in a stilly night bring the light of other days around them, telling her to take her time, to have no fear that the secrets of the confessional will go any further than *The Atlantic Monthly*, the *Sporting Life*, the *Jewish Chronicle* or the *Times Literary Supplement*. White-uniformed attendants adjust the apparatus to accept Case History Number One: Sandra Laffin. Sandra begins reading in a nervous expressionless voice as if giving evidence.

'I lost my virginity on VE night after a party on our street. I was fourteen. After the tea and cake the men brought out crates of beer and then people started dancing when some bandsmen came with their instruments from the official celebrations in the park. I danced with several boys and I got very excited. Not just ordinary excitement, but, well to be quite honest, sexual excitement. I don't know why really. I was a good girl. I had promised my mother never to let boys do anything after I started having periods. But whatever got into me I started kissing the boys and one of them I put my tongue in his mouth. He was about seventeen. His father was a leading light in the church choir in which my auntie also sang. My auntie and-and-and-and he (hesitation at this point due to having first written *him* which had been scratched out by Miss Pym and had had spittle showered angrily on it in the course of grammar correction) sang the leading parts in Handel's Messiah. The boy took me to his house. We didn't switch on any lights. There was enough light coming in from the streets. He hurt me but I still wanted it. When we went out again I went to the bonfire on the wasteground at the end of the street. As the flames died down couples started lying down just beyond the firelight so you couldn't make out exactly who they were. A soldier took me there and lay down with me. He hurt me too but I wanted it so much I didn't care. When he left me I went to my house for a clean pair of knickers as the ones I had on were soaked – I suppose it must have been their stuff running out of me. I went the back way. There was a couple against a yard door. It was an airforceman and a neighbour woman who was a great knitter and could sort out knitting patterns for everybody including my mother. The airforceman's body was moving and they were making regular gasping noises. I wished I could take her place. Further along a man came out of another yard door. It was the father of the boy who had me first. I said hello to him. It must have been the way I said it because he gave me a peculiar look as if debating what to do and then took me into the house where we did it on the same settee in the half dark where his son had done it. He hurt me most of all but he took far longer and maybe because of that I had this well, to be quite honest, terrific climax that I nearly fainted and I cried Oh what's that, what's that. Shush, shush, he says, it is quite normal, don't tell your mother. When I left I suddenly came over so tired and sleepy I went straight home to bed and slept like a log. Next day everybody was back to normal and I was terrified I might have a baby. I prayed to Jesus for my period to come on and promised Him I would be good again. When my period did come I was so thankful I worked harder than anyone giving out the hymn books at the Gospel Hall mission campaign and when I met the boy or his father on the street we said hello the way we always had and soon VE night was just a memory.'

The editor-proprietor is deeply affected by this evocation from the years of his wartime boyhood and requests Vera Lynn singing *We'll Meet Again* on the Forces programme. He says he had a cousin who could do imitations of Hitler, Churchill and Rooseveldt, as well as of Luigi, an ex-Italian prisoner of war who spoke broken English in a Ballymena accent. Mrs Churchill's Aid To Russia Fund, he said reflectively and with affection.

Dried egg, Dig For Victory, We will fight on the beaches, Sidi Barani, collecting Army badges, playing pontoon in the air raid shelters. Here, he asked Case History No. 1, what about that wee English evacuee that hated us making farting noises with our gas masks? But her place on the chair has been taken – despite voluble protests in Gujerati – by the Chief Actuary of the Bulwark Assurance Company who, having spent his lunchtime going from one netball pitch to another in Lincolns Inn depending on which was showing the most knickers is dressed in a shabby white raincoat and is carrying a battered brief case with a make shift rope handle from which he takes out the necessary papers for the tanner-a-week-on-the-auld-aunt wee burial policy risk capital fund to buy two thousand preference shares in the *Clerkenwell Review*. But before dealing with this he expresses himself plaintively in the following terms:

'Terrible day at the office yesterday. Couldn't move in the Bulwark corridors for the scribblers. Sitting with their unsolicited manuscripts on their knees looking for patronage. Of the writing of books there is no end. Scribble, scribble, scribble. Had to send two of them home to put on a white shirt and tie for a handshake with the chief general manager. Awful. Needed a drink before I could face standing in the train for three quarters of an hour. Few people in the pub though filling up. A good looking older woman comes and sits near me. How old? Forties at least. But still attractive. Nice to see that. Rarity value. Wouldn't mind at all with her. To my surprise she speaks to me. She too has had an awful day. In publishing. Sifting through the unsoliciteds. Needed to wind down. Can she buy me a drink? Oh no, let me. I say. And so, in a few minutes we become, well, intimate. You are very attractive, I say boldly. So are you, she says. Oh really, I say, at my age! A spectator sport only now, I'm afraid. Nonsense, she says, I like grey haired men with a tash and a little *cussion d'amour*. I know a place we could go, she says. What on earth could she mean? A hotel room? Oh no, God no, there was no time. The wife had the casserole on. He daren't. Oh but yes, she says. Complete privacy for ten minutes to soft music accompaniment for only twenty pence. I stare at her. Is she round the twist? You pass one every day, she said. These new unisex public toilets. The Superloos. I am taken aback but thoughtful. I had seen them but never been in one. Posh looking aluminium cabins. What happens after ten minutes, I ask, my actuarial training asserting itself despite my excitement now manifesting itself in the form of a growing erection trapped uncomfortably in my Y fronts. Oh, she says, the music stops, the toilet tips up, the floor floods to wash it and the door opens. Ten minutes eh? I gulp down my pink gin and we leave hurriedly. There is a Superloo nearby. It is alongside the railings of the park, ideally secluded for discreet entry. I put in my coin. The door opens. In we flit in a flash and are sealed in. It is clean, soft lighted, and quite spacious. Classical music plays soothingly. She straddles me on the seat, making sure of her own satisfaction before I have mine with three minutes forty seconds still in hand. We even have time to wash our private parts in the charming little stainless steel basin and press the button to slip out into the night discreetly. We part without knowing each other's names. I miss my non-stopping to East Croydon but was only half an hour late home, the casserole unimpaired. Trains dreadful tonight, darling, I say to the wife. Oh you poor dear, she says, *Coronation Street* is just starting.'

The editor-proprietor spoke into the apparatus provided. 'That was case-history number three. Obtainable from the *Clerkenwell Review* for fifty pence plus postage or from a Bulwark Assurance Company agent when taking out a tanner-a-week-on-the-auld-aunt wee burial policy. Roger. Over and Out.'

Then, off the record, he continues. Unsoliciteds, he says contemptuously. Oh don't tell me. The Post Office is never done complaining about my Box Number being choked with unsoliciteds. My arm is nearly dislocated carting them away. Oh quit talking. Here, tell me this and tell me no more. Have you ever met anybody who doesn't believe they could write a book? Oh they all know well enough when they can't sing or dance or do a turn or paint the Cistine Chapel. But *write*? Half the bloody population fancy themselves at it! The painter Degas fancied himself at it would you believe? And couldn't understand why he wasn't good at it as he had 'the most marvellous ideas'. His pal Mallarme, who *was* good at it, had to explain it to him. 'but my dear Degas, poems, novels, writings are not made with ideas, they are made with words.' Collapse of stout party! Oh here, I'm not surprised the pair of you copulated on the streets to wind down after a day looking for a spark of talent among the unsoliciteds though I personally in recent years am more what you might call a gin wallah when knackered than a sexual intercourse wallah.

The editor-proprietor switches on the apparatus again to make an appeal for unsolicited manuscripts about the dream of childhood, the morning light, boyhood innocence in protestant Ulster. The dark figure is again sitting at the bedside and motioning silently not to give away his presence to Army Surgeon Captain Harrison who is heard telling a boy with an unsolicited letter to the editor on the need to reform late-age circumcision that he needs his bloody arse kicked. There is a commotion from the direction of those waiting with unsoliciteds as someone pushes to the fore despite the vociferous protests in Hindi or Gujerati to answer the appeal about boyhood innocence in protestant Ulster. It is someone in the uniform of the Boy Scouts from the 22nd Ballymacarret Troup and at the very peak of life expectancy in the Life Tables of The Bulwark Assurance Company. Perhaps aware that after puberty it is downhill all the way he recites solemnly the Scout Oath and steadfastly refuses both an offer from a peroxide blonde Dublin protestant woman of mature years with good legs to relieve him of the burden of virginity and a snifter from a bottle of gin. The editor-proprietor calls for hush and adjusts the valve of his bedside equipment to the wavelength for Ulster Boyhood Innocence. Further adjustments have to be made to edit out the boy's stammer which he desperately though ineffectually tries to conceal. However the edited version successfully eliminates it from Case

History Number Four: A Ballymacarret Innocent in a Rural Idyll.

'My country cousin in a townland near Ballymena was greatly troubled by lust. He told me that he masturbated every day and sometimes in bed at night as well. He showed me pictures of film stars in swim suits he had cut out of magazines and kept behind the meal barrels in the barn. His favourite was one that showed the swell of her pubis to which he would put his tongue, shocking me. That's dirty! I said in disgust. Oh he said, it would be lovely to lick *her* fanny. When we went to church – they were presbyterians – he would pick out some good looking married woman in the choir or congregation and whisper to me about her having had a big cock up her when her man had come back from his Saturday night's boozing or would have one up her after Sunday dinner. What, on a Sunday! I said, shocked by the idea of it being done on the sabbath, finding it hard enough to believe that the presbyterians ever did it at all. He said that Sunday made it nicer, being wicked. He claimed to know men who told him what they did to their wives. He said that the pig killer from Rasharkin fucked his wife every night without french letters by taking it out in time and doing it up her belly. My cousin spoke of these matters incessantly and I have to confess I listened with more interest than I let on, indeed sometimes bringing them to mind when I myself gave in to the solitary vice of which I was so ashamed and which he referred to as 'flogging the Bishop'.

The farm where he lived had no indoor toilet but a dry privy abutting onto the barn. My cousin said that the girls and women visiting them did not like using it – which I could well believe as I hated using it myself. He showed me a hole in the wall of the privy that you could look through into the barn. You could see a grating beside the meal barrel where he kept the pictures of film stars. I had seen a pig killed there by the Rasharkin man by cutting its throat and the blood had gushed down the grating. That's where they pee, my cousin told me. He said he sometimes watched them. I was shocked when he said he had watched one of our aunts a few days previously. He said they didn't always squat down the right way to see anything. He said he had tried everything instead of just flogging the Bishop – a hole in a turnip or the heel of a loaf but they did not work very well. He said he might even try one of the animals. Oh God no, I said, deeply shocked. Oh, he said, I know a fellow that has fucked a calf and been sucked off by a young pig before it had teeth.

One afternoon his father took us with him to have the cow serviced. I was amazed at the size of the bull's thing when they led it out. It hung down like a gatepost. I was embarrassed when it got up on the cow and my uncle and another man had to help to put its thing in. Oh God I thought that thing will kill the poor cow but it just stood there looking about it till the bull slid off. During these proceedings my cousin told me that he knew a fellow who had been in the Army in Egypt and had seen a woman fucked by a donkey. There were a lot of people in the house when we got back. This sometimes happens in the country just by chance and when it does there's a lot of noisy talk and bantering and gossip that I used to like. My uncle got out a bottle to supplement the tea turning the occasion into almost a party. My cousin was annoyed at having to go off and help a neighbour spray a field of potatoes instead of enjoying the company, especially as the wife of the man who had helped with the bull was still very good looking even though as old as my aunt. She laughed a lot at my uncle's jokes and stories about eccentric neighbours. Some of these were very near the mark considering they all went to church – some of them twice on a Sunday. But they all roared and laughed, the good looking wife especially. I thought of the spy hole in the privy and went to it though full of shame and guilt. I sat on it trying not to think of the awful receptacle under me. Nobody came into the barn for such a long time I got up to leave. Then I heard the sound of someone entering it. Would it be the good looking wife who laughed and flirted with my uncle I wondered with shame and excitement? I put my eye to the hole. No. It was my uncle. At first I thought he was peeing. But his thing was too big and sticking up to be doing that. He was masturbating.

Two white-coated figures are helping the owner-proprietor of the *Clerkenwell Review* to mark the examination papers of the unsoliciteds. One of them is the very distinguished poet and holder of the chair for Pure and Applied Sexual Intercourse at Queen's University Belfast. The other is a more junior examinations invigilator not yet sufficiently experienced to make comments discreet enough not to be overheard by the candidates.

Morbidity of tissue advanced. Very deficient in protein, he whispers loudly, applying ticks to certain boxes one of which says *needs his arse kicked*. This protein remark is picked up and goes echoing down the examination room but in a form changed by translation into and re-translation out of Gujerati. By the time it has reached the queue of unsoliciteds being held back by Sticky Sloan the doorman of Lisburn Picture Palace, resplendent in puce uniform, white epaulettes and bicycle clips, by appropriate gestures of his white gloved hands, it has become something to do with meat.

Not meaty enough, the unsolicteds tell each other, they want more meat. They want stuff with a bit of meat on it. From the street below comes the sound of women singing an old Moody and Sankey favourite hymn with a bit of meat on it.

Pull for the shore, sailor
Pull for the shore.

The sailor is none other than Frank Maguire, ex-Belfast merchant seaman, ex-novelist, ex-literary rough diamond, ex-womaniser, ex-bar room raconteur, ex-brawler, ex-magazine contributor, ex-radio script writer, ex-drinking chum of the famous, ex-damned near everything before good bar talk was ruined by disco pop music.

Ah holy Christ, says the editor-proprietor sadly, Frank Maguire now an unsolicited. Ah Jesus, it was TV and bar amplifiers for disco pop music finished him off more than the booze. He speaks into the microphone cunningly shaped like an oxygen mask with a warning that unsolicited versions of Maguire's Captain McWhirter story purporting to be genuine have been heard in the Kings Head, Chelsea, the Jolly Wrestlers, South Kensington, Henekeys of Holborn, The George, Clerkenwell, The Fox, Knightsbridge, The Athaneum, The Bar of The House of Commons and The Crown and Anchor, Wapping. These spurious versions may be recognised by the terrible Belfast accent attributed to Captain McWhirter and are quite worthless. Permission to reproduce must be applied for to the Joseph Conrad Society accompanied by a hip flask of rum and a twist of baccy.

From the street below the hymn singing women belt out another rousing chorus.

Safe in the life boat sailor, sing evermore
Glory glory Hallelujah. Pull for the shore.

Unsolicited computer print-out is handed out by a junior actuary from the Bulwark Assurance Company listing unclaimed policies on the lives of sailors who fought at the battle of Trafalgar. This causes angry protests from members of The William Hazlitt Society for Perfect Prose

whose inspirer idolised Napoleon as well as greatly fancying
Sarah Walker. Their tempers are further inflamed by an
unsolicited from a PhD researcher in the Pure and Applied
Sexual Intercourse department of Queens University Belfast
claiming that the real reason Hazlitt stamped in rage on
his little bronze statue of Napoleon was because Sarah had
used it as a dildo instead of letting Hazlitt. Salt is rubbed
in their wounds when when a recruiting officer with a
Devonshire accent and a stentorian voice reads from an
unsolicited poster in the Crown & Anchor, Wapping. The
editor proprietor strains his ears to catch the words half
drowned by the effing and blinding of the Perfect Prose
crowd.

'Let us who are Englishmen ... resist ... to make whores
of our wives and daughters ... to murder our King as they
have done their own.

ROYAL TARS OF OLD ENGLAND ... to Lieutenant
... at his rendevous at Wapping ... bounty ... able seamen
ten guineas ... midshipmen...

...All who have good hearts ... love the King ... hate
the French ... AND DAMN POPERY.'

As these proud patriotic words echo down the ward the
menopausal schoolgirl marks time in a very short skirt to
the sound of a flute playing Lilliburlero serving as background for a radio play on the hospital earphones about
the siege of Derry in which are heard the immortal words
of Lord Macaulay first encountered by the editor-proprietor
in the cobble stoned book lined arcades of old Smithfield
in Belfast where he had spent many a happy hour of youth
finding life move in the pages of old books.

He sees the youth whom once he was look up at him
from a second hand book stall. He points out the youth
to the dark figure who is again seated at his bedside with
a weak laugh of amusement in which there is also tenderness
and pity. So absorbed are they in watching the youth look

for life in the words of books that no attention is at first paid to the whispered enquiries of dealers in certain goods about reduced rates for half plate advertisements illustrated in line, halftone or colour. Pope-shaped dildo, they whisper, the infallible contraceptive ... inflatable nuns to suit all sizes ... money back guarantees ... testimonials from satisfied Presbyterian elders and church of Ireland vestrymen. The editor-proprietor tells them wearily to leave samples with Lambton the advertising manager.

The winning entry, he murmurs into the oxygen-mask-shaped microphone. The news that the editor-proprietor is going to reveal the winner of the Baden-Powell prize for the best poem about prepubertal Belfast to be published in the Yom Kippur edition of the War Cry spreads rapidly after first being announced from the bed opposite in voluble Gujerati in which the words 'go private' by God are distinctly heard. Sticky Sloan the doorman is unable to keep back the unsoliciteds and they flood onto the ward waving manuscripts. But when white-coated junior invigilators make it clear to them that their manuscripts will all join the slush pile unless he has a bit of hush they all fall silent and fade into vague outlines. CD speaks softly occasionally coughing.

> Did you never make fun of Jesus, The Lord's Prayer,
>   the Creed?
> Then were you never ten years old in Belfast
> And livened up dull Sunday school
> With whispered naughty meanings to the words?
> Was that not you who fizzed with sniggers
> That Sunday morning, your poor young teacher
>   bewildered
> That her class should find the ten commandments
>   hilarious?
> Were you not the wag who whispered
> Same sounding things for thy neighbour's things
> THOU SHALT NOT COVET?

Like his socks and his arse for his ox and his ass
So that soon the whisper was no longer needed,
A nudge or look would do.
Until a fizzing boy let out a loud guffaw
To the horror of all the classes in the hall
And on the platform a terrible whitecoated figure
        arose
No longer the rector counting the missionary boxes
But JEHOVAH pointing with an outstretched arm.
You there! This is not a circus but the house of God!
Making no distinction between the poor young woman
        and yourselves.
Oh she had now no need to make appeals for order.
You purged impiety not only from your face but from
        your mind.
If now when someone came to ox and ass your mind
        still strayed,
It was to grimmer things than socks and arses.
Struck down from on high for blasphemy
And a right good thumping if word of it got home.
Oh you would be so good, so good, in thought as well
        as deed
Until the awful fear abated.
So hushed in your piety that there could be heard
From the rector's customary table
The occasional faint sharp clink of coin.

He tries to sit up to offer a handshake of congratulation
to a boy of ten now fifty years old wearing a cub scout
cap who is in such grave danger of being lionised that it
takes the united efforts of Sticky Sloan and Miss Pym to
beat back the admiring multitude of academic hacks.

They took their time, CD tries to shout at him in angry
commiseration, the arseholes.

They are driven back and back until they dwindle into

small shadows. Even the senior marshaller Miss Pym grows faint and insubstantial except for her bright yellow cane, frayed at the end from much use, which swishes to and fro like a tail before fading entirely away into the darkness of sleep.

17

He dreams. He is wandering the streets of a semi-strange city that might be London. He is looking for someone he once had the chance to love. He comes to a station that might be a tube station.

The stone steps leading up to the tube station ticket office are narrow and steep with an old wrought iron handrail on both sides. There is moss on the sides of the steps and water trickles down over the dark stone with hollows worn by feet. The ticket office is tiny and the hatch has a wooden door with flaking yellow paint which is closed by an iron hook and eye. What station is it? What line is it? If he knew that he could get into London again. But the man says names he has not heard of and then shuts the hatch door with the hook and eye before he can ask what platform would take him into the city where he would find her. There are many platforms and many trains. He moves with the crowds of people along corridors in some of which are other ticket offices at each of which he buys a ticket in case it should be the right one. He gets into carriages that fill up with people through whom he struggles to get out again when he hears them speak of destinations that are unknown to him. People whom he addresses do not understand him and he tries to break the barrier of communication with humour. The Willynilly Line, he laughs, the Ballyhoo Line he mocks. He should, he jokes, have put a small ad in the *London Weekly Advertiser*: Tube station wanted, any line considered except discontinued ha! ha! But their look of puzzlement is not one whit abated by this. The engine drivers turn away from him in lordly disdain and apply their oil cans to cams and connecting rods of Walschaerts gear and Stevenson's link motion. So he would have to work it out alone. Is there not a way of working out which are the up lines and which the down lines from the orientation of the platforms and the configuration of the points? Was it not in Euclid Part 2? Take whichever route satisfies the X and Y of the quadratic equation. But the bookshops on all the platforms all tell the same story. Euclid has been remaindered along with Shakespeare and the bible. Then he sees the pigeon men with their hampers. Would they not give him a clue in their choice of platform to take them back to the city squares? The pigeon men seem to be gathering on a platform that can only be reached by crossing the tracks. Men fron the pigeon clubs of Belfast are crossing the tracks carrying hampers of birds with labels on them that say Piccadilly, Leicester Square and Tipperary. He keeps finding himself with the wrong ones and having to search for those that, if he stayed close, would take him into the city but fog is making it hard to read the labels and the Belfast men in cloth caps and mufflers pay no more heed to him than any of the other many races and religions who make no answer to his request for directions even when put to them in Spanish and Gujerati. The fog blots out everything except the voices of Cornish railwaymen addressing each other as m'dear. Who better to know which the up line and which the down line than they? He would speak to them in their own tongue, softening their hearts with the sound of it. Oh ah, he calls to them loudly, oh ah, m'dears. Well I be buggered, my old beauties, he shouts genially into the muffling mist that turns everything into vaporous shapes. But there is no reply, not even from the wives and daughters of the Irish shunters repaying drink money debts to the Cornishmen with the oldest barter in the world in the empty carriages being made up into trains while the fog rubs its back against their window panes. He peers at the destination boards of the trains hoping for a familiar name but makes out only stops with names like Rawlters, Histley, Dragglepede which he has never heard of nor will those inside to whom he appeals in sign language tell him where those places are and whether they have a sinister connotation. Then his spirits rise a little when he finds a train that stops at places he once knew well but has forgotten. He repeats to himself the names of tube stations that he knew would be familiar if only he could remember when and where he knew them or what he had done in their vicinity, or had done to him or to whom or by whom or with whom and with what result, good or ill or none at all. The people in this train are likewise those he once knew well enough if only he could place their faces in whatever context or situation he and they had been in together whether domestic or professional, attended by affection or not as the case might be, depending as these things do on mutual empathies and antipathies that would take little account of contracts or promises or declarations of undying love though rather more of how things stood financially and fondnesses for drink. Some of their faces seem faintly multilayered with other similar but different faces discernible under the older one coarsened by life and time. They look back at him frowning in concentration as if something in his own face strikes in them too a chord of memory but not strong enough to identify whoever he might or might not be or might have been had things turned out as once it seemed they would in the morning light and the dream of childhood. Several start up from their seats as if to move towards him only to sink back again though it is not clear whether the brief moment or two of interest soon abandoned is because he is not who they thought he was or because he is and they have no wish to be disappointed in him afresh or let down or neglected or simply forgotten.

The train driver and the fireman are dressed over all in black and the engine has black plumes in flower holders on its smokebox while black ribbons have been tied to every door handle and there is black tape edging on the destinations board from which the fog has cleared to show names such as The Kings Head, The Dog and Groom, The White Hart, but repeated with different inn signs for the different places with the same name which might well be anywhere except Ireland where the public nouses and bars mostly though not invariably take the family name and always without display of debased heraldry on swinging boards.

Something is being awaited. It must be the coffin. The funeral cannot commence without it however much the engine hisses and palpitates and however impatient a boy at the age of puberty and enthusiasm for steam engines is for the excitements of the ride in the black coach, the ham tea gossip and taking down the knickers of a girl cousin for five shillings in applesmelling privacy. Nor can those officiating agree among themselves whether the service is to be Church of Ireland, Presbyterian, Reformed Synagogue or Secular Humanist, the last named adamantly refusing to allow hymns of any description, not even an old Belfast Gospel Hall favourite for old time's sake. On this matter of the denomination of the service to be conducted there is documentary evidence that a boy whose first love was a girl doll belonging to someone else and never to be his, the very same who later had to hand over all his pocket money for viewing the female pudenda had, at or around puberty, been confirmed in the Church of Ireland by a Bishop whose hand had rested briefly upon his brylcremed head and then hovered just above it while he answered questions of the kind:

Question. Which be the ten commandments

Answer. The same which God spake in the twentieth chapter of Exodus saying, 'I am the Lord thy God, who brought thee out of the land of Egypt, out of the house of bondage.'

But the presbyterian padre with the Belfast pigeon clubs, fresh from the singing of a metrical psalm and the saying of a wee prayer over the hampers, objects in a Ballymena accent that the Church of Ireland is a halfway house to popery. There are, he shouts from the footplate of the four-six-two Pacific class engine, ten generations of presbyterian blood in him on his mother's side going back to the bible before the King James still remembered by his great grandparents fondly as the Auld Bible. The padre with outstretched arm points out beyond the station, wherever it is, perhaps out across the great pagan metropolis if it should happen to lie in that direction but certainly homing onto Scotland to where, at a distance of three hundred years his forefathers marched into battle singing hymns against the popish armies of the Marquis of Montrose.

But the Rabbi accompanying the train for Rawlters, Histley and Dragglepede puts in a claim. He is stooped by centuries of persecution and suffering but deeply learned from a long line of scholars famous in the Rabbinical schools of Poland for the brilliance of their discourses on the diaspora, on the Sephardim and the Askenazi, and on the question What Is A Jew? He will not dispute that the circumcision in Belfast was not done according to the laws but firstly he differs from the strictly orthodox in not insisting that it be ritually purified by a mohel with a symbolic blood-drawing nick and secondly the question to be considered is the status of honorary Jew for which there is long precedent for less stringent qualifications. Here the Rabbi produces what at first sight appears to be scroll but is in fact a roll of continuous computer print-out from which, being also a cantor, he sings the following facts in a rich deep voice:

Was circumcised as a shaygets in Belfast.

Learnt to love our food to the extent over a life time of three thousand and nine Matzos, six hundred and thirteen gefilte fish, three hundred and twenty four Vienna Schnitzels, one thousand one hundred and three kreplachs, nine hundred and ninety nine bagels with salt beef.

Out of a life total of one thousand five hundred and thirty-one acts of sexual intercourse sixty-nine per cent were with Jewish partners, six point four per cent Irish protestant, nought point one per cent Irish catholic, non denominational twenty-four point five per cent.

Entreat him not to leave us or to return from following after us; for whither we go he will go; and where we lodge he will lodge; my people shall be his people and our God his god.

The Secular Society preacher with the portable pulpit on which he spends Sunday mornings deriding religions at Speakers' Corner in Hyde park pushes into hands outstretched from the train windows the remaining anti-god tracts left over after attaching them to at least one leg of every homing pigeon from Belfast on platform ten and to both legs of birds with a reputation for having to be coaxed down with corn from the roofs of churches, chapels, manses, presbyteries, Hibernian clubs and Gospel Halls. One of the tracts exposes St Patrick as a slippery trickster chased out of Roman Britain for rascality who engineers 'miracles' to dupe the credulous Irish with the help of a behind the scenes primitive steam engine stolen from the wandering Jew, a device that can also be used to pressure-distil a strong gin-like spirit from the blackberries that are prolific on the slopes of Mount Slemish and with the vast profits from these activities he builds monasteries in which monks re-write the history of Ireland to give him the foremost place in it leaving out any mention of the hocus pocus and the gin. Another tract describes the case of a citizen of protestant Belfast who, though an unbeliever from the age of four when he had nightmares about God, eternity, and the immensity of the universe nevertheless grew up with an addiction to the King James bible and tuneful hymns for which cures have proved only temporary and relapses frequent especially with drink taken. The tract concedes that this condition is met with in people from other regions as witness the recent absurd spectacle of well-known non-believers being signatories to letters of protest in the Times about the new Prayer Book but it takes its most virulent form in those reared in protestant Belfast on every aspect of whose life it casts its long shadow including that of the bedroom.

The representative of the Secular Society, or the Man From The Sec, as he is known around the crematoria and cemeteries of London in which he conducts Humanist burial services with no religious content will accept no responsibility should there be unseemly brawling such as occurred in a case similar to this in which the Humanist service singing of the song 'I Did It My Way' was interrupted by a drunken Belfast man attempting to play at full volume on a ghetto blaster a recording of an East Belfast women's choir singing 'Amazing Grace' for what he called 'old times' sake'.

The catholic Irish shunters do not know where to put with his own a prod non-believer with a fondness for the bible and Jewish women as well as the drink. You should lie with your own at the finish, they tell each other and the Cornish foremen indignantly. Some of the arms reaching for the tracts from the train are those of women and are bare. Their voices are Irish and amused. Ah sure it makes a change to lie with other peoples' they say. Is his engine still in working order at all? Ah sure as long as it can perform the elevation! We'll get him steamed up all right! What about a drop of St Patrick's blackberry gin for us to oil his piston for him! Ah, go on, give us Amazing Grace with your old connecting rod!

But still he is no nearer finding which train would take him back to the city. And where is his briefcase? Oh God, he must have left it in one of the other trains, his old battered briefcase with the rope handle on it. What was in it? What was it that was urgent and important? The unsolicited manuscripts? Oh ballocks to them! The kippers and the gin? He could do with the gin right now. A good noggin or two would soften his unease at the half familiar strangeness of where he was and warm away the dismay of not knowing where the city is. But there was something else. Printers' proofs. Corrections urgent. Typesetting errors turning 'poetry' into 'popery' or the other way round, one as bad as the other, the small presses the worst though none to be relied on not to destroy the subtle meaning of a sentence or the cadence of a line. Was it that and the gin that had the Irish shunters' wives and daughters cackling? Was it the story for the Atlantic Monthly, the one that set him on the road to fame and fortune and many a good literary pissup? He must rescue it quickly and take it back with him to the city where once he had arrived with eagerness and hope.

He spies dimly through the mist the lost property office. There is a notice on the wall saying to specify the identifying features of black umbrellas and that for briefcases the exact words on any documents in them them must be supplied. A man in a white coat is available to administer an injection of sodium pentathol to loose the details from the memory. He eases himself onto a desk gingerly, his backside still smarting from the needle, and begins to fill the form with the words of the lost document.

'The speaker on *The Irish in London* at the Kensington

Historical and Literary Society had unfurled a map of London with the parts where the Irish were most concentrated coloured green. He drew attention to these areas with an ingenious telescoping pointer that he collapsed briskly to pocket size with a flourish, which, while it did not actually imply that the had invented it himself, did not deny it either – in rather the same way that if you wanted to infer that he was the first to discover where the Irish had principally settled he would not stop you from doing so. His biggest patches of green were in the vicinity of, or on the roads leading from, the northern railway termini, especially Paddington, at which many Irish had arrived on the boat trains, especially during the nineteenth century.

After the lecture people lingered in the foyer chatting or fingering the publications offered on little stalls that had been set up to promote the aims of all sorts of societies and bodies, some to do with Irish affairs, some not. A very serious young man with a beard, near a Campaign for Nuclear Disarmament stall was heard to give the earnest advice, seemingly based upon bitter experience, against employing leaflet printers who were not fully unionised, though whether this was in connection with Irish matters was not clear. An elderly man with an Ulster accent gesticulated with an upraised hand into which someone had pressed a leaflet, presumably promoting vegetarianism, headed in very bold type MEAT INFLAMES THE PASSIONS. He was saying very heatedly that of course there must be separation of Church and State if the Protestants were ever to agree to a United Ireland, and later another of the same group, also clutching the tract against meat, said gravely that the Curragh Mutiny had posed the most serious threat to constitutional government since Pitt's bill on seditious utterances.

The connection between the London Irish and the great

age of railways and steam was perhaps the reason for the stall furnished with mementoes such as tea towels on which were famous locomotives with names like Lord Palmerston or Duke of Wellington, and at which signatures were being collected to protest against the plans of a property company to knock down an engine shed designed by the great Isambard Kingdom Brunel himself.

Stanley, a timid bookish railway clerk, stood about for a while listening to these snatches of discussion all around him and wishing he was not too shy to join in. He would have liked to have been able to stand up at the meeting when it was thrown open for comment and say how noticeable it was that many of the railway workers at Paddington station were Irish, though the foremen were mostly from the west of England. He would have liked to tell the man at the Railway Heritage stall that the carriage and wagon office where he worked had also been built by Brunel, and had a little cupola like a Wren church. He was quite a good mimic and had he been able to push himself forward could have made people laugh with imitations of Irish and West country accents that he heard every day. He could have made a party piece out of the way his boss, Mr Trelford, a loud genial little Cornishman shouted affably on the phone to colleagues down the line in Penzance, Reading, Bristol, Cardiff, Holyhead, or less affably debated with the many Irish cleaners, shunters, greasers under his command their foibles, shortcomings, excuses, urgent needs concerning lodgings, early rising, drink, money to send home to Ireland. But Stanley's timidity, while it might have allowed him to reproduce accurately enough the soft Irish shilly-shallying ('Sure, t'was the ould stomach, Mr Trelford, bad luck to it … when I turn on that side there's no waking me'), would have quite destroyed any likeness to little roaring Mr Trelford, whose portrait could have been rendered only with the bold loudness of the original: 'Oh ah, m'dear ... well I be buggered ... oh ah my old beauty!'

On his way back to his lodgings Stanley found crumpled in his pocket a MEAT INFLAMES THE PASSIONS leaflet. *A peaceful world impossible so long as men are carnivores. Territorial aggressiveness, Domination. Lust.* When Stanley was a boy lust was one of the words that gave him a secret thrill of excitement when he encountered it. His mother had once spoken to him about lust. Hoped he would always respect women. No excuse for lust. Should think of his mother and sister. If men weren't encouraged. Hoped no woman would ever corrupt any son of hers. The word again stirred in him a little of that old excitement, now with wistfulness in it. He wondered was it true what one of the Irish shunters had told him about Mr Trelford: that a lot of them owed him money and if they could not repay it, they could in lieu, send a wife or a daughter to visit him when he worked late ... Surely not? Stanley had queried, shocked. And daughters? Ah, sure some of them fellas would have six of them, he was assured, half in pity, half in contempt. The Irish in London speaker had said that Ireland's principal export was people. Male brawn, Stanley thought, female flesh.

Stanley let himself into the hallway of his lodgings, planning to retire early with a library book about great men of the Industrial Revolution. He liked that kind of thing. Railways; canals; bridges; mills; tunnels; engines. He was looking forward to an outing on Sunday to see a beam engine in a pumping station at Brighton, made before Waterloo and still working, though now tended as a hobby by solicitors and accountants who competed for the privilege of shovelling coal and raking out ashes. It was because Stanley knew that much of the English industrial landscape had been hewed by Irish navvies that he had gone to the lecture. Stanley knew that the word navvy was derived from *canal navigator.* He had a drawerful of notes that he dreamed of turning into a book illustrated by prints of early water closets, sewing machines, gasworks. He would make himself a nice cup of cocoa and read his library book in bed. There was a chapter about the great Brunels, father and son. Isambard Kingdom Brunel was Stanley's hero. Reading about him was almost an act of worship. Stanley, timid, sedentary, bookish, venerated the archetypal man of action: engineering genius; wheeler-dealer; fixer of Parliamentary bills; tunneller; inventor; floater of companies; architect; maker of an age; flamboyant to the end; his short packed life as moving as that of Keats.

In the hallway he met his landlady's son. The youth had obviously just spent hours squeezing his pimples and arraying himself in all the splendours of a style called Edwardian: drain pipe trousers; winkle-picker shoes; bootlace tie; side burns; and now like Beau Brumel, he emerged *insolent from his toilet.* Youth, thought Stanley enviously, thoughtless youth, and then from some unaccountable whim translated it mentally into a Dublin accent. Yoot. Tawtless. A tawtless yoot. He nearly giggled. The youth looked at him in surprise and resentment. He was not accustomed to arousing amusement in Stanley, let alone what was to follow, for Stanley had experienced a sudden influx of boldness. It was something to do with the thought of Mr Trelford exacting tribute from his Irish vassals in the form of being pleasured by their women after hours in the IK Brunel building with the pretty cupola.

'Oh ah!' Stanley roared in authentic Trelford accents, conveying by that flexible allpurpose West Country exclamation mock amazement tinged with derision, 'Well I be buggered my old beauty. Oh ah m'dear!'

It was not only the youth who was startled but his mother. Mrs Malloy popped her head round a door in surprise. She was a still good-looking bottle-blonde Dublin woman

SAM KEERY

who could be rather formidable as she was the daughter of a publican and had learnt on both sides of the bar how to be tough with men. Indeed Stanley did not merely read her notices and obey them implicitly – like the one in his room saying *This gas ring is for beverages only* - but imagined them being spoken by her standing with her hand on her hip and he marvelled at the bravery of some of the other lodgers, mostly Irish, having surreptitious fry-ups after what they called 'a feed of drink'. She had summed Stanley up as a quiet man who would give no trouble. She now blocked up the stairs with her hand on her hip and expertly smelled his breath to try to account for the carry on in the hall, and while she was at it she decided to question him about something else it had not occurred to her at the time to be too suspicious about.

'Here,' she said, 'what were you doing in that woman's room the other evening?'

'Well,' said Stanley nervously, abruptly abandoned by the Trelford persona and left to face the consequences, 'I was fixing her gas fire.'

'Her gas fire is it!' Mrs Malloy said scathingly. 'Do you know what that woman is?'

'Well,' said Stanley nervously, 'I understand she does evening work.'

'Oh, she does surely,' Mrs Malloy confirmed bitterly, 'that woman is a tart. Did you not know that?'

'No,' said Stanley in surprise.

'Well you're the only bloody one in the house that doesn't,' Mrs Malloy said, 'I'm going to get rid of her. What the hell were you doing to her gas fire?'

'A burner was blocked,' Stanley explained, a little more confident about technical matters. 'I was poking it.'

'She had two short times in this evening,' said Mrs Malloy grimly, 'and it wasn't her gas fire they were poking.'

Stanley's mouth fell open in a kind of awe. He was the

244

son of a Ballymena Presbyterian minister and thought himself very emancipated to be living in a house full of catholic Irish. Mrs Malloy stood aside to let him pass and watched with amusement as he tried to digest the fact that he was on speaking terms with a prostitute.

'I'm trying to catch her at it,' she called after him, 'so don't you go poking her gas fire again.'

Her feelings of amusement softened her. He was, after all, a nice obliging man who gave no trouble, and if bantering at that eejit of a son of hers meant he could get his paddy up, what harm in it, God help his innocence. She had before then been sometimes moved by maternal feelings to heap up his plate with her good meat stews to put a bit of flesh on him. 'Stuff that into you,' she had urged. 'That'll put a bit of blood in you,' she had said.

But another feeling touched her now that was not entirely maternal. He wasn't a bad looking man when he got you to notice he was there. She patted her hair into shape at the mirror and made a mouth to check the state of her lipstick.

A little later Stanley was in his pyjamas; his book was on his bedside table ready to open at the tooled bookmark that had been a Sunday school prize for bible knowledge. His kettle was already boiled for his cocoa when there came a soft knocking at his door.'

When he has finished writing this on the form he takes it as directed by a series of tin plates depicting pointing hands of which the first has under it a notice saying *please adjust your dress before leaving* and the second another notice advising prompt treatment for VD. He goes down a grubby corridor of small rooms some of which are small home-from-home cubby holes for railwaymen equipped with gas rings, kettles and beds, on the walls of which are texts

SAM KEERY

from the bible and pin ups from the tabloids while in
others shadowy figures in black suits sit upright on a row
of chairs with bowler hats on their knees and warmers of
brandy in their hands and recollect old railway companies
and lines and their rules and regulations differing widely
in what or whom they would carry and when, on the
behaviour that they would or would not tolerate when
there was drink involved as on the annual shoemakers'
outing to the seaside, on whether pigeon hampers and
coffins had to be accompanied in the guard's van by a
sober adult and on the papers, magazines and other literary
matter that they would or would not allow to be hawked
on station platforms, some companies taking a rigid view
on what would have a tendency to deprave and corrupt
while others would turn a blind eye to everything except
the male organ in a state of erection. Finally a hand on
tinplate points to a wooden hatch on which it says
READINGS. 10.30–3.30 w.days ex Mon. and Good Friday.
He knocks. The hatch is opened and the man who takes
the forms from him is vaguely familiar. Didn't he used to
drink in ... use a typewriter that jumped a space at the
letter O ... wave his arms about when speaking of the
Irish literary mafia ... But the man does not reply and
insists on the box being filled in asking for title of document
and writes in block capitals THE CARNIVORES except
that he jumps a space at the letter O. The man hands him
a yellow cloakroom ticket with a number on it, tells him
to wait until the number is called and closes the hatch
with an iron hook and eye. From beyond it comes the
murmur of voices some of them vaguely familiar though
he cannot place them. He presses his ear to a knot hole
in the hatch door to catch bits of what they are saying.

Not it at all ... styistic differences ... use of the semicolon
a clear giveaway ... so many versions ... pre-Chatterley,
post Chatterley, Chatterley schmatterly ... not the one

246

banned by the Railwaymens' Union ... typical Joycean anti-hero ... the Irish version to squeeze past the censorship ... confused symbolism for maternal incest ... the hierarchy would never allow *poked* in Ireland ... deviates from the party line on social realism ... calves testicles poached in new Beaujolais an aphrodisiac ... my PhD on underlying Lawrencian themes in...

He wearies of this mindless academic babble of which the only clear meaning is that his number will never be called and they will never let him have what is his. He notices for the first time that he is not alone. A boy of about the age of puberty is gazing into a glass case in which there is a large model of a locomotive partly cut away to reveal its parts which can be set in motion with a penny. Both boy and engine stir the chords of memory but it is only the engine that he can identify with certainty. It is a Belfast-Dublin express engine, a four-six-nought; three cylinder double expansion; Stephenson's link motion; piston valve; fire-tube boiler. A penny in the slot would set in motion in a flood of light a silent symphony of turnings, noddings up and down, bobbings to and fro, slidings in and out, elegant and harmonious. Does the boy not want to see a moving sculpture, a work of kinetic art that was the pride of the Great Northern Railway? But what is it doing here so far from ... where? Yes. Amiens Street Station, Dublin. In the main hallway during the war. But then moved to Great Victoria Street Station, Belfast, its stately penny dance perhaps better appreciated in a city of mill chimneys created by the age of steam. Boys would put a penny in while their mothers and their aunts spent a penny elsewhere, he explains to the boy studying the exhibit with a pensive air but making no move to insert the penny that would for a minute or so give it the purpose of its being. Perhaps the boy is thinking sadly of it being moved from the main hallway to a platform, its place taken by a speak-your-weight scales or a fruit machine. And moved on yet again, and again, each time replaced by something more in keeping with the heritage-neglecting spirit of the times. From station to station it must have been moved on like the wandering Jew, from platform to platform, corridor to corridor, ever making way for trashy novelties until at last it comes to rest here, wherever here is, among the lost property and the thrown-out artifacts from the days of empire: the big game heads and the penny-peep-shows like What-The-Butler-Saw. He offers the boy a penny but the boy goes on gazing sadly without response. He puts the penny in himself and it falls rattling into an empty chamber. No light comes on and no part moves. It is dead. When he turns to ask the boy if he knows the way back to the city the boy has gone but has dropped a lost document form or perhaps cast it down as not worth handing in. In the space provided for describing it are the words:

'A railway station; going into or coming out of. Before a journey or after it or during it. Or on a street on which there is a station or a railway bridge over it on which a train is passing. Night. Or some other kind of darkness. A light or a lamp. A street lamp or a lamplit window. Or a bedside lamp in a room from which a train can be heard.. Or a station platform lamp. Or a lamp-lit carriage window. As a train rumbles by. Or whistles in the distance comfortingly. Or whistles nearby to warn of imminent departure. Carrying something by lamplight and the sound of a train. Or being carried. Or both. A carrier carried into light from trainsounding dark. Or out of it. Or both. Or'

He studies the boy's form frowning in concentration but comes to the same conclusion as the boy which is that the facts are too uncertain as to be identifiable regarding time, place, or the nature of the happening. He replaces it

carefully on the dusty floor in case the boy should ever
return to add to it some newly remembered fragment that
might illuminate its significance. It is time to leave. A train
is hooting impatiently. It might be the one to take him
back to the city. He cannot reach the platforms by the way
he came. There is a no-entry sign above the door he came
in by and the words Eintritt Verboten in harsh gothic
lettering. He follows another pointing hand on tinplate
saying EXODUS.

He passes through a dark corridor and is suddenly in
the open. It is a place of pathways, flowerbeds and
monuments in stone and marble. A train at the side hoots
impatiently as people descend from it and push trolleys
with coffins along the pathways to open graves. It is the
station cemetery. He notices buildings from which comes
the sounds of people speaking but in unison like chanting.
He enters one of them. The room is filled with people
and a bearded minister in black with a round black hat is
singing something holy in a strange language. All the women
are standing down one side of the room, the men down
the other. A book is put into his hands from which the
people chant in unison in between the minister's singing.
The pages have Hebrew down one side, English down the
other but he can make nothing of it even though some of
the people are chanting in English. Then the man at his
side indicates with sign language that the book reads from
back to front and he sees that the last page is numbered
one. He is conscious of being the object of resentful
attention and he notices that all the men except himself
are wearing something on their heads. With some it is a
little round skull cap but others have on ordinary hats and
are wearing them in a surprisingly casual manner, jaunty
almost, tilted racily to one side, or even pushed to the
backs of their heads. The women are all bareheaded. The
minister stops the service and asks him wearily to cover

his head. He is committing a profanity. What is he to do? It is so far to the door and he would have to run a kind of gauntlet if he leaves. Panic seizes him at the thought of such humiliation. His hand closes over his handkerchief and in desperation he wonders if that would do to cover his head with. He wrestles with the problem of whether holding up the service while he ties knots in the corner of his handkerchief like an old fashioned day tripper at the seaside. Then he sees movements among the women as they pass something from hand to hand and then across to the men who in turn pass it from one to the other till it reaches him. It is a brightly coloured headscarf. Blushingly he drapes it round his head and dumbly waits for the end of the service and to his embarrassment. He tries to hurry away but gets caught up in the mourners as they carry the coffin along the pathways. There is no solemn procession. There are no pall bearers. A crowd of people walking just anyhow and the coffin carried clumsily among them, the women wailing noisily but the men with their hats perched jauntily on the backs of their heads, some with their coats hanging open and their hands in their pockets. All over the cemetery are open graves into which coffins are being hurried. The Jews are burying their dead after some new calamity to their race of the kind that his own race has visited upon them without pity since the crucifixion of Christ. The train hoots loudly, its departure imminent, and he sees uniformed men waving whips. He must find the woman who gave him the scarf. He pushes through the throng, ignoring half familiar faces of people he thought were Church of Ireland, Presbyterian, Methodist, Gospel Hall but who must have had more than one grandparent a Jew even though they protest their bewilderment. Which funeral was it. There are so many. He longs for her. He longs for. He longs.

18

He has returned to boyhood. On the blackstone wall of the school playground there is a love circle saying W. Hazlitt loves Sarah Walker while a group of grinning girls are chewing jelly Napoleons from a brown paper bag which W. Hazlitt with a pale sullen face has pressed upon Sarah as the only way of wooing her that he knows. In the boys' toilets Samuel T. Coleridge sits smoking opium and reflecting upon the meaning of meaning, while Miss Pym the headmistress has just leapt despite her bulk from her table to a desk down the aisle to which, with a skill developed over many years of watching pupils out of the corner of her eye, she has tracked down the bottle of gin that has been circulating among the Eton scholarship boys and with a cry of triumph wrenches it from the mouth of MacFarquar-Forbes to whom she administers chastisement so severe that it leaves her too breathless to play the piano introduction for the annual visit of the representative of the Total Abstinence Society known as the Red Biddy woman who tells the pupils the perils of the demon drink. These she illustrates by the before-and-after-method, calling up a boy who has been tormenting W. Hazlitt with a claim that Sarah Walker in the row behind will push herself forward for him to have a feel of her under the desk. The Red Biddy woman commands the boy to speak in tongues which he does perfectly, reciting 1st Corinthians 13 in Ballymena Scots and Pitman's Commercial English. Then she takes the confiscated gin and pours it down his throat, again commanding him to speak in tongues. But this time instead

251

of the New Testament he chooses Leviticus on the rules for circumcision and speaks only in Yiddish. There, says the Red Biddy woman, LOST TO THE JEWS and wild rumours go the rounds that the shop from which a boy has just bought the cane used on MacFarquahar-Forbes and selected from those marked 'For educational purposes only' is not owned by Jenny Black at all but by a Jew Boy on the Malone Road.

The rows of desks stretch back into the past on either side of long aisles that echo to the sounds of those from the school readers who have long inhabited them: King Henry; the Gorgon Medusa; The Snow Queen; the Hunter Home from the hill, but only a little way into the future where they end at a door marked EXODUS, NO RE-ADMISSION AFTER PUBERTY. Some windows with stained glass fanlights look down upon the playing fields of the Horseshoe Bar where, amid the empty lolling Guinness barrels, some boys swap schrapnel from the 1941 bombing of Belfast with the smell of explosive still fresh on it for American cigarettes obtained from the GIs by their sisters or mothers while others in gas masks defend the honour of the school by aiming a hail of stones at blazered and flannelled third formers from the Royal Belfast Academical Institution who have been taunting them with yiddish insults: fesherstinker! meshuggener! Momzer! shloch! Other windows view the street where an American regiment is passing slowly through the anti-tank barriers accompanied by many of the pupils' sisters and mothers trying on nylons and as it passes a catholic house an old lady puts out a republican flag at a window to which the GIs angrily point their guns until General Stonewall Jackson stands up in the leading jeep in which Sandra Sarah Walker-Laffin is trying on nylons and recites in the high chant adopted by Miss Pym: *who touches a hair of yon grey head dies like a dog march on he said.* The girls in the leaving class gaze impatiently and excitedly at

the door marked EXODUS on the other side of which the
mill horns blow soft organ tunes that promise the girls
lipstick, spinning frames, boys, weaving looms, highheeled
shoes and womanhood and they whisper of things like
balloons that they have seen in alleys on the way to school.

A boy and a girl from Miss Pym's class hurry across the
street between the American soldiers to the boy's father's
shoemaking shop. His father is sitting astride his sewing
stool waxing twist before fixing a pig's whisker, and half
singing half speaking snatches of old music hall songs and
bits of Handel's Messiah. The girl is a London Jewish
evacuee wearing her gas mask which the boy gently but
eagerly removes to reveal her face, dark-eyed and lovely
as that of a doll. Can he take her home and keep her, he
asks his father longingly. His father sighs, blows his nose,
tilts the girl's face up to admire her Jewish beauty, shakes
his head sadly, wonders what the meaning of it all is, frowns
in awe at some dark thought about the state the world is
in, a thought so absorbing he arrests the fixing of the pig's
whisker and stares out of the window in sombre reverie,
forgetting completely his son and the girl whom the boy
promises to protect from the oppressors of her race if she
will come home with him and be his. But she shakes her
head sorrowfully and in the softly twittering London speech
is homesick for Whitechapel and Bethnal Green and Hackney
and for bagels and blintzes and gefiltefish and goy neighbours
who come in to switch on the lights on shabbas. The boy
sees that some sacrifice is required of him, some act of
atonement. He turns to where he has made ships out of
the lasts of long dead customers and takes up the Great
Eastern and Titanic in which he has recently installed a
single-acting single cylinder oscillating steam engine and
boiler heated by a candle. Come, he says, and takes it and
the girl down to the waterside of the Lagan by way of
blackstone steps worn with hollows from generations of

pilgrims. He launches his boats towards where the burning ghats stain red the smooth surface of the great river. He has set them alight with sprinklings of Bushmills whiskey from the bottle that he has taken from its hiding place in his uncle's grandfather clock. They watch solemnly as the blue-flamed Titanic and the Great Eastern steam towards the floating pyres never to return. He has burnt his boats for her. But still he cannot have her until he has done something brave and noble in her sight. So, in the beloved river meadow of his boyhood he climbs the great smooth-barked beech tree that has hitherto daunted him. Higher and higher he ascends into the canopy, far above the shouts of children and the tramp of marching soldiers which grow fainter and fall silent. It is dusk and he suddenly feels alone and afraid. He calls to her to wait for him as he descends, slipping and sliding in fear on the smooth bark like snake skin. Where is she? The street is empty, the playground deserted, the classrooms have fallen into disuse, night and the past are settling on all the buildings, and in his father's workshop dust is gathering on the abandoned stool. She is gone.

Years pass and his father's workshop has been taken over by Major & Blair to produce fine limited editions of erotica bound in hand tooled calf, his father being retained as a consultant to advise on the fixing of the pig's whisker to the waxed sewing thread with spit, wax and a dexterous roll of the hand against the apron. Apprentice writers and failed Eton scholarship boys toil for long hours in rows for a pittance. Work is proceeding on an unexpurgated edition of the Song Of Solomon with photographic plates made in a studio up the yard where Blair, a retired schoolmaster from the Belfast Royal Academical Institution, is inspecting schoolgirls from the sixth class taken by Miss

Pym the headmistress. He is looking for a model for the Shulamite, the Rose of Sharon and the Lily of the valley, picking those who have breasts like two young roes, navels like goblets and thighs like jewels. Major and Blair are falling out over the poses which Major wants restricted to those suggested by the King James version, while Blair wants some from the unexpurgated text otherwise they will fall foul of the trades description act, and Major, who is a solicitor, accuses Blair of teaching his granny how to suck eggs. They are swigging gin copiously as they argue while the girls from the sixth class whisper among themselves about how much the old buggers will give them this time. In another part of the studio an elderly artist has arranged a boy and a girl in a special pose and then retires behind a large camera so that he is hidden under the black cloth. The girl is the dominant one of the two models and has no hesitation in being naked with the boy. She knows that the elderly man will stay hidden behind the camera doing nothing more alarming than occasionally giving out odd little moans and gasps and that when he is finished it will be to her he gives the money, leaving her to give the boy what she sees fit. This is always less than half because it is obvious that the boy enjoys staring eagerly at her more than she does at him when they are directed by the man to do so in scenes he says are from Greek mythology, Shakespeare and the Bible. Today the girl will give the boy nothing. This is because she felt he had been sufficiently rewarded by being touched by her from time to time you know where to keep him in the state the old bugger wanted him in which was to look like Adam about to know Eve in the garden of Eden. This scene will be one of the coloured plates in a special edition of EROTICA for the stall at the General Synod of the Church of England and is expected to be a nice little earner. The apprentice writers look up as the talent hunter MacFarquahar-Forbes arrives to inspect their work and, in the case of the failed Eton scholarship boys to mark it out of ten for Harrow. One of these is learning to write in the idiom of the King James Version but complaints have been received from dissatisfied customers who know their bible that he has not got it right. MacFarquahar-Forbes first reads out a faulty passage and then asks the writing workshop to discuss what is wrong with it.

'And it came to pass that Judith, wife to the governor of Judea being troubled with desire but fearful of scandal, did not lie with men as did other women but took into her service a smooth faced boy that none would think aught of, and him she anointed with oil and put sweetmeats and wine into his mouth and lay with him for her pleasure . . .'

Is the woman, some ask, beauteous to behold, but the Governor comes not onto her because he is old and his loins quicken not for her? Was the boy purchased by her loyal handmaiden for six measures of wine and two of barley? Was he from Babylon beyond the Euphrates so that his foreskin had to be taken from him because Judith abhorred the bed of the uncircumcised and the alien and when he was healed did she watch from a secret place her handmaiden test him that he had come to manhood?

Others, however, point to the similarity between this and another story about the boy in the fourth form of the Baptist college and the headmaster's wife who gives him gin and sympathy after a sixth form girl who is a full back on a girls' rugby fifteen interferes with him in a locked bathroom during her free period. But against this is quoted the truth of the eternal verities: that there are only about six truly original and different jokes and conjuring tricks; all others are variations of these.

Somebody misguidedly calls for more laughs in it.

What, cries MacFarquahar-Forbes in consternation, laughs! Mr Blair! Mr Major!

At the sound of the forbidden word, Blair and Major set aside their differences over the erotic poses for the Shulamite and come rushing into the workshop. Blair is wearing a tattered schoolmaster's gown and Major is urging him to use the cane on any writer who does not take the speciality of the house with the utmost seriousness. No cane can be located so the Shulamite is told to put her knickers on and go to Jenny Black's for one that Miss Pym uses.

In the meantime Blair paces up and down the aisles and tells the writing class that if he catches anybody with the slightest note of comedy in his work there won't be an inch of him that he won't leave the mark of Jenny Black's cane on. It shouldn't be necessary, he says angrily, to have to thump it into them. Did they not recall their own disappointment when they opened surreptitiously the pages of Rabelais in expectancy of erotic stimulation and yet despite the explicitness of the descriptions they experienced no stirring of the groin? Surely they saw why? It was because Rabelais fell into the error of humour. He made it funny the schloomp!

Mr Major, between sups of gin, sighs and groans that funny is the kiss of death in their line of business.

And, continues Blair, after a snifter or two himself and ignoring the snagging of his gown on a bench as he wheels round thus adding another rip to the gown that streams behind him in tatters, had they forgotten how the initial early promise of Joyce's Molly Bloom obtained by a sixth former from his father's toolshed failed to give them the thrill they expected sitting on the school toilets? And why? Because bloody clever fellow Joyce makes Molly reflect upon the bedroom antics of Blazes Boylan and Leopold Bloom in a manner that makes it a laughing matter, the schmuck!

Oh dear, groans Mr Major, shaking his head sorrowfully.

No use whatsoever in our trade. Now tell them about the City Alderman.

Ah yes! cries Blair swinging round and catching his flowing gown on a size 13 RUC bootlast with a ripping sound. The City Alderman! Stand up the writer who did it. You there!

And up stands Cavehill Donard Braidwater looking very sheepish as Blair takes another long swallow of gin to prepare himself to relate the cautionary tale.

This fellow here, he says, turned in this most excellent piece of work in which a City Alderman church elder cunningly exploited the opportunities afforded by taking a dog for walkies for dalliance with a church choir contralto. It was a very big dog. An Irish Wolfhound. Now the bigger the dog the longer the walkies and the longer the time he could be out without explanation to the wife. At the contralto's place the wolfhound would be tucking into a bowl of tasty prizewinner doggy munchies instead of a long walkie while upstairs the City Alderman would be tucking in to treats of a different kind described with great effect, leaving afterwards with a spring in his step and humming bits from Handel's Messiah in a well satisfied tone. Mr Major and myself were at one in recognising CD Braidwater's descriptions of the delights of the flesh that can be commanded by a man of power and influence as having a wonderful appeal to those who have been denied them, often unjustly. We had no hesitation in ordering a double print run. But what does CD here do when he is only supposed to be checking the proofs? He alters the story! The contralto, not content with having her rates and gas bills paid by the City Alderman, starts being mean with the wolfhound's doggy munchies, and changes to a cheaper and inferior brand causing the animal to howl sorrowfully and so loudly as to be heard in neighbouring streets just as the Alderman is at the peak of his performance. This

will not do. But, thinking that it is being left alone that is
making the animal howl, they next time take it upstairs
with them along with the bowl of cheap doggy munchies
which the dog picks over in sullen silence until it leaps
upon the Alderman at the climax of his performance
emitting a howl as loud and long as a siren so that, as the
Alderman leaves the house with a limp and twisted to one
side from a bad crick in his back the curtains are twitching
at every window...

But Blair cannot continue. Ruined it, he says, destroyed
it entirely. Clients wanting their money back. Savaged in
the book pages. Couldn't give it away. Oh a very expensive
lesson indeed for this fellow here. There wasn't an inch
of him Mr Major and I didn't leave a mark on with one
of Jenny Black's thickest canes. Now where's that schmuck
there who suggested laughs? Where's the cane?

But the Shulamite Rose of Sharon from Miss Pym's sixth
class with eyes like the fishpools in Heshbon and a belly
set about with lilies who has just returned says that the
auld bitch only has wee thin canes today not worth a fart.

MacFarquahar-Forbes says his housemaster always used
a cricket stump but Major, on the gin again, says to make
him write a thousand lines. What should they be? You,
boy, set the words. What? The Fun Must Not Be Funny.
Hmm. You, over there, among the postmodernist poets.
They Can't Laugh And Get A Hard On At The Same Time.
Hmm, well. That fellow beside him. Humour Is Hard On
Hard Ons. Better. More feel to it. And you there with the
Baptist College tie. THE COMICAL CANNOT BE
EROTICAL. Ah yes the old Alma Mater always gets it right.
Be upstanding the alumni! Charge your glasses for the
school song!

And up stood Chichester D. Banbridge; Connor Derry
Blackstaff; C. Dundonald Bushmills; Clandeboye D.
Bleachgreen; C. Dungannon Boyne; Crumlin D. Black-

mountain and C. Derry Ballsbridge and others too numerous to mention all in good voice, tonsils well lubricated by the gin passed along the pews by Church of Ireland aislemen, the singing led by the Bespoke Shoemakers Christmas Choir who have all had a good feel up the contralto's dress under the mistletoe.

And we'll all row together
Our shoulders between our knees.

The scene changes. It is the cobble-stoned mill yard as big as a village square with the Red Hand of Ulster on top of the eighteenth century counting house and the mill horn blowing hoarsely the tune Lilliburlero. It is 1913. Men are parading with sloped arms to fight Home rule. There are popery-hating presbyterian shipwrights, true blue methodist boilermakers, Elimite mill chimney riggers, church of Ireland aislemen and a poet with a stammer to record the scene for posterity. They also have their flies open. They are being inspected by army officers from a car that has just swerved to a stop after coming from similar inspections elsewhere with the news that Ulster Will Fight and Ulster Will Be Right. The Officers include Lt. Gen. Walsh-Massingham KCVD MC, Lt. Col. Oliver MacFarquahar-Forbes Eng. Lit. and Surgeon General A. Harrison M.D. Circumciser-in-Chief to the Ulster Volunteer Force, accompanied by Sandra Laffin in a very fetching Salvation Army girl's uniform. Surgeon General Harrison stumps up and down the ranks pointing at the mens' flies and snarling at them to come on, come on, get them out. I'm damned, he says, but they couldn't have left it much bloody longer, every bloody one of them and motions them into the light so that Sandra can see along with the girls from number six spinning room who are making wolf whistle noises except for derisory remarks directed at the poet with the stammer and involving a mysterious doffer called Big Mina. High, Big Mina, they call to her sniggeringly, that wee lad would be no use to you, you'd break your back snapping at it! Surgeon General Harrison says he's damned but he'll have to have appeals for volunteer circumcisers read out in the main Belfast synagogue if he's to have these men ready for the Somme and you know what that bloody well means don't you. Oy veh! the Beth Din says this is not kosher and that's not kosher and the pig's whiskers have to be boiled in separate sterilisers to the waxed thread and all that damned carry on. But Lt. Col. MacFarquahar-Forbes calls out steady on and remembers a chum he has nearby who knows a clever Johnny who might come up with a spiffing wheeze, don't you know, to speed things up. He points to the shipyard gantries towering over the wet spinning rooms where his chum Lord Ismay, heavily disguised to avoid being lynched on the Queen's bridge for being first into the *Titanic*'s lifeboats, is ordering *The Great Eastern* to replace the *Titanic*, and there lolling nonchalantly in a top hat against the starboard paddle wheel is the clever Johnny himself – none other than the celebrated engineer and inventor Isambard Kingdom Brunel who cooly considers the problem and the machinery to solve it. He recommends an adaptation of the first mass production machine in the world designed by his father Mark to turn out pulley blocks for the British navy in the Napoleonic wars. The foreskin harvester would be belt driven from a triple expansion marine steam engine with the exhaust steam from the low pressure cylinder used to play Lilliburlero on the mill horn.

But there are mutterings in the ranks about the name Isambard. Another fucking Jew-boy eh? Wasn't he the one that got the contract for the life boats on the Titanic and pocketed the money for the ones he didn't fit? Though he fitted that false floor all right that helped to sink her.

It was to put the Jewish loot in from the Belfast pawnshops that would give half nothing for your watch and chain on a Saturday night and then bleed you white to redeem it on Monday. Sure it's well known in the Yard that Isambard fella took out a tanner a week policies with the Bulwark on all the Yard men that went down to her. Oh here, he *knew*. There's good protestant blood on that cigar he's puffing at...

The timid young poet at whom Lt Col MacFarquahar-Forbes is pointing his stick purple with indignation at his rifle being sloped on the wrong side and who is being motioned at by Surgeon General Harrison to take two paces forward so that the girls of number six spinning room can see that he couldn't have left it much bloody longer tries to protest weakly that it was an iceberg that sank the *Titanic*. But this is greeted by expressions of incredulous eyerolling, tongue in cheek thrusting, headshaking and forefingers against noses all deliberately exaggerated to underline, mock or even show pity for the naivety of youth. It was Jew ice, the more compassionate ones tell him patiently with a sigh, while others speak darkly of the owners of the Belfast Pure Ice And Cold Storage Company being Jew boys. And what about the White Star Line? Jew money. And the ones in the lifeboats? All Jews, except for one or two shipwrights from Ballymacarret they let in to do their rowing for them – oh they don't dirty their hands – while they sat with their Bulwark policies in their hands ready to collect their insurance money. They say there was Jew money in every hamburger stall on the *Titanic*. Jew money every place. Not a fish and chip shop in Belfast that hasn't Jew money behind it, nor a bar nor a foundation garment manufacturers nor a bookmakers nor a pigeon club nor a greyhound kennels. And that shoemaker, how do you think he took on the order for all the RUC sergeants size thirteens? Jew

money. And him the great church choir man singing The
Messiah – there's a right protestant for you! And that Alfie
Laffin that got the job for the eaves gutters on the *Titanic*
and keeps nearly going bust. It's the Jew money that keeps
him out of Stubb's. And here, I've heard tell your bold
Alfie has Jew blood in him. Sure you only have to look at
him. That big nose and five o'clock shadow and his shifty
look and his wheedling and whingeing. And that daughter
of his over there with the ministers and the officers that
will have their leg over her before you have your next pint.
A right Jewess. There's a woman saw her birth certificate
in the City Hall. Sandra Judith Cohen Laffin.

At this point her father's van appears towing a cement
mixer and a burden of sin with the unshaven shifty-eyed
Jew-boy-looking builder himself at the wheel but
accompanied by a Gospel Hall pilot to steer him and his
load of guilt for the crucifixion safely past the hospitality
room of the mill outside which linen-buying brothel
furbishers whose Jew-boy looks are remarked upon by the
Ulster Volunteers are loafing with large glasses into which
as Alfie passes they ostentatiously pour Guinness from
bottles and take long lip smacking pulls from them to
tempt him from the way of salvation leading to the Jordan
that he has so nearly crossed on many a past occasion.
But the lintel of the Gospel Hall on which the blood of
the lamb has been sprinkled has been put in off the plumb
by one of Alfie's brickies too preoccupied by the racing
results so that Alfie leaps out of the van shouting that any
man on the job he smells drink on will get his fucking
cards, may the Lord forgive them for making him use that
awful word. But the damage is done and the mentor says
it is back to another course of prayer and abstinence from
intoxicating liquor and sexual intercourse before he will
be allowed to have another shot at everlasting life. Sandra
is furious. She says she can take the shloomp of a father

of hers nowhere and her in her best schmattas being shown up in front of the ganzer machers. How, she demands to know, would those shiksas there like it to have a putz like him making a shlemozzel everywhere to shame them, the old shikker, the old schmoo.

Anger enhances her beauty so that the generals shift about in their seats to ease the discomfort of erections which, in the case of the ranks, has the more serious effect of frustrating the workings of the foreskin cutter just patented by IK Brunel and even worse for some of those already processed whose stitches burst with loud twangs leaving them to waddle around bent at the knees bemoaning their virility, to the exasperation of Surgeon General Harrison who complains that they will be late for the Somme and the monstrous anger of the guns.

At the mention of the Somme 1916 the pale young poet with a stammer suddenly recognises and stares in awe at a man in the ranks. Hi, Billy, is that you, he calls, the only one who came back? Don't you remember me, Billy? When you were an old man in hospital and I listened to you remembering on Remembrance Day in Ivy Ward. The pale young poet becomes excited. He now knows what he has to do to commemorate the Ulster Volunteers. He loses his stammer and his diffidence. He strides to the staff car and stands up in it beside Lt. Col. MacFarquahar-Forbes and with confidence waits for silence to speak his narrative. Coughings and rustlings cease in his attentive audience. A last minute rush of poets who have got wind of the reading and want in on it is angrily hushed and entry is adamantly refused to a Welsh poet with a bottle and his flies undone. The pale young official commemorator of the Ulster Volunteers begins:

The two minute silence was observed as well as was possible considering that the patients were all old men with those ailments of old age which make silence and stillness very difficult, even though, as they listened to the Remembrance Day ceremonies on their earphones, they tried to keep to a minimum their coughings, their restless turnings in bed; the chink of urine bottles against bed or locker. One of the old men was in a bad way with his wife sitting at his bed; from the monotonous regularity of his stertorous breathing it was clear he was unconscious.

When lunch was served an old man took a bottle of stout from his locker but delayed starting to eat until he had managed to attract the attention of the woman at the dying man's bedside. He was worried in case the bottle of stout might upset her by its associations with mirth and merry making. He was anxious to let her know there was no question of conviviality. He explained to her earnestly that he had one every day. He meant that it was his only remaining pleasure of the flesh and was of doubtful duration. Have your bottle of stout, she told him, Mr MacDonald would have wanted you to have it and he was so grateful for her reassurance on the matter that when he caught her eye during his meal he half-raised his glass in her direction in an uncertain gesture of sympathy and she nodded back understandingly.

A young boy came onto the old men's ward from another ward. He had been listening to the Remembrance Day poem on his earphones and the recital had moved him.

They shall grow not old as we that are left grow old.
Time shall not weary them nor the years condemn
And in the going down of the sun and in the morning
We shall remember them.

But it was the beauty of the words that the boy liked more than the meaning. He liked beautiful words, especially if they were sad. He liked being made sad by songs and poems. He enjoyed the sadness of the Remembrance Day poem as he had enjoyed the other requiem in his school reader with the lines:

> Home is the sailor, home from the sea
> And the hunter home from the hill.

He had come in hoping the old man with the bottle of stout would tell him more about the 1914–1918 war. The old man had been with the Ulster Volunteers. He always spoke of going up to the front line as *going up the duckboards* and the boy inferred that these were some kind of walkways laid down over the mud. The boy had listened the previous evening to a story about the duckboards. It had been prompted by the appearance on the ward of a black doctor, the first the old men had seen, though they had heard tell of brown ones in The Royal and they had reminded each other of Indians in turbans who used to go round the doors carrying a roll of oilcloth that would last no time on your kitchen floor. The old man had said he was going up the duckboards with an officer when they met this black soldier that must have been off a Jamaican battalion. The officer had pushed the black fella off the duckboards just because he didn't get out of the way soon enough. Says I to him, says I, sir, the day will come when you'll not do that sir.

It seemed the officer had put him on a charge, a young bugger of a lieutenant. He went up before the Captain and the Captain says, what about this, he says, did you say that, he says, and says I, sir, I did sir. Says he, don't let this happen again, next case please. That was all! When they marched him out the big sergeant said to him, said he, well done Billy, that young bugger of a lieutenant will get one in the back if he's not careful!

The other patients had said nothing. Perhaps they had heard it before, but the boy listened enthralled, catching a stirring glimpse of the stern military code: the being marched in and marched out on a charge; the bawling; the saluting; the feet stamping; the encouraging words of an escort whispered sideways on the move. He wanted to hear what happened next. The story seemed unfinished. The old man had merely concluded by repeating what he had said to the officer on the duckboards, as if proud of their prophetic significance. But the boy wanted a tidier ending, a more dramatic one. He had difficulty conveying this as he waited for the old soldier to finish his stout but finally put the question to him straight; had the young bugger of an officer *got one in the back*? Hey, what, said the old soldier, startled, even shocked. Ah no, he said sadly, he was killed not long after. He said it thoughtfully, no longer speaking to the boy but to himself, remembering. And the sergeant, he was killed too. So was the captain. Killed. They were all killed.

In the mill yard the two minute silence is ended by cries of 'Get your copy here' from many voices, 'Special Ulster Volunteer commemoration edition of The Clerkenwell Review'. Sellers move among the crowds with a thick wadge of magazines under one arm from which they whip one out expertly for a purchaser and deftly dispense change with hands blackened by coins. The magazine sellers are unpublished poets and writers who have been recruited by Nigel Lambton with halfpromises to print their stuff so that they are eager to outdo each other in sales and fight for good pitches. Lambton himself has the best pitch at the mill gate where he exploits the opportunity to press upon buyers of the magazine copies of his own Collected Works published privately with his prospective father-in-law's money. As she drives off with the army officers Sandra Laffin gives a shriek at a picture of herself in Lambton's collected works when she sees what he has done to her pubic hair in the darkroom touching up.

But the pale poet distances himself from these dubious practices in the name of literature and wanders up the staircase to No. 6 spinning room with the order book under his arm, revisiting a scene of his youth, placing his feet in the hollows of stone steps worn by generations of women whose teasing voices used to fill him with both dismay and desire. Perhaps now he will find her, his long lost love, the wandering Jewess. He will know her among the shiksas when he takes the orders for No. 6 spinning room since the shiksas will order soda bread and bacon whereas she will order bagels and salt beef. And he will show her his circumcision so that in her sight he will be one of her people and he will wear for her the star of David and be made weak by the beauty of her countenance.

The scene darkens and dissolves into oblivion.

19

He dreams of trying to find whatever it is he is looking for if only he could remember what it is though he will know it when he finds it, whether a place or a time or both or something else not confined to one place or time but present in them all to whatever extent great or small and holding the key to the mystery of why he is who he is and if there was ever a possibility that it need not have been so and whether such a possibility ever came near having a faint chance of being a probability and when that was and where and if the chance was not taken after thorough even if mistaken evaluation of the pros and cons or missed unknowingly through weaknesses and defects whether acquired and therefore reprehensible or transmitted in the genes and therefore inevitable and if the consequence of taking it would have mattered much one way or the other without changes in character necessary to make a go of it and even if this had taken place whether there would have been any guarantee that the difference whether to himself or another or both together would have been worth the effort of transformation involving as it would the abandonment of practices and habits he had grown attached to however unwisely and whether it would not have been possible to have taken different paths but in the same self as the one he was used to and was comfortable with since any other however much an improvement would not have been the self for whose origins an explanation was sorely needed not only on his own behalf but that of others whether changed out of all recognition or having resolutely

SAM KEERY

remained themselves or something in between but in any
case letting him know in which of these categories they
would have considered him to belong and above all if a
way can be found that would lead to the truth of these
matters whether a way in the metaphysical sense of
constructing a system producing a plausible perhaps
convincing theorem of general application as in *I am the
Way the Truth and the Life* or a way meaning a path back
through memory unique to him alone however much shared
by others in certain turnings or diversions or side paths...

...but which way? That must be the entrance with the
big glass door. But where did I cross the street? Maybe
I'll see it if I walk along it a bit. Ah, through the carriage
and wagon workshops. But mind the machine swarf, it cuts
your soles. But they never used to re-tube the engines here,
that was at Swindon. But is here, here? What's that building
I can see the big doors on the other side of that field? I'll
take this lift up to the fifth floor and have a good look
round me. I never recall the lift as small as this, it just
holds one at a squeeze, why doesn't it stop? Here, I can
hardly breathe, I'm going to complain to the bloody
management. Dear Sir, the air in your lift leaves much to
be desired, you'll hear from my solicitors, let me out, let
me out! Ah, that's better. What's this corridor? Oak panelling.
Oh I know now. That staircase. No, wait, it wasn't as grand
as that, it had iron handrails. That's Miss Pym's classroom,
isn't it? No, surely it was on the left. If it has the clay map
of North America on the wall that you can feel the Rockies
on with your fingers it's Miss Pym's. Yes, it's up there on
the oak panelling. She's sitting beside the Fire and Accident
Manager. I'm sorry my lapses and surrenders are up this
year Miss Pym but my new business is up too. It's the
Shankill Road is the worst, Miss. They take out a tanner
a week on the auld aunt and don't keep it up. And the
bit of bother over the roylaties, Miss. I know they haven't

cleared the advance yet but my next book will do it Miss.
I have Sandra Laffin get poked at the back of every Gospel
Hall in Belfast. My God, Miss Pym is getting out the cane!
It breaks on my hand. Yes, Miss Pym, I'll get you one from
Jenny Black's on Chapel Hill. That will be to the left when
I go through that door. Here, I thought corporal punishment
had been done away with at the Bulwark Assurance Company
when they brought in the five-day week and joined the
union? I can't get this damned door open and it's stifling
in here. If only I could get at the valve of that oxygen
cylinder, it's only half on, it's false economy having people
stagger about half choked and can't do their work, it's no
wonder the policy holders complain about the service. I'll
write to the board. Dear Chairman, I took out a wee
endowment on the auld aunt and you wouldn't believe the
half of it. Ah, it's open at last. Here, where the hell is this?
It looks a bit like Ludgate Hill. But the Bulwark isn't on
Ludgate Hill. I'm going to be late back with that cane, was
it a thick one or a thin one Miss Pym favoured? I should
go up St Paul's and have a good look where I am from
that wee balcony at the top of the dome. This can't be St
Paul's. All these coloured statues of bleeding Christs and
Madonnas with candles. Oh trust me to blunder into a
papish church reeking with candle smoke. I'm choking, for
Christ's sake somebody piss on those papish candles, I can
hardly draw breath. Ah, that's better. There's MacFarquahar-
Forbes getting into a taxi with Mrs Lamont and a choirboy
and Sandra Laffin running down from St Paul's cathedral
with semen stains on her nightie but the taxi goes careering
down Ludgate Hill without her, leaving her no option but
to go back into St Paul's and take the choirboy's place at
the ordination service even though they don't use the
Moody and Sankey hymn book she is used to in the Belfast
Gospel Halls. The taxi is stopped but not for Sandra.
MacFarquahar-Forbes is telling an editor chum to put the

word round Fleet Street that the new Irish writer he is
pushing is going to turn up drunk on a TV chat show
using four letter words for the publicity and is going to
claim he's cutting down to five condoms a week out of
respect for the teachings of his church and the pleadings
of Father Mick McQuaid SJ editor of magazines for catholic
family viewing. What's that Mrs Lamont is doing to the
choirboy? He's singing My Soul Doth Magnify The Lord
in a wig and false eyelashes looking like a girl and she is
joining in with her hand up his white surplice to let
everybody know she is a protestant never mind the broad
Dublin accent. She's putting lipstick on him now before
having her wicked way with him. Oh Christ I'm choking
I can't see for smoke. Is St Paul's on fire? It came through
the Blitz an inspiration to us all and now the damned
German tourists with their cigarettes ... what's that smell
of burning meat? Oh Jesus I can't breathe for the stench,
I'll have to get up the dome. Ah that's better, I'm on the
outside gallery. The smoke and smell is coming from over
there in Smithfield. I'll put a fifty pence piece in this
telescope for a closer view. What? Only German pfennigs
taken? Is this what we won the war for? I'll get some
pfennigs of that fat kraut tourist with the iron cross and
the cropped head. Thank you, you fat hun pig. How many
Jews did *you* kill, you teutonic crap bag. Oh my God, I
can see ... Oh Christ that smell of burnt meat isn't the
market on fire ... it's ... Oh God our help in ages past
... it's from people being burnt at the stake in Smithfield
... protestants and Jews. There's Archbishop Cranmer of
the prayer book and Rabbi Shachter of Belfast. There's
the London Fire Brigade arriving. Too late. They are serving
summonses for breach of fire regulations on Cardinal
Macrory and the Inquisition but the protestant and Jewish
martyrs have their feet burnt off, just blackened stumps.
The hoses are just making steam. It's as bad as the smoke,

I can't get a breath. How am I going to get back to ...
Damn this steam like a hot fog. I'll nip into the Daily
Telegraph building. Up these stairs. But they are stone
steps with a hollow worn by generations of women's feet.
I didn't know they had wet spinning rooms at the Daily
Telegraph. Here, I've heard of that fellow coming out of
No. 6 wet spinning room. It's WT Stead. Hello WT I'm a
great admirer. Treat you all right in jail did they? You
should have got a medal for that exposure of child
prostitution. Hazlitt would have been proud of you. Why
is he moving his arms like he is swimming? Can't see him
anymore in this steam. The printing presses are next door
to the spinning room. There's a boy spilling a case of type.
He'll catch it for that! It's WT Stead's revelations on the
supply of child virgins to the West End establishments. A
girl has come out of No. 6 and grabbed that young
apprentice. The steam in the spinning room is catching
my throat. I'm going to write to the editor. Sir, the conditions
the spinners have to work in would have been a disgrace
in the time of Caxton and Gutenberg. They are in their
bare feet and the new overseer is a right bastard who won't
let them boil their tea cans on the tow waste like the old
one did as he has to get the order made up for the bleachers
and dyers. The women are very aggrieved and vent their
wrath upon unfortunate print apprentices who venture too
near them with cases of type. I am witnessing right now
with my own eyes the fate of one such apprentice. Three
bare footed girls that I can positively identify as being the
ones in Red Cross uniforms when I was circumcised are
holding him down while a fourth unbuttons his flies and
exposes his sexual organ to derisive cheers from onlookers
who pass over a can containing a substance too vile for
its recipe to be given in magazines edited for catholic
family reading by Father Mick McQuaid SJ with which they
proceed to smear his member liberally causing such itching

that he cries out piteously until rescued by older women
who wipe his private parts with the tow they were not
allowed to boil their tea cans with while the young ones
go back to their spinning frames singing *You may talk of
your harp your piano your lute but nothing can sound like your
auld orange flute*, Yours indignantly, a fellow editor. Hey,
why are those women waving their arms in slow motion
like WT Stead out there on the stairs? And their hair is
flowing out behind them in danger of being caught in the
spinning frames. And I can't breathe ... it's not the steam
... it's ... ah, that's an improvement. The ventilation in
here is a scandal. It wouldn't have been allowed in Caxton's
time. Where in God's name is the printing room? I want
to keep an eye on the poetry pages. The typesetters keep
tidying the lines. Look, I say to the printers, I know you
have to have a degree in Eng. Lit. to read poetry these
days never mind write it, granted they couldn't rhyme a
Christmas card, but you have to swim with the tide. Hey,
that's my grandfather over there at that hot lead typesetter.
But I thought he was a loom tenter. He is. He's tenting
it with the cards. It's for damask linen tablecloths. He's
slipping a clove in his mouth for the garlic, no, it's for
that bottle or two he had, my grandmother was a tartar
if she smelt drink on him. My God the racket the looms
make, as bad as the printing presses. No wonder my Aunt
Lily who was a weaver got hard of hearing. The weavers
a nicer class of women than the wet spinners. You would
hardly ever hear them effing and blinding. Christ, there's
WT Stead behind that weaver waving his arms in slow
motion. Now the woman is doing it. Hell's bells, one of
the table cloths has got round my mouth choking me.
What hotel has it got in the damask. WHITE STAR LINE.
RMS TITANIC. Oh God that's why the spinners are being
rushed for the yarn and can't boil their tea cans. They
have to fill the order before the Titanic goes down. Get

Why is it hard to walk towards the door? The door seems
to be at the top of a hill. There should be steps instead
of the floor sloping up like this. I'll write to the City
Corporation about this. Dear Lord Mayor … Oh Christ,
that loom is wrenching free from the deck and is sliding.
So are all the printing presses! The weavers and printers
are all going to be killed and I can't breathe. Now I can
hardly see. The deck is getting steeper and steeper. I can't
reach the door. There's WT Stead swimming against a
porthole. That crashing and clanging is the machinery
smashing through the bulkheads. I'm drowning, I'm
drowning! I'll throw this table cloth over the wall with one
end tied round a lifeboat davit. About bloody time too.
This diving helmet is stifling. That fellow up there should
have turned up the oxygen when I tugged the table cloth.
He says is his heart is broke complaining to Belfast City
Hall about the oxygen and damn all they do about it, half
the councillors lining their pockets from the oxygen, their
houses full of it for selling to the papishes, the Lord mayor
as bad as the rest. But mind, he says, I said nothing. I
should have got my grandfather or WT Stead to write me
an excuse for Miss Pym. Dear Teacher, please excuse
lateness as he went down with the Titanic if he gives you
any his old lip there needn't be an inch of him you don't
leave a mark on. I've got to get to Jenny Black's for that
cane. I'm so cold. It must be coming off the ice. No, that's
white marble. If it's the brand new crucifixion outside the
chapel where the papishes cross themselves when they pass
then Jenny Black's should be on the other side. Oh no,
it's the Cenotaph in Whitehall. There's a crowd round it.
Here, I'm not in the mood for a CND demo. I haven't
got the puff to shout Ban The Bomb at Downing Street.
I would need a new set of bellows for that game. My slogan
shouting days are over, sunny Jim, though bliss was it in

275

that dawn. Hey, they are singing Oh God Our Help In Ages Past, that's not the CND hymn, that's the protestant hymn. I know that fellow on the rostrum from his statue in Belfast. It's Carson, a Protestant Land for a Protestant People. He is orating. He is waving at me to do something up. Jesus, did I forget to zip up after those spinning room bitches took out my cock on the Titanic? No. It's to put something on my head. But it's only at Jewish services that men cover their heads. I'll ask that fellow over there. Holy God, it's that old bugger Doctor Harrison that I tried to get struck off the register for the way he made a public spectacle of circumcising me in Belfast. He's wearing his first world war army doctor's uniform and he's got those three hussies with him from the print room of the *Daily Telegraph* got up in uniforms with red crosses. I'm damned, he says, you couldn't have left that much bloody longer, pointing at me with his officer's stick. But not at my flies but at my head. Ah, he means to put on my peaked cap. I'm to fall in. Number from the left. Ranks of five. By the left, quick march, heads right, Carson taking the salute from the steps of Belfast City Hall under the banner FOR KING AND COUNTRY. I'm with the Ulster Volunteers. Here, I know this fellow alongside me, it's old Dodger that was a baler in the yarn store in Taylor's mill. He's opening his trousers and pulling up his shirt to show the nurses the machine gun wound that was a Blighty one that saved his life at the Somme 1916. We're passing the Cenotaph again. Cenotaph my arse, says Dodger, winking, and pointing towards the ship at the docks we are marching towards. It is the RMS Olympic, sister ship of the Titanic. That wasn't the fucking Cenotaph, says Dodger, that was a fucking iceberg. But mind, he says, I said nothing. God help us does Carson know what he's sending us into? It's no good putting lookouts up on the crow's nest. All Belfast knows that. Talked of damn all else till the Somme 1916.

I'll try and tell Doctor Harrison. Left, right, left. We're heading full speed into an ice field, sir, put the look-outs low down so they can see the bergs against the sky at night, that's how the Carpathia got through the ice to pick us up. Left, right, left, For King And Country. No Pope here. Pass the word. Ranks may sing Tipperary.

Farewell Piccadilly, Farewell Leicester Square
It's a long long way to Tipperary

This kit bag on my chest is getting very heavy. I can hardly breathe. Those two full bottles of gin are a ton weight. What was that thumping sound behind the Cenotaph iceberg? Holy Christ, I can't see my feet. It's a London fog, a real pea souper. It's rising. It's over my putees now, nearly at my knees, we'll soon be swimming in it. I'm choking. My throat is burning. I can't get air. Pass the word. Gas masks out. That thumping noise was a gas shell landing! Where's my gas mask? Get it out of my kit bag quick! Oh God I threw it out to make room for the gin after Miss Pym's gas mask drill in the playground, she'll give me such a hiding for that when I get back. Oh God our help in ages past I'm drowning. Old Dodger there has two gas masks from the two world wars. Hey, I'll give you a bottle of gin for one of them. Says he can only drink stout. The auld stomach, he explains. Ah, that nurse is handing me a wet towel, God bless her, it's a bit of a relief. Let that be a lesson to me about the gin. Never again. Easy to say no after such a close shave. Well stone the crows, there's Brendan Behan and Dylan Thomas. Didn't they give them their unit measures at the clinic? No thanks, Brendan, I'm down to fifteen units a day, how's your hammer hanging? Thanks all the same Dylan, but I never drink between drinks. *And as I was young and easy under the apple bows.* In a plummy accent. That's never Cardiff, bach, boyo. What about something for the Clerkenwell review to boost the new talent when the pair of you sober up? Look where Brendan is pissing! Onto the first row of the stalls. He's letting fly onto the critics from the *Times Literary Supplement, The Observer, The Catholic Herald, The Jewish Chronicle, The Sporting Life.* They won't give him good reviews now! He's got Dylan at it too. And there's MacFarquahar-Forbes in the wings waving at me to get out on the stage with them with my cock out. Excellent publicity, he is saying, quite marvellous, would shift two more print runs of paperback at least, five per cent up to five thousand, seven and a half thereafter. Oh dear I can't get mine to go as high as theirs, they must have been on beer, an unfair advantage over gin, I'm straining and squeezing. There should be a handicap system. God, there's Miss Pym heading straight for us! That wee English evacuee I had the crush on must have told her the boys are holding peeing competitions for whose goes the highest at the back of the playground. I must get to Jenny Black's for that cane, I'll have to catch a bus from the City Hall. I feel so cold and damp. I need another blanket. They hadn't got enough for us on the Carpathia. But such a crowd of people pressing me. The whole of College Square is packed. And more pouring down Royal Avenue. Hey, that hurt me. What was that sticking into me. Oh I see, it's for blood. For when we get to the tables where the signing is taking place, the Solemn League and Covenant. Each of us to sign in our own blood. A Protestant Land for a Protestant People. Ulster will fight and Ulster will be right. There's my father leading the bespoke shoemakers, his job cut out to keep them sober till the signing, he can promise nothing after that. Pass the word. Keep your hand bleeding till you get to the Covenant. The Red Hand of Protestant Ulster. Such a crush. Popery hating shipwrights. True blue boilermakers. Off the bottle mill chimney rigger. Tango gold medallist pigeon fanciers. Church of Ireland terrier breeders. Presbyterian gas works retort house deputies. Methodist many daughtered dye house charge hands. Baptist coalmen. Elimite ropeworks foremen. Late marrying church organists. Old arthritic flax scutchers. Yellow whiskered dying out wheel wrights. Hard times remembering bleach green spreaders. Itinerant flax pullers. Sion-Kop-remembering bandy legged Boer War horse troopers. Last of the line bearded venerable pony cart lamp oil men. I can't remember the rest. I've lost them. I'm being crushed. I can hardly draw breath. I'm being pushed among the presbyterian boilermakers by the church of Ireland shipwrights who push me back again and the methodist platers say I'm not one of them and the Wee Free brass foundry men are telling me I should be with the Baptist bleachers and dyers. I'm having to sign as a protestant agnostic along with the Swedenborgians, the Christadelphians, the Mormons, the Lapsarians, the Seventh Day adventists. I'm going to complain to my Orange Lodge Master great grandfather with the Auld Bible beside him older than the King James bible and my sixteen great great great grandfathers and my thirty two great geat great great grandfathers and all my begetters. Hey, my begetters, I'm a bit bit Ireland leaving far wandering Ireland rememberer and … I can't breathe … I'm being suffocated … this throng is pressing the life out of me … I think I'll turn over for a wink or two of sleep. Ah, that was refreshing. I think this is somewhere else.

Here, I know that fellow over there. It's Marcel Proust. I'll ask him how to get back to … where was it I want to get back to? I would know it when I see it. Hi, Marcel, how do I get back to whatdoyoucallit street with the thingamyjig shop in it? What is he shouting? Damn this roaring in my ears I can hardly catch what he's saying. Gone, he says, all gone, not there any more. And yes, yes,

I can hear him better now: Houses, avenues, cities, are as fleeting as the years.

If I cut through here I can catch the tube at Chancery Lane where there's that woman selling papers in the man's cap. What's that it says on her billboard? Churchill dead. The train is painted black and people are lining up to follow it. There's Rooseveldt and Joe Stalin and – my God – Hitler. Why doesn't somebody boot him onto the live rail! I'll do it myself. Hitler is handing me something. It's a clove. For the garlic, he says, breathing into his hand and smelling it and motioning me to do the same. What's it say on the side of the train? Jas Lavery and Son. Dublin Road, Funeral Furnishers and wedding cars. Christ, I'm not going to give that coffin a lift. I'd drop it in the rush hour. This clove is choking me. Did that bastard put cyanide in it? If he did, make it quick, oh make it quick. Ah that's better! Am I dead? Is this being dead? I brought that clove into my mouth from above my teeth and crunched it hard just like it said in the instructions. No, no, there's no garlic smell now. Hey, there's Sandra Laffin buttering bread for the mourners' ham tea. That's MacFarquahar-Forbes chatting to her and what's that on her nightie? That's a semen stain. She'd better not let Alfie, her father, see it! He'll take off his cap and belt her with it and I'll have to comfort her as best I can. MacFarquahar-Forbes is bringing clergymen to meet her, one after the other. That greyhaired Methodist one with the war medals is taking her away somewhere and when she comes back she's got another semen stain on her nightie. At this rate she'll never be ready in time for the social in the Christian Workers Union. What are these stations we are flying through? Etoile, Opera, Arc de Triomphe. We're on the Paris Metro. Ah that explains the bidet Sandra was pointing out to the Moderator of the Presbyterian General Assembly though the Church of Ireland service is just the same as the

Anglican. Oh Jesus it's suffocating in here, I'll complain to General de Gaulle. Mon General, Francais, Francaises, votre air conditioning est bloody awful. Ah, we're out. We're overground. Up, up, up. Lovely view that. Always was. Lisburn cathedral and the Town Clock against the ski slopes of Divis mountain, you can just make out the climbers on the north face of Colin across the grand canyon and all Belfast spread out five thousand feel below, the Holy Jerusalem, descending out of heaven from God, and the streets of the city pure gold, as it were transparent glass, no need of the sun nor of the moon to shine on it for there shall be no night there. But here, they've got cable cars now to cross the city from one hill to another and the hills are so shining blue you could eat them like sugar. But they need to turn up the oxygen in these cable cars or we'll choke to death before we get to the City Hall. I'll speak to the conductor. He says his heart is broke trying to get them to fix it down at the depot. Might as well talk to a brick wall, he says. It's not what you know here, he says, it's who you know, you're nothing here without pull, friends at court, people to put a word in for you, the right connections, well in with the clique. Ah, quit talking, he says, you did the right thing to leave them to it. He nearly went himself, he says, only he's on these tablets for his nerves ever since his play SIMONY was booed off the stage of the Lyric by two rows of presbyterians, one row of Church of Ireland, and a row of mixed nondipping Baptists, Plymouth Brethren and Wee Frees. Hey, that looks a bit like Stormont but that's not the parliament building. What's that dazzling blue colour? My God, it's an Olympic size baptising pool with white marble tiles, chlorine filtration, alabaster columns, gold leaf hand rail, twenty-foot electronic gospel text displayer, seating for twenty thousand, car park for one thousand vehicles being extended by Alfred Laffin Associates, eaves gutters and blocked drains a speciality it says on the text displayer. There's the Christian Workers Union girls' choir, and I can hear Sandra's lovely voice among all the other lovely voices, Safe in the Arms of Jesus, safe on his gentle breast. Ah, the old Moody and Sankey favourites are hard to beat. The rows of women of mature years some very well preserved all in white nighties with semen stains. I can see Bathseba and Ruth and Susanna and Delilah and Hepsibah. They are taking off Alfie Laffin's cap to dip him in the name of the Lord Jesus and he's saying that the U-bends have been put in off the plumb and the first man's breath he smells drink on will get his fucking cards, may God forgive them for making him swear like that, and they are turning up the chlorine to make his garments white as snow in the blood of the lamb. Hey, you've turned up that chlorine too much! I'm choking, I can't get a breath. Let me up, let me up! I'm going to complain to the elders of Mount Zion Tabernacle. Dear Lorenzo de Medici, as well for you you weren't at the grand opening with the Fiosele flute band or you might have been suffocated without a wet towel across your face and you could have spit in the eye of Alfie Laffin saying it would have been a shame to spit anywhere else. The equipment is faulty. That chlorine is killing me. I should have kept my gas mask on from the Cenotaph. I need air for God's sake. A breath of air for pity's sake ... Ah, thanks, angel. Just drop me off here in Great Victoria Street at the Great Northern Station. Hey, what are those children waving? What is that procession? Is it the Jubilee or the Coronation? I can't see which head is on my commemoration mug. A scandal my uncle using a Jubilee mug to shave with. No, there are nuns, and the children are waving tricolours and crosses. Oh God almighty it's the Jews being marched to the station by the IRA. They've got all their belongings in suitcases, Rabbi Shachter is at their head. The nuns are telling the children *They*

Crucified Our Lord. There's De Valera and Cardinal McCrory having a word with Hitler. They're saying, 'but mind, we said nothing'. Oh Christ, there's Miriam struggling with a suitcase far too big for her. No wonder, she's only twelve years old, ah, a lovely wee girl. There's a chalked circle on the school wall saying she loves me. Hey, let me get to help her with that case. Jesus, that IRA man with the swastika arm band is choking me with that pipe you could boil a kettle on full of Mick McQuaid plug. I'm choking. That Ulster Volunteer gas mask was never more needed. I'm going to complain. He shouldn't be smoking with the explosives he's carrying to blow up the Unionists in Glengall Street. Oh God, my chest won't move … I'm suffocating … ah, that's a relief to get into the no smoking compartment. That was Finaghy we just went through without stopping. And then Dunmurry, Lambeg, Derriaghy. Now we are stopping at AUSCHWITZ. But surely that's Barbour's Mill chimney with the plume of smoke coming out of it? Oh God, we're all getting out. Such pushing and shoving and that fellow in the German helmet shouting Raus! Raus! Hey, it's Sticky Sloan the Picture House doorman stopping the matinee queue from leaning against Fusco's fish and chip shop window. He's forming us up into two queues and slapping people and hitting women with the butt of his revolver if they won't part from their children. There's Himmler pointing at people to go in different directions. I'll break this urine bottle over his head and then smash the jagged end into his face tearing an eye out, you Deutsche untermensche! He's smelling my breath! Over there, he says. Here, I'm not Jewish, you schmuk! I just like a bit of chopped liver and rye bread at Blooms in Whitechapel. But you were circumcised, they say. We have eye witnesses. Step forward eye witnesses. Three girls in red cross uniforms step forward with Dr Harrison. He points with his stick and says I'm damned but he couldn't have left it much longer and motions me into the light so they can see. There's Abigail and Anna and Bathseba and Bernice and Deborah and Delilah and Elizabeth and Esther and Hannah and Jemima and Jezebel and Judith and Naomi and Rachel and Rebecca and Ruth and Sarah and Susannah and Tamar and Zipporah. I can't see Miriam. She's only twelve and I'm only twelve. Christ, they are putting me among the women and we are all naked. Their menstrual blood is running down their legs and their tits are suffocating me and they are going to use their hair for U-Boat insulating. Oh God, I can't breathe. What's that hissing noise? Oh Christ, it's Zyklon B gas. Oh, make it quick, make it quick! Everybody is coughing and the mill horn is blowing ... and ... and ... I never ... did ... get...

When they took away the screens there was only an empty bed, flat and blank. They put his things from the locker into a cardboard box for whoever would come to collect them. These included the following items:

A Belfast and Ulster Directory 1942.

An out of date street map of Belfast.

The essays of William Hazlitt which appeared to be a school prize.

A book of Gospel Hymns by Ira D Sankey.

Fifty favourite pub songs with piano accompaniment.

A faded photo of a young woman in a crowd in Trafalgar Square.

Two old post cards: one of the RMS Titanic, the other of the biggest linen mill in the world.

A new notebook in which only the first page has been written on with the word PROLOGUE at the top and on the first line the beginning of a sentence with the words 'I never'.

A half full bottle of gin.